**Olivia Hayfield** is the pen name of British author Sue Copsey. Sue is usually to be found in her office editing other people's books, while Olivia is likely to be in her writing hut at the bottom of the garden, wondering what well-known historical characters would be like if they were alive today.

Sue worked for several years as a press officer at London Zoo, and then became an editor at Dorling Kindersley UK. She and her husband later moved to New Zealand, where Sue continues to work in publishing. She is also the author of several children's books, including *The Ghosts of Tarawera*, which received a Notable Book Award from the Storylines Children's Literature Trust of New Zealand.

Sue lives in Auckland with her husband and two children.

Also by Olivia Hayfield

*Wife After Wife*
*Sister to Sister*

# *Notorious*

## Olivia Hayfield

PIATKUS

PIATKUS

First published in New Zealand and Australia in 2022 by Hachette New Zealand
(an imprint of Hachette New Zealand Pty Limited)
This paperback edition in Great Britain 2022 by Piatkus

1 3 5 7 9 10 8 6 4 2

Extract on ... *Six*

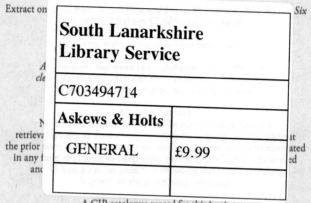

A CIP catalogue record for this book
is available from the British Library.

ISBN: 978-0-349-43101-7

Typeset in Garamond by M Rules

Printed and bound in Great Britain by Clays Ltd, Elcograf S.p.A.

Papers used by Piatkus are from well-managed forests
and other responsible sources.

Piatkus
An imprint of
Little, Brown Book Group
Carmelite House
50 Victoria Embankment
London EC4Y 0DZ

An Hachette UK Company
www.hachette.co.uk

www.littlebrown.co.uk

*For my son James*
*Lover of history, planes, bugs, and repetitive music*

# Preface

Many of us have heard of the disappearance of the Princes in the Tower, but few, if pushed, could give more detail. Yet it remains one of the most intriguing unsolved mysteries of British history. What happened to them? Were they murdered? And if so, by whom? And why?

When I was considering who to focus on for my next historical retelling, Richard III's dark, enigmatic figure wouldn't leave me alone. I knew little about this fifteenth-century English king, and what I did know was mostly based on the character of the hunchback who murders his nephews in Shakespeare's play. But I was also aware of the healthy and growing cohort of people keen to rehabilitate his reputation – the Ricardians. And so I began to read up on this intriguing figure, and the various theories on the princes' disappearance.

I started with an experiment. Without telling them who he was, I sent images of Richard III's portrait to friends, asking the question, *What do you make of that face, that expression?* Their answers (*haunted; judicial; troubled; tortured; some dark secret in his past . . .*) inspired me to delve deeper into the character of this man, and to explore his relationships, in particular with his wife, Anne Neville, with King Edward IV, and with Elizabeth of York, who, after Richard was killed in battle, went on to marry the man responsible for his death, Henry Tudor (Henry VII).

My developing obsession *may* have been influenced by the reconstruction of Richard's skull, created after the discovery of his skeleton in 2012. What a surprise – Richard was a looker! Dare I even say ... sexy? And so, I had my main character.

In *Notorious*, I reimagine the historical figures and events surrounding the Princes' disappearance in a contemporary setting, and speculate as to who might have been responsible. The historical note at the back gives the facts and context behind the real mystery, and discusses what is fact and what might have been Tudor propaganda – the fake news of its time. To this day, the truth of the matter is unknown, and is still hotly debated.

# Cast of Characters

## The Snows (House Of York)

### EMERALD 'EMMA' SNOW

*Elizabeth of York, wife of King Henry VII*

Eldest daughter of showbiz royalty. Reporter for the
*Yorkshire Chronicle*. Bookishly beautiful, passionate
about the environment. Sees the good in everyone.

### TEDDY SNOW

*King Edward IV*

Emma's father. Wildly handsome Oscar-winning actor.
Aristocratic background. A libertine; has fathered
many children, some of them legitimate.

### BELLADONNA 'BELLE' SNOW

*Elizabeth Woodville, wife of King Edward IV*

Emma's mother. Singer with folk-rock band Woodville. Ethereal,
fertile; an Earth mother. Her flaky persona masks a steely core.

# CRYSTAL SNOW

*Cecily of York*

Emma's bubbly younger sister.


# PEARL SNOW

*Mary of York*

The middle child. A little vague.


# ELFRED AND RIVER SNOW

*Edward V and Richard, Duke of York – the Princes in the Tower*

Emma's adorable younger brothers. Fun and feral. Known as Freddie and Riv.


# SIR RICHARD SNOW

*Richard, 3rd Duke of York*

Emma's paternal grandfather. Aristocratic and rather buttoned up.

# LADY (LILY) SNOW

## Cecily Neville, Duchess of York

Emma's paternal grandmother. Kind, old-fashioned; always beautifully turned out.

# MR AND MRS RIVERS

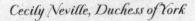

## Richard Woodville, 1st Earl Rivers, and Jacquetta of Luxembourg

Belle's working-class parents. Now resident in Spain.

# The Theodores (House Of Lancaster)

# HENRY THEODORE

## Henry Tudor, King Henry VII

Editor of the *Yorkshire Chronicle*. Classic if somewhat bland good looks. Smiley, good-natured, Bingley-esque; a sharp business mind. A little tight with money.

# LADY MADELINE BEAUREGARD

*Lady Margaret Beaufort*

Formidable mother of Henry. An awful snob. Overly ambitious for her only child. Enjoys blood sports, in particular fox hunting.

# JASON THEODORE

*Jasper/Edmund Tudor*

Henry's father; a property developer. Ex-husband of Lady Madeline, now married to Emma's aunt, Kate. Somewhat hen-pecked. Spends much of his time on the continent furthering his business interests.

# KATE THEODORE

*Catherine Woodville*

Emma's capable maternal aunt (Belle's younger sister), married to Jason Theodore.

# ROWAN BOSWORTH

*King Richard III*

Brilliant writer; protégé of Teddy Snow, who mentored
him through university and beyond. Dark eyes, dark
hair, dark soul; socially awkward. Bullied at school due
to teenage-onset scoliosis (curvature of the spine).

# NEVILLE WARWICK

*Richard Neville, Earl of Warwick –
'Warwick the Kingmaker'*

Teddy's flamboyant manager and theatre impresario.

# JANE WARWICK

*Cecily Neville, Duchess of Warwick*

Wife of Neville. Turns a blind eye to her husband's sexual adventures.

# ABIGAIL WARWICK

*Anne Neville, Queen Anne*

Neville and Jane's daughter. Fragile.

# DS SHORE (LIZ)

*Elizabeth Shore, mistress of Edward IV*

Detective with North Yorkshire Police; Family Liaison Officer.

# ED STUDLEY

*Edmund Dudley, Henry VII's finance
man and administrator\**

Hard-nosed reporter on the *Yorkshire Chronicle*.
\* also grandfather of Robert Dudley, favourite of Elizabeth I.

# BIRCH

*no historical equivalent*

Lady Madeline's butler. Twinkly.

# SUSIE BISHOP

*no historical equivalent*

Plain-speaking features editor at the *Yorkshire Chronicle*.

# MR HAWORTH

*no historical equivalent*

A bluff Yorkshire farmer. Owns the farm next door to the Bosworths'.

## The Animals

### GEORGE

*George, Duke of Clarence – brother of*
*Edward IV and Richard III*

Rowan's black Labrador puppy.

### GEORGE II

Rowan's second black Labrador.

### TEDDY

Rowan's third black Labrador.

### OWEN

Jason and Kate's Welsh Corgi.

# JACQUETTA

*Jacquetta of Luxembourg, mother of Elizabeth Woodville*

Belle Snow's black cat. Special powers. Possible conduit to the dead.

# PERKIN

*Perkin Warbeck, pretender; claimed to
be one of the Princes in the Tower*

Emma's ragdoll cat. Doubtful pedigree.

# STANLEY

*Thomas Stanley, 1st Earl of Derby*

Docile pony from Lady Madeline's stables.

# TUDOR AND JASPER

Horses.

## *At Middleham*

**Mr Zwemmer**: headmaster
**Mr Pickford**: Mr Zwemmer's successor
**Meena Desai**: pastoral care
**Mrs Ollerton**: school cook
**Miles Portman and Ajay Desai**: schoolboys;
best friends of Freddie and Riv.

*He was close and secret, a deep dissembler,
lowly of countenance, arrogant of heart,
outwardly companionable where he inwardly
hated, not hesitating to kiss whom he
thought to kill.*

SIR THOMAS MORE (1478–1535)
*The History of King Richard III*

# NOW

# York, September 2012

*I am always that girl. The sister of the lost boys.*
  She saw it in people's eyes, before they slid away from hers. *Poor thing. How awful, the not knowing. After all this time.*

Her gaze drifted out of the newsroom window, settling on the towers of York Minster soaring into a leaden sky. The sun, up there somewhere, had only just risen. Emma was first at her desk again, having woken before dawn, her mind churning, needing the distraction of work.

*Where are you?*

The sound of the lift descending broke her concentration. The moment was gone, her brothers' sweet faces slipping from her grasp, the echo of their laughter smothered by the hum of the elevator.

Sighing, she reached for her coffee, and noticed her neglected fingernails – different lengths, a couple of them chipped; and she'd been gnawing at the side of her left thumb again. She was losing control of her body, like she seemed to be losing control of her mind.

Her mother wouldn't be impressed. In spite of what she'd been through these past two years, Belladonna Snow, ethereal lead singer of Woodville, had perfectly maintained, witchy nails, which she used to great effect as she performed: twisting her hands, twirling them above her head, running her long fingers through her waterfall of fair curls.

Emma smiled sadly. *We all have our ways of coping with grief.*

To look at Belle, you'd think she floated through life making things happen by casting spells. But behind that beautiful, flaky, Bohemian façade was a remarkably resilient woman who'd carried on in the face of unthinkable pain.

While Emma immersed herself in her writing, Belle had channelled her despair into her last album, *Missing*. The nation had cried along to the haunting lyrics – 'I dream I find you, then your little hands slip from mine' – still unable to come to terms with the disappearance of those two beloved little boys, to grasp the tragedy that had befallen Britain's favourite show-business family.

*When our family of seven became a family of six, and then four.*

Emma rubbed her temples, feeling the effects of the interrupted sleep, the stress of the past weeks; the growing realisation that everything she'd discovered might be pointing to that very conclusion she'd subconsciously set out to disprove.

*Think. Think.*

Her vision blurred as she tried to free her mind, let it follow that elusive scent. She could sense the truth – there, in her subconscious, hovering just beyond her grasp. Like a note too high to hear, a colour on the edge of the spectrum.

The lift clunked to a halt. Henry was probably in it. Normally he was first to arrive; this week's burst of early-birdery was out of character for Emma. But then she wasn't usually gnawing her fingers with anxiety, either.

She put her coffee down. She shouldn't be caffeinating herself, tired or not. The last thing she needed was additional jitters.

Not wanting Henry to find her staring into space, she opened the *Daily Telegraph*, the rustle of the newspaper disturbing the still air of the empty office.

**PARALYMPICS IN PICTURES**

**THE BATTLE FOR HEATHROW**

She found what she'd been looking for, a few pages in:

**2012 – THE YEAR OUR WEATHER
TURNED DANGEROUS**

It was under their own reporter's byline, but they'd credited her: *Emma Snow, of the* Yorkshire Chronicle ... Now all she needed was for *Telegraph* readers to make the connection between their gas-guzzling four-wheel drives and the fact that Britain's weather this year had been a new level of terrible. Driest spring, wettest April, floods, more floods ...

The double doors to the newsroom swung open, making her jump. Yes, Henry. Editor of the *Yorkshire Chronicle*, and Emma's fiancé.

'You beat me to it again,' he called, striding towards her desk, which was on the opposite side of the newsroom to his own private office. *EDITOR* was picked out in gold lettering on his door, a relic from this venerable old newspaper's past. The building was heritage listed, like most in York's ancient town centre, and had been beautifully renovated, retaining the exposed stone walls and timber beams. Emma loved the place, loved the job. It was just her personal life causing the sleeplessness.

Still distracted, Emma found herself viewing Henry as if from a distance, as if assessing a stranger. That friendly, open face; that blue-eyed gaze, apt to skewer you, giving the impression he found your views deeply fascinating, even if they were only comments on the weather. It was the secret of his success. People opened up to him, and before they knew it were sharing their best-kept secrets, which his gaze implied he'd take to the grave.

*Do I really know this man?*

\*

'He's adorable – such a Bingley,' Emma's sister Crystal, a Jane Austen fan, had said, when Emma had first taken Henry home three years ago. 'I didn't think it possible a man could be that good-looking *and* so nice.'

Emma had to admit the comparison with Mr Darcy's winsome friend was spot on.

'Also rich,' Belle had murmured.

'He must have a dark side,' said Pearl, the youngest of the three sisters.

'He's perhaps a little bland,' their mother had remarked, crushingly.

Emma was used to the Snow women passing judgement on absolutely everything in her life. The concept of privacy was beyond them.

'No dark side that I've come across,' Emma had replied. 'Which is a surprise, considering his mother.'

Henry's *nice*ness, together with an uncanny nose for a story, was another secret of his success. His skill as an extractor of truths had seen his star quickly rise on the far side of the Pennines, where he'd started on the *Lancaster Post*, before his mother, the formidable Lady Madeline Beauregard, had bought the failing *Yorkshire Chronicle*, injected a vast amount of capital to bring the technology and premises up to date, then presented it on a golden platter to her only child. Just as well he was such an affable, likeable man, otherwise his staff, mostly headhunted from successful news organisations, would have loathed him on principle.

Reaching Emma's desk, Henry leaned down to kiss her. He smelt of the fresh, damp, autumn air beyond the window. She noticed the faded yellow-green remnants of bruising on his cheek, the result of a recent horse-riding accident.

Apparently.

*Rowan*. His dark image flashed into her head, usurping her ponderings on Henry. Where was he? It was two weeks since she'd seen him, and all her texts and messages remained unanswered.

Emma bit back an impulse to voice her suspicions. That Henry's bruise and Rowan's recent disappearance were connected. The office wasn't the place. She'd tackle him tonight.

'Yes, I woke up early again,' she said, thoughtfully tracing the discolouration with her fingertips. She met his eye. 'Almost gone.'

He frowned, and straightened. 'You're not sleeping again? This investigation ... ' His eyes swept over the piles of paper on her desk. 'You need a break. I was thinking, maybe we should take some time off.'

*No way. Not at the moment.*

When she didn't reply, he reached out, stroked her cheek. 'We could do with a holiday. The staff can manage for a week. How about we slope off to a Greek island? Reckon it'd do you the world of good.'

*I couldn't handle it, being so far away ... not knowing where Rowan is, his state of mind.*

'Hm, it would be nice, but I don't want to lose momentum on the story, now I'm finally getting somewhere.'

He shook his head. 'You're too ... bogged down. It's tough on you, with it being personal. Santorini's lovely in September.'

'I'll take a look at my workload.'

'I'm your editor. I'll genie-fy it away.' He smiled his charming smile.

She smiled back. 'Maybe. Well, I'd better ... '

'I'll leave you to it. Google Santorini. You'll love it.'

She swivelled her chair, tapped the computer space bar. But she wouldn't be googling Santorini.

The last thing Emma needed was more time alone with Henry. No matter what her feelings were – and at the moment, conflicted didn't even begin to cover it – what she needed was space. The chance to think.

*Time to herself.* As she logged on, she reflected that this had been her challenge for as long as she could remember. Growing up, all she'd wanted was time off from her noisy, chaotic, and above all, famous family, and the hangers-on who surrounded them. To be left alone with her books and her writing. But space and anonymity had been elusive.

Emma had hated growing up in public – an acting legend for a father, a rock star for a mother; five blonde-haired, blue-eyed children, like an English version of the Von Trapp family. One Christmas, they'd actually performed 'So Long, Farewell' on a Noel Edmonds BBC Christmas Special.

But of course, you don't know what you've got till it's gone. In what seemed like the blink of an eye, that rowdy, loving family had been shattered forever, its three adorable males spirited away.

She clicked on the opinion piece she needed to finish this morning, on whether the Yorkshire Dales were suffering irreparable damage beneath the boots of a record number of walkers. The cursor blinked on her heading: *Loved to Death?*

Rowan's voice in her head: *Seriously, Ems? Cliché!*

She sighed, her gaze once again drifting out of the window. No matter how hard she tried to lock him out, Rowan was always there.

An hour later, Emma had written only two paragraphs. Henry was right. It was too much, trying to manage her usual features *and* forge ahead with the investigative piece on her brothers' disappearance.

And now, Rowan's, too.

*Focus!*

She typed: *How many is too many? While tourism stakeholders rub their hands in glee, fragile ecosystems are suffering.*

Her desk phone rang. She was *never* going to meet today's deadline.

It was Henry. 'Emma, can you come through?' There was something in his voice.

'What is it?'

'Just come through – and close the door behind you.'

Henry was an open-door man.

She looked across the office, and saw him perched on the edge of his desk, waiting for her. He wasn't looking her way.

*Oh god, he's going to kill the investigation. He's actually going to kill it.*

And for all the wrong reasons.

As she made her way over to his office, Emma was aware of a chill creeping along her veins. *No way am I giving up. Not now.*

'Emma,' he said, as she shut the door. 'Sit down.' Frowning, he raked his fingers through his red-blonde hair.

'What's going on?' she said, not sitting down. If she was going to fight her corner, she'd rather be standing.

'You saw the papers this morning?'

*Oh.* She let out a breath. He was going to congratulate her on being picked up by the *Telegraph*.

'You mean the *Telegraph*?'

'The body found in Leicester. Under a car park.'

'Body?' she said, stupidly. What did this have to do with anything? *Unless . . .*

'Emma . . . '

She sucked in a breath, suddenly petrified by the look on his face. *Oh please god, no. Not Rowan.*

# THEN

# Chapter One

### Thirteen years earlier
### Middleham, Yorkshire

Necks were discreetly craned as Belladonna Snow ushered her three daughters into the front row of Middleham College's ancient, lofty hall.

A whisper from the row behind: 'Mum, it's Belle Snow!'

'Shh! And don't stare,' hissed the mother.

At the age of eleven, Emma was used to the glances, the whispers, whenever the Snow family ventured out in public. Which was rarely, as one parent or the other was usually on location, or touring, or starring in a West End run.

So tonight was special. Her father, Oscar-winning actor Teddy Snow, was returning to his alma mater to guest star in this year's school play, a modern retelling of *A Midsummer Night's Dream*. The hall was packed, every last seat taken, parents crowding in at the back. The air was heavy with anticipation (and expensive scents – a Middleham education didn't come cheap). Acting royalty was in the house.

As they took their seats, Emma's sister Crystal, two years her junior, flicked back her long blonde hair, wriggled in her seat and sighed. 'Honestly, it's like being a Windsor.' Then she gazed around, a gracious smile on her face.

'Eyes forward, Crystal,' said Belle, quietly but firmly, shrugging off her crushed-velvet jacket. She glanced to the side of the hall, and magically a boy in school uniform (optional – Middleham was as liberal as it was expensive) appeared in front of her. 'Can I take your coat for you, Mrs Snow?'

'That's very kind.'

'Gosh, thanks!' Reverentially, he laid the jacket across his arm. 'Can I bring it back to you after?'

'That would be sweet of you.'

'What's a Windsor?' asked Pearl, sitting between Belle and Crystal. At seven, she was the youngest in the Snow party.

'That's the Queen's surname,' said Emma. 'So all her children are Windsors too.'

'Oh,' said Pearl, vaguely. 'I didn't know they had names like us. Queen Windsor.'

'No—' began Crystal.

'We'll explain later, darling,' said Belle. 'Settle down now.'

On Emma's left, her father's manager, Neville Warwick, chuckled. Teddy had invited Uncle Neville (not a real uncle; he was Emma's godfather) to tonight's performance.

'You're in for a treat like you won't believe,' her father had said when they'd popped into his dressing room earlier. He scooped up Pearl and sat her on his knee.

Teddy was prone to exaggerate, as Emma well knew. He was a larger-than-life figure himself, with his resonant, booming voice, his broad shoulders, his handsome, instantly recognisable face.

'Seriously, Teddy?' Neville had replied, bushy eyebrows raised. 'You drag me hundreds of miles to the wilds of – where the actual fuck are we? – *Yorkshire*, for an am dram? A *school* dram? I fear your famously green eyes may be somewhat clouded by sentimentality. But still, an evening in the company of floppy-haired schoolboys ... I suppose one can't complain.' He raised his eyebrows again, in an entirely different way.

'Stop it, you old ham,' said Teddy. 'Just you wait. And don't swear in front of my girls.'

'Are we to be treated to Teddy's Bottom?' asked Neville, winking at Pearl.

The girls giggled.

'No, I'm playing Oberon,' he said. 'But tonight you won't be bothering about me.' He smiled mysteriously.

'What a divine scent,' said Belle. She held back her cascade of hair in one hand as she leaned forward, sniffing delicately at a vase of white roses on Teddy's dressing table.

'From the cast and crew,' said Teddy. 'One of whom is going to blow your socks off, my love. But I'll say no more for now.'

Emma didn't really care whether or not this play was worthy of her father's hype. She was just thrilled her family was enjoying a night out together, like normal people.

The lights dimmed and the noise in the hall died down. Middleham's tweed-suited headmaster appeared on stage and welcomed everyone. 'This play might not be what you're expecting, ladies and gentlemen,' he said. 'This is *A Midsummer Night's Dream* like you've never seen it before. I have a strong hunch Shakespeare would have approved. And so, without further ado ... '

The headmaster was right. And so was Teddy. The production was sensational. Mystical, magical, funky, the language updated to appeal to the teens in the house, while retaining its Shakespearean core. Thanks to Teddy's involvement, no doubt, the acting was exuberant.

The audience was spellbound. There was no shuffling in seats, no coughing, no whispering or fidgeting.

Emma was riveted by the lyrical dialogue. As a bookworm with writerly pretensions, she appreciated a well-turned phrase, a clever juxtaposition of words.

She'd seen her father perform in various Shakespeare plays, and while she enjoyed them, it was always difficult to follow what was going on, in spite of the summaries he gave her. Shakespeare was *hard*. This was different. There was no need to concentrate, the words swept Emma along – their rhythm, their poetry, the emotion they conveyed. She found herself holding her breath.

The play concluded with Cobweb and Moss performing one of Woodville's best-loved songs, 'Dreams', in the moonlit greenwood, dry ice swirling around the faeries' bare feet.

As the curtain fell, the hall was silent for a moment, the air humming with emotion. Belle and Teddy were always talking about that connection with the audience, about moving them, transporting them. Emma now understood – this was what they meant.

Then, the hall erupted into a standing ovation.

'Well well, Belle,' said Neville, looking over the girls' heads to their mother. 'I'll eat my feathered cap. A few tweaks and that play's going straight to the West End. His Majesty's, perhaps. Produced by yours truly.'

'Incredible!' called Belle over the rowdy applause. 'Did you enjoy it, darlings?' she asked the girls.

'Mummy, it was *amazing*!' said Crystal. 'I'm going to be an actress when I grow up.'

'And I'm going to be the cobwebby fairy!' said Pearl.

The cast returned to the stage, led by Teddy, who was whipping the audience up, applauding the young actors as they hugged each other.

Finally, after three curtain calls, the commotion died down to the occasional hoot and whistle, and the actors left the stage. Then Teddy reappeared, and the cheering started up again. After an elaborate bow, he held up his hand for silence.

'Ladies and gentlemen, girls and boys. From your response, I'd guess that you've been as astonished by this production of *A Midsummer Night's Dream* as I was when I first read the script.'

More cheers.

'I must confess, when Mr Zwemmer approached me to perform in the school play ... ' he beamed across at the headmaster, 'I was, shall we say, hesitant.' He pulled a face. There was a ripple of laughter.

'But then I read the script.' He paused for effect, letting his glance fall on random members of the audience. 'And I can say in all honesty, it was up there with the first time I read Shakespeare's original version.'

There were gasps. Such praise, from Britain's most revered stage actor.

'So it's high time I introduced you to the genius behind this play – a young man whose name I predict will one day be up there with the likes of Miller, Stoppard, Wilde . . . '

Emma didn't know the names, but Belle said 'wow' under her breath, so they must have been good.

'Ladies and gentlemen,' said Teddy, looking into the wings. 'Allow me the enormous pleasure and privilege of introducing you to . . . Mr Rowan Bosworth.'

As the applause started again, a boy walked onto the stage, his head lowered, staring at the floor. He came to stand next to Teddy. In the front row, Emma had a good view of this genius her father was so clearly smitten with.

Apart from his pale face, everything about him was dark – curly black hair tumbling to his shoulders, coal-dark eyes; black T-shirt, black jeans and boots. Black . . . bracelets?

As he finally looked up, flicking his hair out of his eyes, she saw . . . the boy was beautiful. She could hardly tear her eleven-year-old eyes from his arresting face.

But . . . Emma's gaze dropped to his shoulders, one of which seemed a little higher than the other. And when she looked some more, it wasn't the way he was standing, it was just how he was. Kind of . . . a bit lopsided. Some of it was an illusion created by the boy's obvious shyness. He looked awkward, embarrassed, as if he'd rather be somewhere else; as if he were turning slightly away from the audience. He probably hated being in the spotlight because of his . . . whatever it was.

'Well, I'll be . . . ' said Neville.

Then Teddy put his arm around the boy and gave him a squeeze, and with her father's big hand splayed across his shoulder, his – Rowan's – face finally broke into a smile, and he straightened, holding his head high as he took strength from Teddy's encouragement.

In spite of the difference in their ages, Emma felt an immediate affinity with this unusual boy, whose natural response to attention was, it seemed, much the same as hers. She found herself willing him to look at her as she cheered and clapped. Those words that had touched her so deeply – they'd been written by *him*.

Teddy spoke in Rowan's ear, and looked down at his family. Rowan's glance fell on Belle (of course), who gave him a sweet smile and a wave. He smiled shyly back, then his gaze moved on to Crystal, Pearl, and stopped on Emma. She felt herself blush. Oh – did she have a crush? Her friends at school were always discussing their crushes (mostly the boys in Take That), but the only grown-up man she'd ever found appealing was Mr Darcy in *Pride and Prejudice*, and he wasn't real.

But Mr Darcy was dark, very handsome, and quite mysterious, too.

Rowan smiled at her, and Emma quietly gasped. Then Teddy pointed out Neville, and the moment was gone.

As the pair left the stage and the audience rose to leave, Crystal said, 'Can we go and see Daddy again? And meet his new friend?'

'No, girls, it's way past your bedtime,' said Belle firmly. 'We have a long drive back to Grandma and Grandpa's, and I need to get back in case Elfred wakes up.' The latest addition to the Snow family – a boy, finally! – was six months old.

They were staying at Sandal Manor, Teddy's parents' ancient country house an hour or so from the school.

'Please, Mummy,' said Emma, quietly. 'I'd really like to ... I want to tell ... Rowan how much I loved his play.'

Belle stopped as the boy from earlier came rushing up with her jacket. 'Thank you so much, that's lovely of you,' she said, taking the pen and exercise book he was also holding out, signing her loopy signature.

'Why don't you take Crystal and Pearl home,' said Neville, 'and Teddy and I will follow on with Emma?'

'Hm. Okay,' said Belle. 'But careful how you go with that boy. I know that look.' She raised her eyebrows at Neville.

'Belle, sweetheart. When one is an impresario, one cannot pass over a talent such as has been presented to us tonight. It would be criminal to let it go ignored, un-nurtured. And if I don't snaffle him, someone else will.'

'You know what I'm saying,' Belle answered, giving him a dark look. 'Keep it professional.'

'Whatever can she mean?' Neville said, winking at Emma.

Emma had no idea, though having recently started at Elsyng Girls' School, where she shared a common room with older girls, she'd begun to look at her parents in a new light. 'Do you know what an open marriage is?' a Year Ten had asked her. 'Cos my mum says your parents do that.'

Rumours about her parents were many and constant, and Emma usually managed to ignore them. But now she was approaching puberty, and learning about all those adult . . . things, she found herself watching her parents with interest.

An open marriage was probably one where the husband and wife told each other everything. Teddy and Belle loved each other very much, everyone knew that. Theirs was a great British love story. Teddy was from a rich, noble family – his parents, Grandma and Grandpa Snow, were a Sir and a Lady! – and he'd married a girl from the local village, which they hadn't approved of *at all*. But now, of course, they loved Belle, probably because she'd given them so many grandchildren.

But that same mean girl who'd told her about the open marriage had also said something very rude about Emma's father and his leading ladies. Well, if you're an actor, you have to kiss other women, of course. It made Emma feel horrible inside, seeing him do that in films, but Belle just laughed about it and said there would have been loads of people on the set watching, and a director shouting things like 'put your hand there' and 'turn this way a bit', so it wouldn't have been at all romantic. And anyway, her parents had just had another baby so obviously they still loved each other in *that* way, so why would her dad want anyone else? Especially when Belle was one of the most beautiful women in Britain – the papers were always saying so.

Uncle Neville and Emma made their way to the dressing room, which was actually the headmaster's study with a special mirror with lights around it, and a dressing screen, brought in for Teddy. A large gold star had been stuck on the door.

Neville knocked and entered, and she followed him in. Teddy was seated in front of the mirror removing his stage make-up; he'd already changed out of his fairy king outfit into a long white robe.

The boy, Rowan, was sitting on the edge of the headmaster's desk, drinking a can of cola. On his middle finger Emma noticed a chunky silver ring with a boar's head.

She found herself staring again. She noticed how his black eyebrows turned up slightly at the inner corners. It made him look sad.

'Ah!' said Teddy. 'Rowan – meet my manager, Neville Warwick. And my daughter Emerald, who prefers to be an Emma.'

Neville shook Rowan's hand, pumping it up and down. 'Marvellous, marvellous. We need to have a talk, dear boy. How much longer have you at school?'

Emma wanted to talk to Rowan too, to tell him how much she'd loved his clever play. But Neville and Teddy were sucking up all the air, all the space, taking over. As usual. She sat down on the leather sofa and watched, instead.

'This is my last year,' said Rowan. He spoke softly, with a Yorkshire accent.

'And then?' said Teddy.

'Uni, if I get in.' Rowan didn't look at the men. Instead, he watched his finger as it traced the gold edging on the leather-topped desk. His long hair fell forward, hiding his expression.

'Which one? And to study what?' said Neville.

Without looking up, Rowan shrugged, and Emma noticed his uneven shoulders again. 'Don't know and don't know.'

'Don't bombard him with questions,' Teddy said. 'You'll scare him off.'

Emma had a strong sense the boy was already looking to escape. The two men could be quite overwhelming.

She cleared her throat, and he glanced over. 'Your play was fantastic,' she said, in a voice that came out a lot smaller than she'd intended – although any voice tended to sound small if it followed her father's. 'I want to be a writer too. I think it's amazing that you wrote a Shakespeare play I could understand.' She felt herself blushing again.

She saw the interest spark in his eyes. He hopped down from the desk and came over, sitting down beside her. 'Yeah, Shakespeare's awesome, but it can be a real pain at first. Takes ages to understand it. Don't give up. Watch some movies, start with the easy ones, like *Twelfth Night* and *As You Like It*. Save the biggies, like *Hamlet* and *Richard the Third*, for later.'

'Oh yes, I will,' she said. 'Thank you.'

He smiled, and it transformed his face, from dark to light.

'Rowan,' said Neville. 'We need to talk, dear boy. Obviously you should do English or drama at university, and I would very much like to take you under my wing. You can write alongside your studies; Teddy and I will open doors for you – beautiful, gilded, West End ones. Do you have other scripts, treatments, as well as what we witnessed this evening?'

'No,' said Rowan. The light had faded. He wasn't looking thrilled at the prospect of working with Neville. Emma wondered why that was. 'Just poems,' he said, head down again, picking at a thread on his jeans. 'I'm focusing on my A levels now.'

'Of course,' said Neville. 'Perhaps we should speak to your parents about how we might sponsor your studies and lock in optioning rights on your work.'

Emma felt Rowan go still beside her. He didn't reply. The silence lengthened.

'Are they here tonight?' said Neville.

More silence, then, 'Nope.' He started picking at his jeans again. Then he suddenly stood up. 'I'm going now. But thank you for being in my play, Teddy. It was . . . ' he took a breath. 'I'll never forget it.'

'And there will be many more!' announced Neville. 'Come, be our wunderkind, our protégé. Together we'll conquer the West End with your *Midsummer Night's Dream* and then onward to theatrical legendry.'

'Goodbye,' said Rowan. He looked down at Emma and said, 'Keep writing, girl.' Then he headed to the door, yanked it open and left, not shutting it behind him.

'Rather rude?' said Neville. 'We just offered him a stellar career on a plate and he walked out.'

'You blew it,' said Teddy. 'Neville, you have to tread carefully with Rowan. He's a tricky one. There are issues, obviously.'

'Is there something wrong with his back, Daddy?' said Emma.

'Yes, sweetheart. He's got scoliosis. It's when the spine doesn't grow quite straight. Rowan's isn't too noticeable, but it would have been hard for him standing there under the spotlight tonight.'

'Does it hurt?' said Emma.

'Not that he's ever said. But he's quite sensitive about it; it's probably why he's so shy. This school – it's meant to be inclusive and whatnot, but bullying happens. My guess is it happens to him. Teenagers can be brutal.'

'I know,' said Emma, thinking of the comments the girls at school had made about Belle and Teddy. *God, your mum's clothes! Move on from the seventies, why doesn't she?*

'Poor beautiful boy,' said Neville.

Yes, poor Rowan. Poor, poor Rowan. So clever, so nice looking, and he'd been lovely to her. But he was bullied for having a not-quite-straight back. And his mum and dad didn't come to his show.

As they drove home, Emma gazed out of the window into the darkness. She often wished for normal parents, who didn't attract attention wherever they went. But even though Teddy and Belle were often away, Crystal, Pearl, Emma, and even Elfred, knew they were loved.

No one from Rowan's family had come to see him. No one. How would that feel, to write something so brilliant, and the only people who told you how great it was were other children's mums and dads?

# *Chapter Two*

Glastonbury, summer 2004

'Far too cute,' said Rowan, watching Emma's brothers.

'Monsters, Inc,' replied Emma, pulling a face.

The Snows were renting a rambling old manor just outside Glastonbury. Woodville were headlining at the music festival, and Emma's father was between movies, so they were spending three months in the depths of the Somerset countryside – along with many, many guests, some of whom had also been appearing at the festival.

One was Marty Christian from the band Heat, who, according to Belle, had been the festival's stand-out act. Marty had been invited for Sunday lunch, and afterwards played a few songs with Elfred and River on the baby grand piano in the music room. Emma was impressed – he was the only grown-up who'd managed to get her brothers to sit still for more than five minutes all week. Discipline was way below self-expression on Belle's list of childrearing priorities.

Elfred, now five, was on grade 1, and had just played Marty his latest piece.

'That was great, Freddie!' the singer said, as the boy finished thumping the keys. (Like Emma, Elfred had ditched his full name as soon as he'd become name-aware.) 'The best "Mary Had a Little Lamb" I've heard in all my life.'

Emma was leaning on the piano watching, along with Rowan. She'd met Neville and Teddy's protégé again several times over the years. Neville had finally lured him into his fold, and during Rowan's time at Cambridge he'd made his mark as part of the Footlights team, and at the Edinburgh Fringe, with two productions that had launched his career as a playwright. His success didn't seem to have changed him; he still avoided the limelight, still dressed in black, still took the time to chat with Emma about her writing. And since Teddy and Neville had become his mentors, that awkward shyness had morphed into quiet self-confidence.

Rowan had been adopted as a baby, Teddy had told Emma on the way home from the play that night. His childhood had been lonely. He'd been brought up on a remote farm on the Yorkshire moors, his only friends the farm dogs. (Emma's heart had broken a little at that part.) He'd been expected to help out, but, as Rowan had put it, he'd been more of a farm hazard than a farm hand.

Dick Bosworth, his father, was a down-to-earth Yorkshireman who didn't hold with non-productive occupations like reading, and his mother, Celia, just agreed with everything Dick said. Rowan suspected their happiness at adopting a child had been short-lived, when that baby had turned out to be 'less than useful'.

But then he'd won a scholarship to Middleham, and the three of them had breathed a collective sigh of relief when the school had offered him board, including holidays if required. By then, the first signs of scoliosis had been making themselves noticed. Celia had made a half-hearted attempt to see if something could be done, but baulked at the thought of helping Rowan through treatment. There was far too much to do on the farm. They simply didn't have the time to be toing and froing to hospital, miles away.

In Rowan's second year at Middleham, Dick had suffered a debilitating stroke. The farm had been leased, and the Bosworths had moved south to live with Celia's sister. Rowan hadn't seen them since.

'Very cool, Freddie,' Rowan said, clapping. He glanced at Emma and smiled, and her heart flipped. 'How about you, Riv?' he said. The youngest Snow, aged three, was perched next to Freddie on the piano stool. 'You got anything for us?'

Riv said, 'Yes!' and shoved Freddie, who fell off the stool.

Freddie hopped back on and pushed Riv off.

Emma intervened. Her brothers' love–hate relationship was hard work.

When they were sitting properly again, Riv played 'Chopsticks'. Emma smiled – on the rare occasions when they weren't trashing whichever room they were in, they looked like a pair of cherubs, with their long fair curls and sweet faces.

'Very good, maestro,' said Rowan, ruffling Riv's hair.

'Well, *I* can play "The Grand Old Duke of York"!' said Freddie, loudly.

'Shit song,' said Marty. 'Shall I teach you "Orange"?' It was Heat's big summer hit.

Neville Warwick came into the room, pausing theatrically in the doorway. He was wearing a cream-coloured linen suit, and his long silver hair was tied back in a ponytail. 'Would you look at this room full of such sweet boys,' he announced. His eyes appraised Marty, swept across Freddie and Riv, then settled on Rowan.

Neville had recently come out as gay, which was probably the least-surprising revelation of the decade. But he and his wife, Jane, were still together – just – and Rowan was now dating their daughter, Abigail. All three Warwicks were here for the weekend.

'He and Jane will work it out,' Belle had said airily, when she'd told Emma about Neville's coming out. 'Jane must have suspected, when she married him, and they've rubbed along all these years.'

Hm. Emma now knew enough about her parents' marriage to understand where that statement was coming from.

However, Neville and Jane's marriage problems, and Neville's ongoing media notoriety – in particular his preference for beautiful men about half his age – had deeply affected their daughter.

'Poor Abigail,' Belle had said. 'She was fragile to start with, always an anxious little thing. I hear she's ... well, she has issues. But it's lovely that she's dating dear Rowan.'

Emma agreed. She liked Abigail, who'd always been kind to the Snow children. She wondered what Abigail's issues were.

Emma went over to the sofa, and Rowan followed, sitting down next to her as the boys watched Marty, entranced.

'How's your summer going?' he asked.

'Exhausting,' she said, looking over at her brothers. 'Mum and Dad said something about the peace and quiet of the English countryside. Maybe it was, until the Snows arrived. And I'm expected to babysit the monsters.'

'Don't knock it, Ems. Your family's awesome. Teddy's been like a father to me.' He smiled, and she felt the familiar knotting of her stomach. His black eyelashes were so long – it wasn't fair.

'You probably see more of him than I do,' she said. 'And even when we're together, he's always ... ' In an attempt to hide her crush, which her eyes must surely be betraying, she looked out of the French doors to the terrace, where their guests were gathered ... and saw her father's hand move down from the slim waist of an actress whose name she didn't know, but who was always in things like *Midsomer Murders*, to her pert behind. The actress turned slightly to look at him, a small smile on her face.

Rowan had followed her gaze; he noticed Teddy's hand too, and his eyes moved back to Emma's.

'Yeah. He's *really* awesome,' she said, her voice flat.

'Try not to ... ' Rowan stopped as he noticed Neville's eyes on him. 'Fancy a walk?' he said quietly. 'You been up the tor yet?'

Her heart lifted. 'No. I mean yes, I'd like that. Will Abigail come?'

'She's having a nap.'

'Oh, right. I totally get her exhaustion.'

Rowan chuckled and stood up. 'Your footwear all good for a climb?'

They set off down the lane in companionable silence. The sky was a gentle blue, with the odd puffy cloud aimlessly floating about, and from somewhere high above them the sweet notes of a skylark's song fell like a benediction. It was the only sound, and Emma breathed deeply, experiencing a burst of pure happiness.

Rowan glanced over at her. 'Good to have some space?'

'This is perfect.'

He looked at her some more. 'Your dad . . . '

She could tell he was weighing up whether to broach the subject. 'I hate him for it,' she said.

'Try not to.' He touched her arm, and a little thrill ran through her. 'You and me – writers – we try to understand behaviour, right? What motivates people to act in certain ways.'

'Well – I *don't* understand him. They make out they're this lovey-dovey couple, but everyone knows he's . . . he's not faithful.'

'It doesn't mean he doesn't love Belle, though,' said Rowan. 'Humans are complex. Who knows why he feels the need to act that way. Maybe he's proving something to himself.'

'How can Mum stand it? She pretends she doesn't care, but she so does.'

'You know what though, Ems? She's the strong one in that relationship.'

They passed through the kissing gate marking the start of the ascent to St Michael's Tower.

'Do you know about this place?' said Rowan, as they stopped for breath on the way up. Below, the flat, green patchwork of the Somerset Levels reached to the hazy horizon. 'The Isle of Avalon, so they say.'

'God, yes. Mum's obsessed with this bloody hill,' said Emma, hands on her hips, gazing out at the view. 'She's been meditating in the mornings, facing the tor, banging on about absorbing its energy.'

Rowan grinned. 'Perhaps she is in fact a reincarnation of the Lady of the Lake. She looks like every cover of a fantasy novel.'

The warm breeze whipped his long, dark hair across his face, and he pushed it back, tucking it behind his ears. His cheeks were rosy from the climb. Emma tried not to stare.

'She reckons she's got an actual river goddess in her family tree,' she said. 'Her maiden name was Rivers – that's why she called the smaller monster brother River. Sometimes I think she's properly mad. Oh yes, and we're on a ley line, apparently. Whatever the fuck one of those is.'

She probably shouldn't have sworn, but she wanted Rowan to know she wasn't a child any more. She was sixteen, the same generation as him, practically.

'Don't be too quick to dismiss all that,' he said. 'This place has a lot of power, even if that's only because of its history. And you can't deny it's quite magical, when you see it sticking up above the plain from miles away. All those people coming here, for thousands of years. Pilgrims, pagans—'

'Weirdo stoners,' said Emma, 'dancing naked at the solstice. Oh my god, I bet Mum will.'

'Seriously,' he said, 'we should watch the sunrise one morning – you'll feel it then.' He moved to the side of the path to allow a middle-aged couple in windbreakers past. 'While the anoraks are still asleep in bed.'

He rolled his shoulders and took a deep breath, grimacing a little.

'Does it ever hurt?' she blurted, without thinking. 'Oh, I'm so sorry,' she said immediately, horrified she'd drawn attention to his back. 'I didn't mean to pry.'

He smiled. 'Don't apologise for caring, Ems. It's better than pretending not to notice. It aches sometimes, but it's no big deal.'

'Dad said . . . he said you were bullied at school about it. That must have been horrible.'

'They called me a freak.' He watched a bird of prey wheeling above them.

'That's so cruel. And you can't even notice it, usually.'

'It's just part of who I am. I don't really think about it any more.'

Emma was quiet for a moment. 'I'm glad you have a nice girlfriend.'

'Yep.' He fished in his hoodie pocket and produced a KitKat, snapping off half and handing it to her. 'I'm in a good place right now. The writing's going great; Neville does the wheeling and dealing so I don't have to. I have Abigail. I'm lucky.' He put his arm round her shoulder and gave her a squeeze. 'And I bloody love your family. Right – come on, girl, let's summit this creepy old hill.'

When they reached the top, they sat on the grass in the sunshine, a short distance away from the tower and the people milling around it.

'You still writing?' he asked.

'I've just done my GCSEs, so I haven't had much time, but yes. I think ... I want to do journalism.'

'God, you sure?' He grimaced. 'You've got to be tough for that gig. They start you off knocking on doors asking parents how they feel about losing their children in motorbike accidents.'

'I want to be an environmental reporter. I run the school eco-committee and edit their newsletter. We've got to stop people killing the planet. I mean ... look at it.' She gazed out at the fields stretching into the distance, the green and gold squares stitched together by ancient hedgerows. 'It's so beautiful, and we're destroying it. There are people down there killing badgers, foxes; ripping up woodlands, poisoning the bees. I don't understand how anyone can do those things. Maybe our generation can still turn things round.'

Rowan smiled, and it was a little sad. 'Don't lose that voice, Ems. Why don't you show me some of your stuff. Email it to me. I'll help you with it, and then we can get it under the right noses. You're never too young to make a start.'

'Gosh, thanks. I will.'

'Shall I let you into a secret?' he said, nudging her with his shoulder.

'What?'

'I've asked Abigail to marry me, and she's said yes.'

She couldn't help the crushing disappointment. Why did she have to be so much younger than him? Six years! If only she were a sophisticated twenty-one-year-old.

'Oh – so you're engaged. Congratulations,' she said, wistfully. 'I hope you'll be very happy.' It seemed like the right thing to say.

'Probably not,' said Rowan.

'Huh?' She looked at him in confusion.

'What I was saying before, about relationships often being … well, not what they seem. Happy on the surface, but kind of complicated underneath. Like your mum and dad's.'

'Oh, I see.' She didn't, not really.

'Love … it's as weird and magical and inexplicable as this old hill.' He ran his fingers across the grass beside him. 'Sometimes I wish I hadn't fallen in love; life was a lot simpler without it. But I did, and so … I just gotta go with it. Because I can't imagine not being with her, now.'

'But why wouldn't you be happy with Abigail?' Emma was mystified.

'When it looked like her parents might split, it messed her up. I helped her, but she's still working through it. Neville. He … ' He shook his head. 'He's a shit, Emma. It's like me and her won the world's worst dads competition.'

'Not forgetting mine,' Emma said. 'When I found out about all his other women … well, I wanted to kill him, to be honest.'

He took her hand, gave it a squeeze. 'Crap dads for all, eh? Must've been hard for you.'

'Do you know, Rowan, he's got two other kids? Mum says probably more, he's … had … so many women.'

'I know. Most people know. It must be difficult for your mum, too, but she's one tough cookie, right?'

'She is.' Emma shivered; the breeze had cooled.

Rowan put an arm round her and rubbed her shoulder. 'Shall we go?'

She didn't want to. She wanted this afternoon to last forever. But he stood up and held out his hand, pulling her up.

'I guess Belle had a pretty stark choice,' he said, as they started on the path down. 'Leave him, and bring you lot up by herself, or put up with it and keep the family together. He's never going to change his ways. His behaviour makes no sense to me, but . . . the complexities of human motivation, right?'

'That's not an excuse. He's a shit too.'

'I've watched him, with my writer hat on. I try to figure him out. That eternal battle between good and bad, dark and light. We're all fighting those internal battles; we're all flawed, Ems.'

'*Nobody's perfect* isn't an excuse either, Rowan.'

The path widened, and he fell into step beside her.

'But it's a truth. And when you get deep into writing, you find you're exploring your own internal landscape too. God, the stuff I find out about myself when I'm in the zone.'

She looked over at him. 'Like what?'

'I'm . . . well. The dark side. We all have thoughts and emotions we're trying to suppress. Sometimes they bubble through when I'm writing. My own fucked-up-ness is undoubtedly the result of my shit childhood. Adults have this horrible habit of messing up their kids' minds. If your dad's always telling you you're a useless waste of space, you tend to believe it.'

'Well, *my* dad's right obviously lost out to his wrong. And I don't honestly think there was much of a battle.'

Rowan held out his hand as they reached a slippery part of the path, helping her down. Then he didn't let go.

'He really loves your mum, though,' he said. 'The others never last, he's always straight back to her. And maybe love's the redeeming thing? It ultimately triumphs? He adores you lot, he'd never want to hurt you.'

'But he has.'

They reached the kissing gate again. Rowan passed through then turned as he flipped it back. 'You're cool, Emma Snow,' he said. He leaned over the gate and kissed her cheek.

Emma felt as if her heart might burst. She stared hard at the gate as she swung it away from her, as if it were a complicated thing, so he wouldn't see her blush.

As they reached the lane, she said, 'Rowan – why don't you think you'll be happy with Abigail?' She really needed to know.

'She's just not a happy person. I've kind of accepted that. I have to. I've downgraded my expectations from making her happy, to making her not *un*happy, if that makes sense?'

'But what about you? You need to be happy too.'

'If she's not unhappy, I'm happy. I love being with her; we're into the same things – books, dogs, country walks. She's not into parties and all the shallow bullshit that goes with this business.'

'But if she's not happy, you're not happy?'

'Bottom line is, I love her, so I need to be with her. That's just how it is.'

In years to come, after everything changed, Emma would look back on that afternoon, sitting on that magical tor with Rowan, and she'd think . . . *That was the last time I was truly happy. Nobody had died, or disappeared, yet. It was such a perfect afternoon. Even though he'd just told me he was marrying someone else.*

## Chapter Three

London, summer 2006
The Snow Residence, Hampstead

Emma's A level results were in – three As! – and she'd been offered a place at the London School of Economics to study media and communications. But as she flew down the stairs to share her news, she was ambushed by the sight of the detritus from last night. Her smile faded, and she wrinkled her nose in disgust. What fresh level of depravity had these grand, high-ceilinged rooms been witness to?

She picked her way past discarded bottles, glasses and trodden-in food to the kitchen, where Belle was alone at the table reading the morning paper.

'That's lovely, darling,' her mother said without looking up, when Emma told her the happy news. 'While you're here, can you get me a coffee? Black. Mrs Burbage has gone AWOL again. Really, Emerald, I don't know what's going on with the staff these days.' (Her mother was the only person who still used the full and ridiculous version of Emma's name.)

Emma could probably answer that one. Who'd honestly want to work for the Snows in any capacity that involved cleaning up after them?

She'd been hoping for more. A hug? A *Wow, that's amazing!* Or a *Let's make a special celebration breakfast – pancakes?* Surely this was exciting news. Grandma Snow had said she'd be the first girl in the family to go to university.

'Actually,' said Belle, finally looking up. 'Can you fetch me a couple of aspirin while you're at it?'

'Big night, was it?' Emma snapped, filling the kettle via the spout. She turned the tap on full, feeling a grim satisfaction when the water blew back, going everywhere.

The after-show revelry had yet again gone on into the early hours. This house was big, but not big enough that the thumping of the stereo and the guests' raucous laughter didn't keep her awake.

Teddy, the loudest of them all, hadn't yet surfaced. And there was no sign of Pearl who, like her father, probably wouldn't materialise before lunchtime. But she was a teen now, so that was to be expected. Crystal was in Spain, staying with Grandma and Grandpa Rivers, and Freddie and Riv were ... who knew? Playing with fire? Falling out of a tree? Terrorising squirrels on Hampstead Heath? Seven and five now, they were feral, free to do pretty much as they pleased during the holidays.

Emma had put her foot down this year. 'If you want a babysitter, you can hire one. I'm unavailable.'

The Snows were staying in their London house, a three-storey Georgian mansion on the edge of Hampstead Heath, while Teddy appeared in Rowan's new play, *Twisted*, which had taken the West End by storm. The *Guardian* had called him 'the Guy Ritchie of London theatre'. Emma considered that way off the mark. Yes, it was full of Cockney wide-boy gangsters, but that was where the similarity ended.

Emma had been disturbed by the darkness in this play. Proper darkness, not mostly fun darkness, like Ritchie's. The language was ferocious, the characters tearing each other apart. She compared the production to that exuberant *Midsummer Night's Dream*, seven years ago at Middleham. That had been magical, light-hearted, whereas *Twisted* was unrelentingly violent, both emotionally and physically. Was Rowan experimenting? Or was this a reflection of something inside him? She remembered their conversation on the tor, about exploring your dark side through writing, the internal battle between good and bad.

She made Belle's coffee and poured herself a bowl of muesli. Dirty glasses and empty bottles were scattered over the worktops, and the floor was sticky.

'Mum, this is gross,' she said. 'For god's sake, can't you give it a wipe round?'

'Your father can do it,' said Belle. 'He didn't tell me he and Neville were bringing all those hangers-on back last night. Oh . . . Rowan was here, by the way. He was asking after you.'

Emma's heart leapt at the mention of his name. He'd been downstairs, and she hadn't known! She had a boyfriend now – her first proper one (sort of) – and Rowan and Abigail were married, but she still hadn't quite kicked that crush.

She busied herself pouring the milk, in case she was blushing. 'How is he?'

'Troubled, according to Dad,' said Belle. 'You know how tricky he can be. Dark moods, apparently. The play's doing great, but . . . I don't know what's going on with him. Abigail's fallen out with Neville, so Rowan's relationship with him has become difficult. Neville's . . . god, that man. No wonder Abigail's messed up.'

'Messed up how?' said Emma, sitting down opposite Belle. With her fingertips, she pushed aside a bowl of dead crisps.

'I don't know, exactly. I heard drugs – class A ones – but that could just be gossip. Also she's looking terribly thin, like she's wasting away. It's not good.'

In her dressing gown pocket, Emma's mobile beeped. It was a message from Carly, who lived close by.

Fancy going to Camden Market to celebrate?

Emma replied: Yes! Lunchtime?

Cool – c u at Camden tube about 12?

OK :)

'I'm going out,' she said. 'We'll probably get food, so don't worry about dinner.' She looked around her again at the kitchen. 'And for god's sake, Mum, phone an agency or something. Before someone dies from botulism.'

Emma put on a short black dress with shoestring straps and a ruffled skirt, teamed with a wide, metal-studded belt slung round her hips, and calf-length boots. Rather than brushing her long fair hair, she pulled her fingers through it. She was aiming for tousled, like Sienna Miller. It was so good to release her tresses from their term-time constrictions, and to hang up her school uniform – forever!

Looking in the mirror, she was pleased to see that the eye bags she'd woken up with, courtesy of last night's revelries, had deflated. She applied liner and mascara to open her eyes further. Emma was still experimenting with her look, forever aware of being compared with her iconic mother. Rather annoyingly, the Bohemian style Belle had adopted way back at the start of her career had recently become on trend. Emma didn't want to be seen copying her own mother – god forbid – but did enjoy the increasing number of people telling her she was turning out to be just as beautiful as Belle.

As she walked to the tube, Emma pondered her mum's words about Rowan: *troubled . . . I don't know what's going on with him*.

She'd give him a call. Maybe they could have lunch or something. Now she'd left school and was heading to LSE, she could call herself a student. She was ready to join the adult world of catching up with friends for coffee or a glass of wine, nights out on the town . . .

Suddenly overwhelmed with the need to find out how he was, she flipped open her phone. They hadn't been in touch a great deal over the past two years, but he'd done as he promised and read through a couple of pieces she'd written for the school magazine.

One of those had argued in favour of the proposed fox-hunting ban, which to her delight had become law last year. Result! (Not that she could take *all* the credit.) The other had started life as a solemn piece begging the 'Elsyng family' to think about whether they really needed to take all those fossil-fuel-burning flights to the Caribbean when there was so much beauty on their own doorstep. Rowan had suggested she lighten it up, make it a 'For and against the Great British Holiday'.

He'd sent the rewritten article to a contact at the *Guardian*, and they'd run it! Her elation at being discovered as a future environmental features writer was somewhat dampened by the editorial introduction: *Teddy and Belle's eldest daughter, Emma Snow, a pupil at exclusive Elsyng Girls' School, explains why the common people should shun flying to the Caribbean and instead consider a week in Frinton-on-Sea.*

Oh. But it was a start.

'Yup?' came Rowan's voice.

'Hi! It's Emma – how are you?'

'Hi, Ems. Bit shit, since you ask. Big night at your place last night. You were wise to avoid. And you?'

'I'm great! Hey – I got my A level results. Three As. I've got a place at LSE!'

'Wow, that's brilliant.' He sounded genuinely pleased. 'Congratulations. You're far and away the brains of that family. I bet Teddy and Belle are thrilled.'

'Oh, you know. Mum managed to look interested for a millisecond. Dad was still in bed asleep when I left.'

'Benefits of being on the stage. You get to sleep until lunchtime.'

'From the mess, it looked like a good party.' She took a breath. 'Was Abigail with you?'

There was a pause, then he said, 'No, she's not going out much at the moment.'

'Is she okay?'

'What have you heard?'

'Nothing much. Well . . . that she wasn't getting on with Neville?'

'You could say that. It's making life difficult. Thank god for Teddy – he's a buffer between me and Neville. Look, sorry – I need to go, Ems. But I'm glad you rang—'

*Don't go, not yet!*

'Can we have lunch, or a drink, or something?' she asked. 'Sometime? I mean, I can drink now. I'm a student! Not a schoolgirl any more.'

But she was aware she sounded like one. A bit desperate.

'I'll text you. If you're celebrating tonight, have one for me. Congrats again, my clever girl.'

He ended the call.


It was the last time she spoke to him before her world fell apart. Her phone rang as she and Carly were flicking through racks of boho-chic dresses on Camden Market. It was Belle, and she was hysterical.

'Emma, come home! You have to come home—'

'Calm down, Mum. What's going on?' Had Freddie and Riv set fire to something again?

'It's Dad, Emma. I can't wake him up! Oh my god, Emma, I think . . . I think he's dead!'

She and Carly had taken a cab home; the ambulance had already been there when they arrived. It had been too late to help Teddy. He'd died in his sleep, in the early hours of the morning. So as not to wake Belle, who'd gone to bed at something approaching a normal time, he'd slept in a guest bedroom, and there he'd slipped away.

There was an autopsy, and the results were a shock. His heart had been in bad shape, and there was evidence of sustained, prolonged drug abuse. Alcohol was a factor, too.

'Well, if one's going to pop one's clogs,' said Neville when he heard, 'I'd say debauchery's a good way to go.'

# Chapter Four

Teddy's funeral was an enormous, excessive affair at St Paul's in Covent Garden.

Predictably, it was a 'celebration of Teddy's life', with theatre and film greats sharing their memories and their tears. Neville cried noisily, while Belle was quietly tragic, her lovely pale face and hair contrasting with the floaty black of her funeral outfit. Outside the church, as the celebrity congregation mingled on the steps, the roped-off press jostled for position.

Emma and her siblings stuck together in a tight huddle, the three sisters standing protectively around their little brothers. Emma was numb, unable to take in her father's sudden demise. She tried to block the cause of death – and the image it conjured – from her mind, superimposing memories of the jolly figure who'd loved playing with his kids, picturing him dressed as Santa Claus, or in his favourite armchair, telling them stories.

Tears filled her eyes again as she stood on the church steps. She wished she had Belle's strength. How was her mother holding it all together so well?

Someone touched her arm. 'Emma.' It was Rowan. His eyes were red.

At the sight of him, her tears spilled over.

'I didn't hate him, I loved him,' she sobbed.

He pulled her into his arms, and for one fleeting, beautiful moment, she forgot why she was here.

'I know, of course you did,' he said, gently rubbing her back. 'I did too. He was the dad I never had.'

He held her tight and she leaned her head on his chest, putting her arms around him. She felt the unevenness in his posture, the way his back curved a little in the middle.

He lifted a hand and stroked her hair, which hung loose down her back. 'We'll miss him,' he said, 'but he'll go down in history as one of the all-time greats.'

'I can't believe he's dead,' she said. 'I can't believe . . . so many drugs? So much alcohol?'

'He took care around you guys.'

'Is Abigail here?' she asked, looking up at him through her tears.

'No.' He didn't offer an explanation. 'Look, I'm not coming to the wake. I can't stomach it. And Neville's . . . ' He glanced over at his father-in-law, who was standing with a group of actors, ostentatiously dabbing at his eyes with a large handkerchief. 'I can't be round him right now.' He looked down at Emma, who'd rested her head back on his chest. 'You'll be okay. So will Belle. You're both strong women. But if you need to talk, just call me, okay?'

'Thanks, Rowan.'

Emma was reminded again of their conversation, about dark and light. Today had been dark; the funeral had been so hard. But now, with Rowan holding her close, she felt a burst of light, pushing back against the sadness.

He released her. 'I need to go. Good luck, Ems, I know you'll do great.' He smiled, then all at once his eyes filled with tears. Hers spilled over again and she reached out a hand, but he walked away.

Belle's younger sister Kate and her husband Jason stayed with them in Hampstead the week after the funeral, to help Belle sort out Teddy's affairs (the business kind). Aunt Kate was a sleeker version of Belle – same hair, but a fraction of the length and blow-dried into a tidy bob; practical-length nails, well-cut clothes that didn't float when caught by a breeze. Kate took charge while Jason hovered, waiting for orders.

Kate had married Jason Theodore only recently; it was a second marriage for both. She had no children, while Jason had a grown-up son. This was the first time Emma had met her new uncle, as he was often away – he had a construction company that operated mainly in France and Germany. Apparently his long absences, which didn't seem to bother Kate, had been what ended his first marriage, to 'a right battle-axe'.

'She's *frate*-fully rich, Emma,' Kate said in a pretend-posh accent, as the two of them cleared up the breakfast things. It was the morning after the funeral, and Belle was sitting at the table staring into space. As Emma took in her vacant expression, her dark-ringed eyes, she hoped Rowan's prediction that her mother would have the strength to get through this was correct.

Kate prattled on about Jason's ex-wife. She was beginning to annoy Emma, but at least her aunt's non-stop chatter filled the silence. It was a new experience, a quiet Snow house. It was the housekeeper's day off; the boys had gone to stay with a friend of the family, and Pearl and Crystal stayed mostly in their rooms, glued to their computer screens. Belle seemed to have lost the ability to speak in anything other than monosyllables. Suddenly Emma longed for the old, noisy, chaotic version of her family.

'She's got a title,' continued Kate, clattering plates into the dishwasher. 'Lady Madeline Beauregard – but I call her Lady Mad. She's very intense. She lives on a massive country estate in the Yorkshire Dales – just one of her many residences. She's actually quite terrifying; it's no wonder Jason spent all his time in France. I've sent him out to mow the lawn, by the way.'

'We have a gardener,' Emma said. 'He doesn't need to do that.'

'Oh, he just wants to feel useful. Does what he's told. Hey, Emma. I've now got the most *gorgeous* stepson.' She winked. 'Henry. You two should meet!'

'I've got a boyfriend,' Emma replied. Though 'boyfriend' was probably an exaggeration. Aaron was nice, but he was far too starry-eyed about her famous family. On their third date, a couple of days before Teddy had died, she'd struggled to keep the conversation going, and had been relieved when he finally kissed her so she didn't have to think about what to say next. The kiss had been pleasant, but ...

Maybe Rowan had ruined all boys for her. Those around her own age seemed altogether too immature, too ordinary.

'Is he a serious boyfriend?' said Kate.

'Not really. It'd probably be better if I started uni single, to be honest. Less complicated.'

Life returned to a new version of normal. Belle coped with her husband's death by going on tour. Every concert sold out in minutes, as Britain was desperately sad at the loss of Teddy, and wanted to show their support.

Pearl and Crystal returned to their Gloucestershire boarding school, and Freddie and Riv to their prep school in Ludlow. In the blink of an eye, the Snows were once again scattered across Britain. Teddy was scattered near the Yorkshire village of Towton, in the meadow where he and Belle had picnicked on their first date.

Emma loved student life. Living in hall, joining clubs and protest marches, dating other students, hanging out in the LSE bar with her new friends. But she missed her family, mourned her father, and wondered about Rowan, who never answered her emails or texts.

Then, a year or so after Teddy's death, she received an email from Belle, who was on tour in Europe.

> Emerald, sweetheart,
>
> I hope you're well. I'm so sorry to have to tell you this, but I just heard from Jane Warwick that darling Abigail has died. I don't know the details, but it seems it wasn't unexpected.

She'd been in and out of hospital for a while.
Jane is devastated, of course. I'm afraid
Neville's blaming Rowan, which is absolutely
unjustified. Poor Rowan's beside himself,
Jane says.

I'm sure you'll want to contact Rowan, but do
be careful what you say. He's very close to the
edge, blaming himself for Abigail not making
it through (but I do know it wasn't suicide,
sweetheart, whatever you might hear).

I'm so sorry to be sending you such awful
news. The tour's going well, I'm doing okay.
Missing Dad so much, but connecting with my
fans, putting my emotion into my singing, is
really helping. I hope you're still enjoying
university – make the most of these happy
times, my darling.

With love and hugs

Mum xxxx

Emma closed her laptop and stared out of the university library window. What had happened to Abigail? Nobody had ever told Emma what was wrong with her, except that she was sad, too thin, didn't like going out, and maybe had a drug problem.

Emma remembered a pretty, quiet girl with expressive brown eyes and a spiky pixie cut. Several years ago, Abigail had introduced the Snow children to her menagerie of pets – mainly rabbits and guinea pigs. She must have been about eighteen, because Emma remembered her saying she was going to study veterinary science at university.

She took out her phone, wanting to reach out to Rowan.

*Be careful what you say. He's very close to the edge.*

After a minute of typing and deleting, she gave up and packed away her laptop and books. Leaving the building, she headed south towards the Thames. She needed some air, to think, but the wind was biting. Hunkering down in her wool coat she walked briskly until she reached the river, then turned east, beneath the arches of Waterloo Bridge and into Embankment Gardens, where she found a sheltered bench.

Pulling off her gloves, she fished her lunch out of her backpack and munched on a tuna sandwich, absently watching a twitchy squirrel foraging on the grass.

The words were forming in her head. Swallowing the final mouthful she took out her phone again and started to type them in.

*Hi Rowan.* No. The 'hi' was all wrong. Delete.

*Rowan – I just heard. I'm so sorry . . .* No. Everyone would say that. She needed hers to be different.

*I don't have the words.* Well, that was true. She didn't. She deleted them.

Would Rowan even care whether or not she sent him a message? He hadn't replied to any of those she'd sent this past year. That was probably because of whatever had been going on with Abigail (though really, how hard was it to send a couple of lines? Like Teddy had always said, Rowan was difficult.)

But what was Emma to him, after all? The kid daughter of his old mentor. If he bothered to keep in touch, it was only because Teddy had been 'the dad I never had' for a while. So that made her a kind of ex-honorary sister. That was all.

She started again.

> Rowan – I remember what you told me about
> Abigail, that lovely afternoon on Glastonbury
> Tor. She was very lucky to have you love her
> so much. I'm sure any not-unhappy times she
> had were because of you. I hope I can see you
> sometime. I know I'm just some kid from your
> past, but I'm here for you if ever you need to talk
> or something. Love, Emma xxxx

She pressed send, wiped away a tear and set off back for afternoon lectures.

As she passed underneath the bridge again, her phone vibrated in her pocket.

Emma – you're not just that kid from the past. I can't
think further than a minute ahead at the moment, but
it's good to be in your thoughts. Maybe I'll see you
again someday. R x

Emma heard some time later that Rowan had left London. *Twisted* was still running, but he'd taken himself off. No one seemed to know where.

# *Chapter Five*

## Spring 2008
### Kent

The Snows were spending Easter with Aunt Kate and Uncle Jason at the couple's quaint, black-and-white cottage, tucked away down a lane in a pretty Kent village. It was Sunday afternoon, and after eating far too many chocolate eggs, Freddie and Riv, now aged ten and eight, seemed to have run out of steam and were sitting quietly on the living-room floor building a Tower of London out of Lego. Uncle Jason was helping.

The room was quiet, apart from the rattle of Lego and the crackle and spit of the log fire. Emma's sisters had taken Kate's dog for a walk, and Belle, Kate and Emma, comfortably full after one of Jason's legendary Sunday roasts, were slumped by the fire, reading.

Kate tutted at her newspaper. 'It says here that quite a few fox hunts have been ignoring the ban.'

'Yes,' said Belle, looking up from *A Game of Thrones*. She loved her fantasy novels. 'Teddy's parents told me there are still a number happening in Yorkshire. It makes my blood boil. They think just because they're land-owning gentry they're above the law. As if anyone really *owns* land. The Earth and its creatures belong to no one, it's—'

'How are they allowed to get away with that?' interrupted Emma. 'Why aren't they being arrested?'

'I expect the saboteurs will be back on the case,' said Belle. 'I'm thinking of saying something to the press. I'd like to lend my support.'

'What can I do?' said Emma. 'Something in the uni newsletter?'

Freddie looked up from his Lego. 'Foxes are awesome. People shouldn't be allowed to kill them.'

'I like *Fantastic Mr Fox*,' said Riv. 'Why do people kill foxes?'

'To control their numbers,' said Jason. 'If a fox gets into a chicken run it looks like a bomb has gone off. Not pretty.'

'Boom!' said Riv, lobbing a handful of Lego onto the fortress wall Jason had been carefully building.

'It's more for sport, River,' said Belle. 'The thrill of the chase. Riding a big fast horse across the fields for fun. Except it's not fun for the fox.'

'They chase it and chase it until the fox is too tired to run any more,' said Freddie. 'And then it falls over and it's ripped apart by the fox hunters' dogs. Until it's *dead*.'

Riv's mouth dropped open in horror.

Emma shook her head at Freddie, but he was on a roll.

'And they wipe the dead fox's blood over children's faces.' He lifted a hand and dragged it across his brother's cheek.

Riv swiped it away. 'Stop it!'

'No, Freddie,' said Jason, gently but firmly. 'That was in the old days. They don't do that any more.'

'Usually not,' said Kate darkly. 'Jason still hunts.'

Freddie and Riv gasped.

'We follow a scent trail,' he said. 'There's no real fox involved.'

'I believe you,' Kate replied, shaking her head. 'Jason's ex, Lady Mad, prefers the real thing, right, Jason? I can just see her lopping off the brush and throwing the carcass to the hounds.'

'Kate, *please*,' said Belle, flicking her eyes over to Riv.

'Sorry. But I bet she's up to her neck in illegal hunting. She's the master of her local hunt.'

An idea was forming in Emma's head. 'I need a topic for my final assignment – an investigative piece with an environmental theme. Maybe I'll look into whether the new law is being upheld, get some reaction from people like Lady Mad who might think they're above it. I could interview her.'

'Jason can introduce you,' said Kate. 'Can you get on to that, darling?'

Uncle Jason did as he was told, as per, and emailed his ex-wife to explain Emma's university project. But Lady Madeline ungraciously declined the opportunity.

'Sorry, Emma,' Kate said over the phone. 'She won't be persuaded. To be honest, it's probably because you're related to me, rather than any reluctance to discuss fox hunting. According to Jason, she can talk about that till the cows come home.'

'That's okay. Thanks so much for trying.'

'She was keen until Jason explained who you were – the family connection,' Kate went on. 'Let's just say, although they split before I came on the scene, I'm not her favourite person.'

'Oh dear. But I can quote what she's publicly said on the subject. It won't be as good as a one on one, but it'll still be a strong piece.'

As she typed it up, she remembered the article she'd written for the school magazine, the one Rowan had helped her with. It had begun life full of emotive, purple prose about the rights of wild animals and the barbarity of noble native foxes being ripped apart by baying, bloodthirsty hounds bred for their . . . well, their bloodthirstiness. Rowan had whipped it back covered in red, adverbs deleted, margin notes crammed down the side:

*Cite! What's your source?*

*Calm down – kill these exclamation marks*

*Delete delete delete*

*Nope*

*FFS Ems*

But also:

*THIS – yes* ❤

She remembered how she'd felt – the mixture of dismay and elation at his feedback, hearing his voice in her head as she read through the comments: *Take a breath. Commas are your friends, girl.*

'Don't lose that voice,' he'd said, back at Glastonbury. She'd quickly learned to strike a balance between authoritative, persuasive and passionate. And much of that was thanks to Rowan.

She missed him.

'Why don't you come down for a weekend, when you've finished your exams?' Aunt Kate said. 'I feel like I owe you, having failed to bag Lady Mad.'

Emma accepted. Another dose of bucolic Kent countryside would be very welcome after weeks in the city.

Jason met her off the train. 'Lovely to see you again,' he said, loading her backpack into the Range Rover.

'It's good to be out of the Big Smoke.' She breathed deeply.

'I'm delighted you'll be meeting my son at last,' he said, driving slowly and carefully down the narrow road.

'What? Oh!' Emma's heart sank. She'd assumed she'd be the only guest. Now, instead of curling up with a book in some cosy corner of Aunt Kate's cottage, she'd have to make polite conversation with a stranger.

'Did Kate not say? Sorry about that!' said Jason. 'But I'm sure you and Henry will get on.'

The son of Lady Mad? But in spite of herself, Emma was curious.

She ducked her head as she entered the old, beamed living room.

'Emma!' said Kate, coming in from the kitchen, wrapping her in a hug. 'So good to see you. I spoke to your mum this afternoon; promised her I'd look after you this weekend.'

'Thanks for inviting me.'

The front door slammed, and Kate's Welsh Corgi, Owen, rushed into the room and over to Emma.

'Hello, boy!' She bent down to pat him, and on straightening up . . .

*Oh!*

Standing just inside the door was a tall, rosy-cheeked man, maybe twenty-five, twenty-six, with red-blonde hair and startlingly blue eyes. His expression was open and friendly, and he was . . . gosh. He was very, very good-looking.

'Hello, Emma!' he said, holding out his hand. 'It's great to meet you. Glad it's not just me and the olds this weekend.' He spoke beautifully – just the right side of plummy.

'Olds?' said Kate, punching him on the arm.

Emma took his hand. 'Hello – nice to meet you too.'

The handshake was firm. 'I hear you're at LSE?'

Kate returned to the kitchen, saying, 'Jason – can you give me a hand, please.'

'Yes, my second year,' said Emma, as Henry watched them leave, an amused smile on his face.

He shook his head. 'Your aunt's got my dad well under the thumb.'

Emma laughed. 'She's quite bossy.'

'Poor Dad. Having said that, Kate's a lot gentler with him than my other mum.'

'Lady Mad . . . Madeline?' Emma felt the heat rise in her cheeks at the faux pas.

Henry grinned. 'Correct the first time. Mad as a bag of ferrets.'

'Mine is too,' said Emma.

'Ah, the divine Belle Snow. I do hope our mums meet sometime. That would *really* be something to see.' He chuckled. 'Want a wine? Or a G&T? What's your tipple, Emma?'

'A wine would be lovely. White, please.'

'Sit yourself down, I'll be right back.'

As she parked herself by the fireside, Emma was aware of her heart racing a little. Holy heck. As Kate had said, Henry was indeed 'gorgeous'. (And she had *definitely* engineered this, no two ways about it.) And he was charming, and nice, and . . . she blew out a breath.

He returned with the wine, and sat down opposite her. 'How do you like LSE? A couple of my mates went there.'

'It's great. I'm doing media and communications. I'm hoping to become a journalist.'

His eyebrows shot up. 'Seriously? I'm working at the *Lancaster Post*, up in Lancashire. Obviously.'

'Oh! I didn't know that.'

'It's only a small paper, but hey, Andrew Neil started out on the *Paisley Daily Express*, right?' He raised his beer in her direction. 'Cheers – here's to the weekend.' He sat back in his chair and crossed one long leg over the other.

'I'll drink to that! I'd like to write features – investigative. Especially on the environment. I just did an assignment on the anti-fox-hunting legislation. Actually, Jason asked your mum if I could interview her, but she said no.'

He pulled a face. 'God, why would you want to?'

'What's it like, working on a regional paper?' she said. She remembered what Rowan had told her that day in Glastonbury. 'Do you have to ask parents how they feel when their children die in road accidents?'

'Death knocks? There's a bit of that, yes. But sometimes they really want to talk about it, strangely.'

But maybe that wasn't, in fact, strange. Henry was so engaging, so . . .

She was having trouble looking away from his eyes. The thought occurred to her, almost subconsciously, that they were the polar opposite to Rowan's. Bright versus dark; open versus guarded.

'I'd hate to do that.'

'Oh, you're put on far worse things when you start,' he said. 'My first assignment was the Garstang Vegetable-growers' Association's annual pumpkin competition.'

She laughed. 'Quirky rurals showing you round their allotments? Sounds fun.'

'Don't be fooled,' he said. 'Vegetable growing is viciously competitive. And flower shows are even worse – absolutely brutal.'

'Wars of the Roses?' said Emma.

'Utter carnage.'

They smiled at each other, rather stupidly.

Owen loped along ahead of them, zigzagging across the path as he investigated interesting smells and intriguing holes in the hedgerow. Kate and Jason were half a field ahead of Henry and Emma, and the gap was widening.

Kate glanced back at them as she climbed over a stile.

'Subtle,' Henry remarked.

It was Sunday afternoon, and Emma was due to leave Aunt Kate's soon. In the two days she'd known Henry, they'd progressed from friendly chat to full-on flirting. It was delicious. He was far and away the loveliest man she'd met since leaving school. Fun, intelligent, mature, thoughtful, beautiful manners, and – yes, heir to a fortune, but that was by the by. The Snows weren't exactly poor.

He opened the dog door next to the stile for Owen, then climbed over and held out his hand to help Emma down.

When her feet landed on the ground, he didn't let go. 'Shall we do this?' he said, looking down at her hand. 'Make Kate's day?'

Emma wasn't sure what he meant by 'this'. The holding hands, or what the holding hands implied?

'Works for me,' she said, smiling up at him.

'So, Emma,' said Henry as they set off walking again. 'I've been listening hard all weekend, and I haven't heard mention of a boyfriend. Is there such a person in your life, if I may be so bold as to ask?'

Emma's heart was racing again. *He's going to ask me . . .*

'No one special. And you? Is there some bonnie northern lassie in Henry's life?'

'I live in Lancaster, not Scotland. But no. In which case, might I trouble you for your phone number?'

'You might. It would be fun to keep in touch.'

'I should imagine my stepmother will organise things so we do.'

He stopped walking, and gently pulled her towards him. 'And to be honest, I really hope she does.' He released her hand and put his arms round her waist. 'You're lovely, Emma. I expected you to be some bratty celebs' kid. I thought you'd be absolutely revolting, in spite of Kate talking you up all the time. But – well. You're ...'

Just before his lips met hers, he said, 'Okay if I do this?'

'So polite, Henry,' she said. 'Of course it is.'

It was sweet and delicious. If that kiss had been food, it would have been a cream slice, she thought, later. One of those layered ones where you just can't bear to finish it, and in the middle there's a sudden exquisite burst of jam, and you let out a little moan, because you can't help yourself.

'Next time I'm in London,' he said, as they set off walking again, 'can I see you? Take you out?'

'Yes, please.'

'And ... that phone number?'

Emma stopped and took out her phone. 'I'll text it to you. What's yours?'

As she flipped it open, she noticed the message icon, and pressed read. Her heart skipped a beat. *Rowan.*

'Is everything okay?' said Henry. The shock must have shown on her face. It had been a year since she'd heard from him.

'Fine, I just ... I need to read this.'

Emma – sorry, been off the grid for a while. I've left London for good. Back in Yorkshire. Call me sometime. R x

In a flash, his face was back in her mind's eye, knocking her off balance. His expression at the funeral, just before he'd hugged her, on the church steps. Wrung out, his eyes red. And then ... that sublime moment of connection, when he'd held her tight. She could still feel his warm chest against her cheek, the curve in his spine when she'd slipped her arms round him.

'Emma? Is it bad news?'

'No, no, just . . . an old family friend. Someone my dad used to work with. You know . . . any mention of my dad.'

'Oh, right. Of course. I'm sorry.'

She took a breath. 'What's your number, then?'

He told her, and she texted: Call me soon! Emma xxx

His phone beeped and he typed something in.

Is tonight soon enough?

She grinned.

No! But it'll have to do. Till then xxx

On the train back to London, she stared out of the window, thinking back over the weekend. And the kiss. Kiss-*es*. He'd kissed her again, on the station platform, after she'd said goodbye to Jason and Kate in the car park. 'We'll wait here,' Kate had said with a knowing smile.

Henry lived hundreds of miles away, but he'd said he came down regularly, so . . . maybe it would work?

And then her thoughts returned to Rowan. He'd been there, in her heart, for so long. It was time to let go of that girlhood crush. Dad was dead, there was no real reason to be in touch any more. He'd probably only texted her, after all this time, out of a sense of doing the right thing by Teddy. It was in the past. Rowan was done with London; he'd gone back to Yorkshire.

*Both so far away. One in Lancashire, one in Yorkshire.*

Her phone beeped as the train pulled in to St Pancras.

Missing you already. H xx

## Chapter Six

August 2009

'Are you and Bingley a proper thing now, then?' asked Crystal. Emma sighed. She'd known it would only be a matter of time before the inquisition began.

'Well?' said Pearl, when Emma didn't reply immediately.

She shook her head slightly at her sisters, as they sat with their mother round the kitchen table drinking wine. They were mini versions of Belle, with their blue eyes, long wavy blonde hair and delicate features. Crystal had inherited their father's height, while Pearl was petite, like Belle.

'Sort of,' she said. 'We're probably too occasional to be actual boyfriend-girlfriend, but I really, really like him.'

Belle was staying in their Hampstead house while she recorded a new studio album, and Crystal and Pearl were home for the university holidays.

Henry, visiting Emma for the weekend, was freshening up after his long train journey. He and Emma had been meeting up whenever they could. She loved spending time with this easy-going, clever man, who treated her like a princess. But the part-time, long-distance relationship was frustrating. Henry's career was taking off, and he was usually up against deadlines, forever chasing the next big story, so he only made it down to London occasionally.

The sounds of explosions and machine-gun fire floated along the hall to the kitchen. The boys, also home for the holidays, were in the TV room, deep into a video game.

'I suppose virtual explosions are preferable to actual ones,' said Pearl, after a particularly loud boom. 'Mum, I told you not to let them near my gerbils.'

'Sorry, darling. I think it was from fright. We'll get you some new ones.'

'Have you glimpsed Bingley's dark side yet, Emma?' said Crystal.

'Nope. A little tight with money, maybe, but that's about it.'

'But he's got shedloads of the stuff!' said Crystal. 'Or at least, his mum has.'

'It's fine, I'm not interested in his money.'

In spite of Teddy's extravagant lifestyle, their father had left his children well provided for, and Belle was still raking it in thanks to the lasting popularity of Woodville's classic albums. *Whispers* even surfaced in the Top 100 every now and then, after all these years, and their tours continued to sell out.

Henry was rising quickly up the ranks at the *Lancaster Post*. He'd broken several stories that had been picked up by the nationals, and had been thrilled when, as a result, Terri Robbins-More, editor of *The Rack*, Britain's most respected current affairs magazine, had commissioned him to write a piece on the behind-the-scenes politics at Manchester United FC, and had then offered him a full-time position.

Emma had encouraged Henry to make the move. It would be a fantastic step in his career, surely, working for media giant Rose Corp? Maybe he'd even get to work with Harry Rose himself! And, of course, he'd be near her, in London. Emma had recently graduated and would soon start as a cub reporter on a local paper.

But Henry loved the culture of the regional daily. 'And Harry Rose is an exceptional media man, yes,' he'd added. 'But my god,

I can't imagine working full-time for Terri. She's an absolute dragon. She reminds me of my mum.'

Emma still hadn't met Lady Mad. 'We'll save that for later,' Henry had said.

'I'm going up to Yorkshire in a couple of weeks,' said Belle, stroking the family cat, Jacquetta, curled up in her lap.

'To see Grandma and Grandpa Snow?' said Emma.

'Yes, I'll be staying with them. But I've decided to send the boys to Middleham. You remember going there for Dad's play, the one Rowan wrote? It's Dad's old school, and I think he'd have wanted Elfred and River to go there.'

That jolt to the heart at the mention of Rowan's name. Emma still sent the occasional email, letting him know how she was doing, but never received a response.

*Maybe I'll see you again someday.* His final text had been a brush off. He was done with her family, now Teddy was gone. Emma had tried to consign him to the past, but her reaction to Belle's mention of his name hinted she wasn't quite there yet.

'That's great,' said Crystal. 'Yes, Dad would have wanted them to go there.'

'It's a very liberal school, nicely in line with what we always wanted for our children,' said Belle. 'Though ... sometimes I wonder if the boys wouldn't benefit from a little more discipline.'

Emma snorted. 'What, Mum? Are you un-mellowing in your old age?'

'Mr Chatterjee from two doors down buttonholed me about them today,' said Pearl. 'Honestly, Mum, you need to tell them they can't just go into people's gardens without asking first.'

'They were probably fetching a ball,' said Belle dismissively.

'No – it was after dark. They were hiding behind his bins. He got the fright of his life. They told him they were on fox watch.'

The four women smiled guiltily at each other as they pictured it.

'Little monsters,' said Emma. 'But, Mum, I'm glad they'll be going to Dad's old school.'

'Yes. And of course, Rowan's there,' she said, 'so that'll be nice for them, to know someone when they start.'

'*What?*' said Emma, her smile disappearing. 'Rowan's there?'

'He's teaching. Didn't you know? I always assumed you'd stayed in touch. You and Teddy – and poor Abigail, of course. I felt you were the only people he ever properly connected with. He was such a loner.'

'Mr Darcy,' said Crystal. 'All brooding and dark looks. Bloody gorgeous, too. I would.'

'No, not Darcy – Heathcliff,' said Pearl, dreamily. 'Darcy was on the level, just a bit socially awkward. Rowan's your legit beautiful fuck-up. Remember his play we went to see? *Twisted*? Holy shit, that was intense.'

'Girls!' said Belle. 'Can we stop the swearing, please? And Rowan is not a – what you said, Pearl. He's a lovely man who's had a very difficult time. He lost his wife, remember? She was only twenty-two. Rowan was devastated.'

'Wasn't she a fuck-up too, though?' said Pearl.

'For heaven's sake,' said Belle. 'When did you two become these teens?'

'Yes – stop it!' said Emma. 'Please, don't talk about him like this. Mum – how come you know he's at Middleham? What's he doing there?'

'I'm still in touch with Jane Warwick. She hears from him from time to time. I think it's the right thing for him to do. He's a Yorkshire boy; I don't think he liked London, not really. He wasn't happy here. He's teaching English—'

'Oh, he'd be so good at that,' Emma interrupted, remembering how he'd helped her.

'Jane said he's doing fine,' said Belle. 'He loves teaching.'

'He taught me a lot about writing.' Emma smiled at the memory.

'Watch out, Henry,' said Crystal. 'Emma's gone misty eyed.'

'I emailed him about Elfred and River starting at Middleham,' said Belle. 'He's looking forward to seeing them again. They'll have to stay there during the holidays, when I'm on tour, and he's said he'll keep an eye on them for me.'

Emma was still processing the fact that Rowan and her brothers would soon be together at Middleham; this renewal of the family connection. She felt a churning combination of anticipation and dread at the thought of seeing him again. She wanted to reconnect, while fearing that it might kick-start those feelings she thought she'd managed to leave behind.

But she couldn't help herself. 'Mum, can I come with you to drop the boys off?'

She ignored the knowing look that passed between Pearl and Crystal.

'Of course,' said Belle. 'It would be nice to have company on the drive up. More to the point, someone to keep the boys under control. We'll spend a few nights with Teddy's parents – they'd love to see you.'

Henry came into the kitchen, smelling fresh after his shower, dressed in a crisp, clean shirt and jeans.

'Greetings, Bingley,' said Crystal. 'Looking lush.'

Henry grinned. He now knew about the nickname – Crystal had forced him to watch *Pride and Prejudice* the last time he'd visited. 'As are you, Ms Bennet.'

'Jane Bennet – that's me!' said Crystal, fluttering her eyelashes and raising her glass at him. 'The hottest Bennet sister.'

'No – you're Lydia,' he replied, pouring himself a wine.

'Rude!' Crystal said, and cackled.

Jacquetta looked up at the noise, fixing Henry with her green-eyed stare. He leaned across and stroked her black, furry head. 'Honestly, it's like walking into a coven.'

Crystal cackled some more.

'You are *so* right,' said Emma. 'I do apologise for my family.'

'There was a frog in the shower, by the way,' said Henry. 'I re-introduced it to the wild.'

'Oh dear. That was Prince Harry, the boys' pet,' said Belle.

'Serves them right,' said Emma. 'Horrible little pranksters. Come on, Henry, let's go find dinner.'

\*

The next morning, Emma was only half awake as Henry gently brought her to life, stroking, kissing, finally moving on top of her as she sighed with pleasure and opened her eyes, smiling lazily up at him. 'Mmm, good morning, lovely Henry . . . '

The door burst open and Pearl called, 'Sorry! Just need to borrow your hairdryer, mine's packed up. I'm not looking . . . '

'Chrissakes,' muttered Henry, rolling off her.

They waited, neither saying a word as Pearl scuttled across the room and into the bathroom, then back again.

'Thanks!' Pearl slammed the bedroom door behind her.

Henry pulled Emma towards him again; there was a knock on the door, and a giggle. 'We know what you're doing,' came Riv's singsong voice. More tittering.

'Okay, I give up,' said Henry.

She looked over at him. He was staring up at the ceiling, but he was smiling. Good-natured didn't begin to describe this man.

'Sorry,' she said. 'At least we had last night.' And it had been wonderful. Henry was a gentle, considerate lover. Not that she'd had many lovers to compare him with. Just one, in fact, and that had been more the result of curiosity than desire. The second-year law student had lasted only three weeks.

'Your siblings don't seem to understand—'

'Privacy? No. But I think . . . when we were kids, we were only together during the holidays. It was always exciting, so we were all rather in each other's faces. That doesn't seem to have changed.'

'You were lucky,' he said, as she snuggled into his chest. 'There was only really me and Mother, when I was home from school.'

'What about your dad? Jason's lovely.'

'He was hardly ever there. He was usually on the continent for his work, especially later on. Mother doted on me; it was . . . smothering.'

'Is she really that scary?' said Emma. Dragon or not, surely it was time he introduced her?

'You want to meet her?'

'I think I'd like that.'

'I think you wouldn't like that, to be honest. She's on to you.'

'What?' Emma turned to look at him.

'She knows you're an anti-blood-sports campaigner. Hunting's her thing. She was apoplectic when the ban came in. She was behind a lot of that lobbying about the rural way of life being under threat, ignorant townies having no right, etc., etc.'

'Ah.'

'Anything – any*one* – who draws attention to the fact that hunts with actual foxes might still be happening—'

'Which would be me.' Emma had been on the universities' anti-blood-sports campaign team, and continued to write passionate (but better-worded, these days) articles on the rights of wildlife to be safe from guns, hounds, traps, poisons, and farmers with a bad attitude.

'And, well, Kate . . . ' continued Henry. 'Mother still loves Dad, and they're actually on good terms. I'm afraid . . . Dad's not great with money. Mother helps him out. She always hoped they'd get back together. When she discovered Dad had a new girlfriend, and that she was Belle's sister—'

'Mum also being very publicly on the side of the foxes—'

'Yep. Let's just say my mother's the polar opposite to Belle. She was so upset when Dad remarried. She's horrible to Kate, she can't help herself.' He turned onto his side and traced a finger down her cheek. 'I have an inkling she might be the same with you.'

'But it's not like I had anything to do with her marriage failure. And neither did Kate.'

'Mother takes against people.' He cupped her chin, brushed her lips with his. 'You're Kate's niece and Belle's daughter, and Belle's a figurehead for the hunt saboteurs. God, that photo call she did, when she was sitting on that horse, whipping the demonstrators along. She looked like bloody Boudicca. Mum would have happily set the hounds on her.'

'Yikes.'

'I'm sorry, Emma. I don't mean to be so negative. But if you're going to meet her, I want you to be prepared.'

'I'll lay on the charm,' said Emma.

'No need – utterly charming is your default.' He kissed her again, deeply this time, and pulled her closer.

Melting, Emma pressed herself against the length of his beautiful body, hooked a leg round his thigh . . .

The door flew open and Riv called, 'Breakfast's ready! Mum says come and get it.' Then it slammed shut again.

'Okay, I've revised my position,' said Henry. 'I'd officially like to murder your brothers.'

# *Chapter Seven*

## September 2009

For once the boys were quiet, as Emma sat between them in the back of the Rolls-Royce.

The pair had argued and fidgeted as far as Nottingham, when they'd stopped at a service station for burgers and fuel. Then the boys had disappeared while Belle and Emma had been delayed by selfie-seekers in the Ladies'. (Belle was always too gracious to refuse.)

Emma had found them in the amusement arcade. She stopped and watched them for a moment, noticing other people doing the same. Freddie and Riv always attracted attention, with their arrestingly pretty faces and white-blonde hair. A couple of years ago they'd appeared in a TV drama series with Teddy, and the British public had gone wild for them. Neville had tried to sign them up, seeing future tween idols, but Belle had refused. They were too young, she said, and the TV thing was just for fun.

Teddy had backed her up. Emma had been impressed, for once, at her parents' good sense.

'And as if I'd let *Neville* manage our boys,' Belle had said. 'It'd be like asking a hungry wolf to look after a couple of spring lambs.'

As Emma watched them trying to grab a toy in the claw

machine, she remembered Rowan's instinctive dislike of Neville, how he had bristled at the mention of his name. Had something happened there?

She marched over to her brothers. 'Hey, I told you to stay in the café! You can't just wander off! Stranger danger – remember?'

Freddie rolled his eyes. 'I'm *eleven*, Em-er-ald. Nearly twelve. And there are two of us. I think someone would notice if a perv tried to abduct us from a service station.'

'I'll miss you, Emma,' said Riv, the (slightly) quieter of the two, as they continued north. 'I wish we didn't have to go away.' He snuggled in to her and put his head on her shoulder.

A lump pushed its way into her throat.

'Can you tell us one of your stories?' he said.

So she told them a Yorkshire folk tale, of a giant, ghostly dog, with eyes that burned like coal, who was said to lead lonely travellers astray. 'If you're walking on the moors at night,' she finished, 'and you see two glowing eyes, be sure not to leave the road ... ' She looked down at Riv; he'd fallen asleep. Freddie had too. Slipping an arm round each, she rested her head on Riv's soft curls.

They arrived at Middleham School late afternoon. The boys piled out of the car, and Belle stood by her open door, breathing in the crisp, fresh, autumn air. 'I love it up here,' she said.

Emma was still in the car, a little mirror in her hand, brushing her hair which she'd released from its ponytail. Her stomach was churning. It was ridiculous. The thought of seeing Rowan again had her behaving like that star-struck teen on Glastonbury Tor.

Deep breaths. She was twenty-two, about to start her first proper job, and with a steadily growing following on her blog about environmental issues. She wasn't a child any more.

'Come on, Emerald,' called Belle, unloading the boys' bags from the boot. 'I can't carry all this gear myself. River! Elfred!' But the boys had disappeared up the front steps of the school, which looked like a cross between a stately home and a castle. Battlements ran along the roof high above, and there were square towers at either end of the imposing façade.

'I don't remember this,' said Emma, hauling out a holdall and dropping it beside the two large cases. 'I guess it was a long time ago.'

'Oh, Emerald,' said Belle, gazing around her. 'Think of Dad, at school here. I do miss him.'

Emma's feelings about her father were still conflicted. 'I do too.'

'He was an old rogue,' said Belle. 'But he was my rogue.'

She couldn't help it. 'But not only yours, Mum?'

*What am I saying? Why now?*

Belle didn't respond for a moment. Then she picked up Freddie's battered old teddy and hugged it to her. 'Love is a strange beast, darling. Your father's behaviour was appalling, yes. I died a little death each time I found out about his latest affair. But I learned to cope. He was what he was, and I loved him. And if he hadn't been living that life, maybe he wouldn't have been such a great actor.'

Emma made a small noise in the back of her throat.

Belle pursed her lips. 'People of Teddy's calibre rarely live by the same rules as the rest of us. He lived life to the full – to excess. Don't be so judgemental. Your Henry may be delightful, but he's . . . never mind. We need to get inside or those boys will get themselves expelled before they've even started.'

Emma wanted to ask what Henry was, but thought better of it. *Normal, probably.*

Two older boys came down the steps and politely introduced themselves. Watching them, Emma guessed they weren't aware of Belle's rock-star status. Woodville were before their time, old enough that there were tribute bands.

'Mr Pickford has asked us to show you to his study,' one said. 'We'll get the bags taken up to the dorms.'

The other boy was surreptitiously eyeing Emma. She smiled at him, and he blushed.

In the headmaster's study, Belle filled in forms while Emma looked around her with interest. There were tapestries and portraits on the walls, and the furniture was antique. The ancient, traditional feel of these surroundings didn't seem to fit the famously liberal attitudes of the school.

'I'd like to see Rowan Bosworth before I leave,' said Belle, putting down the pen. 'He's an old family friend.'

'Of course,' said Mr Pickford. 'I'll see if he's available now.' He picked up his phone, and after the brief call continued to make polite conversation with Belle.

Emma wasn't taking in a word. Her heart was in her mouth.

There was a knock on the door, and Rowan came in. Belle jumped up with a squeal, and hugged him. 'Oh my goodness! How absolutely wonderful to see you. We have *missed* you!'

He wasn't wearing black. His hair was shorter, curling over the neck of his midnight-blue sweater, worn with jeans and boots. He was the same, but different. He looked ... comfortable in his skin. Happy.

He looked over Belle's shoulder at Emma. She saw the momentary surprise.

*Yes, Rowan, I'm grown up now!*

Then his smile widened into a grin. 'Emma Snow, what in god's name are you doing here?'

'Delivering monsters,' she said. 'Hello, Mr Bosworth.'

He released Belle and came over, holding out his hands.

She took them, drinking in that striking face. The square jaw; the long, straight nose. His dark, dark eyes fringed with long eyelashes.

Those eyes – she'd forgotten their depth. How there was little delineation between the pupils and irises. It was like drowning. All over again.

The headmaster gave a discreet cough. 'Rowan, these ladies have had a long drive. Perhaps you'd like to take Mrs Snow and Emma for a brief tour, then get them a cup of tea?'

'Sure,' said Rowan.

He let go of Emma's hands. It was as if someone had turned off the power.

Rowan ushered them along a wide hallway with more tapestries and paintings. It smelt of polish and something ancient.

'It's like a proper castle,' said Emma.

'It was, at one time,' he replied.

'Does it have a moat and a portcullis?' said Emma. 'You might need those to keep the monsters in.'

Rowan laughed. 'I'm looking forward to seeing Freddie and Riv again. Belle – I promise to keep an eye. I know how it feels to be lonely in this place.'

'They've got each other,' she said.

'Yes, but they're in different houses. That's the system; I'm not sure I agree with it, splitting up siblings. I think Freddie's in the White Tower and Riv's in the Red. But they'll be able to hang out together outside school hours.'

Rowan held open a door as they reached the end of the corridor. 'Remember this?' It was the vast hall in which Rowan's play had been performed.

'*A Midsummer Night's Dream*,' said Emma. 'It was brilliant. You sparked my love of Shakespeare that night.'

'I remember meeting you. And Neville.' A shadow passed over his face. 'I guess it was the night that changed my life.'

'Neville offered to make you a star and you walked out,' said Emma. 'He was properly pissed off.' She sniggered. 'But I was so impressed, because Neville and Teddy were such a couple of overpowering luvvies when they were together. I thought you were the coolest, just getting up and leaving.'

They stood side by side at the back of the hall, as Belle wandered along looking at the portraits of venerable old boys. She stopped at the one of Teddy, and wiped a tear from her eye.

Rowan noticed. 'How's she doing?' he said quietly.

'Like you once said, she's a tough cookie. It's good that I'm in London. I go home most weekends when she's not touring. I miss him too.'

'Those were wild times. Crazy.'

Emma saw him remembering. 'Are you happy here, Rowan?'

'Buried in the country, you mean?' His eyes stayed on Belle. 'Yes. I love teaching, and I'm writing again. Less ... let's say, fraught, themes.'

'Oh, I'm so pleased! You're brilliant at it. I learned so much from you.'

He looked at her, saying nothing for a moment. 'Ems – I'm sorry I didn't call ... ' His voice tailed off.

'It's okay, I think I understand.'

He smiled. 'You're ... sweet as you ever were.'

*And you still do all the things to my heart.*

He called over to Belle. 'Seen enough? The rest of the school's pretty much rows of desks and chairs; whiteboards, not a lot else, unless you're into science labs. I could show you the grounds?'

'You two go,' she said. 'I'll ask that nice headmaster's secretary for a cup of tea and have a rest before we leave. Text me when you're ready to go, Emerald.'

The playing fields rang to the shouts of pupils and sports coaches, and the short, sharp bursts of whistles, as gaggles of boys in hooped shirts thudded up and down the rugby pitches. Beyond the grounds, woods and farmland rose quickly to the moors and valleys of the Yorkshire Dales. In the far distance were purple hills.

'Is that the Lake District?' asked Emma, pointing. Her geographical knowledge of the north was sketchy.

'That's further over. Those are the Pennines.'

'Ah, the backbone of England,' said Emma.

'Straight as a die,' said Rowan. 'Unlike mine.'

Emma gasped. 'Oh, Rowan, I didn't mean to ... oh my gosh, I'm so sorry.'

He laughed out loud and put an arm round her shoulders, pulling her close. 'Emma Snow. Still apologising. You haven't changed at all – apart from in the obvious way.' He released her. 'All grown up. Look at you – you're full-on beautiful. Got yourself a boyfriend?'

Her face was on fire, she knew it. He'd called her beautiful, he'd said she was grown up – but he was still treating her like that gauche teen.

'Yes, I have,' she said, aware of her defensive tone. 'Henry. He's a journalist. Just across the Pennines, in fact, in Lancaster. He's my aunt's stepson.'

'Keep it in the family, eh? I hope he's nice; he'd better be.'

'He is. Very nice. Crystal calls him Mr Bingley.'

Rowan laughed again. 'How very suitable for the winsome Miss Emma Snow.'

Now he was mocking her.

'And she called you Darcy, by the way.'

'Darcy? That pompous arse? Tell me you don't think I'm a Darcy.'

'No, not at all. You're like . . . no one else. In real life or literature. Except, maybe . . . '

'Maybe who?'

She ran her eyes over his tousled dark hair, and cocked her head to one side playfully. 'Heathcliff?'

'Fair comment,' he said, smiling.

'And if you ghost me again, I'll go all Cathy and haunt you,' she said.

'So you promise to be mine, even after death?'

*Oh my god, he's actually flirting with me!*

'Always.'

His expression turned serious. 'Emma, look.' He rubbed the back of his neck. 'I *am* sorry I lost touch. I was . . . it's taken me a while. Losing Abigail – I was a big mess. I cut myself off from my old life. You – the Snows – were part of that.'

'I missed you,' she said.

The path led into the woods beyond the sports fields. It was a mild autumn afternoon; birdsong filled the air, and there was the gentle murmur of a hidden stream.

Rowan pulled a few blackberries off a bush, holding them in his palm. He picked one up between a finger and thumb. 'Here you go – afternoon tea.'

She opened her mouth and he popped it in. The burst of sweetness hit, and it seemed like the most delicious thing she'd ever tasted.

'How much longer at uni, Ems?'

'I'm done already. Starting my first job soon, on a local paper.'

'In London?'

'For now. I'd like to be nearer Henry, though. He wants to stay up here. He's doing well at the *Lancaster Post*.'

Rowan frowned. 'You're too young. Concentrate on *your* career; plenty of time for all that later on.'

'I'm not *that* young. Anyway, you married young.'

'Yep, but it wasn't healthy. None of it. Should have run a mile, but I couldn't bring myself to.'

'I'm so sorry. Abigail was lovely.' She took a breath. 'Rowan . . . what happened to her? No one ever told me.'

Emma had asked Belle about Abigail's death, but she'd dodged the question, hinting only at drug abuse. Emma had assumed she was protecting the Warwicks from blame.

'She gave up on life,' Rowan replied, looking straight ahead. 'She just didn't want to carry on. Fell into a dark place and couldn't get out. I tried, I tried so bloody hard.'

'Was it . . . do you mean drugs?'

'She was a user, but that wasn't why she died.' He met her gaze for a moment, then looked away again. 'She had anorexia. Had it for years, even before we started dating. Came right for a while but then . . . that last year. She just stopped eating; she wasted away.'

Emma was quiet, remembering Abigail. Her pixie cut and her slight, boyish figure.

'When a person you love falls into a dark place,' he went on, 'you blame yourself for not being able to pull them out of it. You feel like such a failure. You think – if they only knew how much they were loved, they'd get through. But they have to *want* to help themselves, to have faith. She never had that.'

*How could you not want to live, if you had Rowan's love?*

Without thinking too much about it, Emma linked her arm through his. 'I'm sure you never gave up trying. Did everything you could.'

'I should never have got involved. I don't know why I loved her so much, I've never worked it out. Maybe I just connected with a fellow fuck-up.'

'You're not a fuck-up, Rowan. I think you're great ... well. You know I do.'

He gave a small laugh; it was slightly bitter. Then he stopped walking and turned to face her. He lifted a hand and gently stroked a tendril of hair back from her face. The gesture was at once intimate yet detached.

She felt his touch as an electric shock.

It was as if time had slipped, and she was back there with him on Glastonbury Tor, a teenager drawn like a stupid, unthinking moth to a flame. Again, she didn't want this to end, didn't want to leave. Just wanted to be here, with him.

'Well,' he said, 'I guess there's no accounting for taste.' He took a step back.

He'd shut it all down; she felt a stab of hurt, right there, in her heart.

'We should get back to your mum,' he said. 'And you'll want to say goodbye to the boys.'

'I'll text her.' She pulled out her phone, glad of an excuse to hide her expression as she typed in the message.

This feeling was so familiar. She glimpsed the future. She'd be off-kilter again, for days, weeks, maybe months. Constantly wondering whether to text, message, email. Waiting for his replies. Feeling anxious and sad when they didn't materialise.

She should never have come.

The Snows stood by the Rolls on the wide expanse of gravel in front of the school. Riv was crying, and buried his face in Belle's skirt, embarrassed.

Belle hugged him. 'Darling, you'll be home for Christmas

soon. Think about what you'd like. And we'll play all your favourite games and have a huge tree again.'

Freddie looked on, and Emma waited for him to make fun of his younger brother, but he didn't. Instead he squared his shoulders and said, 'I'll look after him. Now Daddy's dead, it's my job.'

Emma thought about how Freddie had quietly matured. 'Hey, come here, give Big Sis a hug.' She squeezed him tight, then she and Belle swapped and she leaned her head on Riv's as he wrapped his arms around her, his soft hair against her cheek. He wiped his tears on her jumper; he smelled of boy.

Her own eyes filled. This wasn't like Riv at all. Their father's death must have affected him more than she'd realised.

She met Rowan's eyes as he stood watching. They were slightly narrowed, inscrutable. Given his own childhood, did he secretly disapprove of the boys being sent away from home, especially now they'd lost their dad?

He noticed Emma's tears and his expression softened. 'They'll be fine. Goodbyes are rubbish, eh boys? But I find cake helps. Shall we go find some?'

Riv untangled himself from Emma and looked up at Rowan, swiping at his cheeks. 'Is it chocolate?'

'You bet. And I'll introduce you to Mrs Ollerton, who's in charge of the kitchens. Make her your friend and you won't ever want to leave. Go wait for me on the steps.'

The two boys did as he asked.

'You've got them in the palm of your hand,' said Belle. 'They always liked you.'

'I'll make sure they're okay,' said Rowan. 'Goodbye, Belle. Drive safely.'

'I feel so much better, knowing you're here. Thank you, Rowan.' Belle gave him a hug and got into the car.

'Ems.' He came closer and she looked into his eyes, waiting to feel his arms round her, holding her breath. 'Safe journey.' He took a step back and looked over to where the boys were waiting. 'Keep in touch.'

Again, a stab of hurt.

'I will.'

'I hope things work out for you and your Mr Bingley.' He gave a small laugh and walked away.

# Chapter Eight

Emma and Belle were subdued that evening as they picked at their dinner in Sandal Manor's lofty dining room.

'Buck up, ladies,' said Emma's grandfather. 'The boys will be fine. Teddy loved every minute of his time at Middleham. I'm sure that El ... Elfred and River will, too.'

Emma smiled inwardly as Sir Richard struggled to say the boys' unusual names. He was a dear, old-fashioned thing, and was still coming to terms with the fact that his son, instead of joining the Army as per family tradition, had gone on the stage and married a local girl from a working-class family who became, of all things, a rock singer.

Another Snow tradition was to pass first names down through the generations. The family tree was replete with Richards, Edwards, and Georges (male babies being the only ones that counted). But Teddy had happily gone along with Belle's compulsion to name each new baby as if it had materialised not from her womb, but from the pages of a fairy tale.

'I know Middleham's what Teddy would have wanted,' said Belle, sighing. 'It's just ... I'll miss them. I always do – all of my children. The thought of that empty house waiting for me, everyone away at school or university. Thank goodness I still have my work – though I sometimes wonder if I'm not getting a little long in the tooth for it all.'

'Oh, Belle,' said Lady Snow – Lily. 'You're what, forty-eight?

You're still young! Perhaps you'll meet someone else, darling. You're still very beautiful.'

'I can't imagine it,' Belle said. 'Not after Teddy. Most men are so dull in comparison. It'd need to be someone wildly interesting and creative.' She grinned. 'And devastatingly handsome, of course.'

She looked sideways at Emma. 'Pity I'm not ten years younger. Rowan is the most beautiful, intriguing man. Do you think I'm too old?'

'Mum!' Emma spluttered.

'Works for Madonna,' said Belle.

Lily was chuckling, but Sir Richard looked horribly uncomfortable.

'He'd never . . . Mum!'

'Darling, I'm teasing you,' said Belle, laughing. 'Talking of lovely men, why don't you invite Henry over? It's – what? An hour across the Pennines from Lancaster?'

'Nearer two,' said Sir Richard, looking happier now the subject had turned to drive times.

It was a good idea. Why hadn't Emma thought of it before? She needed somehow to keep her emotions suppressed, locked away. The moment she let her attention drift, the sensations rushed in – the touch of Rowan's finger as he'd brushed back her hair, that jolt of electricity pulsing through her body.

*I shouldn't have come. I knew this would happen.*

'Two hours? It's probably too far, but I'll speak to him after dinner.'

'So it's okay for me to invite Henry?' Emma said to Belle as they made their way to the drawing room.

'Your grandparents would be charmed,' said Belle. 'Nothing to worry about there. Not like when Teddy brought me home for the first time.'

'Henry is charming, isn't he?' Emma said the words with a sigh.

Belle looked at her thoughtfully. 'Come and sit with me for a minute, while Richard and Lily are busy with the coffee.'

*Oh no.* Belle was on to her. Her mind-reading antennae were frighteningly well-tuned.

'You're still very young, Emerald,' she said, as they sat down in the deep window seat overlooking the sweeping lawns. 'Henry's delightful, yes. But he's your first proper boyfriend. Take the time to work out how you feel.'

'I think I do love him, Mum.' Until today, there would have been no 'think'.

'He's very lovable.' She smiled, and cocked her head to one side. 'But I can see . . . you were always a big fan of Rowan.'

As Emma opened her mouth to respond, Belle continued, 'It's okay if you still have some of those feelings, it's quite natural.'

'It was just a teenage crush.'

'Was it?' Her eyes searched Emma's. 'There's something about that boy . . . well, man, now. He's hard to know – there are walls, and it's tempting to want to break them down. But I'd say, don't. Don't even try.'

'Why not?' If Mum had rumbled her, she may as well enjoy the opportunity to talk about him. She'd bottled it all up for as long as she could remember.

'Oh, I know he's irresistible,' said Belle, 'in his way. Lord, he's . . . well, let's be honest, he's incredibly sexy.'

'Mum! Don't objectify him.' Emma couldn't help laughing.

'Isn't it our turn now? I remember at our parties, in London – women falling at his feet.' She paused. 'And men, actually.'

Emma opened her mouth to respond, but Belle carried on. 'That aloofness, that awkwardness. It seemed to make him even more appealing. But of course, he was desperately in love with Abigail.' She sighed. 'What an awful business that was. You know the police questioned him? Neville accused him of psychological abuse. Said it contributed to her death.'

'What?' Emma was shocked. 'That's ridiculous! He did everything he could to make her happy; it was all he wanted.'

'I know,' said Belle. 'But theirs was a strange, intense rela-tionship. Quite unhealthy. To be honest, darling, I don't want anything remotely like that for you.' She took Emma's hand in hers. 'Rowan's a very complex person. There's a lot of darkness there. Henry may be a bit . . . ' She paused.

'Bland? That's what you called him before.' Emma pursed her lips.

'Did I? *Safe*, maybe. But he's up front. What you see is what you get. Whereas Rowan . . . '

'He calls himself a fuck-up, but he's always been lovely with me.'

'I think he sees in you what he can never be. You're sunny and sweet, and you see the good in everyone. You're a positive person. Rowan – he's moody; he's suspicious of people, doesn't trust them. You have to gauge his mood before you can talk to him.'

'I've never seen him like that.'

'Certainly he was on form today. Maybe he's changed. But I remember how he was. Teddy had a real time of it with him.' She patted Emma's hand before releasing it. 'You're best off with Henry, and don't worry too much about the distance. Give it time, go out with your friends, enjoy your life in London.' She tucked a lock of Emma's hair behind her ear. 'And if those feelings for Rowan are still there, don't worry too much about them. We never forget our first proper crush.'

'Mum, they *are* still there. I don't want them to be, but they are.' To her dismay, Emma's eyes filled with tears. 'I can't help it.'

'Acknowledge them, but don't act on them. Leave him be. He's a difficult man.' Belle looked out of the window; she seemed to be weighing up whether to say something more. 'He's . . . damaged.'

'Damaged?' Emma blinked back the tears.

'A loveless childhood; bullied at school. What he went through with Abigail. And then . . . ' She stopped. 'These things leave their mark, and they don't make for easy relationships.'

Belle was holding something back.

'And then what, Mum?'

She looked at Emma for a long moment. 'How much has Rowan shared with you, about what happened with him and Abigail?'

'He said she had depression and anorexia, that she used drugs?'

'Nothing else?'

Emma gave a small laugh. 'There's more?'

Belle was quiet again, then she said, 'They had a baby, Emerald. A little boy, the year after Teddy died. He only lived a few weeks.'

'*What?*' Emma stared at her mother.

'They called him ... ' She stopped and took a breath. 'They called him Teddy. It was a cot death.'

'Oh, Mum, oh no ... ' The tears came back, running down her cheeks.

'The night little Teddy died, Abigail ... well, she was in a bad way, by then. Depressed, couldn't cope with the baby. Jane was away for a few nights doing a seaside show thing, and she'd kicked Neville out by now. Rowan was up for a theatre award for *Twisted*; Neville insisted he went, and Abigail apparently told Rowan she'd be fine for a few hours – she encouraged him to go.'

Emma braced herself for what had happened next.

'When he got home, he found the baby dead. Abigail was asleep – or more likely she'd passed out after taking something.'

'No, Mum.' Emma swiped at her cheeks. 'This is too awful.'

'It was a terrible tragedy. And after that, Abigail ... well. She just faded away. Stopped eating again, in and out of hospital. She died within the year. Rowan ... he tried his best. He and Jane got her all the help they could. But she didn't want to live. And you can imagine what all this did to Rowan. He probably needed help as much as she did. He blamed himself; said he should never have left her alone with Teddy. He was never a healthy baby.'

'I can't ... ' Emma shook her head. 'How would you ever get over that, Mum? He lost his baby boy, and then he watched his wife die from grief.'

'I don't think you could. And so – you understand why I'm telling you – Rowan's not for you. I don't want you taking him on. Keep your lovely heart safe from that boy.'

'How strong are you feeling?' Henry asked when she phoned later to invite him over, admitting that the drive to Sandal Manor might be two hours long.

*Not at all strong, actually.* She'd been sitting alone in the window seat, thinking about her mother's heart-breaking revelation. Now that she'd roused herself sufficiently to phone Henry, his cheery voice was perking her up a little.

'Strong-ish, why?'

'We could meet at Mother's. It's about halfway for both of us.' He paused again, to let it sink in.

Through the window, Emma watched a peacock strut across the lawn.

'Meet Lady Madeline?'

'Would you like to?'

'Well, Henry, you've hardly built her up. But yes, for some reason, I'd like to.'

'Right. I'll organise a day and time. I'll meet you in the local pub so we can turn up together. You can leave your car there.'

'Will it be safe, though? It's the Rolls.'

'We'll put it in the pub garage.'

'Will they allow that?'

'Mother owns the pub.'

'Oh!'

'Also the village.'

'Ah.'

'And the farms.'

'Right. Now you're just showing off.'

'It's true, I am. Let me call her; I'll get back to you.'

# Chapter Nine

When Emma saw Lady Madeline's country mansion looming in the distance, she felt like Elizabeth Bennet setting eyes on Pemberley for the first time. Henry's gleaming sports car – a Maserati – swept past the gatehouse, and as they crested a hill he pointed. 'There she is. Welcome to Montfort Grange.'

An enormous stately home of honey-coloured stone sat overlooking a vast, rolling parkland, with woodlands and hills behind. It was three storeys high with an enormous portico over the entrance. At least twenty windows along the front glinted in the early afternoon sun.

'Holy fuck,' said Emma.

Henry grinned. 'Mother enjoys a big house.'

'Let me get this straight. She lives there by herself?'

'Currently, yes. Unless you count all the staff, horses and dogs, in which case it's fairly well populated.'

'Jesus.'

'Oh yes, I should mention she's on good terms with the big man upstairs. Very religious.'

'Anything else you need to share in the – let's see, a mile? – before we reach the front door?'

'Emma, just be yourself. Apart from the anti-blood-sports part. If Mother raises it, I'll try and divert her. Safe topics are gardening, horses—'

'About which I know nothing—'

'. . . the history of the house. I'd avoid politics.'

'Henry, I'm feeling intimidated.'

'I'll be right there by your side.' He squeezed her knee.

'Hello, Birch!' said Henry, as a door-within-a-door opened and a middle-aged man in a smart grey suit appeared. 'Emma, meet my mother's right-hand man and butler. Birch, this is Emma Snow – my girlfriend.' He grinned widely at the man.

'Girlfriend, is it, Henry?' said Birch, smiling at him fondly. 'Well, I'm very pleased indeed to meet you, Emma.'

'Is the dragon in her cave?' said Henry.

Birch chortled. 'Now now, Henry. No, she's out riding, but she said to serve you tea in the green drawing room.'

'Oh.' Henry's smile disappeared. 'I see. Well, hold off on the tea, I'll give Emma a quick tour while we're waiting. Can you let me know when she's back?'

'Will do, Henry. Enjoy the tour, Emma.'

'I'm sure I will!'

'We'll just take in a few highlights,' said Henry.

Their footsteps echoed into the void of the entrance hall as they crossed the black-and-white tiled floor. There was a cavernous stone fireplace to one side, and directly ahead of them a wide, carpeted staircase with ornate gilded rails, leading up to an archway that promised bedrooms on an epic scale. Above the fireplace was possibly the largest oil painting Emma had ever seen. It depicted a hunting meet in front of the house.

'Good grief, what's going on with the ceiling?' she asked, craning her neck. Painted in wild shades of turquoise, red and gold, it was crowded with curly-haired men, bare-chested women, and . . . swans. Apart from the odd cape or toga, all the figures were completely naked.

'It's a hot mess,' said Henry. 'Mother's pride and joy, though. She spent a fortune having it restored. It's Ancient Rome, I think.'

'I feel that if I look too closely, I might see something unsavoury,' said Emma.

'Fear not. Mother had those bits painted out.'

They passed into a long gallery lined with portraits. Henry stopped in front of a ruddy-faced man wearing armour, the visor of his helmet raised. 'Venerable ancestor John Somerset. And this one is also a John,' he said, moving along. 'There were many Johns.' The painting was of a dark-bearded man with steely eyes. 'This John is responsible for the family fortune, which has remained surprisingly intact over the centuries. He made an absolute killing serving Edward the Third, and also knew how to marry well. Several times, in fact. Not a bad-looking chap, wouldn't you say?'

Emma regarded his flinty black eyes, hollow cheeks and black beard. 'He's a little gaunt,' she said. 'Looks like he's seen a few battles.'

'He was good at them,' said Henry. 'Okay, that's probably enough of the ancestors. I think you'll like the library, it's just along here.'

'Oh,' she gasped, as they entered. The back wall was lined with books, and a balcony with a carved balustrade ran along the top. Huge windows looked out over the parkland. Persian rugs covered the floor, and there were a dozen or so desks and tables, each with a lamp.

'I thought you'd like it,' said Henry. 'Look at this shelf – these are all my first editions. Mother gives me a new one for my birthday every year. I got my first one when I was five.' He took out *Thomas the Tank Engine*. 'See? Nineteen fifty-five.'

'Oh, that's special. Freddie and Riv used to love *Thomas the Tank Engine*.'

He replaced the book and took out another. It was *The Cat in the Hat*. 'Worth about three grand, with the jacket.'

'Wow. But priceless, really.'

'Sorry, I didn't ask – how did it go, dropping off the boys?' said Henry. 'Glad to see the back of them?'

'No, it was sad. Riv was really upset – I didn't expect that.'

'But they've got each other.'

'And Rowan,' said Emma, without thinking.

'Who?'

*Shit.* Emma bent her head over *The Cat in the Hat*. 'He's the English teacher there. Friend of the family. The boys like him.'

'Oh, I see.' He paused, and she looked at him. That gaze of his, the one that saw things. How did he do that?

'Not ... Rowan Bosworth? The playwright? The guy who was part of your dad's clique?'

'Yes, that's him.' She tried to keep her voice impassive, holding his gaze. 'He and Dad were both Middleham boys – at different times, of course. It's how they originally met. Dad was sort of his mentor. Rowan's returned there to teach. He fell out with Neville Warwick after Dad died; I think it was all too hard. He lost his wife, too.'

'Hm.' Henry took the book from her, returning it to the shelf. 'I remember Kate mentioning it. And I saw his play, *Twisted*. That was a new level of angry. Not my cup of tea, really.' He returned his gaze to her face. 'What's he like? I'm not sure I'd want him teaching any kid of mine.'

'Oh no, he's ... he likes to explore the human psyche through his writing, that's all. He's not like that in himself. Well, he maybe has a few demons, but he's ... ' She'd been about to say 'lovely' but thought better of it. 'He's a very clever man. Dad was like a father to him, and Mum's really pleased he'll be keeping an eye on the boys.'

Henry's phone beeped. 'Ah, Mother's back,' he said, reading the message. 'We should wend our way, it's a ten-minute walk to the green drawing room.'

Henry opened a door leading off the gallery. Beyond it was another vast, if slightly cosier room, with chintz sofas, floral wallpaper, and coffee tables stacked with books and magazines.

'Henry, darling!'

Lady Madeline was seated in a wing chair, one long, slim, jodhpur-clad leg crossed over the other, reading a copy of *Horse & Hound*. She still wore her shiny black riding boots, and a black jacket over a cream-coloured polo neck. Her dark hair was scraped into an immaculate bun.

Emma was completely thrown. In her head, Lady Mad had been a fifty-something, stern-faced matron, dressed in a sensible blouse and tweed skirt. Brogues on her wide feet, probably.

But the real Lady Mad was svelte, crisp, attractive. Noticing the riding crop on the table next to her, Emma couldn't stop the word *dominatrix* popping into her head.

And Henry's mother was young! She didn't look a day over forty. Emma remembered Henry saying she'd been a teen when he was born, and how Jason, quite a few years older, had 'done the decent thing'. He probably hadn't taken much persuading.

As Emma readjusted her preconceptions, Henry took her hand and led her over.

'Mother, this is Emma,' he said. 'Emma, meet my dear mama, Lady Madeline.'

As she met Lady M's eye, Emma was reminded of the portrait of John in the gallery, the one with flinty black eyes and hollow cheeks. The family resemblance was striking.

Lady M lifted her chin and inclined her head slightly to one side, and Henry bent down and kissed her cheek.

'Birch is organising tea,' she said. Her clipped, upper-crust accent could have sliced glass.

'I'm so pleased to meet you,' Emma said. 'And your house is amazing.'

Lady M smiled a small smile, finally meeting her eye. Briefly. '*Amazing*? I suppose it is.'

The pause that followed was surely a judgement on Emma's choice of adjective.

Henry headed to the sofa opposite his mother, and Emma sat down beside him. She perched, back straight, hands in lap, smiling nicely. *Oh god, I'm Eliza Bennet facing Lady Catherine de Burgh.*

'Emma's been delivering her two younger brothers to Middleham,' said Henry. His jolly tone sounded forced, as his eyes flicked between the two women. 'She's staying with her grandparents, Sir Richard and Lady Snow, over at Sandal Manor.'

'I know them, a little,' said Lady M. 'Sir Richard's well respected. Such a shame they only had the one son, who . . . well.' She gave a small shake of her head.

A woman in a smart blouse and skirt appeared through the doors, pushing a wheeled contraption in front of her.

'Oh!' said Emma. 'A tea trolley! That's so . . . ' She stopped herself.

'Quaint?' finished Henry. 'Honestly, it's such a distance to the kitchens that if we didn't have this baby we'd be drinking our Earl Grey stone cold.'

'Will that be all, m'lady?' said the woman.

'Thank you, Alice, yes.'

*I've actually fallen into a costume drama.*

'I'll be mother,' said Henry, getting up.

Lady M smiled, watching Henry, but his words made Emma uncomfortable.

'How's work, darling?' said Lady M.

'Busy,' he replied, handing her a cup of tea.

*Shouldn't you be serving your guest first?*

Lady M then offered her opinion on the mayoral race for Lancaster, and they talked for a while about that. Emma tuned out. Lady M was ignoring her. But then, she'd been warned.

'Wouldn't you agree, Emma?' said Henry.

'Sorry, what?'

Lady M raised her eyebrows. 'Your guest appears bored, Henry. We must do better. So, Emma. Shall we talk about you?'

'Sorry, Lady Madeline, I was busy admiring this room. Um, well, I've just finished my journalism studies. I did media and communications at LSE—'

'An interesting choice. I'm not *au fait* with these . . . new subjects.'

'I want to be a journalist; it was the best foundation for that. Then I—'

'Henry's a journalist, and he studied English at Oxford.' She watched Emma over the rim of her teacup.

Emma wondered if Henry would care to back her up, but he said nothing.

'Yes,' she said. 'But LSE is great too. Eventually I'd like to write features. I'm particularly interested in the environment.'

'As am I,' said Lady M. 'You'll know all about land management, then?' Her gaze moved out of the window, no doubt to remind Emma of the vast tracts she owned.

Emma's heart was beating uncomfortably. 'I'm learning more. I'm especially interested in sustainable farming – reducing the use of pesticides, creating wildlife corridors ... '

Lady M made a dismissive gesture. 'English landowners have been doing very well for centuries without interference.'

'I beg to differ.' *In for a penny* ... 'The decline in native bird species is really alarming. Insect numbers are in free fall. And ... dormice! We've lost nearly fifty per cent, most of those quite recently. Almost five per cent, year on year.'

'Door ... mice?' said Lady M, slowly. She took another sip of her tea, her little finger cocked.

'Yes, dormice.'

'I read your piece on fox hunting.'

'Oh!' *Oh god.*

'Perhaps I should have taken the opportunity to talk to you about that, after all.'

'Uncle Jas—'

Henry nudged her with his knee, and she stopped.

'It was full of inaccuracies, Emma. But then it was only a student piece. I don't suppose many people read it. I *would* take the time to explain the importance of controlling fox populations, and the hit the countryside has taken, thanks to the ill-informed prejudices of people who have probably never lived outside of a town or city, but ... ' She did the small headshake thing again. Clearly such people weren't worth her time.

'Mother, let's save this discussion for later?' said Henry. 'Emma's an excellent writer—'

*Finally!*

'—she obviously writes about other things too. She managed to get an interview with Helen Mirren, to talk about her role in *The Queen*. Quite a coup.'

Emma smiled at him gratefully.

Lady M gave a short, sharp laugh. 'Goodness knows what Her Majesty made of *that* film,' she said. 'I must ask, next time I see her. There's so little respect for the Royal Family these days.'

She put her cup down on her saucer and returned it to the trolley. 'Right, well, if you've finished your tea, I need to change. I have a function tonight in York, so if you'll excuse me? Henry, you'll be over for Sunday lunch next week?'

'I should be, yes.'

'Good. Well, it was interesting to meet you, Emma. Perhaps our paths will cross again.'

'They will,' said Henry.

'Well, London's a long way away,' said Lady M.

'Much too far,' said Henry, squeezing Emma's hand before standing up. 'Okay, Mother, we'll be off. Thanks for the tea.'

'It was nice to meet you, Lady Madeline.'

'Goodbye, Emma.' Without a backward glance, Henry's mother swept from the room.

# Chapter Ten

That Christmas was the last time Emma saw her brothers. The Snows spent the festive season at Sandal Manor, and the boys were full of tales of high jinks in the dorms, midnight feasts, and the end-of-term concert, which their grandparents had attended.

'They've certainly inherited your singing talents, Belle,' Lily said over Christmas dinner. 'There wasn't a dry eye in the house when they sang "In the Bleak Midwinter". Like a pair of little Christmas angels.'

Emma imagined their sweet, high voices soaring into the lofty rafters of that great hall. She wished she could have been there, but her new job was keeping her busy and she hadn't been able to get away until Christmas Eve.

Christmas at Sandal Manor was always special. The boys were their usual exuberant selves, and were confined to their room only once, following an incident with an antique vase during a game of 'Bomb Duke' (Duke being Lady Lily's Persian cat).

Emma couldn't help prodding the wound. 'Do you see Rowan much?'

'Oh yeah, Rowan's the coolest!' Freddie said. 'He lets us hang out in his lodge at weekends, and play with George.'

'Who's George?'

'His dog. He's very friendly. Rowan sometimes lets us come when he takes him for walks.'

'What kind of dog is George?'

'He's a Labrador. A black one,' said Riv.

Emma smiled. 'Black. Of course he is.'

She loved the image this conjured in her head: Rowan dressed all in black, striding across a moor, his hound by his side, the two boys bounding along in front (they never seemed simply to walk).

Before leaving Sandal, she texted him: *Bringing the boys back to school today. Hope we can catch up! Emma x*

She actually got a reply, her first since . . . well, forever. *Brace positions. Look forward to seeing you.*

Crystal and Pearl were staying with the grandparents for a few more days, along with Belle, but Emma had now left the world of university holidays behind. In fact, she was keen to get back to work. She was growing into her role at the small London newspaper, and hadn't yet been required to do any door-stepping or death-knocking. It was mostly fetching coffee, proofreading, and reporting on planning applications. All junior stuff, for now, but she was loving it.

Her tyres crunched on the wide semicircle of gravel in front of Middleham. She was driving a smaller car this time – her Mini with a Union Jack roof, a graduation present from Belle.

She tipped the seat forward so the boys could exit. They quickly ran off towards the main building.

'Hey! Your bags!' she yelled. They ignored her.

She hoisted them out of the boot – a backpack each, a box of edible goodies from Lady Lily's housekeeper, Freddie's teddy, and the fluffy toy fox Emma had given Riv for Christmas.

She texted Rowan: *Here! I'm out the front.*

A minute or two later a black Labrador loped up to her, its ears flapping up and down, its tongue hanging out.

'You must be George,' she said, bending down and holding out her hand. The big dog looked up at her with soulful, dark-chocolate eyes. 'Oh,' she said, melting. 'You've got your master's eyes. Aren't you gorgeous!'

'Ems!' She looked up and saw him coming towards her, a wide grin on his face.

She returned it. 'Hi, Rowan. Happy New Year!'

'And to you, Emma Snow.' He kissed her cheek, creating a little pool of heat. 'I was just walking the dog – where are the monsters?'

'They ran off, leaving me with all their stuff. They seem to love it here – and they tell me you're the coolest.'

'True enough.'

He called to a couple of passing boys, asking them to take Freddie and Riv's bags inside.

'Come for a walk – if you've got time?'

'I have! Yes. That'd be nice. How are you? You look very well.'

*Too enthusiastic! And I'm gabbling. Why does this always happen?*

'Fine, just fine.'

He looked fine. He looked better than fine. His hair was longer again, falling over the leaf-green scarf wound around his neck, and he was fresh-faced after his walk. He wore a dark green rain jacket, and jeans tucked into green wellies.

'You always used to wear black,' she said, as they set off. 'You've diversified.'

He laughed. 'My Goth phase. I'm a lot less dark than I used to be. In many ways.'

'You're still enjoying teaching, then?'

'Yep. It suits me – plenty of time off for writing.'

'What are you working on?'

'We'll come to that. Tell me all about you, first. Are you at work now?'

As they walked across the sports fields, she explained about her job and what it entailed. 'I'm hoping they'll let me write some feature-type stuff soon, but I don't want to push it.'

A few boys were kicking a football around, and one wolf-whistled. 'Is that your girlfriend, Mr Bosworth?'

'Might be,' he said, grinning.

'She's hot!' said the boy.

'Totally,' said Rowan. 'And now shut up, Portman. A little more respect, if you please.'

'We'd never have got away with speaking to a teacher like that!' said Emma, giggling, while also acknowledging that his reply had made her heart sing.

'Freedom of expression all the way at Middleham. So – do you have much in the way of spare time?'

Emma thought he was about to ask her to stay for dinner or something. 'Oh! Well, I have a bit of a drive, but I suppose—'

Rowan laughed and shook his head. 'Not now. I mean ... this novel I've been working on. A psychological thriller, I suppose you'd call it. I could do with a first reader. Would you be interested?'

This was almost as good as dinner. A chance to keep the lines of communication open. 'Of course – I'd love to!'

'I'll send it to you.'

'Great!'

'Possibly not. Be honest, Ems. You're my target reader – well read, intelligent, enjoys a good yarn and a well-drawn character.'

'I'm really flattered you've asked me.'

Rowan whistled to George, who was heading off towards the woods. The dog did an about turn.

'You still with Mr Bingley?'

She tittered. 'You remembered. Yes. I haven't seen him over Christmas, though. He was with his mother, the very terrifying Lady Madeline Beauregard. She doesn't approve of me.'

Rowan gave her a look of exaggerated surprise. 'Why ever not? What could there be to disapprove of in the impossibly perfect Emma Snow?'

'Perfect?' She pulled a face. 'Actually, that's an easy one. My banging on in my blog and such about how the countryside's being trashed. It displeases her. Especially my musings on blood sports. Picture Lady M with a shotgun, or on the scent of a fox ... you get the picture.'

'I've come across her. I had no idea she was your Bingley's mother. How bloody hilarious.'

They were quiet for a moment as they negotiated the stile over the school boundary fence. Beyond it, a public footpath stretched away towards a high, flat-topped hill.

George squeezed through a gap.

'How long have you got?' Rowan asked. 'Are you up for an ascent of Middleham Tor?'

*I'd drive through the night if it meant I could climb another hill with you.*

'A tor – again?'

'A proper one, with fuck-off slabs of Yorkshire rock at the top instead of a poncy pretend-Avalon tower.'

'Yes! Let's do it.' She did a little hop and a skip. 'So – how come you're familiar with Lady Madeline?'

'She's a big cheese in Yorkshire. Owns an awful lot of it. Fingers in many pies. Luckily, this school isn't one of them.'

He stopped to throw a stick for George. 'There you go, idiot dog. Something for you to pointlessly chase after and pointlessly bring back.' He gazed after the bounding dog, then turned back to her. 'Sorry, Ems. Got caught up in my own metaphor there. You were saying?'

She looked at him. 'I don't need to talk about Lady M. Let's talk about you. Any nice lady teachers in the picture?'

'The occasional stolen afternoon with Mrs Ollerton, the cook,' he said. 'Worth it for the cakes.'

'Rowan!'

'And a brief fling with my agent, but that didn't end well. She was far too intense. Bit inconvenient – I had to find a new one. Anyway, I'm fine by myself. Let's say I'm overly cautious about any entanglements, given past experience. I'll no doubt end up that tragic single English teacher in tweeds, mouldering away, out of touch with the real world ... '

'No, you'll be a famous author going on book tours and appearing at literary festivals during the school holidays. A nice life! And you'll meet a lovely lady author and you'll live together in one of those cosy masters' lodges and have cute kids.'

He smiled and shook his head. 'If we could write our

own endings, eh, Ems? And what would yours be? Does it include Bingley?'

The path had grown steeper, and Emma stopped for breath, looking back over the flat, crenulated roof of the school below.

'I don't see that much of him, to be honest. I don't know. He *is* lovely.'

*But he's not you.*

*Oh my god, Emma. Get over him!*

'So you said.' Rowan stopped beside her.

'Hey—' Emma touched his arm, and grinned. 'Mum was joking that she thinks you're hot. How about an ageing rock star? Then you'd be my stepdad!'

Rowan snorted. 'Belle? Wow, that'd be a result. Snagged by a beautiful rock goddess.'

'She said all men seem boring after Dad – but not you, apparently.'

'Not boring. I'll settle for that.' He set off again, then turned round, walking uphill backwards. 'C'mon, city girl, put your back into it or you'll be leaving in the dark.'

He held out his hand, and she took it, and he hauled her up the slope. As they climbed higher the wind picked up, whipping their hair across their faces. George ran ahead. They reached the top, scrambling up a huge, flat slab of granite, and the landscape opened up around them; treeless moorlands stretching into the distance, higher and higher into the Pennines.

'It's so beautiful,' said Emma, gasping for breath. 'It makes me feel—'

'Alive?' finished Rowan. 'I come up here a lot. Sometimes I wonder ... if I'd come to Middleham earlier, brought Abigail ... '

'Maybe. Nature's a great healer.'

He put an arm across her shoulder, and they stood side by side looking out across the hills and dales. Emma breathed deeply, trying to imprint it all on her brain. The earthy smell of the bracken; the ancient dark rock beneath her feet. The wind whistling in her ears, tugging at her hair, buffeting her coat, cooling her warm cheeks. The clouds scudding across the sky; the way the sun pierced them, sending a burst of golden rays onto a patch of farmland below, lighting it up in shades of green. The smudge of purple heather on the distant moors.

The weight of his arm across her back.

She turned to look at him, just as he turned to her. She opened her mouth to speak, but he stopped her with a kiss. And all those heightened sensations were suffused with a fierce inner heat, the like of which she'd never known. He pulled her to him; her back arched as she wound her arms round his neck, tangling her fingers in his hair, wanting him closer. The kiss deepened, and Emma felt herself falling, falling. The ground seemed to drop away beneath her feet.

Later, driving home, she thought about her first kiss with Henry – the cream slice. That delicious lightness, soft and sweet.

If she was going with the cake analogy, Rowan was darkest chocolate infused with strong alcohol. Rather than taking small nibbles, licking the cream delicately, savouring every delicious morsel, with Rowan she'd wanted to cram it all in her mouth at once, gobble it up, bite after bite after bite, saving none for later. It had been overwhelming; it had left her breathless, and dizzy with desire.

'Christ,' he'd said. 'That was a surprise.'

All she could manage was, 'Yes.'

He noticed her shivering, and assumed she was cold. He unwound the scarf from his neck, and looped it around hers, slowly.

'Ems,' he said, tucking the ends in. 'Delightful as that was, it's probably best we forget it happened. You're far too nice for me, with all my baggage and general fucked-up-ness.'

His tone was flippant, but his eyes hinted at an inner battle being waged.

He was trying to shut it down again. This time, she wasn't going to let him.

Belle's words came back to her: *Keep your lovely heart safe from that boy*. She'd tried (okay, not that hard), but it had always been a lost cause.

'No, I'm not too nice,' she said, 'but I need to think—'

'Nothing to think about. I'm not an option.' The scarf sorted, he took a step back, shoving his hands in his pockets.

'Why not?'

'Look what happened to the last one.'

'That wasn't your fault! Stop taking the blame.' She wondered whether to tell him she knew about baby Teddy, but decided against it. If he'd wanted her to know, he'd have told her.

'Mum told me Abigail had always suffered from anxiety,' she said, 'even before you were around. You know that. You're just—'

He looked away. 'We should go. The weather's closing in.' He whistled to George.

'Rowan,' she said, moving in front of him. 'Don't be like this. You can't just—'

'Sorry. Truly. I shouldn't have done that. I was carried away with the moment. Like I said, let's forget it ever happened.'

She'd never forget it. She already knew it would be a defining moment in her life.

He moved past her and set off down the hill. No hand was offered. After a while she followed, on the verge of tears. The climb had been a perfect moment in time. Then on the summit, it had been sublime, like touching heaven. The kiss had released a depth of feeling she'd never experienced before. A subconscious recognition that everything had been leading up to this, for so long.

And then he'd slammed on the brakes – again. Why? There was Henry, but he was *her* reason to say no, not his.

She'd always felt Rowan understood her, even more than Henry did. They'd clicked, right from the start. And he'd guided her, taught her, for a little while, before Abigail had died. But he'd always kept that distance; always been reluctant to get too close.

Was he cleaving to the great love he'd lost, convinced no one would ever take Abigail's place? Was he punishing himself for not being able to save her and the baby? Had he convinced himself he wasn't worthy of love? Didn't deserve a second go? Or was he afraid of that darkness inside himself, wanting to keep Emma safe from it? Because, in fact, he *did* care about her – surely? Could he really have kissed her like that if he didn't?

The thoughts went round and round in her head as she descended the hill, her gaze moving between the ground in front of her and his back. That not-quite-straight back, that beloved back.


'Say goodbye to the boys for me,' she said, bleakly, as they stood by her Mini.

'Shall I go get them?'

'No. It's fine.'

They were like polite strangers. How had this happened?

'Safe journey,' he said.

Would he kiss her again, even on the cheek? It seemed not.

She bent down to pat George. 'Goodbye, lovely dog. Look after your master. Someone needs to.' She looked up at Rowan. 'I'm glad you let *him* love you, at least.' Then, before she said anything else she might regret, she hopped in the car and drove off. Without saying goodbye to the boys.

She would never see them again.

# Chapter Eleven

A kiss like that should have changed everything. But it changed nothing.

She texted him on her return: *Thanks for this afternoon, it was lovely. Give the boys a hug from me and also Gorgeous George. Looking forward to reading your magnum opus! E xx*

The tone was way too cheerful, considering his behaviour, but she couldn't help wondering if now he'd had some time to think, he might be regretting that abruptness.

No reply.

That night, she couldn't sleep. She relived every moment of that walk: each backwards glance, the memory of her hand in his as he pulled her up the hill, his arm round her shoulder as they stood on the summit. The intensity in those coal-dark eyes; the sensation of his lips on hers. Fierce, passionate – surely? There was *emotion* in that kiss! No way was it a well-done-for-reaching-the-top kiss.

After hours lying in the darkness trying yet again to work him out, a flicker of anger began to take hold. What right did he have to treat her like this? Playing with her feelings, like she was some ingénue unworthy of serious consideration. The way he mocked her – both overtly and subtly – for being the way she was: 'the impossibly perfect Emma Snow'. No hidden depths, no troubled psyche; just normal, straightforward, what-you-see-is-what-you-get Emma. Always wanting to please, always hoping to make people happy, trying to save the planet one campaign at a time.

How naïve she suddenly felt. Lady M thought she was ridiculous; Rowan probably thought she was ridiculous. Cool, enigmatic, clever-clever Rowan with his troubled past. The clichéd tortured writer, the angry young man. All those patronising pats on the head he'd given her over the years. Helping her with her writing – sometimes, when the mood took him. Then month upon month of silence, never deigning to reply to her schoolgirlish emails, full of exclamation marks with kisses at the end. One minute warm, friendly and affectionate; the next cold and remote, like she was an irritation. He made her feel like an idiot.

Did his general 'fucked-up-ness' include hurting people for pleasure? Had his own life been so difficult, so full of tragedy, that he felt the compulsion to mess up other people's? Did that make him feel better?

*The occasional stolen afternoon with Mrs Ollerton.* He was sleeping with the cook – *worth it for the cakes.* She'd laughed, but now she thought about the cruelty in those words.

*Brief fling with my agent . . . far too intense. Bit inconvenient – had to find a new one.*

Were their hearts breaking too?

Had he in fact been cruel to Abigail? Blown hot and cold with her, as well? Had Neville's accusations of abuse been justified? *Look what happened to the last one.*

And then there was his attitude to 'Bingley'. He didn't care that she had a boyfriend (if only a part-time, long-distance one). He thought it amusing that she was seeing someone so *suitable.* And it was 'bloody hilarious' that Henry's mother was hateful.

The tears finally came, before she fell into a restless sleep.

In the morning there was still no response to her text. But there were three messages from Henry. Dear, reliable, upfront Henry.

Rowan and his hang-ups could go take a running jump.

*

Two weeks later, on a grim Monday morning, Emma set off for work under cover of her umbrella, well wrapped up in a camel coat bought in the New Year sales. She lived within walking distance of the *Voice* offices, having recently moved into a house in Kentish Town shared with two friends from university.

She was at last feeling less off-kilter. After days of further introspection (during which she'd heard from Henry every evening and from Rowan not at all), her head had finally inched ahead of her heart.

Discussing the situation with her friends had helped. Normally she shared little about her private life with anyone other than her nosey sisters and mother, but Isabel had prised her dilemma out of her over Friday wines.

'What's eating our Emma, then?' she'd said.

'What? Nothing! I'm fine.'

'No, you're not. Your head's been in a galaxy far, far away. Is it work or is it Henry?'

*Don't tell her!* said her brain.

*Do it!* said the wine.

'Well . . . I kissed someone who wasn't Henry.'

'Oh. That explains a lot. And?'

'I liked it far too much.'

It had been a relief to share. Summarising the situation strengthened her resolve. She'd described her father's former protégé, who was brilliant and beautiful and kind of understood her, but who had a ton of baggage and wasn't properly interested, anyway. He hadn't even replied to the single text she'd sent since. And he lived a million miles away, buried in the depths of Yorkshire.

'Is he called Heathcliff?' said Greta.

'Sister Pearl already cracked that one, but it's beginning to feel bang on.'

'The messed-up ones can be so appealing,' Isabel had said, dreamily. 'They make you want to mother them. But seriously, why would you even consider it when you have blue-eyed Mr Perfect with his winning smile? You've just got to persuade your Henry that London's where it's at.'

Emma jumped back as a car whooshed through a puddle, admonishing herself for not watching her step. In spite of her sensible conclusions and her friends' advice, her head was still far too much in the clouds (they were so low, it didn't have far to go).

The green man lit up and she crossed, skirting puddles. The wind hurtling down the road picked up one end of her scarf – Rowan's scarf – and flicked it over her shoulder. She fought to tuck it back in with the hand that wasn't trying to keep the umbrella steady. She'd forgotten to return the scarf before leaving Middleham, and in spite of resolving not to revisit that moment on the hill, in spite of her determination to be utterly pissed off with Rowan, she couldn't help reaching for it each time she left the house, winding it round her neck, imagining his mouth, his lips, against the soft wool.

*R Bosworth* was penned in large black letters on the label. She assumed it was his little joke, being a teacher.

She reached the opposite pavement, scarf and umbrella back under control, and her thoughts took off again.

Now she'd had some time to think things over, she could be more objective. What if Rowan hadn't cut her dead, had wanted a relationship with her? Would she have followed her heart, ignored her head?

'I'm not an option,' Rowan had said.

She was eaten up with guilt. Was it fair on Henry, to carry on as normal when she couldn't get Rowan off her mind? When she suspected she may have only just found out what being in love *really* felt like?

But probably, there were different kinds of love. Her feelings for Henry were wholesome and healthy. They made her happy, and brought out the best in her.

There was nothing much healthy about her feelings for Rowan. They made her insecure, sapped her confidence, filled her with self-doubt. Had Abigail felt the same?

*Stay away*, her mother had said.

Belle was right.

If only they hadn't kissed.

She arrived at work, made a coffee and began reading through her emails.

The *North London Voice* was housed in a non-descript office block on Highgate Hill. The staff was small and tight – half a dozen reporters, the editor, a couple of subs, two advertising reps and a receptionist.

Emma, while enthusiastic, and willing to do the dogsbody jobs, was aware that they treated her differently. All she wanted was to be Emma, trainee reporter, fan of books and country walks and a good gossip in the pub. But she was still Emma Snow, daughter of Belle and Teddy, with all their money and their glamorous, notorious lifestyle.

She clicked on a press release from the local wildlife trust, about a scheme to reintroduce bats to pockets of woodland. She resolved to speak to the editor about a feature, something on re-wilding the city, perhaps. It was time she moved forward, started to make her mark.

But first she needed to distribute the post. It was something she enjoyed doing, menial as it was, because it gave her the chance for a quick chat or two, to improve her people skills, make further inroads into being just a regular office worker.

She picked up the pile from the post tray, asking after the receptionist's son's first day at school.

'Oh, he'll be fine. I won't be, though!' said Imogen. 'It was so hard, saying goodbye.'

'I know,' said Emma, perching on the desk and leafing through the post. 'I dropped my kid brothers back at their boarding school after Christmas. They're the devil's spawn, but I do miss them.'

'How old?' asked Imogen.

'Twelve and ten.'

'Ten's quite young to be away from your family.'

'It's a good school, kind of opposite to Dickensian. Like, if the boys set fire to their dorm, which is entirely possible – likely, even – we'd probably be told they had a small issue managing their impulsivity and the school would be teaching them coping strategies.'

She'd reached the bottom of the pile, where there was a large white envelope addressed to *Emma Snow, c/o London Voice* . . .

She turned it over, and her heart missed a beat. *Sender: Bosworth, Middleham College* . . .

All that resolve, that determination, flew at the sight of his name.

She scooted round the office dumping mail on desks, before sitting down heavily in her own chair and ripping open the envelope.

Inside was a sheaf of A4 paper held together with elastic bands, into which was tucked a folded-over sheet with *Emma* written on it in black pen. Slowly she pulled it out and unfolded it.

His handwriting was beautiful – tight, the words sloping slightly backwards, the upper case initials overly large.

*Emma – my manuscript, if you have the time and inclination to read it. Come at it like you don't know me & be as brutal as you want, like I was with you. No rush, return envelope included.*

*Also, I'm sorry. I'm completely shit at relationships, as you know. But stating the obvious doesn't excuse the way I treated you and it's been playing on my mind. I'm going to work on my attitude.*

*You're by far the loveliest person I know and much too nice for me. Bingley is the sensible choice. Stick with him.*

*And Emma – that was one hell of a kiss. You never cease to surprise me.*

*R x*

The letter sent her straight back to square one. By the end of the day, much of which she spent on autopilot, she knew it off by heart.

*I'm going to work on my attitude.* Was he attempting to change, so he was less 'shit at relationships'? Did this mean he might, in fact, be considering one with her? The 'much too nice for me' implied he'd thought about it, surely?

*Stick with Bingley.* Somehow, she sensed a challenge in that short, sharp sentence. As if he was saying, *Have you got the guts not to? How brave are you, Emma Snow?*

That evening she made a start on the manuscript. Isabel and Greta were out, and Emma was tucked up on the sofa with Jacquetta on her lap. (The cat was a guest while Belle was on tour in the States.) When Rowan had said 'psychological thriller', she'd assumed the novel would be along the same lines as his play, delving deep into a twisted psyche. She'd expected violence; rape, perhaps. But this was lighter than *Twisted*; still dark, but more Stephen King, less Stieg Larsson.

It was a page-turner with bestseller written all over it. Emma felt herself breathing out in relief as she recognised the old Rowan in its words. This was a rewind from the angry young man, edging back to the playful author of that exuberant retelling of Shakespeare.

She read on into the night. About halfway through, she sent him a text: Hi - got the m/s. 25 chapters in. Winner! Need to sleep but can't put it down. E xxx

Then after pressing send, she thought for a moment and, shooing away guilty thoughts of Henry, sent another: Also thanks for note. Have been quite mixed up since seeing you tbh. Apology for shit behaviour accepted and look forward to meeting new improved version. PS You shouldn't have kissed me but I *think* I'm glad that you did. X

# *Chapter Twelve*

'We're short-staffed this week. I need you to answer the phones,' said Kyle, the *Voice*'s editor, when she asked about reporting on the bat project.

'I know, and I'm happy to, but – I'd really like to interview this guy in person. Take some photos of him with his bat boxes. This project, it's part of something bigger.' She felt the rush. 'It's all about rewilding, reclaiming city space—'

'It's bloody bats, Emma.' He stopped what he was doing and looked at her over his little round glasses.

'Please?' She sensed he was caving.

He shook his head. 'Two hours max. Including your lunch break.'

An enthusiastic conservation volunteer, known locally as Batman, told her all about London's burgeoning bat population as she helped him check the bat boxes on Hampstead Heath. Afterwards he asked, tripping over his words and blushing, if she'd like to join him for a cup of tea in Costa, but she explained she had to get back to finish a piece on the lack of remaining space for burials in Highgate Cemetery. 'What you might call a *dead*-line,' she said, to soften the blow, but he didn't laugh, just looked terribly disappointed.

*You may be living closer to a bat than you think*, she wrote, the following morning. She'd been taken by surprise at the size of

London's bat population. Perhaps she'd try to negotiate an extra column inch or two, for a 'Build your own bat box' add-on.

Her phone beeped, and she saw that, more than two weeks since she'd messaged Rowan, she had a reply. Finally. It had taken at least one of those weeks for her not to flinch every time she heard the text message alert.

> In London to meet new agent. Quick drink before I head back? Need to be at Kings X by 8

Her heart did its thing again.
*Calm down.*

What time was it now? Eleven thirty. Could she leave work early this afternoon? Give herself time to go home and wash her hair?

*Wait.* Why was he texting her only now? Why hadn't he given her a couple of days' notice? Was she an afterthought?

She had to stop asking 'How high?' every time he said 'Jump!'

She gave it five minutes. During which time she decided yes, she could go home first, but no, she wasn't going to leave especially early.

> Hi!

She deleted the exclamation mark.

> Hi. Yes – earliest can do is 6. Where?

That sounded a bit cold.

> Hi, yes but earliest can do is 6 :( Where?

She pressed send.
Her phone beeped again:

> Dog & Duck, Bateman St

She replied:

See you there!

As she finished putting on her make-up (subtle – it needed to look like she hadn't tried too hard), she glanced over at the manuscript on the chest of drawers by her bed. She'd finished reading it, notes scribbled in the margins, but he probably wouldn't want to lug it back with him. She doubted he was carrying a briefcase; she couldn't picture it, somehow. And his scarf, draped over her chair ... she might just forget to take that with her.

On the tube, Emma opened her copy of the *Standard* and took in hardly a word as the train rattled south.

As she exited into the biting cold at Tottenham Court Road, the brightly lit streets were bustling with late-night shoppers. She walked briskly through Soho, mostly to keep warm, but also because ... Rowan's *here*. In London!

Butterflies were partying in her stomach, but she reminded herself that this was just a meeting between friends. It didn't have to be awkward. They could talk about his book, the boys.

The tiny bar of the Dog and Duck was packed, and she craned her neck, looking for his dark head. Rowan wasn't particularly tall – maybe five ten. He was a fair few inches shorter than Henry, who was way over six foot.

*Henry.* She felt a stab of guilt.

She looked at her watch – 5.55 p.m. Early. *Uncool as ever.* She squeezed her way through to the bar, and waited to be served.

A tap on her shoulder. 'Emma. Have you ordered?'

Heart in mouth, she turned round. He was looking beyond her to the barmaid.

'Um, no, not yet. The barmaid's ignoring me.'

'I'll get them.'

He was wearing a dark wool coat over a black polo neck.

'Black again,' she said. 'Very meeting-my-agent-in-Soho.'

'Gotta look the part,' he said, as the barmaid came over. 'Pint of Old Peculier and . . . ?' Finally he looked at her, raising his eyebrows. His gaze was inscrutable.

She turned to the barmaid. 'I'll have a sauvignon blanc, please.'

Emma waited for him to speak, looking him in the eye, her head on one side.

'What's that look for?' he asked.

'I thought you were working on your attitude.'

'What?'

'A "Hello, Emma, lovely to see you" would be a start.'

He laughed. 'Ah. Sorry. Apologies for fuckwittery. I was too focused on my beer – it's been a long day.'

'Not good enough, Rowan.' She gave him a small smile.

His eyes widened a little. 'I see. Must try harder?'

'Probably a B minus for general rubbishness of greeting.'

His eyes held hers, and she saw him thinking, readjusting. 'Suggestions for improvement?'

'A hug? A kiss on the cheek?'

'Four pounds eighty, please, love,' said the barmaid.

Rowan handed over a five-pound note, barely taking his eyes from Emma's. 'Keep the change.'

She continued to hold his gaze. She needed to move this forward – or maybe it would be backward. But his eyes suggested forward.

She was determined. There would be no more wondering, no more pointless crush. It had gone on long enough; it needed resolving. And oh boy, did it feel great to be the one pushing.

'What have you done with the real Emma Snow?' he finally said.

It was cheesy, but she couldn't resist. 'You melted her. Don't you remember?'

He smiled, shook his head a little. 'Jesus, that was unforgivable. But yes, I do remember.' He slipped an arm round her waist, bent down and kissed her cheek, then didn't pull away. 'Better?' he murmured.

His lips were a tiny turn of the head away; she resisted an overwhelming impulse to kiss them.

'Yes. B plus.' She moved away, and picked up her drink. 'So, you have a new agent. Will you be behaving professionally with this one?'

He blinked. 'Okay, what's going on here, Ems?'

She took a breath. 'You tell me, Rowan. You kiss me, then you blank me. You send me a nice, if confusing, note, then you don't respond to my texts.'

'You've got a boyfriend.'

'Yes, I do, and he doesn't deserve to be mucked about. So maybe *you* should tell *me* what's actually going on in your head.'

He frowned, then noticed a couple leaving a table in the corner. 'Over here,' he said.

She sat down beside him. 'So? You told me to stick with Henry, but I'm not sure you meant it. Did you?' She sipped her wine, trying to keep her face impassive as she waited for his response.

He raked his fingers through his hair, staring at the table. She remembered how it had felt when she'd tangled her fingers in it.

He picked up a beer mat and started fiddling with it, pulling the layers apart at one of the corners. After a pause, he said, 'Would you be surprised to learn I'm having therapy?'

She was. 'Really?'

'Not a full-on proper psychiatrist, just the school counsellor. Meena. She's a friend. I think it's helping.' His eyes remained focused on the beer mat.

'So you really *are* working on your attitude?'

'I'm not sure she's up to the task.' He gave a small laugh. 'She thought it was all about dealing with grief – she had no idea of the depth of shit in there.' Finally he looked up, meeting her eye. 'Jesus, Ems. I wouldn't touch me with a bargepole.'

But he was daring her to try.

She was actually getting somewhere. She hesitated, then put her hand on his. 'You can talk to me too.'

Emma wanted to say she knew about the baby, but she couldn't seem to speak the words. Her instinct was to wait until he told her himself. Or did he assume she already knew?

'No. Not yet.' He removed his hand from hers and sat back a little. 'Tell me about your job, how's it all going?'

She remembered Belle's words: *There are walls, and it's tempting to want to break them down. But I'd say, don't. Don't even try.*

There was barely a brick dislodged, but he'd opened up a crack. She'd probably pushed it far enough, for now.

So she told him about her work, and then they talked about Freddie and Riv.

'I love thinking of you three yomping across the moors with George. What an adorable dog.'

'Idiot hound. George the Second, to give him his full name.'

'Because he's loopy?'

'C'mon, Ems. What did they teach you at that expensive school? George the Third was the mad one. But my George is also a big stupid lump.' He went to lift his beer, then hesitated and put it down again. 'George the First died,' he said, not taking his eyes from the beer.

Emma didn't reply, sensing there was more to come.

'My mum gave him to me for my ninth birthday, when he was a pup. Dad drowned him in a water butt when I left a gate open and the sheep got out. He made me watch.'

Emma stared at him in horror. 'My god, Rowan. That's—'

'*Enjoyed* making me watch. I'll never forget the look on his face. Like he wished the pup was me.'

'Surely not—'

'I realised in that moment, there are people driven by the need to hurt, who enjoy inflicting pain.'

'I can't imagine—'

'No, Emma, you can't.' He glanced at her, then frowned at the table. 'You and your wholesome life. You have no fucking *clue.*'

He picked up the beer mat again and folded it in half, squeezing it between his palms.

The silence stretched out between them. Emma felt helpless, out of her depth. She desperately wanted to hug him, but everything about him said *Don't touch me.*

'Sorry,' he said finally, meeting her eye. 'I shouldn't have landed that on you. Meena got me to talk it through. And now I guess I've told you.'

'I'm glad you did,' she said. 'I want to understand you. I want so very much to help.'

He unfolded the beer mat and dropped it on the table, then sat back in his seat. 'Anyway, enough of that. Let's lighten things up. I'm pleased to say, my new agent loved the book.'

The abrupt change in tone took her aback, but she followed his cue. 'Oh, that's great! But I'm not surprised; it's absolutely brilliant. So you don't really need my feedback, then?'

'I do. She's waiting on the final version, so send me your thoughts.'

The conversation remained on safe ground, and then, another drink later, it was time for him to leave. As they exited the cosy warmth of the pub they were assaulted by the raw February chill.

'God, it's bloody freezing!' she said, linking her arm through his and snuggling close. *Thank you, weather!*

'It was snowing in Yorkshire when I left,' he said. 'Hope the trains aren't stuffed.'

She loved how he said *stoofed.*

'Oh, I bet it's beautiful up on your tor. I wish I could see it.'

'I'll go check it out for you tomorrow.'

Now, all she could think was, would he kiss her goodbye?

He suddenly stopped. She held her breath, but he said, 'Ems – look.'

A fox was trotting across the road ahead of them, its fiery red coat briefly illuminated in the yellow pool cast by a streetlamp. It glanced towards them, then was swallowed into the shadows of Soho Square.

'Oh!' said Emma. 'What a beauty. Isn't it amazing how they've recolonised the city?'

'Their numbers are up in Yorkshire too, since the ban. Freddie's doing his environment project on how foxes are adorable and hunting is evil.'

'Good boy,' she said, as they started walking again.

'Mean bastards, though, foxes,' said Rowan. 'Used to wreak havoc on the farm. But better a clean shot than ripped apart by the hounds of upper-class twats on big horses.'

'Like Lady Mad. Horrible woman.'

'The unspeakable in full pursuit of the uneatable,' said Rowan.

'Oscar Wilde.'

'Well done.' He patted her hand. 'Which tube?'

'Tottenham Court Road.'

'I'll walk you, then jump in a cab.'

'That's okay, you don't want to cut it fine. You can get a cab from here.' To her dismay, she saw one coming towards them, its yellow light an unwelcome beacon in the darkness.

He waved it down and turned to her. Smiling, he pulled up the collar on her coat. 'Stay warm, lovely Ems.'

'I still have your scarf at home.'

'Keep it.'

'Confession – I thought about bringing it for you, but I decided not to. I like wearing it.'

His hands moved from her collar to cup her face, and he kissed her, gently, on the forehead. 'Lucky scarf. I don't suppose I'll see you for a while. Listen – I'm sorry, about what I said earlier.'

'Don't be. I want to know everything about you.'

'No, you don't. But thanks for coming to meet me.'

'Rowan—'

*Kiss me.*

He stepped back. 'Got to go.'

Her face fell. 'Don't—'

He opened the cab door and hopped in, saying, 'Text me.'

And then he was gone.

# Chapter Thirteen

'Anybody fancy going out for brunch?' said Emma on Saturday morning, as she shuffled into the kitchen in her dressing gown and slippers.

Isabel and Greta looked at each other.

'Was rather hoping not to get out of my PJs before midday,' said Isabel. 'Weather's disgusting, why would you want to?'

'I could make pancakes?' said Greta.

'Yes! I'll help,' said Isabel.

'Pancakes?' said Emma. 'Since when have we cooked hot food that isn't toast on a Saturday morning?'

'Since today,' said Isabel. 'Anyway, we wouldn't be able to get past the deluge of Valentine's Day cards that will be spilling through our letterbox any moment now.'

'Val—oh shit,' said Emma.

'Oops, did you forget Henry's card?' said Greta.

'No, I sent it in good time, actually,' she said. 'It's just ... I was going to ... Dammit.'

Belle had pulled strings to get Emma two best-in-house tickets to see Radiohead in June. In Paris. They were Henry's favourite band, and she'd been so excited about this brainwave of a gift. She'd intended to courier them to him, along with details of flights and romantic-Parisian-hotel accommodation, in some sort of fancy red packaging, but everything was still sitting on the chest of drawers by her bed.

She didn't think too hard about why she hadn't in fact found the time to send it all northwards. If she did, she'd be forced to confront the disquiet eating away at her. Again.

Rowan was having therapy. He was attempting to come to terms with his past, to move on, and Emma wondered if her reappearance in his life might have prompted those efforts. And if she had, did that 'I'm not an option' still apply?

*Did you get your train ok?* she'd texted before bed on Thursday. No reply.

*Was your tor snowy and sublime?* she'd texted the next day. No reply.

He was ghosting her again. Rowan was impossible.

She'd dumped him in the 'too-complicated' basket and was now attempting to get on with her life. She would show Henry his present on Skype, tonight.

The pancakes were a hilarious disaster, so Isabel whipped up a pile of scrambled eggs while Greta and Emma dealt with the toast, bacon and coffee.

'You can't beat a full English,' said Greta, as they finally sat down to eat.

'This is more your half-English,' said Isabel. 'No sausages or tomato . . . '

'No baked beans or mushrooms,' said Greta.

'Or black pudding, if you were up north, probably,' said Emma.

'Congealed animal blood for breakfast. Yum,' said Greta.

'It's a super-food, apparently,' said Emma. 'Antioxidants, or something.'

'Pudding should never be black,' said Greta. 'Yellow is the natural colour of puddings.'

'And what in god's name would a pudding be doing on the same plate as bacon, anyway?' said Isabel.

'Like Yorkshire pudding,' said Emma. *I'm obsessed with Yorkshire.* 'Why do they call it pudding?'

'Northerners,' said Greta, as if that explained everything.

There was a knock on the front door.

'Flowers!' said Greta, 'I bet. Please-be-for-me, please-be-for-me.'

'From who?' said Isabel. 'And is anyone going to actually answer that?'

'From hot bookstore guy,' said Greta getting up. 'When I ordered *Eat, Pray, Love*, he took my address. He *so* didn't need my address. And he definitely looked me in the eye when he repeated the "Love" part.'

Emma snorted. 'This explains the toppling pile of new unread books on the coffee table.'

'Emma!' came Greta's voice from the hallway. 'For you! Come get!'

For a moment, she wondered if it might be flowers from him. The thoughts rattled through in quick succession ... But he didn't have her address. Although ... the boys would know it ... But she couldn't see him as a sender of flowers. But! He was working on his attitude.

They were probably from Henry.

Tying the dressing-gown belt round her waist, she made her way into the hall. Greta was standing in the open doorway grinning, and behind her was ... Henry.

An internal battle erupted, between joy and consternation.

'Oh my god! Henry!'

'Surprise!' He stepped inside and wrapped her in his arms. As she leaned into his broad, familiar chest, joy inched ahead of consternation, and her relief was profound. Dear, gorgeous, loveable, uncomplicated Henry. Surely he was the answer to her unspoken prayer.

*Eat, pray, love.* Indeed.

She hugged him tight. 'What the hell?' she said. 'But this is wonderful!'

As Greta disappeared, tittering back down the hallway, he kissed her. It was sweet and lovely and ... grounding.

'Oh god,' she said, suddenly stopping. 'I haven't cleaned my teeth yet.' And then, 'My hair! Shit. Henry, this is such a lovely surprise, but I need to go shower.'

'Emma,' he said, running his eye over her bed hair. 'I have seen you dishevelled before. I love you dishevelled. I love you full stop. Happy Valentine's.'

He resumed kissing her, pulling her close.

'Shall we go to bed?' she whispered, as things became increasingly passionate.

He looked a little shocked. 'I just got here! I've had a four-and-a-half-hour drive.'

'So?'

He laughed. 'Wanton. Well, yes, but maybe a coffee first? And I should check in with my co-conspirators, who were enthusiastic participants in my cunning plan to keep you home.'

'Ah, that explains the whole pancakes scenario.'

They sat around the kitchen table chatting, as Isabel organised more eggs and bacon, and Emma smiled as she watched her friends responding to Henry's charm. Those winning blue eyes, that irresistible smile.

She left them to it while she showered. When she returned to the bedroom, he was sitting on the bed, waiting for her.

'This is such a lovely surprise,' she said, sitting beside him.

He took a corner of her towel and pulled it open. 'Are you glad I came?' he said, running a finger down from her neck to her breasts.

She lifted a hand to his head, gently combing her fingers through his hair. 'Of course I am.'

She was relieved to discover it was true. She kissed him, and as it deepened he lowered her back onto the bed and began to explore her body.

He was tender, loving. 'Do you like this?' he murmured, looking up at her.

She lost herself in his touch. 'Yes, god yes . . . ' she whispered, closing her eyes. But as the intensity increased, it uncapped some deep well of emotion, and tears ran down her cheeks.

'What happened there?' he said later, as they lay quietly. 'You were crying.'

'I don't know,' she said, truthfully. 'Sometimes when I . . . you know. I get a bit overwhelmed.'

'Should I take that as a compliment?'

'Yes, do.' She quickly changed the subject. 'I have something for you. I was going to show you on Skype, but . . . ' She looked up at him and smiled. 'I still can't believe you're here! I really needed to see you. Long distance sucks.'

'It does. Where is this something, then?'

'On the drawers next to you.' She'd put everything in a red envelope and drawn a large heart around Henry's name.

He reached over. 'I actually saw this, but I got distracted.'

He lay on his back and opened it up. 'Holy shit!' he said, an enormous smile spreading across his face as he worked out the connection between the Eurostar tickets, the email confirming the hotel reservation, and the Radiohead tickets.

'You're welcome.'

'Wow, thanks, Emma.'

'Feel free to properly show your appreciation,' she said, stretching like a cat.

'Oh, I booked us a table at Christopher's tonight, by the way,' said Henry, later.

'Lovely. Have we got time for a walk on the Heath first?'

'I suppose we should earn our dinner.'

'I want to show you the bat boxes.'

'The what?'

'I'm writing my first feature for the *Voice*. It's on London bats.'

Henry chuckled. 'Bats? Big time, Emma.'

She frowned. 'Bats are important. And they're part of—'

'Oh dear, I squashed my present,' he said, pulling out the sheets of paper from beneath him and putting them back on the chest of drawers. 'What's this?'

She looked over. *Shit!* It was the manuscript. Luckily, Rowan's note was tucked away in her handbag.

'Bosworth?' he said, picking up a few sheets. The page header read: © *R Bosworth: Bent V1.1 for Ems.*

'I've been doing some beta reading,' she said, attempting to keep her tone nonchalant.

'For *Rowan Bosworth*?'

'Well, yes, obviously. He asked if I would, when I dropped the boys off.'

He lay back on the bed, flicking through the pages. 'Not exactly wholesome reading?'

'Oh no, it's quite different from *Twisted*.' She wished he'd put them down. 'More mainstream; commercial. It's really good.'

He carried on leafing through. Her heart was thumping. She tried to remember her margin notes. There was nothing incriminating, surely?

He read one out: '*Lol, Mr B. This is NOT how a young woman would respond!*'

'Men are rubbish at women's introspection,' she said weakly.

He read out another. '*What did you teach me about commas? I'm totally out of puff. Though that may be because you just took my breath away.* Heart heart. *Love this.*' He raised his eyebrows.

'Okay, can you stop now?' she said. 'It's actually quite personal. He helped me with my writing when I was young, and I'm just returning the favour.'

'Good, is it?'

'Brilliant. He should have a deal for it soon. Watch it go straight into the *Sunday Times* bestsellers.' She couldn't help the pride in her voice.

'Right.' He smiled. It didn't quite reach his eyes. 'Shall we take that walk, then?'

Fifteen minutes later, as Emma opened the front door to leave, Greta called, 'Wrap up well, children. It's brass monkeys out there.'

'True,' said Henry. And before she could grab it herself, he pulled Rowan's scarf from the coat stand. 'Okay if I borrow this? Is it yours?'

'Um ... yes. Actually, can I wear that one?' The thought of Henry in Rowan's scarf made her uncomfortable. 'I'll get you another.' She rifled through the muddle of outdoor clothes on the stand.

*Oh god.*

Henry had caught sight of the black lettering on the label. 'R Bosworth,' he read out. He looked at her. '*R Bosworth*?'

She could feel the colour rising in her cheeks. 'It's Rowan's, yes. He lent it to me when I dropped the boys off ... we went ... we all went for a walk, up the tor behind the school. I forgot to give it back.' She busied herself with the coat stand, fishing out another scarf.

They swapped, and left the house.

'We'll take the car, we can park up on the Heath,' he said.

'Okay.'

They were quiet as they set off.

'How old is Rowan?' he finally said, as they pulled out into the traffic on Highgate Road.

'Twenty-seven, twenty-eight?' she said. 'You can see where I work! It's up here on the right.'

'I thought he'd be older.'

'He was really young when he wrote *Twisted*. Just out of uni.' She wished she didn't blush so easily.

She needed to address this. Apart from anything else, Henry deserved some version of the truth.

'Okay, Henry.' She took a breath. 'I'll be honest. I may have had a crush on him when I was a teenager. He was a close friend of Dad and Neville's; they took him under their wing. I thought he was the coolest person ever. He was kind of like ... I don't know ... Kurt Cobain, maybe. Brilliant, beautiful, full of angst, the clichéd tortured creative, maybe. I guess I'm still a bit ... in thrall to his talent. But that's all.'

Henry looked over at her, his expression inscrutable. He waited for her to go on.

'He had this girlfriend – he married her, eventually. She

suffered from depression, and I think ... they kind of fed off each other. It was really unhealthy. She was Neville's daughter, so I knew her. She was actually lovely, but very messed up. And then she died.'

'Died?'

'It was so sad. And Neville accused Rowan of emotional abuse, but that was bollocks. Rowan's not like that – at least, I'm pretty sure he isn't, and he did everything he could to help Abigail. He told me all about their relationship, even though I was only sixteen. It was very intense. He went through hell with her.'

'He shared that with you, when you were only sixteen?'

'We've always got on. But even before he met Abigail ... Rowan had his own issues too. Terrible childhood, cruel father ... ' She couldn't help picturing it – a young Rowan, being forced to watch his beloved puppy drown. 'And he was bullied at school—'

'That brutal play he wrote is making more sense to me now,' interrupted Henry.

'He's ... complex. Dad used to call him "tricky". Dad meant an awful lot to Rowan; I think he'd have wanted me to keep in touch. It's why Mum sent the boys to Middleham – for Dad's sake, and because Rowan's there. It's just ... family stuff.'

He took one hand off the steering wheel and squeezed her knee. She glanced over at him. He was looking more relaxed.

'So – it was just a teenage crush?'

'Yes. Him and Mark from Take That. I've moved on.'

He laughed. 'Good. You had me worried there. But I guess it was about time I introduced you to my jealous streak.'

'So you *have* got a dark side! That's quite a relief, actually.'

'Even Bingley had a dark side.'

'Look! There's my office!' Her voice was far too enthusiastic. 'Feel free to be unimpressed,' she added, as they swept past the seventies monstrosity.

'Small newspaper offices look like shit, it's a tradition,' he said. 'But they're not the same since workplace smoking was banned.

Those were the days. The wall of smoke as you entered; the yellowed walls. Those hard-bitten newsmen ... '

'And women.'

'Not many, in those days. And they were terrifying. Jean Rook, Lynda Lee-Potter ... '

'Terri Robbins-Moore.'

'The ultimate bloodhound. From the wrong side of the Pennines, though.'

'You should've taken that job.'

He glanced over at her. 'Maybe I should have. The move south is becoming ever more tempting.'

They strolled over the Heath, Emma trying not to brood on the conversation about Rowan, happy she'd put Henry's mind at rest yet experiencing a nagging guilt.

She felt disloyal, like she'd betrayed Rowan's trust – which seemed a fragile thing at best. The words she'd said about his relationship with Abigail, even hinting that he *had* been abusive, just to throw Henry off the scent.

But she could hardly have told him the whole truth. What even *was* the truth? She didn't know any more. She'd never be free of that crush. It was a curse, still a long way from being broken. She'd pushed Rowan, made dents in his walls, but he still wouldn't let her close.

Today had helped her reach a conclusion: it wasn't worth risking her lovely relationship with Henry for a maybe-one-day with Rowan.

They stopped on Parliament Hill, looking out across the spectacular view of London. Henry pulled her close, kissing her hair. 'London's okay, I suppose,' he said, in response to her sigh of pleasure. 'I guess ... seriously, if one of us *were* to move, as in, to be nearer to the other, that should probably be me. The next step on the ladder would be a national. What would you think about ... if I were to start having a proper sniff around?'

She put her head on his shoulder. 'You'd do that for me?'

'I would.'

'I think that would be an excellent career move. Lancaster's too small for Henry Theodore. It's time to head south, for sure.'


'You're too beautiful for your own good,' said Henry later, in bed, nuzzling her neck. 'That waiter was dazzled. Probably why he completely cocked up the champagne.'

Emma laughed and pulled up the duvet, thrown off in the considerable heat they'd generated over the past half hour. 'That dress was a bit risqué for me, to be honest.' She'd borrowed Isabel's Valentine-red mini dress with a plunging neckline.

'You took my breath away,' he said, as she snuggled into his chest.

'Aw, Henry. Thank you. But I'm not really beautiful – not like Mum. I wouldn't want to be.'

'You are. Just in a less obvious way. Quietly beautiful as opposed to in-your-face beautiful. With Belle it's like, *boom*. You – you play it down. But every time I'm with you, I see it more.' He twirled a lock of her hair round his fingers.

'I think Mum's looks, they're almost a burden. The way people respond to her – they can't see past her beauty. Like Dad ... whenever he spoke about when they first met. It's this corny family legend – she was standing under an oak tree on the village green on May Day. He always said how she knocked him sideways with her beauty. How he couldn't sleep, blah blah blah.'

'Love at first sight?'

'Apparently. And they married young, and they stayed married, but then there were so many other beautiful women.' She looked up at Henry. 'So ... if that's why you fall in love, it's only going to be until the next beauty comes along, right? And what happens when it fades? There's got to be more. A lot more.'

'You've obviously thought about this.'

'I have.'

'I guess your dad was famous for his love of beautiful women.'

'Exactly. So in her case, maybe it wasn't such a great thing.'

'Well, Emma. You're as lovely inside as out. And that's a rare thing.'

She felt a warm glow, and tried not to compare it to the self-doubt Rowan always seemed to generate. 'As are you, Henry. I would love it if you got on and looked for that national newspaper position at your earliest opportunity.'

Emma was just dropping off to sleep when there was a crash outside the window below. Henry went to leap out of bed, but Emma stopped him.

'It's just the foxes. They raid the bins.'

'Fuck's sake, I thought we were being burgled.'

'No.' She remembered the moment in Soho Square, that burst of auburn fur in the street lamp, how the fox had glanced over at them. *My home as much as yours.*

Henry chuckled.

'What?'

'I just had a vision, in my head. Mother on her horse with a bunch of hounds, charging through the streets of London.'

'Urban fox hunting. That would actually be something to see.'

There was more crashing, and a bloodcurdling yelp.

'You know you can get alarms?' he said. 'They emit a sound too high for us to hear, but it sends the foxes packing. Keeps them out of your garden.'

'But why would I want to do that?' she said. 'I love seeing foxes in my garden.'

'Foxes are vicious beasts, Emma. They're vermin. You're going to have to lose that sentimental streak if we're going to make a hard-nosed journalist out of you.'

'They have as much right to be here as we have. Maybe more.'

'City girl. Maybe Mother was right.'

'Henry!'

'It's probably time I took you to Montfort Grange again. You know, if we're going to take this thing further. If you're going to lure me south.'

'Won't that just be another reason for her to hate me? If you make the move?'

'She has houses here too. She'd probably spend more time in London if I was down here.'

'Oh. Whoop-de-do.'

He laughed. 'Mother. The final frontier. Maybe I can reconcile the two of you yet.'

Somehow, Emma doubted that.

# Chapter Fourteen

*What a difference a week makes*, reflected Emma, as she walked to work on Monday morning. The sun was out; the crocuses were poking their heads up, wondering if they could come out now. It had been a perfect weekend. Henry had left yesterday lunchtime, and she'd floated through the rest of the day on Cloud Nine.

(Why Cloud Nine? What happened on Clouds One to Eight?)

For the first time in a while, she felt settled, able to see the way ahead. Henry was going to explore finding a job in London. It was exciting; it was for the best. *Stick with Henry*. Rowan was happy teaching in Yorkshire. She'd serve her time as a trainee reporter and then she'd spread her wings, and they'd both be journalists, him a newshound (the BBC, maybe – he'd be perfect on screen), her a features writer. Perhaps they'd get a place together. She smiled happily at the corner shop guy arranging his fruit and veg.

At the office, Kyle beckoned her in as she distributed the mail.

'Emma,' he said. 'The bats piece was good. We've had a few reader letters asking for more on local wildlife.'

She beamed at him. 'Oh, that's brilliant!'

He gave a small laugh. 'I enjoy your enthusiasm. Long may it last. You've got yourself a regular column. Let's call it something like Nature Watch. Tell readers what to look out for, where to find things. Feature more local nutters, like your Batman.'

'I will – oh, thank you! I can't wait to get started. Foxes. Can I start with foxes?'

'Only if you tell me how to keep the buggers out of my garden.'

'I can, actually . . . '

Back at her desk, she texted Henry: I've got my own column!! Nature Watch (or something). Can't quite believe it! And thanks again for coming down. Love you xxx

She was missing him already; she wasn't sure when she'd see him again. But today was a good day.

She kept her phone handy, waiting for his reply, and ten minutes or so later it rang.

It was Rowan.

*Rowan?*

It's amazing, she thought, watching herself in wonder, how many words and thoughts can be processed by the human brain in a matter of seconds. Was he coming down again? Did she want him to? Why else would he be ringing? Maybe he wanted to see her again! But she'd only just recovered from his last visit . . . *I don't need this.* But no way could she say no. Not to him.

'Rowan!'

'Hi, Emma.' His tone was serious. 'Where are you?'

'At work, of course! Where else would I be, now I'm a wage slave?'

'No – I mean, are you at your desk? Are you alone, or are there people with you?'

She went quiet. What was going on?

'I'm at my desk, but no one's listening.' The reporter who sat opposite her, Nick the Sport, wasn't in yet. 'Rowan – what's up?'

She heard him take a breath. 'I wanted you to hear it from me. Emma – look. Try not to panic, you know what they're like. There's probably a simple explanation. But it's Freddie and Riv – they've gone missing.'

Her heart skipped a beat. *'Missing?'*

'Since yesterday. They haven't been seen since Sunday breakfast.'

Emma went cold. For a moment, she couldn't think.

'I don't understand. How can they be missing?'

'I'd told them we'd take George for a walk in the afternoon. They didn't show up. I thought nothing of it – they're always off somewhere. They're not allowed out of the school grounds unless it's with an adult, but those two don't have much respect for the rules. I thought maybe they'd gone up the tor – they always like that walk.'

'But . . . where could they be?'

'The police are out looking. When they didn't show up for dinner last night we searched the school and the grounds, then we called the police. Look – where's Belle?'

She thought hard, trying to retrieve the information, but her mind was blank. 'I don't know. Dallas, maybe?'

'Shall I speak to her, or would you rather do that yourself? Because if the boys don't show soon, the police will contact her. It'd be better if she hears it from one of us. And with the police swarming all over the place – it's only a matter of time before the press get hold of it.'

'Rowan . . . ' She was still processing what he'd told her. 'Where do you think they could be?'

'I don't know, I just don't know. Shit, Ems. I was meant to be keeping an eye. I feel responsible.' His voice was low and worried. 'I was hunkered down writing all day; I just forgot I was meant to be walking the dog with them. Emma, I'm sorry. I'm so sorry about this. But you know what they're like. I'm sure they're okay; they'll be off on some adventure—'

'But Rowan, it's February. And you're saying they've been out all night? They have to be indoors somewhere, otherwise they'd freeze to death.' The thought occurred to her. 'Oh god. Could they be lost up on the moors?' Panic was rising. She picked up a pencil, and the lead snapped as she pressed it into her notepad.

'We have to hope not. The police were up there all night, and they're taking a helicopter up today.'

She pictured it. A helicopter. This was serious. 'No. Oh no.'

'We checked their lockers. It looks like they were setting off on something – big coats, gloves, hats, all gone. They took their backpacks.'

'An adventure, yes. Rowan, what should I do?'

'Sit tight. I've given the police your number. Will you ring Belle?'

'Yes, and I'll tell Crystal and Pearl too. Like you say, once the press get wind of it . . . But by the end of today . . . surely, Rowan, they'll find them today, won't they?' Her voice was pleading.

'I'll phone the minute I hear anything. Or just to update you.'

'Right. My god, Rowan. I can't believe this is happening.'

'Try and stay calm, Ems. The waiting's awful, but carry on as best you can. I . . . you're in my thoughts. All the time.'

He ended the call, and she sat staring into space.

It felt unreal, like a terrible dream. Freddie and Riv getting into scrapes was par for the course – but *missing*, overnight, in freezing February temperatures. Where were they? What on earth had they planned? Had they run away from school? Surely they'd have told Belle, or Emma, if they were miserable. And at Christmas, they'd been full of love for Middleham.

No, the most likely explanation was that they'd set off on a walk and got lost. Perhaps the mist had come down. Or it had snowed, and they'd missed the path. Perhaps they'd spent the night shivering in a barn somewhere, and were even now trying to find their way back. A helicopter would spot them soon. Or a line of policemen crossing the moor . . .

She roused herself, sitting up straight. What time was it in Dallas? She checked on her computer – 5 a.m. She sent a text: Mum, when you wake up can you ring me? Important. X

Then she called Crystal and Pearl, repeating what Rowan had said, asking them to sit tight, wait for news.

'Everything alright, Emma?' Nick the Sport had arrived and was looking at her in concern.

She thought quickly. This was a newsroom. Her brothers going missing would be big news. 'Fine, thanks. Just family stuff. Shouldn't bring it to work – I know.' She gave him a weak smile.

'When it's *your* family, I guess it's difficult to ignore,' he said.

'Yup.'

'Okay, doll. I'll leave you to it. Cuppa?'

'Oh, that'd be lovely, yes, please. And congrats on Chelsea's win.' She marvelled at her ability to sound normal.

'Epic.' He chuckled. 'Shame about Leeds.' The team had been one of Teddy's big loves, so Emma sort of followed them.

Nick left for the kitchen.

Emma tried to carry on as usual, but she couldn't write a word, couldn't even usefully proofread, and was relieved when Kyle sent her off to review a local amateur art exhibition. She scooted round it in half an hour, taking a few notes, her phone heavy in her pocket, then went home.

Alone in the house, she tidied up, made a sandwich she couldn't eat, tried and failed to watch TV. Belle finally rang, and Emma filled her in, trying to keep her voice steady and matter of fact. 'I'm sure they'll turn up soon, Mum, like they always do. It's been less than twenty-four hours ... ' *Including one whole freezing-cold night.*

Emma's words seemed to reassure Belle. 'You will let me know, the minute you hear anything?'

'Of course. Do your concert, try not to worry ... '

At three o'clock, Rowan texted: No news. Big search up on the moors. Weather not great but above freezing. Piece scheduled for tonight's local TV news if no sign. Want me to call you?

She replied: Thanks. Yes please.

His voice was reassuring. 'There's been a small development. Two students' bikes have disappeared from the bike sheds. The police think the boys probably took them.'

'Oh! Right.'

'It means they planned this, and they were more than likely on the roads – not the moors. That's good, Emma. And surely – two blonde boys on bikes, people will have seen them. If word gets out on the news tonight we can expect plenty of information to come in.'

'Rowan – if it's on the local news ... I mean, they're Snows.

Teddy and Belle's sons. This is going to be huge, right? I need to warn Mum.'

There was a pause, as they both contemplated what lay ahead.

Emma knew what she had to do. 'I'm coming up. I can stay at Grandma and Grandpa's. I have to be there.'

'Come tomorrow.'

'No. I'm leaving as soon as possible. I can't just sit around here waiting for news. Maybe ... by the time I get there, they'll be found.'

'There's got to be a good chance of that.' He sounded genuinely hopeful. 'The police say most missing kids are found within forty-eight hours, and within a few miles of where they went missing. And there's two of them, that's got to up the chances.'

'I'll see you tomorrow.'

'Drive carefully, Ems, for god's sake. Promise me.'

'Of course. Ring if you hear anything?'

'Yep.'

As she ended the call, her phone beeped. *Missed call.* It was Henry's number. It beeped again. Call me asap H x

She should let him know. With a heavy heart she returned the call.

He didn't waste time on the preliminaries. 'Emma? Has your brothers' school been in touch?'

'What? Yes – but how did you know?'

'A contact at the *Yorkshire Chronicle* told me about the police search. Are you okay?'

'Oh god,' she said. 'Everyone knows?'

'You can't keep something like this quiet. The nationals will be on it by now. Probably the TV news. You'd better be prepared. Does Belle know?'

'I've told her, yes. I'm about to leave for Yorkshire.'

'No. Stay in London. It'll be crazy over there, once word's properly out.'

'I can't! How can I, when Freddie and Riv are missing!' Her voice rose to a wail. She took a breath. 'I have to go. I need to pack. Can I call you later?'

'Emma, go tomorrow. Don't drive up in the dark.'

'I'm going today; I've made up my mind. I'll be okay, I'll take it slowly. I'll stay at my grandparents'.'

'I'll come over.'

'No! Don't, Henry.'

'Emma, it's a big story. Apart from anything else . . . I can report on it. You'll need as much press coverage as possible, for the search. Don't speak to anyone else, right? Wait for me. I won't print anything you don't want me to.'

For a moment she was speechless. He was thinking about the story. All her worry, the gnawing anxiety for her brothers, coalesced into a burst of anger. 'You want an *exclusive*, Henry? How could—'

'Emma! Don't be ridiculous. It's going to be huge – you'd rather have me there than some random reporter, wouldn't you? And I can support you, keep the newshounds at bay.' His voice was steady, reassuring.

'I'm rather hoping they'll be found well before you could make it across the Pennines.' She was breathing quickly. 'But perhaps that would spoil your story?'

'Look. You're worried, of course you are. But don't lose sight of the big picture. The key thing is getting word out, so people can phone in. Maybe the boys are sheltering somewhere – farmers can go check their buildings. But they won't be doing that until they learn the boys are missing.'

She took a breath, tried to calm herself down. 'They're making an appeal on the news tonight.'

'Did the police tell you that?'

'I haven't spoken to them yet.'

'Did the headmaster ring you?'

She hesitated. 'No, Rowan did.'

There was a pause. 'Emma, you need to be speaking to the police. Get a police contact. Not him.'

'He's their teacher. I'd rather talk to him.'

'Look – you mustn't. He's being questioned . . . '

*Questioned?*

'My contact said Bosworth was meant to be supervising them yesterday afternoon. Emma – he didn't even report them missing until way after dark.'

It sounded like Henry was accusing him of something.

'I know. But . . . they're always off somewhere, Henry.'

*They're questioning Rowan.*

*Well of course they are, if he was the last person to see them.*

'It was negligence, at the very least,' said Henry. 'That school's not going to come out of this well.'

This was going nowhere.

'I have to leave, Henry. I don't want to be driving late at night.'

'I'll need your grandparents' address.'

'No! Please. Wait until I'm there. I promise I'll ring you. Surely by the time I get there they'll be found? Surely they will, Henry?' She swallowed back the tears.

*Freddie, Riv, my darling brothers. Where are you?*

# Chapter Fifteen

By the time Emma arrived at Sandal Manor, the evening news had run the piece about Elfred and River Snow, aged twelve and ten, pupils at exclusive Middleham College, feared missing with temperatures expected to plunge below zero tonight. The police appealed for anyone who'd seen the boys, or with information as to their whereabouts, to contact them.

Richard and Lily had recorded the appeal, and showed it to Emma as she sat down with them in the drawing room.

'*The boys are the sons of rock singer Belle Snow, currently on tour in America, and the late actor Teddy Snow,*' said the reporter, standing outside the school, her breath forming little clouds in front of her face in the chill evening air. '*We believe their eldest sister, Emma, is on her way to Yorkshire this evening.*'

'How did they know that?' asked Lily, pausing the recording.

'I expect Rowan told them,' said Emma. 'Rowan Bosworth. He's their teacher. It was him who rang me.'

'Bosworth? What's he doing there?' said Sir Richard, frowning. 'I assumed he was still in London.'

Lily unpaused the recording, and a lump formed in Emma's throat as a recent school photo of the boys appeared on the screen, along with the number to ring.

The piece ended, and Lily switched off the TV.

'Bosworth,' repeated Sir Richard. 'Why didn't Belle tell me he was there?'

Why did he sound so concerned?

'Do you know him?' Emma asked.

'No,' said Sir Richard, glancing at Lily, 'but I remember Teddy talking about him, and I went to see that play of his, the one Teddy was in.' He shook his head. 'Dreadful. All that swearing and shouting; quite the worst night at the theatre I've ever endured.' He paused. 'What's a man like that doing teaching young boys?'

'Honestly, Grandpa. Rowan's fine! He was just, I don't know, exploring that genre, experimenting with violent language. I think it was cathartic for him; he was having such a horrible time personally.'

'That business with his wife? Didn't she kill herself?'

'No. She had anorexia.' *No wonder Rowan cut himself off from this bloody family!* To Grandpa, eating disorders were probably as unfathomable as Rowan's prose.

'But she attempted it, I remember,' he went on. 'And she took drugs, I'm sure Teddy said. There was some business with Neville too. Everything got very ... unsavoury, didn't it, Lily?'

Lily was looking upset. 'I'm afraid it did, yes. But I'm sure we don't need to bring this up now. We have more serious concerns.'

'Well, I don't know,' said Sir Richard. 'I wish Belle had told me he was teaching there. I can't think what that school is doing, putting my grandsons into his care.'

*Enough!* 'Grandpa – that's one of the reasons Mum wanted them to go there! Because they like him. And actually, I think you'll find Dad's behaviour was far worse than Rowan's. He's a good man.' She needed to get away from her grandfather's accusatory stare. 'Grandma, is it okay if I go have a shower?'

'Of course,' said Lily. 'And I can rustle you up some supper – we'll see what Mrs Berry has left.'

'No, it's fine, I stopped to eat on the way up.'

'Alright, dear. A hot chocolate?'

'Oh. Yes please. With marshmallows?'

At the mention of the sweet, comforting drink that Grandma had been making her since she was a little girl, Emma found herself in tears, all at once overwhelmed by the events of the day.

Lily hugged her. 'There there, darling, they'll turn up.'

The tears spilled over.

'I've never known such a pair of scallywags,' said Lily, rubbing her back. 'When they come back they'll be full of their adventure, and I'll give them the biggest telling-off of their lives.'

In her room – the chilly, pink flowery bedroom she always stayed in when she came up here – Emma wiped her eyes, took some deep breaths, then checked her phone. There were two messages. The first was from an unrecognised number:

Hi Emma,
Please call me at your earliest convenience, I'm here
to help you.
Warmest regards,
DS Shore, Family Liaison Officer,
NYorksPolice

The other was from Henry:

Hope journey was okay.
Pls call when you arrive
H x

Nothing from Rowan.

She rang DS Shore, who offered to drive over from York, even though it was gone nine o'clock.

'Can you tell me if anyone's seen the boys?' Emma asked, her heart in her mouth.

'We've had a few calls to follow up on, after the TV appeal, but they all relate to yesterday morning. No credible reported sightings since then.'

'*Nothing?* No one might have seen them today?'

'We're hoping for a wider response when the papers run it.'

'But the papers – that's tomorrow!'

'The search is continuing, Emma. We have officers coming in from other areas to help. We're doing everything we can to find your brothers.'

'The helicopter didn't find anything?'

'I'm sorry, no.'

'There's no need to come over tonight, but you'll call me if you hear anything?'

'Of course. I'll see you tomorrow, then. Would about nine suit?'

'I'd like to see the boys' teacher, so I'll need to go over to Middleham first. Can we make it later?'

DS Shore hesitated. 'Mr Bosworth is assisting the police at Middleham. But I'll arrange for you to see him, if you want to. I understand he's well known to your family?'

'Yes, he's a family friend.'

'I'll let the team know. And Emma – I'd like to have a chat, about your brothers. The more background we have, the fuller picture we can build . . .'

'Of course.'

Next, she rang Henry, who asked how soon he could come over.

'I'm going to Middleham first thing, then to the police at York.'

'I'll meet you in York.' He proceeded to fill her in on developments. She learned far more from him than from DS Shore.

'There's been quite a response,' he said. 'Two boys on bikes in various locations – latest one was near Aysgarth. It sounds like them, but nothing definite beyond yesterday morning.'

'Aysgarth?'

'Local beauty spot.'

'Yes, I know it. The waterfalls. We went there on a family outing one time. Henry – that must be it. They must have gone to see the falls.'

'The police are on to it. They're searching the area. Look, Emma. Let me come over now? I'll be there before midnight.'

'No, Henry. I'm going to have one of Grandma's special hot chocolates and them I'm going to try to sleep. I'm exhausted, and I need to be up early tomorrow.'

Finally, she rang her sisters. Pearl was at Bristol University, and Crystal was at Oxford; both wanted to come up the next day if Freddie and Riv were still missing.

Surely, by this time tomorrow . . . She pictured it. A piece on the news: '*The boys were found suffering from exposure and hungry, after losing their way on the remote Yorkshire moorlands . . .* ' A quick shot of them with those silvery warm-up blankets round their shoulders, being bundled into an ambulance which would be taking them to hospital, just to be sure . . .

Later, as she wrapped her hands around Grandma's liquid comfort, she wondered why she hadn't wanted Henry to come over tonight. She could've curled up in his arms, slept on his broad, soothing chest. She thought back to their earlier phone call, when she'd accused him of wanting an exclusive. He was only doing his job, she supposed, and with the best of intentions – spreading the word, getting people looking. But she remembered his tone of voice: *He's being questioned.* There had been a note of triumph in there, hadn't there?

*It was about time I introduced you to my jealous streak.*

Emma had ever been wary of those wanting to be close to her – wanting to befriend the girl with the famous parents, hoping some of that glitter would rub off on them.

With Henry, it had never felt that way. Until today, when something had been triggered. An instinctive need to protect herself and her family – and Rowan – from those same outsiders with an appetite for the gossip that had always surrounded Teddy, in particular the truths that had been exposed after he'd died.

For Henry, it was all about the next big story. Would he resist the temptation to use this situation to his advantage? And what about that 'jealous streak'? Had it been a flippant comment, or was it something she needed to be concerned about? She was well acquainted with the power of the media. The thought of Henry coming into Rowan's proximity made her uncomfortable. She probably shouldn't have called him 'the coolest person ever'.

Maybe she was overreacting. A lifetime of holding people at arm's length – it was difficult to adjust. Henry loved her for who she was, not what she was. She imagined how reassuring it would be to have this calm, competent, intelligent man watching her back in days to come.

'Grandma,' she said, 'would it be okay if my boyfriend stayed over tomorrow? I think it's time you met him, and he wants to help.'

'From Lancaster, is he?' said Sir Richard, looking up from his newspaper.

'Yes, that's where he's living at the moment.'

'And he's a newspaper man? As long as he's not expecting to get the inside story.'

*Actually, I asked Grandma, not you!*

'I don't think so. Though he's keen to involve his paper in a good way.'

'Then yes, of course, on the condition he doesn't air this family's dirty laundry. We don't want all that stuff with Rowan and your father dragged up again. Make that absolutely clear to him.'

*What stuff, exactly?*

'I will. And you're both going to love Henry. Everyone does.'

*And hardly anyone I know seems to like Rowan*, she realised. *Just me, Mum – and the boys.*


Emma tossed and turned in the lumpy single bed, unable to banish the image of Freddie and Riv, huddled together against the cold in the cellar of a – kidnapper? Holding them for ransom? Or an abductor? She chewed over the possibilities, again and again.

There were two of them, and they weren't small any more. Could one man tackle them into his car and abduct them?

Unless … they'd been lost, and an opportunist had spotted them, offered help. But they'd had stranger danger drummed into them. No, they wouldn't have got into a car with a stranger.

But if they were desperately cold, lost, hungry …

How deep were the waterfalls? Could one of them have fallen in, the other trying to save him?

But it was a popular spot, especially on a Sunday, even in February. What were the chances of no one noticing if a boy fell in and another jumped in after him?

Lost on an adventure? This was surely the most likely explanation. But for all this time? If they'd taken the bikes, were on a road – well, it couldn't be *that* far to the next village, or a farmhouse? Had they stopped to ask for directions, and the farmer had just happened to be the local paedophile ...

The bark of a fox pierced the dead of the night, like a supernatural scream.

'You're not going out without breakfast,' said Grandma firmly, from her seat at the kitchen table. 'Mrs Berry can do you some eggs, or you can have toast and cereal if you don't want cooked.'

Mrs Berry, standing at the kitchen sink, smiled over her shoulder at Emma.

'Okay, Grandma, just toast and coffee, then.' Though she had zero appetite.

'Let me do that, dear,' said Mrs Berry. The kind, plump little housekeeper had been with the Snows for as long as Emma could remember. Her cakes were Snow family legend; she'd loaded the boys with sponges and cupcakes when they'd returned to Middleham after Christmas.

Emma sat down opposite her grandmother, who looked as if she was about to chair a parish council meeting, or something. Always immaculate, always in a blouse and skirt or well-tailored trousers, standards only easing when she was gardening. Grey hair swept up into a pretty bun; little pearl earrings. And she always smelt of something old-fashioned and floral. Grandma was like a heritage rose.

'I thought you might want to see the morning paper,' she said, passing it over.

It was the *Yorkshire Chronicle*. She remembered – it was a contact from this paper who'd alerted Henry to the boys' disappearance.

She spread butter and marmalade on her toast, from the little ceramic pots in the middle of the table. (Lily didn't tolerate jars or bottles or tubs.) Each piece of crockery and cutlery, the brand of marmalade (Rose's English Breakfast), even the clanking of the plumbing when Mrs Berry turned on the tap – everything was reminiscent of her childhood visits here. It was soothing.

She read the piece. There was nothing new, except for the fact that the teacher who'd last seen the boys hadn't reported them missing until several hours later, having apparently spent the afternoon alone in his master's lodge.

That teacher, the article helpfully informed the reader, was Rowan Bosworth, writer of the ground-breaking play *Twisted*, memorable for its ferocious language and violent themes. It finished by speculating on the reasons why Bosworth, a friend of the Snow family, would abandon a career as an award-winning playwright for a position teaching at an all-boys' school. Perhaps it was a response to losing his young wife, who'd died 'after a battle with mental illness'. And of course, Bosworth had also lost his mentor, Teddy Snow, having been part of that actor's notoriously wild circle.

Emma didn't recognise the reporter's name. What were the police doing discussing Rowan with the press? Or had someone else fed them that information?

Later, as she drove north, Emma listened to the hourly news bulletin on BBC Radio Leeds. More of the same. The boys had been missing for two nights; the police believed they were likely to be somewhere in the Aysgarth area.

Cars and TV vans lined the road as she approached Middleham, and – oh no – reporters were milling around the school gates. Her Union Jack mini wasn't exactly inconspicuous. They came swarming out as she approached, shouting her name.

A woman wearing a lanyard over a navy puffer jacket was waiting, waving her forward into a space alongside two police cars. She had a moment – *here I am again*. Hugging Riv as he cried his heart out. Saying goodbye to Rowan that last time when, within the space of an afternoon, they'd gone from easy companionship to passionate kiss to polite strangers.

*How will it go with him today? How will he be?*

She took some breaths and got out of the car, and the woman came over. She was young and black, with warm eyes and a reassuring smile.

'Emma? I'm DS Shore, family liaison officer. Please call me Liz.' She held out her hand.

'Oh!' Emma shook it. 'I thought we were meeting in York.'

'I wanted to introduce myself sooner. Let's go inside. Shall we have a cup of tea?'

All Emma wanted was to see Rowan. 'I'm fine, thank you. It would be great if you could update me, though.'

They made their way inside just as a bell rang, and for a moment Emma was surprised to realise everything was carrying on as normal, with herds of schoolchildren moving noisily along the corridors from one classroom to another.

But why wouldn't they be? People died, and the world carried on. Children went missing, and the world carried on.

'They've just had assembly,' said Liz, as they attempted to navigate their way through the oncoming tide of boys. 'Mr Pickford reiterated that anyone who might have known Elfred and River's intentions on Sunday should tell their teacher. I hope we get some response.'

'Surely *someone* will know what they were up to? Liz – you should know, ever since they were little they've been off on adventures. My parents weren't great on discipline; it was a battle to keep them under control. But they had it drilled into them about stranger danger, especially after the TV series with Dad, when they became quite famous for a while.'

'Yes, we've taken that into account, that they're well known,' said Liz, showing Emma into a room just along from the headmaster's study. She shut the door, cutting off the hubbub from the corridor. 'A stalker is one possibility.'

Liz sat down on a Chesterfield sofa, indicating the space beside her. 'One of the masters has kindly lent us his study for as long as we need. We can be private in here. Is it okay if I ask you a few questions – not an interview as such, just building a picture.' She took out a notebook and pencil.

Emma instinctively trusted Liz, and was happy to share more thoughts on her brothers. But as she described them, relating the scrapes they'd got into over the years, she found herself in tears again. 'I can't understand it,' she said. 'How can they have just vanished?'

Liz said again that they were doing everything possible, repeating the forty-eight hours statistic Rowan had mentioned. 'Are you quite sure you wouldn't like a cup of tea?'

'No, I don't want tea!' Emma tried to calm herself, to swallow down the panic. 'Can I see Rowan now?' she said, sniffing as she fished in her little backpack for a tissue.

Liz hesitated. 'I'll see if I can organise that.'

*He's being questioned.*

'I *must* see him!'

'Emma.' Liz laid a hand on her arm. 'We're trying to establish the sequence of events between when Mr Bosworth last saw the boys, and reported them missing. There are some question marks.'

'I've spoken to him,' said Emma, shaking off the hand. 'He was writing in his study. They'd run off somewhere.'

'Can we talk about Rowan's relationship with the boys? We've established he spends a lot of time with them, outside of school hours.'

Emma tried to keep her voice steady. 'He's known them since they were tiny.' She explained how Teddy and Neville had taken Rowan under their wing, his progression through university and his career as a playwright. 'When my father died, and then Rowan's wife, Abigail, he . . . well, he didn't want to carry on with that life in London. He returned to his roots here in Yorkshire and took up teaching. He's been so much happier since he did.'

'And how well did he know the boys?' Liz pressed.

Emma described his visits, his delight at the boys coming to

Middleham. 'He had no family of his own, so he loved being part of ours. And the boys adore him; they told me he's the coolest teacher. They walk his dog with him, he tells them stories, it's a lovely relationship. Liz – there's absolutely nothing sinister about it, I can assure you.'

'Right.' Liz held her gaze. 'I'll go fetch him. But Emma, you should be aware, he's quite . . . stressed.'

Emma sat alone, waiting, her heart in her mouth.

Then the door opened, and she was flying across the room and into his arms.

He held her close. 'I'm sorry,' he said, his words muffled as he spoke into her hair. 'I'm so sorry.'

'No, it's not your fault, Rowan.' She held him tight.

'They were in my care. I shouldn't have left them alone. I promised Belle I'd look after them.' His words ran together in his distress.

'No.' She tightened her arms round his waist. 'They've always been feral.'

He stroked her back, kissed her hair. It was as if he was trying to absorb her.

'They're a nightmare,' she said. Their impish faces pushed into her mind, and her tears – for them, for Rowan – came back in a rush. 'I know you love them, and I won't let you beat yourself up.' She looked up at him. 'But where are they?'

He searched her eyes, and there were tears in his, too. Then he gently pushed her away. 'Everything I love turns to shit.' His voice was flat.

'Stop it!'

'It's true.'

Should she tell him she knew about the baby? Would this be a terrible time to say, or would it help?

She laid a hand on his arm. 'Mum told me about baby Teddy,' she said gently. 'I'm so, so sorry. I can't imagine how that must have been for you, the very worst thing.'

She flinched at the pain in those dark eyes.

'I wondered if you knew.'

'I've known for a while, but I was waiting for you to tell me.'

He took a breath. 'I'm glad you found out.'

She nodded. 'We can talk it through when the boys turn up. Look, Rowan – Freddie and Riv – you really mustn't blame yourself. They're two naughty boys on an adventure. If they're in trouble, it's mostly their own fault. Not yours.'

He shook his head. 'How are you like this?' He sounded calmer now.

'Like what?'

'Always seeing the good in people, looking to excuse their failings.'

'It was *you* who taught me to try and understand people, remember? And I thought you were working on your . . . demons.'

'Not going so well. Look, you'd better know, the police suspect me. I have no alibi for the afternoon in my study. The boys are known to spend a lot of time hanging with me and George. Ergo, pervert child-molesting teacher. It seems the best they can come up with.'

Emma sucked in a breath. 'That's ridiculous! What about the sightings on Sunday morning?'

'Minor detail. Could've been any two boys on any two bikes.'

'Rowan—'

'Ems, think hard, about what they might have been up to. You know them better than anyone.'

'Yes.' She looked him in the eye. 'And I know you too, Rowan, demons and all, and I *won't* let them . . . ' Her voice tailed off, as the air between them changed.

'My lovely Ems,' he said, softly. 'You really do believe in me, don't you?' He reached out a hand and cupped her cheek. She leaned her head into his hand, closing her eyes. Then she felt his lips on hers. It was a sweet, beautiful, comforting kiss; a promise, for when all this was over.

'You know I do,' she said, leaning her forehead against his. 'You know how I feel, how I've always felt.'

'Yes, I do know. But we'll have to put this on hold, until the boys are found.'

'And then?'

'Then you can tell Henry to fuck off home to Lancaster, and come back to me.'

# *Chapter Sixteen*

Her Mini was hemmed in on all sides by thundering juggernauts, but Emma was glad of the heavy motorway traffic. Focusing on staying alive kept the worry and guilt at bay.

Unable to face a phone conversation, she'd texted Henry from Middleham:

> Police liaison came to school so don't need to
> go to York. Sorry if you're already there. Heading
> home to Sandal – entrance off Manygates Lane just
> past Castle Café. G&G looking forward to meeting
> you! PS Nothing new to report from Middleham.

He'd replied:

> No problem, popped into Yorks Chron, always good to
> scope the comp! See you at Senior Snows xx

The traffic eased as she left the M1, and back it all came, the relentless, gnawing worry about her brothers. Her feelings for Rowan – all so familiar, switched yet again from backburner to full heat. And it was all entwined, like strands of wool, into one big ball of angst.

The simplest thing would be to put aside thoughts that weren't relevant to the matter at hand. She had to focus on what was important right now: Freddie and Riv. And in the meantime, she'd carry on as normal with Henry. She couldn't possibly address her future with him – or lack thereof – while the boys were missing.

Arriving back, she spotted Henry's car parked out the front.

Mrs Berry opened the door. 'Your young man's here, dear,' she said. 'They're all having tea in the conservatory. How did you go at Middleham?'

'Nothing new to report,' she replied, hanging up her coat, 'but it was good to meet with the police.'

They walked down the hallway together.

'I'm sorry to hear that. This is so very hard on you all, this waiting for news. I do love those boys.'

Emma smiled sadly. 'In spite of . . . '

Mrs B chuckled. 'Yes, in spite of the trail of destruction.'

'And they love you, Mrs B.'

'I'm glad your Henry's here to look after you. On brief acquaintance, I'd say you've got yourself a lovely lad there, Emma.'

Henry. Soon to be her ex. She blocked that thought.

'Did you make him a special cake, Mrs B?'

'A Victoria sponge.'

'Then I would expect the liking to be entirely mutual.'

The conservatory was a beautiful space. Lady Lily was a keen gardener and it resembled a giant greenhouse, full of tropical plants kept cosy by heaters and the rare winter sun shining on the south-facing glass walls. The earthy smell took her back to days helping Grandma with her watering and spraying.

Henry was chatting with her grandparents, and judging from their expressions, his approval rating was comfortably in the upper nineties. No surprises there.

He leapt up, and she closed her eyes as he hugged her.

*I don't deserve you.*

The emotions rushed in again – mostly guilt – and she couldn't help the tears.

'Oh, my poor love,' said Lily. 'Not good news?'

She shook her head, leaning on Henry. 'Nobody's seen them since Sunday morning. The police seem to have no ideas at all.'

'I heard they're questioning Bosworth,' said Henry.

'What did I tell you?' said Sir Richard.

'No!' said Emma, sharply, moving away from Henry. 'They're *speaking* to him – of course they are! He's the boys' teacher and their friend and he's known them forever.'

Henry held up his hands. 'I'm just repeating what I've been told.'

'He's beside himself with worry, and he's blaming himself. But he shouldn't be. And can we stop ... Grandpa, look – just because Rowan wrote a powerful play about unhappy people and went carousing with Dad doesn't mean he's a potential abuser of children, for god's sake!'

She stopped, breathing quickly, and there was silence for a moment.

Grandpa looked uncomfortable, Grandma looked distressed.

Emma wiped beneath her eyes.

Sir Richard cleared his throat. 'Right. Well. Why don't you sit down and have a cup of tea. I'm sure it's been a difficult morning for you.'

Henry was looking at her in that way again. Like he was reading her mind. Then he smiled. 'I remember you telling me about Mrs Berry's cakes.'

'What?'

'You were absolutely right. What you need, right now, is a cup of tea and a slice of Victoria sponge.'

Why did everyone think she needed tea? What she needed right now was to find her brothers, but she went along with it, sitting down on the cane sofa beside her grandmother.

'We're all tense,' said Lily. 'It's only to be expected. There's no point in speculating; leave that to the police. Let's just try and get through this, and pray for good news soon ... '

'And eat cake,' said Henry, passing Emma a dainty plate with a slice of sponge.

He was trying to be nice. But she could tell, he was mulling over her impassioned defence of Rowan.

'Come on, Richard,' said Lily, standing up. 'Let's leave these two to talk.' She gave Emma a reassuring smile as they left.

'Your grandparents are lovely,' said Henry, moving to the spare space beside her. 'And Belle will be here soon. She caught an overnight flight and someone's driving her over from Manchester.'

'Oh, that's good,' said Emma. 'Poor Mum, she must be frantic.'

'You okay with me sticking around?'

She turned to face him, and saw only concern. 'Yes. I'm a bit of a mess. I'm feeling completely useless. I don't know what to do.'

'Just be here for your mum. I can help with the press stuff.'

Emma nodded. 'DS Shore, the family liaison officer – she's great. She didn't tell me much, but I think that's because they have so little to go on. Henry – they've vanished. How can two boys just vanish?'

He took a breath, looked her in the eye. 'Can I be honest?'

She braced herself. 'What are you thinking?'

'If they were lost, they'd have been found by now. If they'd had an accident, chances are someone would have come across them, or one of them would have gone for help. If they'd run away . . . same. Two blonde boys, someone would have seen them.' He paused, and took her hand. 'The fact that there's no sign . . . it's all pointing to an abduction. My guess is they got into a car they shouldn't have got into.'

Her heart plummeted, and for a moment she couldn't speak as a wave of nausea hit. But she recognised the sense in his words. 'They know all about stranger danger, though.'

'Could have been someone very clever. Or a person they'd trust, like someone in a uniform. Or . . . maybe it wasn't a stranger.'

'What?'

He shrugged. 'Someone they knew, who'd realised they were missing from the school and went to look for them. Perhaps.'

'But no one knew they were missing until dinner time.'

'Emma . . .' He paused to let his words sink in.

He was treating her like an idiot. 'Henry. Of *course* the police are talking to Rowan. He knew them better than anyone at that school. And guess what? He's only human. He was deep into his writing, he forgot about them for a bit. And now he's distraught. He needs bloody support, not accusations!'

'You saw him, then?' His voice was steady; there was little warmth in it.

'Of course I saw him! He's a friend; he's going through hell. He *loves* those boys! And they're missing, and he was meant to be keeping an eye. How would *you* feel, Henry?'

'Okay, I'm sorry.' She caught the look. Like he'd got the answer he'd been waiting for.

If that was the case, what had been his question?

'I need to go freshen up.'

'Wait.' He took her face in his hands and kissed her, and she gave in, closing her eyes, soothed by its tenderness.

'I'm sorry,' he said, wiping away the traces of her tears. 'I didn't mean to upset you even more. Let's start over. How about a cup of tea to go with that cake? And then maybe you could show me round this incredible old house.'

She welcomed the return to safe ground. 'Good plan. I don't know how I'm going to get through this, but attempting a modicum of normality would be a start, I guess.'

'It's not quite on the scale of Montfort Grange, but I reckon it's older,' she said, as they came back down the ancient staircase, half an hour later.

'I love it,' said Henry. 'And I love Richard and Lily.'

'Seems to be mutual.'

He smiled. 'They've given me my own room. Does this in fact indicate disapproval?'

A burst of relief. 'Not at all. They're pretty old-fashioned.'

Lily's voice floated up from the hallway. 'Emma! Your mother's here!'

They hurried down the remaining stairs and followed Lily into the drawing room, where Belle was sitting on the sofa with

Grandpa. She looked pale and tired, and Emma wondered for a moment at her mother's stamina. All the touring, night after night; carrying on without Teddy. Trying to hold her family together, while rarely seeing them. And now, after an overnight flight and a long drive, having to face this.

'Darling!' Belle got up to hug her. 'And Henry. Thank you for being here for Emerald.' Her eyes moved between them, and Emma saw her distress. 'Well, all this. I don't know ... those wretched boys.' She waited, the question hanging in the air: *What do you know?*

'Emma's doing brilliantly,' said Henry, kissing Belle's cheek.

'I spoke to your sisters this morning,' Belle said. 'They wanted to come up, but I've told them to sit tight for now. The boys will turn up soon, I'm sure of it.'

Nobody replied.

'Won't they?'

Henry glanced at Emma.

'Mum ... it's not looking good.' She met her mother's eyes. The positivity in them quickly faded as Emma's again filled with tears. 'They haven't been seen since Sunday morning.'

'More than two days. That's so long, when you're only a child.' Belle sat down heavily on the sofa. 'I can't believe this is happening. Where can they possibly be?' She began to cry.

Emma sat down beside her, pulling her into a hug. She told her about the missing bikes, the sightings near Aysgarth.

Belle took a breath. 'Yes, I've read the papers.' She glanced from Emma to Henry, then back to Emma. 'What did Rowan say?'

Emma tried to keep her face impassive. 'He says they're always off somewhere – no surprises there. But this time ... He's beside himself, Mum.'

'Why did you not tell me Rowan was at Middleham, Belle?' said Sir Richard, from behind his *Yorkshire Chronicle*.

'Why?' Belle's eyes met Lily's, and Emma saw her grandmother frown. 'Because I knew you'd take umbrage.' She was regaining her composure. 'I don't honestly know what you've got against him.'

Sir Richard made a scoffing noise.

'I know you hated his work,' Belle said, 'but Rowan meant a lot to your son. He had no one, when Teddy took him on. Our family was very important to him. Sending the boys to Middleham – it's what Teddy would have wanted.'

'But Rowan was part of that ... that *circle* of Teddy's,' said Sir Richard, putting his paper to one side. 'And don't tell me you didn't loathe all that, Belle.'

'That was down to Teddy and Neville, not Rowan,' said Belle.

Lily spoke up. 'Richard, this is hardly the time to be dragging all that up again.'

'I'd say it's highly relevant. God knows what ... behaviours Teddy and Neville introduced that boy to, at such a young, impressionable age.'

Emma was in the dark, and happy to remain so, for now, but she felt the need to intervene. 'Rowan hates Neville.'

Henry was quiet, but Emma sensed him taking it all in, making mental notes. So much for not washing that dirty laundry.

'That's quite enough,' said Lily, visibly upset.

'Yes,' said Belle. 'Let's have some respect for Teddy's memory. And a little less sanctimony, perhaps, Richard.'

'What?' he spluttered.

'Slinging mud at your own son,' Belle went on, 'when perhaps he learned at his father's knee? Sorry, Lily, but I can't abide hypocrisy.'

Henry cleared his throat. 'I need to make a couple of calls. Perhaps Belle would like to talk to Emma alone. I'm sure that would be helpful to them both?'

'Yes,' said Emma gratefully. *My god, forty-eight hours in and we're all losing it.*

She and her mother made their way to the smaller sitting room just along the hallway.

'Have I done it all wrong?' said Belle, sinking down onto the sofa. 'Should I have stopped touring, kept the boys with me, not sent them away?'

'Of course not, Mum. That's who you are, and you love it. And it's not like the boys are littlies. Freddie's practically a teenager – and they have each other.'

'But they've run away, haven't they?' She was trying to convince herself. 'Why would they do that?'

Emma sighed. 'I don't think so. They'd planned something, for sure. Rowan said they took warm coats, hats and gloves, their backpacks, so they were off on an adventure, maybe. But not running away – they were happy at Middleham. Remember how full of it they were at Christmas?'

Belle frowned. 'Could someone have been bullying them? Because of their parents, maybe? I remember you telling me—'

'No one's mentioned that. Rowan thinks they're happy. They'd probably have told him if they weren't. They hung out with him a lot.' She paused. 'Which seems to be the reason the police are suspecting him of . . . ' She shook her head. 'They need to investigate others in the area who might have shown an unhealthy interest in two beautiful, famous little boys. Other masters, groundsmen, locals . . . '

'Yes,' said Belle. 'I know they're only doing their job, but Rowan? He loves those boys – they're like the kid brothers he never had.'

Emma sighed. 'I feel so awful for him, Mum. He's blaming himself, for not keeping an eye when he promised. I told him, he mustn't do that.'

'Poor Rowan.' Belle slowly shook her head.

'He said . . . ' Emma closed her eyes for a moment. 'Everything he loves turns to shit.' She opened them again. 'Mum – I know we need to focus on the boys, but . . . can I talk to you about him?' She felt a desperate need to confide.

Belle frowned, then nodded.

'He's been having therapy. He was doing well; he was great, when I dropped the boys off after Christmas. He was more like the old Rowan, before everything went wrong with Abigail.'

Belle gave a small laugh. 'Therapy? Good luck to whoever's taken *him* on.'

Emma turned her face away, looking out of the window. The gardens were monochrome; skeletal trees and shrubs, perennials hacked off at ground level, the only signs of spring the muted green spears of new daffodil leaves, huddled in clumps around the lawn.

'Sorry,' said Belle, covering Emma's hand with her own. 'That was the stress talking. Of course it's great that Rowan's finally working on his grief.'

'It's okay. I'm sorry. We're most certainly not here to talk about my love life—'

'*Love?*' interrupted Belle. 'For heaven's sake, Emerald. Did you not listen to a word I said, when we last had this conversation?'

When Emma didn't respond, she said, 'Look, I'm here if you need to talk, you know that. All I'll say is, Henry's perfect for you, and Rowan most certainly isn't. Rowan grew up never knowing love. He's what happens when you neglect a child and throw the damaged result into situations even a well-balanced person would struggle to cope with.'

'I love Henry, I do. But I can't kick the feelings for Rowan.' She saw the dismay in Belle's eyes. 'I've tried so, so hard. Time and again. I *know* he's difficult. I know he's moody and awkward. But I can't stop wanting him, I just can't.'

Belle thought carefully. 'What you and Henry have is very special. You light up when you're with him, and he adores you, it's plain to see. But Rowan ... what you feel for him, I don't think it's love, darling.'

'But what else would it be?'

'You've always been in his thrall, ever since you were a girl. He's brilliant, he's charismatic, he draws people in. But he doesn't care too much about them. Rowan's all about himself.'

'Mum—'

'I only want what's best for you, which is a man who puts you first, who's dependable, steady, caring. *Henry*, Emerald. Not Rowan.'

Emma sighed. 'I guess that makes good sense.' *But it's too late.*

Belle brushed Emma's hair back from her face. 'You've got such a good, wise head on your shoulders. Do yourself an enormous favour and listen to it. And ignore that soft heart of yours. Because if you don't, my darling, he'll break it.'

Emma arranged to take the rest of the week off work as compassionate leave.

'Emma, love, I'm so sorry about what's happened,' said Kyle. 'And I wanted to let you know, we're running a piece. The Snows are well-known in Hampstead so . . . you know. Do you want to give us a quote?'

'Not really. Can you just make something up about how grateful we are to the North Yorkshire Police and for everyone's support at this difficult time, etc., etc.?'

Dinner was a muted affair, Henry filling the sad silences with small talk, asking Belle about her tour, listening attentively to Lily's plans for the garden, and showing enthusiasm for Sir Richard's minor obsession with military history.

'Sandal was the seat of a couple of Dukes of York, Henry, back in the days of the Wars of the Roses,' he said.

'More of a Lancaster boy myself,' said Henry with a grin.

Emma yawned as Sir Richard droned on about Sandal's appearance in Shakespeare's *Henry VI* (Part Three, apparently). 'No thanks,' she said, as Lily dished out Mrs Berry's apple crumble. 'I'm bushed. I think I'll just go to bed.'

Later, Henry crept along the landing to her room, and squeezed into the single bed. 'Okay if I do this?' he said, nuzzling her neck and slipping a hand between her legs.

'I can't,' she whispered. 'I'm sorry, I just can't.'

She was grateful to the dark, for hiding any truths that might have been there in her eyes. The heavy curtains at the ancient windows let through only the smallest amount of light, and Henry was just a silhouette, hovering over her.

'I understand,' he said. 'I'll go back to my lonely bedroom, then. Tell me, why do olds think single beds are acceptable for men over six foot?'

'I know, it's like being swaddled,' she said, relieved as he slipped out and shrugged on his robe. 'Goodnight, Henry, and thanks again for today – for everything.'

Half an hour later, with no hope of sleep, she slid out of bed and made her way down the ancient landing to the bedroom her brothers stayed in when they visited. Picking up the fluffy toy rabbit that lived on Riv's bed, she burrowed under the duvet and curled up, burying her nose in the rabbit's fur with its remembered little-boy smell, soaking it with her tears.

'Where are they, Bunny?' she whispered. 'Where are our boys?'

# Chapter Seventeen

On Wednesday, Pearl and Crystal arrived, and the four Snow women's TV appeal for help assured prime-time news slots and front-page coverage in the nationals.

## BRITAIN HOLDS ITS BREATH
## AS BELLE WAITS FOR NEWS

The incident room at the police station was busy. They were still working through the calls, but none had resulted in anything significant or new coming to light. Many had been from cranks. The Snows were used to those.

Henry's journalist tentacles reached far and wide, and he was head down, following leads, efficiently sifting speculation from fact, evidence from gossip. His updates for the *Lancaster Post* were authoritative, well reasoned, and included moving quotes from the family. He didn't name Rowan, restricting himself to vague references to staff members helping police with their enquiries.

While hundreds of extra officers had been drafted in to continue the search, a team of police was still based at the school, interviewing employees and pupils.

Henry may have been restrained in his reporting, but as he mentioned, repeatedly, to the family, Rowan was at the centre of it all. There was most certainly a cloud of suspicion, he said, and it was hovering directly over Rowan's head.

'Based on *what*? It's all purely circumstantial,' snapped Emma.

'Unanswered questions,' said Henry. He ticked off the points on his fingers. 'Can't prove his whereabouts on the Sunday afternoon. No alibi. Last person to see them. Meant to be supervising them, but sent them away from his study without asking where they'd be. Didn't report them missing until after dark. *Way* after they were meant to be back at his study.'

'But how is it *his* fault the boys sneaked off?' Emma countered. 'They were never taught why rules might actually have a purpose.' She couldn't stop herself glancing at Belle.

'And motivation, Henry?' said Belle. 'No way is Rowan an abuser of boys.'

'People once believed Catholic priests were above sin,' was Henry's response.

'Yes – you could be wrong, Mum,' said Crystal, not meeting Emma's eye. 'Rowan is quite weird. All that suppressed anger. And he's certainly very interested in the whole subject of abuse. I mean – that play!'

Emma closed her eyes for a moment. 'You don't know him at all.'

**HOPE FADES FOR BELLE'S LOST BOYS**, read Sir Richard's *Telegraph* on Thursday.

Emma now knew how despair felt. It was as if a huge shard of glass was wedged in her heart, causing a constant, nagging pain.

That afternoon, she, Belle and Henry went to Aysgarth Falls, because it felt right to do so. They sat on the riverbank, wrapped up against the cold.

Belle's eyes were squeezed shut. 'I'm trying to open up a connection,' she said. 'Maybe we should get in a psychic?'

Henry answered. 'No, Belle. Let's stick with good old-fashioned detective work.'

'I don't think they were here,' said Belle. 'I feel like I'd know if they had been.'

A young couple with a baby in a backpack appeared beside them. 'Sorry to interrupt,' said the woman, 'but we just wanted to say, how sorry we are about—'

Belle's eyes flew open. 'Leave us alone! For once in my life, I'd just like to be left in peace . . . '

Emma gasped.

'Oh, we're so sorry,' said the man, looking mortified. 'Of course.' The couple moved quickly away.

'They were only being kind, Mum.'

Belle burst into tears. 'I can't stand this, Emma. I can't do it . . . '

'Oh, Mum, I know.' Emma rubbed her mother's arm.

'Give her a minute,' said Henry, holding out a hand to Emma. She took it, and he led her a short distance away.

'How do we get through this, Henry? Just . . . how?'

He put an arm around her shoulders. 'Emma, I think—'

She knew what he was going to say, and cut him off. 'No! I can't go back, I can't leave. How can I do that?'

'But now you've done the press conference, what else is there? Sitting around with your family, waiting and worrying – it isn't helping anyone. If you were back at work, it'd take your mind off things.'

It was as if her life had been paused. She couldn't think more than half a day ahead. The waiting; imagining the possible scenarios – it was pushing her to breaking point. Henry's words made sense, but returning south with nothing resolved was unthinkable. She couldn't turn her back on her brothers.

And then there was her mother.

And Rowan.

She looked away from Henry, towards the falls. Rowan hadn't been in touch, and she'd resisted the temptation to contact him. He was there, waiting for her, waiting for the boys to turn up so the two of them could be together, whatever form that relationship might take.

She'd tried to picture it, when she couldn't sleep, in an attempt to divert her thoughts. He could come to London – maybe write full time, see how that worked out. Get another teaching job if he needed to. He'd continue with his therapy; they'd work together towards a normal, healthy relationship.

And yet ... her heart, already aching, died a little more each time she contemplated losing Henry.

Her feelings for the two men were so different. Henry lifted her up, made her feel good; she never worried that he'd let her down. Everyone loved him, and with good reason.

But Rowan ... the intensity of it all. The angst, the longing. His trickiness, his baggage. Could a person really trust their heart to another after an abusive childhood, a loveless life?

And strangely, she couldn't picture the years ahead with Rowan. She found it almost impossible to imagine the two of them doing normal things, like the weekly supermarket shop. Not so with Henry. She could see them at forty, reading their newspapers at the kitchen table, sipping their coffee, discussing the weather, mustering their two children for the school run before leaving for work.

'I'm going back to Lancaster at the weekend,' Henry said. 'I have to, I'm afraid, for work. And I said I'd stop over at Mother's on the way. I don't suppose ... '

'No.'

He raked his fingers through his hair. 'Fair call.' He looked disappointed. 'You've been through enough. I don't suppose Mother's views on liberal schooling would be helpful.'

On Friday, the police sent divers into a canal, following a report of two boys smashing the ice on it last Sunday. Another team was searching a flooded gravel pit not far from the school. It seemed they were now looking for bodies, as well as runaways. The thought was unbearable.

Liz Shore was updating the family on these searches, but Henry invariably knew about them first. Emma had the uneasy sense he was enjoying being chief comforter of women and bringer of news, and didn't miss the way he slipped in innuendos about Rowan's guilt at every opportunity. She'd stopped pushing back; now she simply stayed silent.

On Saturday morning, when there was nothing new to report, Henry said his goodbyes. Upstairs in his room he held Emma tight. 'I feel like I'm abandoning you. This is horrible.'

'I couldn't have got through it without you,' she said, taking comfort in his warm, muscular chest, aware of how different it felt to Rowan's lithe, wiry body.

They gathered outside, and Henry hugged Crystal and Pearl then received a heartfelt squeeze from Lily and a firm, prolonged handshake from Sir Richard.

'Thank you again, Henry,' said Belle, reaching up to hug him. 'It means so much to me, knowing you're here for Emerald.' Her eyes met Emma's before returning to his. 'Come down to London as often as you can. You two – you can use the house, any time you like, whether I'm there or not.'

He kissed Emma goodbye, and as she watched his car disappear down the driveway her despair grew heavier, settling like a rock in her stomach. It suddenly felt so final.

Emma knew there was nothing more she could do up here.

She texted Rowan: Leaving tomorrow. Can I see you first? Miss you, hope you're OK XXX

The reply came: Best stay away. I'll be alright. Will be in touch x

She'd do as he asked; no doubt he had good reason. She helped Grandma with her plants in the conservatory, then took a solitary walk round the grounds, noticing how the daffodils had already grown an inch or two during the five days she'd been here.

*Only five days?* It came as a shock. She watched a squirrel searching for something it had buried deep against the scarcity of winter. Maybe Freddie and Riv were buried somewhere. If so, whoever had taken them would have had quite a task, digging a large grave in the frozen Yorkshire soil.

She squeezed her eyes shut against the image, and headed back to the house.

On Sunday morning, there was a tap on her bedroom door. 'It's me, darling,' came Grandma's voice. 'May I come in?'

Grandma's routine was unchanging: tea in bed with the paper; shower, quite some time to dress and do her hair, then down to breakfast. Never in her dressing gown. Robes were for the bedroom and bathroom, possibly the late-night news, if she'd had an evening bath.

Why would Grandma be coming to her room now? Emma could think of only one reason.

Hope wrestled with fear as she sat up, her eyes fixed on the door. Time seemed to slow down, and she was hyperaware of the moment – this moment, the last moment of not knowing, before her life changed, either for the very best, or the absolute worst.

'Yes, come in, Grandma.'

The door opened. 'Good morning, sweetheart.' Lily read her expression, and quickly said, 'No, no – it's not the boys.'

Emma let out a long breath. 'Oh, thank god.'

'I brought you this,' Lily said. 'I'll leave you to read it. No rush to get up.' She walked over to the window and drew back the heavy curtains. The sky outside was its habitual grey.

She looked over at Emma, and her eyes were full of sympathy. But Emma saw something else in them, too, as she turned to leave. A hint of anger?

As the door closed, Emma sat up straighter, frowning, and picked up the paper – the *Yorkshire Chronicle*, Sunday edition.

**MIDDLEHAM MASTER SEEN ON MOORS WITH LOST BOYS**, said the headline. There was a school photo, with Rowan and the boys circled.

Emma started to read, her heart in her mouth. Immediately she realised – the headline was misleading, sensationalist; it was there simply to sell more copies. A Middleham local had come forward to say she'd often seen Rowan out walking with the boys and his dog.

She breathed a sigh of relief – but then her eyes widened as she read the next paragraph.

*Theatre producer Neville Warwick, Bosworth's ex father-in-law, told the* Chronicle *of his deep concern for the safety of the boys, who are his godsons. 'Clearly Rowan only got the job at Middleham because he was an old boy. Did the school not check his credentials? He never trained as a teacher – he's a writer. He's a volatile man and not, in my opinion, suited to teaching. He has anger issues, as my poor late daughter learned when she was married to him. I regret not taking more of an active role in my godsons' lives.'*

*Abigail Bosworth died in 2007, after battling drugs and mental illness . . .*

Emma lowered the paper and stared into space. She felt nauseous. *Oh my god, Rowan.*

Why did Neville hate Rowan? Did he really blame him for Abigail's death?

She mulled over the article as she showered, dressed, and finished packing.

In the kitchen, Sir Richard was busy by the toaster. Mrs Berry had the weekend off. Belle, Pearl and Crystal hadn't emerged yet.

'Oh, sorry, I left the paper upstairs,' said Emma.

'It's fine, darling, we have the *Sunday Times* too.' Lily looked at her, waiting for her to say more.

'I don't know what Neville's problem is,' she said, sitting down. 'It's one thing to let rip to the police because you're grieving your daughter and need someone to blame, but it's not okay to slander that person in the press.'

'Slander?' said Sir Richard, turning round.

'Look,' she said. 'Neville came out as gay, and he was notorious for . . . his promiscuity?'

Sir Richard made a small harrumphing sound.

'And as a result his marriage nearly broke up, and Abigail found all this hard to cope with. *That's* what sent her out of control, not Rowan.' Emma wasn't going to mention the baby – her grandparents might not know.

'Are you sure, dear?' said Lily.

'That's what Mum said.'

'Belle always loathed Neville,' said Sir Richard. 'And it was mutual. Neville hated the power she had over Teddy, when he wanted Teddy all for himself.'

Emma's jaw dropped. 'What? You don't mean . . . '

'No, no,' said Sir Richard hurriedly. 'Teddy wasn't . . . like that. But Teddy was Neville's meal ticket. As long as he was Teddy's manager, he was a major player in theatre circles. Belle attempted to split them apart, but – well. You remember how Teddy was. He liked to keep everyone happy, hated disagreements. Buried his head in the sand. He thought he could carry on regardless and things would work out.'

'I see.'

'I'll tell you what, Emma,' he continued, bringing over a rack of toast. 'At first I didn't approve of your mother, because she was . . . what I suppose we used to call a commoner.'

'Honestly, Richard,' said Lily, helping herself to a slice of toast.

'But she's proved herself a tower of strength over the years. I have enormous respect for her now, I have to say.' He put his hand over Emma's and squeezed it.

Emma resolved to talk to her mother about Neville before she left. Belle was giving it a few more days, and if there was no progress on the search, she would return to London. The remainder of Woodville's tour had been postponed.

There had been no new leads; fewer calls had been coming in. More rivers had been searched, the moorlands had been scoured. Woodlands had been examined for freshly turned earth. Farmers all over Yorkshire had searched their outbuildings.

Nothing.

Sir Richard and Lily took themselves off to church, and soon after, Belle appeared in the kitchen, her eyes puffy and red, her face pale. It was as if she'd aged several years in a week.

Emma fetched the newspaper article, and Belle shook her head as she read it. 'Emerald, how on earth did the paper find this out, about Neville and Rowan?'

'They must have phoned Neville. He probably knows as much about Rowan's past as anyone. And he's obviously ready and willing to share his bile.'

'That dreadful, dreadful man.'

Emma took a breath. 'Mum ... tell me, honestly. There's no truth in Neville's accusations about Rowan, is there?' Emma trusted Rowan, but, she realised, she didn't quite trust herself. Where her feelings for Rowan were concerned, there wasn't a great deal of logic involved.

Belle was quiet for a moment. 'It was the grief, I suppose, making Neville lash out. But Teddy ... ' She paused.

'What, Mum?'

Belle was clearly weighing up whether to tell her something about her father. Had Grandpa been in denial about his son's sexuality? But Emma needed to know the truth. 'I'm a big girl now. There's little you could tell me about Dad that would shock me.'

Belle's eyes widened. 'Oh, no! Not that. Goodness me, no.' She laughed, nervously. 'Oh, for sure, he and Neville did that whole camp luvvies thing, but Teddy was ladies only. No, what I'd been going to say was, Teddy told me, when they first took Rowan on, when he was only seventeen, that Neville was infatuated with him.'

'What?'

'I think he was. I saw it, the way he'd watch him. I worried about that boy, constantly. He was a vulnerable youth with no one to turn to. Something may have happened. I think ... well, to be honest I'm almost certain – Neville tried to seduce him.'

Emma's hand went to her mouth. 'Oh no.'

'But I soon realised,' Belle went on, 'Rowan was stronger than I'd thought, and perfectly capable of looking after himself. Teddy watched out for him too – he knew Neville's game. When it all got too much, Rowan would just walk away, disappear for a while.'

Things were beginning to make sense. 'So that's why Abigail fell out with Neville,' said Emma. 'Because he was infatuated with her husband. And presumably this didn't help with her own issues.'

'Exactly. Teddy said Neville was in love with Rowan,' said Belle, 'but I doubt if Neville's actually capable of love. I think he's a complete narcissist.'

*Best stay away.* Emma thought she understood why Rowan would rather not see her yet. He was protecting her. She wondered if he'd seen the newspaper article. How would that have affected his state of mind?

He'd asked her to stay away, but maybe a phone call . . . she was suddenly overwhelmed by the need to connect with him.

He didn't answer.

She tried again, immediately. And then a third time.

Finally, he picked up. 'Emma. You okay?'

For a moment she couldn't speak, floored by the sound of his voice. 'Hi. Not okay, no. But I'm driving back to London today, and I wanted to talk first. How are *you* doing, if it's not a stupid question?'

'I'm packing. Pickford fired me. Job no more.'

Emma gasped. 'What? But . . . why, Rowan?'

'Days of outraged parents emailing about evil Mr Bosworth who's clearly unfit to look after young boys. They have a point. Then today's newspaper – did you see?'

'Neville. Yes. God, Rowan, there's so much we need to talk about.'

'Now's not the best time. And you've got enough on your plate.'

'You're important too. What are you going to do? Can you keep your lodgings for a bit?'

'I'll clear out this week; lie low for a while. Look, Ems. Don't fret about me. If there's one thing I've learned in life, it's how to be on my own. I'm just going to do that again. I've got George – uncomplicated, idiotic George. We'll go for walks, I'll write, we'll be okay.'

But she couldn't bear to think of him living all by himself. 'Can I come up and see you?'

'I'll summon you, lovely Ems. When the boys are found.'

## Chapter Eighteen

B ack in London, Emma retreated into herself as the days passed
with no further news from Yorkshire. People at work didn't
know how to act around her. She saw the question in their eyes:
*How would you cope with that?*

Her flatmates were kind; they couldn't do enough for her, and
she was grateful for their girly chat, for their attempts to carry on
as normal.

The only ones who understood were her sisters. The three girls
spent a weekend together at Pearl's place in Bristol. They cried a
lot, pored over family photos, shared memories. It helped, a little.
When Crystal returned to Oxford and Emma to London, she felt
very alone. Everyone she loved was so far away.

Henry phoned in the evenings, and promised to come down
next month.

At first, Rowan replied to her daily texts.

She said: I feel like I'm in a bubble, separate from everyone else.
I hate how the world carries on as normal. I miss you so much xx

He replied: I know that bubble well. Take it one day at a time x

On her second week back, she pressed him for news on his plans.
He didn't reply for several days, then: Doing something I swore I
never would. Going back to the farm. My old man died, Mum gave
tenants notice, says I can stay while she decides whether to sell.

Leasing land as zero farming skills or desire to learn. No mobile coverage. Need to sort internet. What's your address? x

She texted it by return, finishing: Landline? What will you be doing there?

Rowan: No landline. Writing and walking dog x

It sounded lonely and bleak, but he'd told her he was fine by himself. And it was only until ... Emma sighed as she put her phone down on her bedside table. It was beginning to feel like the boys would never be found. She was in limbo, her life still on hold.

At what point should she attempt to move forward? And what form would 'forward' take? Carry on as now? Kyle was enabling her to coast through work; she wasn't busy. It was just as well, because the creative part of her brain had shut down. She'd forgotten how it felt to have ideas; she was no longer able to free her mind to let them in. Every sentence she wrote was an effort, like dragging words from quicksand, and she found herself staring into space, unmotivated, disconnected.

What was the point? She'd wanted to save the world. This beautiful planet. But now, that world was a place where loved ones vanished without trace, where that man over there could be a sex offender, an abuser of boys, or a person who enjoyed cruelty for its own sake. Someone who'd drown a little boy's pet puppy in front of him, because he was pissed off about a gate being left open.

Before, she would jog across Hampstead Heath at dawn, taking pleasure in the solitude, in nature; flying along, freeing her mind, ideas rushing in, feeling her heart soar. Now, being alone on the Heath frightened her. When she could summon the energy, she ran the streets at lunchtime instead.

March trudged on, and then it was more than a month since the boys had disappeared. Press coverage had dwindled to the occasional mention. And Rowan had stopped texting.

She waited.

Henry came down for a weekend. The weather was cold and

wet; going out didn't appeal. He said no more about looking for a job down south, and Emma didn't bring it up. There was an unspoken understanding – no major life changes until there was news on the boys.

Emma's response to being with Henry again took her by surprise. She felt the angst, the despair, easing, like he was lifting the weight from her chest. Cuddling up with him on the sofa made a big difference. She'd been fixated on hearing from Rowan, had taken Henry's nightly check-ins for granted. Now she appreciated all over again his steadying presence.

Henry knew how to handle her. He talked to her about the boys, about what next, if there continued to be no news.

'With every day that passes, the chances of finding them alive diminish,' he said. 'You know this, so you're losing hope, but you can't bring yourself to admit that's happening. If you give up hope, it's like you're abandoning them.'

'Yes, that's how it feels.'

'Baby steps,' he said, then suggested some, like writing down her feelings, and getting outside, maybe helping out on the Heath with Batman. 'You're strong, Emma. You'll get through this.'

Henry, she thought, blinking in the first rays of sunlight, was a wonderful man.

Then, a week later, a letter arrived from Rowan. It was waiting for her on the doormat when she arrived home from work. She recognised his distinctive handwriting on the envelope, and took the letter into her bedroom, quickly unzipping her boots, kicking them off and hopping up onto the bed, a smile on her face.

Inside was a single sheet of A4. No date, no address.

*Emma,*

*Not an easy one to write, but I've never found it easy, knowing what to say to you. All these years, you've confounded me. I'm bad at all of it, but you refuse to see that. You still hope I'll come right, be that person you want me to be.*

*Being here by myself, having this space, just me and the dog, I've been searching my sorry soul, Ems. And it's not in great shape. You deserve better. So I've decided – no more.*

As Emma stared at those last two words, her heart seemed to twist, and then stop. She forced herself to read on, and her hand started to shake.

*When Abigail died I cut myself off from your family and everyone associated with that painful time. But then, for a brief moment, before the boys went missing, I thought we could connect again. I even thought I might come to terms with my past. I loved teaching at Middleham – you were right, I was happy. You came back into my life and suddenly, I saw the possibilities. But you know what happened next.*

*With no news, we have to assume the worst. That they were taken, and I have to accept the blame for that. I promised Belle I'd look after them and I failed. Just like I failed my own boy.*

*I can't see a way forward for us, Ems. I'm up here, you're down there. I don't want to be in London again, I'm done with that. I might just stay a recluse. It kind of suits me right now. Can't really see myself as your partner, suburban man with kids. Honestly – could you?*

*Those things that happened between us, I shouldn't have let them. I tried to resist, but you were too lovely. Much too lovely for me, like I keep saying. FFS Ems what were you thinking, really? Take a step back, look at what you could have.*

*Coming to terms with the boys' disappearance is going to be long and hard, and I can't be the one to help you with that. I'm so fucked up we'd probably annihilate each other. I've been there before and I'm not going there again. It wouldn't work – I think you know that, in your heart. Your Henry will do a far better job of it than me. You'll live your best life.*

*So this is me saying goodbye. It's over, and for god's sake don't be coming up here or trying to persuade me otherwise, because it hasn't been easy coming to this decision, I've thought long and hard and may have shed a tear, because I do love you, my lovely Ems, you know I do. Enough to let you go, to wave you off on your life with Henry.*

*Don't shed too many tears, don't get angry, just think of me sometimes, and know how much it means to me that you believed in me. I'll never forget that you did.*

*Don't know how to finish this. Maybe just – sorry.*

*Rowan x*

She sat staring at the page, the final, crushing words blurring as the tears came. In the same letter he'd told her he loved her, and had ended it.

She lay down on her side and curled up, pulling the duvet over her. Her hot tears ran into her hair and onto the pillow. Her mother had warned her, but she wouldn't listen. She'd given Rowan her heart, and he'd broken it.

But later, as she finally managed to rouse herself enough to get up, splash water on her face, brush her hair and change into jeans and jumper, she acknowledged that he'd resolved her dilemma; that now she wouldn't have to choose. Here was the way forward. He'd given her that – he'd finished with her, because he loved her.

She took a long breath and blew it out, grimaced at her reflection in the mirror, and headed for the living room, where she could hear Greta and Isabel chatting.

'Aha! There you are,' said Greta. 'Allow me to pour you a Friday one.' She reached for the bottle of wine and empty glass on the coffee table.

'Make it an extra large, would you?' Emma said, plopping down next to her on the sofa.

She saw the look her friends exchanged as they took in her swollen eyes.

Greta passed the drink over, and with her other hand stroked Emma's arm. 'There you go, gorgeous. Get that down your gullet. Lovely body, aromatic and pretty damn rich, just like your Henry.'

Emma took a large gulp. 'Sheesh, that's good. I think I need to get extremely drunk tonight.'

'We're here for you with that,' said Isabel.

*

Easter marked two months since the boys' disappearance. Belle was back in London, and the girls and Henry were joining her at Hampstead for the long weekend.

Emma was first to arrive.

'I haven't moved anything,' said Belle, seeing her eyes on the boys' wellies as she let her in the front door.

'Of course not, Mum. Why would you?'

The sight of those boots, still muddy from the Christmas holidays, undid Emma. 'Sorry, I'm going to cry,' she said, her hand pressed to her mouth.

'Oh, Emerald, it's unbearable. I've done little else but cry since I got back. Thank goodness you're here.'

'Tea,' Emma said shakily. 'Apparently this is what we need at these times. I'll make us some.'

More reminders of the boys ambushed her. The photos on the hall walls; their video games stacked next to the TV. In the kitchen, as she made the tea, the boys' Coco Pops in the cupboard. Marmite. Cartons of Ribena in the fridge. Out of the window, the planks they'd wedged in the old apple tree for their 'treehouse'. She could almost see them, aged about five and seven, balancing in the higher branches as they played pirate ships.

There was no way she could face going in their bedrooms yet.

As they sipped their drinks, Belle asked if she'd heard from Rowan.

Since receiving the letter, Emma had tried not to think about him. It was too painful.

'We spoke on the phone, that last Sunday in Yorkshire. Mum — he lost his job.'

Belle looked horrified. 'I had no idea! I've been in touch with Mr Pickford; he didn't mention it.'

Emma scowled. 'Probably too embarrassed. From what I understand, Rowan was a brilliant teacher and Pickford didn't have a choice. Angry parents thinking Rowan's the most likely culprit in the boys' disappearance. God, how could people be so cruel, to jump to conclusions when they know nothing?'

'It must have been the newspaper coverage,' said Belle. 'I'm just going to trust in karma to deal with bloody Neville. But . . . how did Rowan seem?'

'Surprisingly resigned to it,' she said. 'It's like he wants to be punished. He feels responsible; he thinks he's let you down.'

'Poor Rowan. I should go see him – maybe next week. I can't let him think that way.'

'He's gone. He's living on his parents' farm, by himself. Writing. He said he'll be fine. But I don't know if he is . . . ' Her voice caught. *Don't let me cry again.*

'You've lost touch?'

'He was always rubbish at all that. There's no mobile coverage; I don't think there's Wi-Fi. I have no idea where the farm is – maybe the school would know. But he said he's fine with being a recluse for a while.'

'And things between the two of you?' Belle's eyes searched hers.

'Resolved, Mum.' She sighed. 'You were right, of course. Henry's the sensible choice.'

# Chapter Nineteen

The weekend marked a turning point. That evening at dinner, Emma registered the change. Henry had managed to lift their spirits, from melancholy to ... not happy – no, not quite that. But they were able to push the boys' disappearance to the backs of their minds for a while, to take pleasure in each other's company again.

Winter was finally over, and bright, enthusiastic young leaves were bursting out on the trees on Hampstead Heath, their green haze a promise of the long, warm days of summer to come.

'I may have some news for you soon,' said Henry, as he and Emma walked hand in hand on Parliament Hill the next day.

'Oh!' This must be to do with that postponed move south. 'Does it involve working somewhere over there?' She nodded towards London's distant towers.

'No. But it does involve more Henry and Emma time.'

'Oh, c'mon Henry.' She let go of his hand and turned to face him. 'You can't say something like that and then go all mysterious on me.'

He smiled secretively. 'Yes I can. I just wanted you to know that I'm working on it ... on us.' He pulled her to him, encircling her with his arms. 'I don't want to push it, or move too fast. I know things are still really hard for you. Just keep hanging in there, you're doing so well. One question, though.'

'Go ahead.'

'Will you come spend a weekend at Mother's with me? Soon? I want you two to get to know each other better.'

They hadn't talked much about that time she'd met Lady M. 'I don't think she liked me, Henry.' She took hold of the loose sides of his jacket, absently pulling them together. 'But I can try again.'

'She was just coming to terms with having a serious rival for my affections.'

Emma snorted. 'Also, I don't think she was sold on my plans for the countryside.'

'Seriously, she just needs time. Why wouldn't she like you?' He shook his head a little. 'How could anyone not?'

Emma thought back to the woman who'd managed to convey condescension and disapproval with one tweak of a perfectly arched eyebrow. She'd made Emma feel utterly unworthy of her precious son, in the brief time it had taken to drink a cup of tea from that ridiculous trolley.

'Did she discuss me with you?'

Henry grimaced. 'A bit. I don't think it's personal. I think it's more ... your family.'

'Ah yes. Them. Well, I kind of see her point of view. But maybe now ...'

'Right,' said Henry. 'Who *wouldn't* be feeling awful for you all. Mother's only human.'

Things were picking up at work. Emma's colleagues were more confident about striking up a chat, less worried about treading on eggshells. Nick the Sport was flirting with her again, taking the mickey, making her cups of tea that weren't loaded with sugar and sympathy. Kyle was back to bollocking her for lazy writing, or overblown prose, and most of all for her unashamedly biased coverage of all things green.

'What the fuck's this?' he demanded, pointing to the Nature Watch piece she'd sent him. '*In defence of rats?*'

Their numbers in North London were ballooning, thanks to weekly bin collections becoming fortnightly.

'Have you read it?'

His eyes scanned the screen: '*There's a reason rats are used in scientific research . . . they have high levels of emotional intelligence . . . Rats are in fact cleaner than cats.* Fuck's sake, Emma, that person coming face to face with a rat in their kitchen doesn't give a toss about their emotional intelligence. Tell them how to get rid instead.'

She folded her arms. 'I'm just getting people to see the other point of view. We don't own this planet, we share—'

'I want three hundred words on how to control rats.'

'But—'

'Bullet point the rat apologist crap in a breakout box, and give me three hundred on pest control. And tell Sales to ring Rentokil about an ad.'

Back at her desk, Emma sighed. She was never going to change the world one small breakout box at a time. But she realised . . . she *was* caring again. She was edging back towards the light, thinking positively.

Emma arranged with Henry to head north for the spring bank holiday. She gazed out of the train window at the countryside, resplendent in its May garb. Hawthorn frothed in the hedgerows, newly green fields and woodlands were vibrant and fresh. Black and white cows, horses; cars pootling along winding roads; brightly painted narrowboats chugging along canals. A red post van, a country pub . . . alpacas? Kites wheeling above farmland, church spires rising above villages. The industrial sprawl of the Midlands . . . Birmingham, Stoke-on-Trent . . . distant cooling towers puffing steam into the blue sky. Nearing Manchester, row upon row of red-brick terraces . . .

And all the while, she was aware of travelling north again. Somewhere up here, her brothers were waiting to be found.

The land became hillier; the Pennines rose over to the east, dark shadows on the horizon.

*The backbone of England, straight as a die, unlike mine.*

Over there, on the other side, Rowan was maybe sitting at a desk, writing. Or strolling across farmland or a moor, with George. *How's he doing?* She'd learned to shut him out. He was off the back burner and into the freezer. She was doing as he'd asked – finding a way through, inching her way back to living the best life she could. Without her brothers; without him.

Henry met her off the train, and she felt a burst of happiness when she spotted him on the platform. He swept her up and they kissed, and then kissed some more. 'Okay,' said Henry, coming up for air. 'I might just let that dinner booking go. A quiet night in suddenly has more appeal.'

Henry owned a beautiful, centuries-old house in the centre of town, not far from the dark, imposing shape of Lancaster Castle. A few doors down was Ye Olde John O'Gaunt pub, and music from a live band floated in through the open bedroom window.

'I suppose there's something to be said for long distance,' said Henry. A gentle breeze slipped through the window with the music, caressing Emma's still-tingling skin. 'It's like I fall in love with you all over again every time I see you.'

'Absence makes the heart grow fonder?' she said, drawing circles on his chest with a finger. 'So, Henry. That thing you mentioned, about being less long distance. Do I get to find out this weekend?' She'd been thinking about it; what he could have meant. TV news? Radio? Another regional, closer to London?

'Can't say yet, sorry.' He kissed her hair. 'Looking good, though. Should have news soon.'

Next day, the weather was glorious, so they drove up early to the Lake District. The fell tops were clear, and Emma was happy to accept Henry's challenge to climb The Old Man of Coniston.

Reminders of Rowan came at her thick and fast – the dark hills of the Pennines coming into view as they climbed higher; her hand in Henry's as he helped her up the tricky parts. The cool mountain wind on her cheeks, blowing her hair across her face. But she was conscious of handling the memories, anticipating them, like a batsman facing a fast ball, hitting it away, tapping the ground in preparation for the next.

They picnicked on the summit, their backs against the cairn, enjoying panoramic views as far as Yorkshire to the east, and the Isle of Man, hazy across the Irish Sea, to the west.

Henry seemed to read her mind as she gazed across at the Pennines. 'Emma ... '

His tone of voice had her turning to him.

'I thought you should know, I've been keeping track of the investigation, through my Yorkshire contacts.'

Emma's heart skipped a beat. That anxiety was always there, just below the surface, no matter how 'well' she was doing.

'They'd have told Mum if there was anything new,' she said.

'No, nothing new. Each and every lead turned cold. But unofficially, Bosworth's prime suspect.'

Emma gasped. 'How *stupid* are they? Chrissakes! Of course it wasn't him.'

Henry stroked her arm. 'I know you don't want to think the worst, and they can't officially accuse him because there's no ... well, there are no bodies.'

'Thanks for that, Henry.' She shuffled away from him, scowling.

'The police impounded his car for forensic testing. The boys had been in it.'

'So they'd been in his car? Big deal.'

'They questioned him about it. He said he took them on a day trip to Robin Hood's Bay, looking for fossils. Other boys corroborated that.'

She pictured it for a moment, the three of them on the windswept beach, the boys lolloping along with George, Rowan showing them where to look for ammonites. Tears pricked the backs of her eyes. All three were lost to her now.

'Thing is, he shouldn't have done,' continued Henry. 'You can't just be taking two boys off for a day out without permission. He didn't even tell anyone – just took them.' He shook his head. 'That

school isn't coming out of this at all well. And as for Bosworth . . . '
He glanced over at her.

She stared resolutely ahead. He was waiting for a response. *Why all this, now?*

'Rowan doesn't really do rules,' she said.

She was no longer used to speaking his name out loud. It hurt.

'He'd have been sitting in his lodge with them,' she continued, 'talking about dinosaurs or something. He'd have said, there's a great place to look for fossils, and then he'd have said, let's go see it. It's how he is. Spontaneous.'

She looked at him, and frowned. 'Henry, why are you bringing this up now? I was having such a nice day.'

He took her hand and kissed it. 'Because I can see, you being up here, it's brought it all back.'

She nodded, fighting back those tears, looking away from him and into the distance.

'A lot of things have been left in limbo,' he said. 'My guess is that something will turn up; someone will remember something, notice something, and things will open up again. But now you've had a bit of time and distance, it'd be as well to be a bit more . . . open-minded about the probabilities.' He was watching her, waiting for her to respond.

He was trying to make her see Rowan from a new perspective, from an outsider's point of view. His tone was patronising; he was implying her judgement was clouded.

She snapped. 'Henry, I appreciate what you're saying, but I know Rowan, Mum knows Rowan. He's quite messed up, through no fault of his own, but he's not a bad person. No way. He's lost his bloody job because my appallingly behaved brothers took themselves off without telling anyone, and then probably got into some evil man's car and I really, really, don't want to think about what happened next, so can you just shut the *fuck* up about Rowan.'

She squeezed her eyes tight shut for a moment, then went on, 'As if it's not hard enough for me – he was my friend, a dear friend, and now he doesn't even want to know me, because of all the associations. He's cut me off, he's told me to fuck right off, and I miss him.'

Henry's eyes widened, and it seemed a little theatrical. '*He* told *you* to fuck off?'

'Yes, in so many words.'

That penetrating gaze. 'But doesn't that imply he feels a terrible amount of guilt?'

'Yes! He does! Because he was meant to be looking after them. He told Mum he would; I was there when he promised. And then he did exactly what Mum and Dad did for all those years – he let them do whatever they bloody wanted. And look what happened. So yes, he feels guilty, we *all* feel guilty. And it's hell. But whoever took my brothers, it wasn't him. It was someone who didn't love them. Rowan loved them. We all bloody loved them. And now they're gone. Dead, probably. After going through god knows what horrors.'

She burst into tears. 'I feel like I'll never be properly happy again, Henry. Never. And my family and Rowan are the only people who understand that.'

She stood up and walked off down the hillside.

Henry came hurrying after her. 'Emma, stop. For god's sake, stop.' He grabbed her by the arm. 'Sorry, I'm so sorry. I just needed to . . . I need to understand, as best I can.'

'Well, obviously you don't. You can't.' She swiped at her tears.

He pulled her into his arms. 'Emma, please forgive what I said. I messed up really badly.'

The fight left her, and she let him hold her, feeling it all drain away, leaving her empty.

'This is not what I meant to happen,' he said. 'That back there – that might just have been the biggest botch-up of my life.'

'What was?' she said, taking a breath, looking up at him.

'That was meant to be me, asking you to marry me on the summit of Coniston. How wrong could I have got it?'

'Marry you?'

'Yes, marry me. I needed to know first . . . that you were ready to move on with your life. But I messed it all up. I'm so sorry. Can I start over?'

She looked into his eyes and saw his frustration, his anger at himself.

*He just asked me to marry him.*

How did she feel about that? Reassured, safe. But the joy she should have been feeling had been blocked by the emotions unleashed when he'd forced her to think about Rowan and the boys.

'Not yet, Henry,' she said in defeat. 'I'm sorry, it's too soon.'

'Understood,' he said. 'My bad. Can you pretend all that never happened, and forget I was going to propose? Just pretend. And I'll try again when the future's looking like a happier place.'

'Yes.' Her voice was flat. 'That sounds like a sensible plan.'

His smile was so sad, and her heart went out to him. 'Let's rewind,' she said, trying to rally herself. 'Back to the summit for the chocolate part of the picnic, then onwards to the next leg of this fun-stroke-knackering day before going home for more bed-based activity, or possibly exhausted sleep?'

He laughed, and she saw the relief. 'Absolutely. And not forgetting the ultimate challenge.'

'Which is?'

'Second encounter with possible future mother-in-law tomorrow.'

'Oh fuck, I'd almost forgotten.'

# Chapter Twenty

'Emma,' said Lady Madeline, rising in one fluid movement from her chair. She gently put a hand on each of Emma's arms and kissed her on one cheek and then the other. She smelled of something excessively expensive.

'My dear, it's been a while. I'm so terribly sorry about your siblings. It must all be taking an awful toll on you and your family.'

'Yes; yes, it is, Lady Madeline,' said Emma, attempting to adjust to this softer version of Henry's mother. Lady M was dressed in a pale blue cashmere jumper and white trousers, her dark hair loosely tied back. She was beautiful, immaculate, and against the backdrop of the green drawing room, like a template for gracious country living.

'Please, call me Madeline. I'm so glad you're staying over. It's high time we got to know each other.'

'I'd like that,' said Emma.

'Do sit down.'

Emma perched again on the chintz sofa, and after kissing his mother, Henry sat down beside her.

'How is your mother coping?' said Madeline. 'Belle, isn't it?'

'Yes. She's getting through. I don't quite know how – I guess she's a very strong person.'

'I'm acquainted with her sister, through my husband. Ex-husband. Henry's father.'

'Aunt Kate and Uncle Jason, yes.'

'Have you seen much of Dad?' Henry asked.

'Not for a while,' said Madeline. 'He's been in France. Have you?'

'I saw him and Kate just after Christmas. He was working in the Midlands, I think, but then yes, he said he'd be in France for most of the rest of the year.'

They continued with the small talk, and Emma found herself warming to this previously chilly woman. What was it like, she wondered, living in this enormous house, all by herself? Divorced; her son absent. Maybe she was lonely, afraid that Emma would lure her only child south and she wouldn't see him at weekends any more.

'I've put you two in the Queen's room,' said Madeline. 'I had it redecorated when Her Majesty last visited,' she added by way of an explanation.

'Both of us?' said Henry, looking surprised.

Emma dipped her face to hide her smile.

'Well, yes. I'm perhaps not such a prude as you think, Henry,' she said, looking amused. 'And I'm not actually that much older than you.'

'True,' he said.

'I think we have an imposter,' Henry said later, as they relaxed on the four-poster before dinner. 'What on earth's happened to Mother?'

Emma was flicking through a copy of *Country Life* from the pile on the coffee table, where there was also a beautiful arrangement of red roses. There had been a box of truffles, too, which were now on Emma's bedside table, and as she popped another into her mouth, she wondered if Her Majesty had also had trouble stopping at one or two.

'It sounds horrible, Henry,' she said, 'but I think you'll find it's the missing brothers effect. People are just kinder to me.'

'Ah. Maybe. But still.'

'She's got quite a sense of humour under that steely gaze. She kind of reminds me of Princess Anne.'

'The Princess Royal, you mean. Don't mess up your titles in front of Mother.'

'Whoops. Yes, she's certainly one for protocol and etiquette. Will I have to call her My Lady Mother-in-Law, if . . . '

Henry turned to look at her. 'Emma! Is that a yes?'

*Oh my god, what did I just do?*

'No, it's a maybe. And it's an ask me again, but not for a while.'

The local vicar and his wife, a charming young couple, joined them for dinner, along with Montfort Grange's estate manager, Gerald, and his partner, Lauren. The long mahogany dining table, watched over from the walls by more of those venerable ancestors, was polished to a mirror-like sheen that reflected crystal glasses, floral arrangements and weighty silver candlesticks. The food and drink was served by uniformed staff, supervised by Birch, who gave Emma a friendly wink each time he topped up her glass.

In spite of Lady Madeline's earlier easing of hostilities, Emma couldn't help but be aware of her scrutiny, as she sat straight-backed at the head of the table, dressed in black, her glittering eyes narrowing slightly each time they alighted on Emma, which was often.

Emma grew increasingly nervous under her gaze, and compensated by drinking her wine far too quickly. Having Birch regularly top it up meant she lost track of how much she'd drunk, and she suddenly found herself giggling as she took stock of herself sitting here in this ridiculous country house setting, being assessed on her suitability by Henry's mother.

'Do the women later retire gracefully to the drawing room while the men pass the port and talk politics?' she said in a low voice to Henry, on her left, trying to stifle another giggle as the staff paraded in with the main course. Henry was looking lush in a Prussian blue jacket, white shirt and grey silk tie, his hair neatly swept back. Henry's lovely hair was always so tidy, she reflected, gazing at it. He never allowed it to grow long enough to blow artistically about in a strong summit breeze. Like . . .

She admonished herself. *Stop that thought about beautiful men on mountain tops.*

Emma was wearing a dark red silk dress, low cut but not indecently so, and had pinned her hair up into a messy bun, little tendrils pulled loose around her face. She'd caught the sun on their walk up Coniston Old Man, and felt her face glowing in the candlelight – partly suntan, partly alcohol, partly because of the way Henry was looking at her.

'Of course,' he said, quietly. 'Not forgetting the cigars. I hope you remembered to bring your after-dinner embroidery.'

'Oh, I can't sew for fuck,' she said. It came out far louder than she'd intended, and as the vicar's eyes alighted on her, she added, 'Oops, I'm terribly sorry.'

Henry swallowed a smile. 'Well, clearly I'll have to look elsewhere for a wife,' he said. 'You can't sew, you swear like a trooper . . . '

Emma felt the needle pricks of Lady M's glare. The warm welcome was cooling.

'Oh, are you getting married?' said Caroline, the vicar's wife.

'Not yet, under the circumstances,' Henry said. He hadn't taken his eyes from Emma. 'Maybe one day, when the time is right for her.'

'Oh, I see. Yes, of course,' said Caroline, looking uncomfortable. 'I'm so sorry.'

'It's fine,' said Emma.

The vicar asked if there was any news on the boys, and she had the conversation she'd had so many times these past months.

An artistically arranged plate of lamb rack was placed in front of Emma, and her heart sank. Seeing her frowning at it in consternation, Harry beckoned Birch over.

'Yes, Henry?'

'Sorry, Birch – did the message about Emma not eating red meat fail to make it through to the kitchen?'

Birch looked horrified. 'Oh my goodness, my deepest apologies, Emma. Let me have a word right away.' He went to whisk away the offending plate, but she stopped him.

'No, no,' she said, as dishes of roast and green vegetables were set down along the centre of the table. 'Seriously, look at all these lovely veggies. Yum! I'll just load up on those, this poor little lamb here can scoot over to the side of my plate.' She nudged it across with her knife.

She would, in fact, have enjoyed the succulent local lamb, perfectly roasted with garlic and rosemary – the aromas were tickling her nose – but she'd recently decided the planet would benefit from her giving up meat.

'You're vegetarian?' said Lady M. She made it sound like a communicable disease. One to which only unsuitable girls were susceptible. One you had to go to a special clinic for. Before they infected proper ladies' precious sons.

'I'm still finding my boundaries on this issue, Lady M . . . Lady Madeline, I mean. Madeline. Sorry.' She took a sip of her wine.

Lady M pursed her lips; the vicar and his wife exchanged a nervous glance.

'I eat fish, and I'm still on the fence about whether free range, ethically raised and humanely killed meat is okay. I'm researching it. I have a column, Nature Watch – I'm hoping my editor will let me do a feature, eventually. I'm sure this little lamb,' she swung her wine glass in its general direction, 'had a very happy life, if it lived here on your magnificent estate. And I'm sure it was killed nicely.'

'Our sheep have it very cushy,' said Henry, looking amused. 'And I'm sure Gerald would be happy to discuss the ethics of animal husbandry with you when I give you the full tour tomorrow.' He looked over at the estate manager. 'And Gerald, be prepared to fight your corner. Emma knows her stuff when it comes to the environment, and she won't let you off lightly if she suspects sheep abuse.'

'Which paper is it you work for?' asked Caroline, nicely diffusing the mounting town-versus-country tension.

As Emma explained her role to the vicar's wife, she heard the estate manager say something about 'hounds', and she tuned Caroline out, pricking up her ears.

'And Chigley over at Garsdale is selling a good hunter,' Gerald went on. 'We could go take a look, if you're interested. And he's keen to buy your horsebox, though you should really be asking a lot more—'

'Yes, phone him,' interrupted Lady Madeline. 'Stafford can't manage the higher fences any more, and at the rate he's slowing, I'll have no chance of being in at the kill next season.'

'*Kill?*' said Emma, before she could stop herself.

She felt Henry's leg squeeze against hers.

Lady M looked over. 'My apologies, Emma. It slipped my mind that you also don't participate in country pursuits.'

*Translation: What are you doing with my son?*

*Stop!* said Emma's brain.

*Go for it!* said the wine.

'Killing animals for fun has never appealed, somehow,' said Emma, ignoring the increasing pressure of Henry's knee. 'Especially when those animals might have more right to live on the land than those people who just inherited it, from ancestors who were given a big, fat shire for being good at . . . well, killing? Recent debate implies the majority of British people would agree with me on that.'

There was a pregnant silence, then Lady M turned back to her estate manager. 'Gerald,' she said, 'we'll talk some more tomorrow.'

'Yes, my lady.'

He sounded like Parker off *Thunderbirds*.

'Henry,' said M'lady, turning to her son. 'Have you discussed your plans with Emma?'

A look of trepidation passed over his face. 'No, it's not . . . definite, yet. I'll talk to her about it when it is.'

'It's near enough definite,' she said. Her eyes flicked over to Emma. 'You should share it with us all; we can drink a toast.'

'I'd rather not,' said Henry, frowning. 'I'd like to do this in my own time.'

'Henry, that won't do at all!' she said. 'If you don't tell, I will. After all, it was my idea. And it's so *very* exciting.'

What on earth was going on here? Even in her wine fog, Emma was aware of strong undercurrents. Lady M wanted to spill about Henry's mysterious plan, but Henry wanted to save it for later. But most importantly, Lady M wanted Emma to know that she knew what it was, and Emma didn't.

'Don't tell, Henry,' Emma said recklessly, loud enough for everyone to hear. 'Not until you're good and ready.' She put her hand over his and squeezed it.

'My dear friends ... and Emma,' said Lady M. 'I'm delighted to let you all know that I have bought the controlling interest in the *Yorkshire Chronicle*, and as from later this year, Henry will be its new editor.'

'Shit,' Henry muttered under his breath, as everyone turned to look at him.

Emma's jaw dropped. 'Henry?'

'Surprise,' he said, weakly.

## Chapter Twenty-One

'What marvellous news!' said the vicar. 'The *Chronicle* used to be such an excellent read, but over the years it's really gone downhill. It's just sensationalist headlines and lots of adverts now.'

'So very true,' said Caroline, nodding.

'How absolutely wonderful,' he continued, 'that a respected local family will be taking it over. Congratulations, Lady Madeline and Henry.'

'Thank you,' said Lady M, with a benevolent smile. 'Yes, Henry and I will be getting it back on track. It will be all about Yorkshire issues that matter. Far more news, a lot less gossip. Right, Henry?'

He nodded, but said nothing. He hadn't yet met Emma's eye.

'We'll be letting go most of the existing staff, perhaps bringing over a couple of Henry's Lancaster colleagues but basically recruiting an entire new team,' Lady M continued. 'Only the very best will do.'

'Where is the *Chronicle* based?' asked Lauren.

'York,' said Lady M.

'Oh ho, Henry,' said the vicar, wagging a finger at him. 'You'll be going over to the other side.'

'York's much nicer than Lancaster,' said Lauren.

'Birch?' said Lady M, over her shoulder. 'Could you serve dessert now, please?'

Emma sensed Henry's desperation to talk to her, to explain, but all eyes were still on them. She wasn't thinking too hard about what this news meant for her. She was more focused on wanting to rescue poor Henry after his devious mother's pre-emptive move. How dare she steal his moment. He'd been building up to sharing his exciting news with Emma for so long.

She turned to him. 'Henry, this is so great!' she said, a wide smile on her face. 'You're going to be the best editor *ever*! Congratulations!' She raised her glass. 'To Henry, everyone. The best editor Yorkshire and probably England could have.' A bit OTT perhaps, but as she mentally ran through England's news-paper editors, it felt like a real possibility.

'To Henry,' said the others, raising their glasses.

Lady M's expression was inscrutable.

'Thanks, everyone,' he said, his eyes now on Emma. His gaze was amused, and full of relief. 'I was going to tell Emma this weekend. I was waiting for the right moment.' His eyes flicked over to his mother.

*Take that!*

'You'll all appreciate,' he went on, 'that Emma has been through a tough time recently, and I needed to consider her feelings, to time it right. I didn't want to load more onto her things-to-worry-about pile.' He put down his glass and put an arm round her shoulders, pulling her close, planting a kiss on her head.

'This amazing girl has been through so much, and she's stayed strong. She's the one that holds her family together, keeps every-one's spirits up, looks after her mum, who's also incredible – I can see where Emma gets her strength from.'

'Aw, Henry,' she said.

He grinned. 'And her rather beautiful hair, but it's a shame about the singing.'

She laughed. Yes, she'd missed out on the singing gene, as Henry loved to point out when she was in the shower.

'Emma, I want you to be part of this next phase in my career, but I'm completely aware it's too soon for you to be considering a move. I won't be going to York for some time yet, and I'll be talking to you about that. You're doing really well in London, but London . . . ' He pulled a face. 'I think you'd make a lovely northerner, but like I say, that's something we can discuss later.'

Lady M was examining her long, red fingernails.

'Let's have another toast,' Henry said. 'To this lovely woman who never ceases to surprise me. Who I love to bits. To Emma . . . '

The words struck a chord. *You never cease to surprise me.* They were Rowan's, in the letter he'd sent with his manuscript. Not that they were still imprinted on her brain.

Emma raised her glass, and as the wine-induced mood flipped from warm glow to something else, she realised Henry was going to ask her to work with him at his new paper. In York. If she said yes . . . and that was one big, fat *IF* . . . nepotism rarely went down well with co-workers, surely, and your boyfriend as your boss? Not ideal. But maybe . . . freelance?

The thoughts tumbled through her mind, and she focused on them, mustering them to block the other thought, the one that was elbowing its way aggressively to the front. The one that was saying – *you'd be back, just up the road from him.*

'I can't believe Mother did that,' said Henry, gently lowering the zip on her dress.

'She was just reminding me who's boss,' Emma replied, unpinning her hair and letting it tumble across her shoulders.

'You're boss,' said Henry, sweeping her hair aside and kissing her neck as the dress fell to the floor. 'You were wonderful tonight.'

Emma laughed softly, inclining her head as his kisses grew more insistent. 'I was *drunk* tonight. Sorry about that, it was the nerves. Did I disgrace myself?'

'Emma,' he said, between kisses, 'watching you battle it out with Mother has turned me on in a totally inappropriate way.' He scooped her up and dropped her on the bed, divested himself of his clothes in a flash, and then he was on top of her, kissing her hungrily, from her lips, neck, breasts, all the way down to . . . he quickly removed her underwear, and she gasped, her eyes open, fixed on the rich red velvet of the four-poster canopy.

'Oh god, Henry,' she whispered, as her hands dug into his hair and he took her higher, intent on her pleasure, insistent, not letting up for a moment. Then he was inside her, and she wrapped herself around him, swept away by his urgency, until he collapsed on top of her, spent.

After a while he propped himself up on one elbow and said, 'Sorry if that was . . . hasty. You were far too irresistible tonight. And you handled my surprise news so well. I don't know what Mother was thinking. She knew I was planning to tell you this weekend.'

'It's okay, Henry,' she said sleepily. 'We can talk about it tomorrow. You said later in the year, there's plenty of time.'

'I want you to come with me to York. But yes, you don't have to decide yet.'

She thought about opening her mouth to reply, but decided she was too tired.

'Goodnight, my lovely Ems,' he said, when she didn't respond. He lay back down, snuggling into her.

Her eyes flew open. 'No, please don't call me that.'

'Why not?' he mumbled.

'Just . . . I don't like it,' she said, closing her eyes.

The summer months passed with no further news from Yorkshire. Belle was in Hampstead, writing an album on the theme of loss. Emma couldn't bear to listen, on her visits home. She wondered where her mother found the strength to write those lyrics, those melodies.

Lady Madeline was apparently wrapping up the *Chronicle* deal, with a view to taking the reins before Christmas. Henry's involvement was still hush-hush, but it was only a matter of time before news reached the *Lancaster Post*'s editor. In the meantime it was business as usual.

Kyle was giving Emma more weighty assignments. She reported on court hearings, continued with her nature column – now she had a dedicated half page with images – and wrote about matters of local importance. When a property development company applied to build five houses on the fringes of Hampstead Heath, Emma took up the cause. Concerned locals rallied behind her, organising a petition, and the planning application was thrown out on environmental grounds.

Henry came down every few weekends, and they stayed with Belle, who seemed besotted with her possible future son-in-law. Emma had confided in her about his botched proposal and his plans for her to join him in Yorkshire.

'I couldn't ask for more for my lovely Emerald,' Belle had said, with a smug *Mother knows best* smile.

It was a hot and humid August afternoon, and Emma was on her way to meet up with Isabel and Greta, who both worked in town. They were going to see Shakespeare's *Richard III* at the Globe. She'd finished work early, and decided to treat herself to a book or four from Foyles before heading to the South Bank.

Exiting the Underground into the noisy bustle and the traffic fumes, she set off down Charing Cross Road, enjoying the summer buzz of the West End.

She glanced at Foyles' window display . . . and halted abruptly. It was as if her heart had stopped, too. A stack of books, artistically arranged like a mini spiral staircase, had caught her eye. A large poster beside it displayed the bold, black-and-white cover of *Bent*, by R. P. King.

It was the title of Rowan's book.

Heading inside, she found the new releases table. Her hand trembled a little as she picked up a copy.

She took a breath before turning it over and skim-reading the back cover – yes, it was definitely his book. There was an endorsement from another well-known thriller writer: *Kept me up all night! A compelling debut.*

She opened the cover and flicked over the title page. The dedication read:

*For my lovely Ems, who believed.*

Emma looked up, blinking quickly to dispel the tears already brimming.

A woman close by looked at her sideways.

Emma steeled herself to look again, and allowed herself to picture Rowan, sitting at his desk, scribbling the dedication on his manuscript. Thinking of her. Wanting her to know he hadn't forgotten her.

She turned the page, and there was a quote:

> *Since I cannot prove a lover*
> *To entertain these fair well-spoken days*
> *I am determined to prove a villain.*
> – William Shakespeare, *Richard III*

It was the perfect quote for Rowan's tortured lover-turned-stalker protagonist.

She flicked to the back, looking for the acknowledgements.

There weren't any. And there was no *About the author*, either.

Clearly Rowan had decided to remain anonymous, using a pseudonym – R. P. King – which, she realised with a smile, would place him squarely next to Stephen King on the bookshelves. Clever Rowan. She wondered what the 'P' stood for.

She picked up two copies, one for herself and one for Belle, and took them to the till.

'Oh, that's a cracker,' said the assistant. 'You won't be able to put it down. Just make sure you read it with the lights on.'

'I know the author,' said Emma, unable to resist. 'I don't suppose . . . he's not doing any signings?'

'Not as far as I know. That's nineteen ninety-eight, please.'

'Oh, fuckety fuck,' whispered Greta, as Act One got underway. She put her hand on Emma's and squeezed it. 'Sorry, sorry.'

'What for?' whispered Emma.

'For choosing this play. I forgot about the two murdered brothers part. Shit, I'm the dumbest.'

'It's fine, no nasty surprises. I did it for A level.'

'You know it's all bollocks,' whispered Isabel. 'Tudor propaganda, aided and abetted by Shakespeare, who was just sucking up to Elizabeth the First – cos I reckon Richard was innocent. Lizzie's grand-daddy Henry the Seventh did it.'

'Sh!' said someone in the row behind, and the girls tittered and were then quiet.

Later, Emma started to reread Rowan's book, interested to see how different it was from that first draft. She could hear his voice as she turned the pages deep into the night. It was there in the sharp, clever prose; in that sardonic, suspicious tone, those moments of blinding insight, when he understood your very soul. His grasp of the darker side of human nature, of the flaws inside us and what happens when there's nothing – no love, no social constraints – to inhibit them.

He'd taken on board almost all of her suggestions, and the realisation that he had, that he valued her opinion, had her crying into her pillow again. He did rate her, he did care. *Had cared*; past tense.

*I do love you, my lovely Ems, you know I do.*

His face swam in front of her as the book fell from her hand onto the floor. She remembered how it had felt, being held by him, being kissed by him.

It was six months since she'd seen him, five since he'd sent her the letter. She'd boxed it all away in the memory part of her brain labelled *Fragile – Do Not Touch*, and had focused on Henry, on her work, on supporting Belle. And it had mostly been going fine, until today.

Ah well, she thought, pulling a handful of tissues from the box on her bedside drawers. I'll allow myself a small wallow. One small wallow in six months. Surely I can have that.

# Chapter Twenty-Two

It was Halloween, and Henry was visiting, wanting to talk properly about the move to Yorkshire. He was starting full-time at the *Chronicle* in the New Year, and was making good progress recruiting his team. Lady M was leaving staffing matters to him, but was involved in a redesign of the paper, and in the financial side of things.

Henry was intending to take two reporters with him from the *Lancaster Post*, and was interviewing existing *Chronicle* staff to decide who would go and who would stay. He had his eye on other talented journalists in his network, and now wanted to talk to Emma about her role.

They were sitting by the window in a Highgate pub, half-watching gangs of small ghosts, pirates, Disney princesses and the like passing by.

'Bet Highgate Cemetery will be buzzing tonight,' said Emma.

'With real ghosts or pretend ones?' said Henry.

'Probably both. And bats. Oh, I should've done a piece!'

'But back to business,' he said. 'I want to bring you in at about the same level or slightly higher than you're on now. I can't really give you a senior role—'

'Of course you can't, how would that look? And I don't actually have the experience yet.'

Truth be told, Emma had been putting off thinking about the

move north. The *Voice* was a local institution she loved being part of. She was well-known in the area now, as 'Emma from the *Voice*' who, yes, also happened to be Emma, daughter of Teddy and Belle, sister of the lost boys, but equally Emma who they rang if they were worried about council plans to chop down an ancient tree, or needed coverage of their London Garden Bird Survey. Children wrote to her about their pets, Batman relied on her to help check the boxes on Wednesdays.

And she was near Belle, which was comforting for them both.

'Perhaps,' she said, 'we should give it some time. You'll need to establish yourself with your team, get to know the local people who matter, schmooze advertisers. Once you're known, all settled in, surely *then* it would be better to haul me north, rather than having me there from the start?'

She saw him considering it. He was too sensible not to.

'I suppose that makes sense. But ... ' He sat back and sighed. 'I just want you with me, Emma. This long distance thing, it's not great, is it? When you come up, we can get a place together—'

'Work together *and* live together?'

He frowned. 'It would seem the obvious thing to do?'

She sighed. 'But how would that look to your staff? Here's your new colleague, and by the way she's my live-in lover? I wouldn't properly be one of them; they might treat me like a spy! That'd make my job really difficult.'

Henry looked up at the ceiling for a moment. 'Right, I see. Well ... you could have your own place for a little while?'

'That would probably be better. And honestly, I don't think being together twenty-four seven would be healthy. From long distance to no distance. We should probably do the normal "going out together" part first.'

'You like your space. I know that. Just let me stop over six nights a week, then.'

'Five?'

He laughed. 'And I promise to keep it strictly professional at work. If you think you'll have a problem reporting to me, we'll work it out so you report to the deputy editor. Or the features editor.'

Emma thought for a moment. 'I could write features? Proper features? Investigative ones, like, more than a column on hamster management?'

'Absolutely. Look, I know you're a good journalist, I know you can write. You can start off buddying up with a reporter who knows the area and the people who matter, then we'll slide you into your own investigative pieces, if that's what you want.'

*Investigative pieces.* She pictured her brothers.

Suddenly it was sounding more appealing.

She squeezed his knee. 'I can't wait. How about provisionally we say April or May? In time for summer in Yorkshire.'

'Could be a plan,' said Henry.

Yorkshire. Where the boys were still waiting for someone, somewhere, to spot something. Where Rowan sat writing on his remote farm with his dog.

Henry wanted her to join him at Montfort Grange for Christmas, but Emma explained that she needed to be with her family in Hampstead. Sir Richard and Lily were coming down, Uncle Jason and Aunt Kate would be there, and Grandma and Grandpa Rivers were on a rare trip home from Spain. It would be their first Christmas without the boys, and it was going to be hard.

Emma tried to persuade Henry to join them, but he wouldn't abandon his mother. And apparently, Lady M wouldn't entertain the prospect of him missing the 'Boxing Day meet', the highlight of her winter social calendar.

'What?' Emma said, as they spoke on the phone. 'A hunt?'

'They do a scent trail thing now. No actual fox.'

She remembered Lady M's comment about being 'in at the kill'.

'You sure about that?'

'Bearing in mind the increasing carnage in the free-range-chicken sheds, I'd say yes.'

'How can they be free range if they're in sheds?'

She heard Henry sigh. 'Emma, my lovely, if you're going to be a reporter in a largely rural area, we're going to have to bring you up to speed on how it all works. Yorkshire farmers – blunt doesn't begin to cover it.'

Emma put on a Yorkshire accent. 'I like what I seh an' I seh what I like?'

He laughed. 'Exactly. They won't hold back if they meet the pretty, privileged southerner wanting them to swap their sheep for swathes of wild flowers. And I should also mention, for future harmonious relations with my dear lady mother, you're going to have to learn to ride properly.'

'Oh my god. You mean actual big horses?'

'Absolutely. But you'll love it. The bridleways across the Dales – we'll sort you a nice well-behaved mount from the stables.'

The prospect of riding the hills and dales with Henry would have been a lovely one, were it not for the expectation of spending weekends with Lady M.

'I'll come up for a visit when the weather's warmer. And maybe we could have a look at some flats in York? So I can get a feel for the place?'

'Good plan. Mother has a few rentals in town. I can have a look at the tenancies, see if any are becoming available.'

Lady M as her landlady too? Emma was beginning to feel … *owned.* She remembered Rowan's words: *She's a big cheese in Yorkshire. Owns an awful lot of it.*

'I'll have a look online. Like I say, just to get a feel.'

Pearl and Crystal arrived home for the holidays, and the four women set about putting up the Christmas decorations. Unpacking the boxes from the attic was hard, each and every bauble and string of tinsel resonating with memories. They gave up trying not to cry as they rediscovered the boys' homemade tree ornaments – Freddie's woolly-haired, smiley angel; Riv's snowman, made from ping-pong balls and randomly glued-on cotton wool. Emma found its red pipe-cleaner scarf in the bottom of the box, and gently replaced it around the snow-man's neck.

On Christmas Day, the sheer number of Snows and Rivers and Theodores helped them get through without the boys, though it was exhausting, trying to be jolly when all Emma could think of was Christmases past ... Teddy in his Santa hat, reading them *The Night Before Christmas*, his beautiful voice bringing the story alive. Being woken at some ridiculous hour by the boys thudding down the stairs, ripping the paper off their presents, the living-room floor scattered for days with Lego lying in wait to cripple those who forgot their slippers.

Now there was no Teddy and no children, and the magic had gone. Emma felt it would never come back. Not until she had her own children, maybe.

And then it was January, and all the while the anniversary of their disappearance was growing closer.

At the end of the month Emma headed north again, staying the weekend in Henry's new apartment. It was a penthouse, on the top floor of a converted warehouse on the banks of the River Ouse, and was luxurious, spacious and airy. Also neat, tidy, and spotlessly clean. Very Henry. Whenever they were together, he was always picking up after her.

'Oh, this is absolutely lovely!' she said as he showed her round.

'We got fifty-thou off the asking price,' he said. 'Should be a good investment.'

'We?' said Emma, looking out of the enormous arched window of the living area. From up here she could see Clifford's Tower, the last remnant of York Castle, peeping over the buildings on the far side of the river.

Henry joined her at the window. 'Mother thought it would be a good addition to her portfolio. And a journalist's salary doesn't stretch to riverside penthouses.'

'No, I suppose not.' They hadn't discussed her own pay yet. 'Might have to tap the Bank of Belle myself, I guess.'

'You sure I can't tempt you?' he said, his gaze sweeping over the Arctic Sea of white. 'It's a bit big for one.'

'Oh, I'll be stopping over plenty,' she said, turning to him and putting her arms around his waist.

He bent to kiss her. 'Want to see the bedroom?'

On the Saturday it snowed, and the picturesque old town was transformed into a silent, romantic, days-gone-by version.

They ate in cosy pubs, browsed the shops and estate agents' windows, and explored the medieval Shambles, arm in arm. And all the while, Emma couldn't help but notice that dark head on the street; that person in black, striding along; that black Labrador in the park.

Did Rowan come into York? How far was it from his farm? Was York even his nearest town? When she lived here, would she bump into him one day on the street? In a shop? Getting petrol? And if she did, how would that go? Would they smile and hug and chat like old friends, catch up over a coffee? Or would it be awkward?

Or would one spot the other and pretend they hadn't? Because it would be too hard?

'What shall we do now?' she said on Sunday morning, as they finished walking the city walls, stopping beside a board displaying a large map of York. She read the list of attractions down the side. 'The museum? Or there's "The Richard the Third Experience". How about a spot of tyranny, murder, usurping?'

'Richard was popular in these parts – still is,' said Henry. 'York's more for him than for Henry Tudor.'

'Isabel says Henry trashed Richard's reputation. She thinks Richard was alright, and that he didn't actually kill the Princes in the Tower.'

'Henrys often have a talent for spin,' said Henry, with a grin. 'Actually, I have a plan. It's time I showed you the *Chronicle* offices. We're mid renovations so it's a mess, but I'm sure you're going to love them.'

The ancient building was all rugged stone walls and lofty beams, which were being stripped back to bare oak by workmen perched high on ladders. It was a new experience for Emma, seeing Henry interacting with people in his employ, watching how they responded to him. He was well informed, interested; those sharp blue eyes missed little. She smiled inwardly at the difference between his clipped tones and their broad Yorkshire accents. Henry's made him sound rather high-handed. He also closely quizzed the foreman about costs; as she went off to explore, he was suggesting ways to keep them down.

Stepping carefully over the wires criss-crossing the dust sheets, she couldn't deny this would be a lovely place to work. The tall windows running down one side let in plenty of natural light, and looked out over York Minster. The mellow yellow of the York stone walls created a gentle ambience. Compared to the fluorescent lights, old plasterboard and ancient carpet tiles of the *Voice*, this was newspaper office heaven. She pictured herself in this bright corner, here, writing her features, gazing out at the Minster's gothic towers as she searched for that perfect word . . .

She made her way back to Henry, who properly introduced her to the foreman, Jack, and she saw the recognition, that moment of consternation when he realised. The boys' disappearance was still a cause célèbre in Yorkshire – according to Henry, it was regularly resurrected in the local press.

'Sorry, love, penny just dropped,' said Jack, not quite meeting her eye. 'Henry says you'll be working here soon. That'll be good for you, eh? To be closer to where it all happened, with it all still being unsolved.'

She smiled at him, trying to dispel the awkwardness. 'I have family up here too – both my parents are from Yorkshire and my grandparents live near Wakefield.'

'Teddy and Belle. I'm a big fan of your mam's.'

'Thank you. And yes, if any new information comes to light it'll be good to be here.'

Now that she'd put him at ease, Jack was keen to share his opinion. 'Has to have been the master. Used to invite them to his rooms, can't account for his movements on the day they went missing, got fired from the school. A *bachelor*. I hear he lives up on the moors all by himself. The locals avoid him.'

Henry glanced at Emma. She waited for him to speak, to tell Jack this was misinformed speculation, but he said nothing.

'Actually, Jack,' she said, 'he's a widower, and no one in my family believes he had anything to do with it. Rowan's been a friend for many years. If the locals are giving him a hard time, then that's the very worst news.'

'No smoke without fire, though. And didn't his wife die in mysterious circumstances?'

Emma felt her heart rate increasing, and tried to keep her voice steady. 'Uninformed gossip. And that is *just* the sort of thing we'll be aiming to push back against here at the *Chronicle*. Right, Henry?'

'Indeed, Emma,' he said, a little patronisingly. 'But it's always good to keep your finger on the pulse, know what the locals are saying. News-gathering is very much a two-way thing between reporters and the person on the street.'

Emma said nothing. Were the locals really giving Rowan a hard time? Was he being bullied, all over again?

She was quiet as Henry drove her to the station to catch the train back to London.

'I'm sensing this weekend has brought it all back again,' he said eventually.

'Yes. And the fact that it's been almost a year. I can't quite believe it.'

He squeezed her knee.

She stared out of the window. 'Sometimes I think I see them. A glimpse of a blonde head in a crowd, or I hear a giggle like Freddie's. For a few seconds I'll think, maybe it's them, but of course it isn't, and then I die a little more. And I dream about them, that they've been found, and then I wake up and it hits me all over again.'

'There's a slim—'

'No,' she interrupted. 'I think the best I can hope for now is closure.' She turned to look at him. 'Don't you think it's odd, that there's been nothing since those first few days – just *nothing*. How is that possible?'

Henry shook his head. 'It's different to London. There are still wild, remote places up here. Not so many people.'

'But those places all belong to someone. People walk their dogs on them, climb the hills, go running.' She swallowed. 'Rivers, canals – things come to the surface.'

'Emma – it's not like on the TV. Missing persons, murders . . . a huge number of these cases are never solved.' He pulled into the station car park and found a space. There was a heavy silence as he switched off the engine.

'I can't believe people are saying it was Rowan.' She kept her eyes straight ahead, afraid of what he might see in them.

Henry didn't reply.

'Imagine, people thinking that about you.'

Finally he responded. 'I should imagine that will remain the case unless something new turns up.'

'It's not right. What about being innocent until proven guilty?'

'People always look for someone to blame,' he said. 'There's no one else in the picture. And even if he didn't do it—'

Emma's anger, which she hadn't been aware was there, bubbled over. 'Henry! What do you mean, *if*. It's like you *want* him to be responsible! Just because he's . . . ' She stopped abruptly.

'Because he's what, Emma?' His voice was steady.

She wasn't quite sure what she'd been about to say. 'I don't know. Because he's different. Hard to get to know. But anyone who does, knows he could never have hurt my brothers. The only thing he's guilty of is forgetting to walk the dog with them. That's it.'

'And the hours between when he should have been doing that and reporting them missing?' His eyebrows were raised; that penetrating gaze was fixed on hers.

'I've told you! He thought they were just off somewhere. They were always off somewhere. For god's sake, Henry, you met them.

You know what they're like.' She huffed a deep breath as she felt tears threatening.

His gaze softened. 'Sorry. I shouldn't have brought it up again.' He opened the car door and slid out.

She calmed herself for a few moments before opening her side. She didn't want to leave things like this.

He was unloading her case from the boot. She stood beside him, waiting.

'I just . . . I can't not get emotional about it,' she said when he didn't speak. 'Can you understand?'

He slammed the boot. 'Of course. It's a terrible situation. I'll be keeping in touch with the police, making sure we're first to hear of any developments.'

'After Mum, you mean.'

'Well . . . yes, I guess so.' He set off for the station building, wheeling her case for her.

He kissed her goodbye on the platform, but things still didn't feel right. She couldn't help holding back.

'I did it again, didn't I?' he said, stroking her cheek. 'I'm sorry. It's just . . . '

'Your jealous streak?' she finished. 'You're being a bit ridiculous.'

The London train was announced, and people moved towards the edge of the platform. She grabbed the handle of her suitcase.

He pulled her back towards him. 'Emma, sorry. Things will be better when you're properly here. I can't wait. Think of it, after all this time. Not having these pain-in-the-arse journeys.'

'Thanks for a lovely weekend. I'll miss you. Maybe come down once more, before I make the move?'

'Yes, I'll do that.' He kissed her again. 'And I'll keep an eye out for flats.'

'Cool!' she said, as the train halted. She hauled her case on board and turned round.

He smiled and waved; he looked sad, and her heart constricted. She blew him a kiss. 'I'll call you tonight. Love you.'

As she took her seat she was aware of a sense of relief. It was true, she would miss Henry. But she welcomed the space, the time the journey would give her to think.

She mulled over Henry's blind spot when it came to Rowan, and his refusal to back up her response to the foreman's speculation. She'd opened up to Henry about her need for closure, and he'd turned the conversation into an insidious attack on Rowan.

Emma wondered for a moment ... was she ready to leave her friends, her job, her mother, to be nearer Henry? What if things didn't work out?

*Except ... that's not the real reason.*

She rested her head back against her seat.

Surely her new job would enable her to push for more answers? In all this time, there must have been leads, even if they'd led nowhere. What were they? Was anyone checking they'd been properly followed up?

When she was established at the *Chronicle*, Emma would reconnect with DS Shore. She drafted an introduction in her head: *More than a year after Elfred and River Snow disappeared, the* Chronicle *asks, why has nothing come to light in all this time? Emma Snow, sister of the missing brothers, investigates ...*

# Chapter Twenty-Three

Winter dragged on, cold, dark and miserable, reflecting Emma's state of mind as the anniversary of Freddie and Riv's disappearance loomed. Belle's haunting album, *Missing*, was released to rave reviews. It prompted a flurry of articles revisiting the mystery, and there was a second wave of requests for press and TV interviews. Belle's beautiful, sad face, and photos of Emma's brothers, were everywhere again.

Emma wondered if this new burst of publicity might jog someone's memory, or encourage them to look at something in a new light.

'Hey, your mum's at number one,' said Isabel over Sunday breakfast. The entertainment section of the paper was open in front of her. She swivelled it round and pushed it over to Emma.

'Go Mum,' said Emma, munching on a piece of toast.

She read the review: *An instant classic . . . Unforgettable melodies and searing lyrics in this heart-breaking masterpiece from Britain's queen of soft rock.*

Her eye was caught by a cover in the Books section on the opposite page. *Bent* was at number five in the bestsellers. It had been in the top ten for months now. Emma hoped the sales meant that Rowan could indeed afford to eat, now that he'd lost his job and presumably wouldn't be offered another teaching post any time soon.

And his heating bills. She pictured an ancient stone farmhouse with drifts of snow banked against the walls, Rowan and his dog huddled inside by the fire. For a moment she imagined herself sitting by that fireside with him, talking books and writing, the dog at their feet. How lovely would that be?

*Can't really see myself as suburban man. Honestly – could you?*

'I bought your mum's album,' said Greta.

'I haven't heard it yet,' said Emma. 'I just can't bring myself to listen.'

Greta scraped her chair back and went over to the boom box sitting on the worktop. She flipped open the lid and took out a CD. 'Here. It's the anniversary this week, right?'

Emma nodded, a lump in her throat.

'Listen to it – maybe it'll help. Just make sure you stock up on Kleenex.'

So on Tuesday evening when she got home from work, she did.

'*. . . I see your shadows in the apple tree,*
*hear your sweet voices on the wind,*
*I touch your baby faces . . .*
*On the street and in the park,*
*I see someone like you . . .*
*Someone like you . . .*'

Emma lay on her bed, tears streaming down her cheeks, forced again to confront the random cruelty of life. Thinking about the toll the not-knowing was taking on Belle, on herself and her sisters, her grandparents. On Rowan.

She picked up her phone and through her tears typed out a text: Don't know if you'll get this, but you're in my thoughts today. And every day actually. I miss you and hope you're doing okay. Congrats on the book. I'll always believe in you. xxxxx

She listened to the rest of the album, and by the end she knew. She couldn't sit back, do nothing. This waiting, this not knowing; it was too hard. She needed to act, to find a way to bring closure. For the sake of the family, for Freddie and Riv's sakes. It was time to move to York.

She picked up her phone again and texted Henry: Sorry – can't face calling tonight. It's been a year and I've been listening to Mum's album and I'm a complete mess. I need to move on, make the change. I'm going to hand in my notice. XXX

The reply came immediately: Brilliant – been waiting for this news, didn't want to push it. And re today, have a good cry, it'll do you good. Call me tomorrow. Love you v much. H xxxx

Emma looked at her diary to work out the timing. Greta had organised a girls' trip to Morocco in April; there was also Crystal's twenty-first birthday party. She decided June would be good. Summer would be well on its way, it would be a new beginning. It felt right.

She handed in her resignation just before heading off to Marrakesh.

'Oh, that's completely shit news,' said Kyle. 'You're a proper part of the furniture now.'

She supposed that meant he was sorry to lose her. 'I've been offered a post at the *Yorkshire Chronicle*. I think it's a good move for me.'

'The *Chronicle*, eh?' he said. 'Sit down, Emma.'

She pulled a chair up to his chaotic desk, already feeling a pang at no longer sitting here, arguing her case for more words on wildlife.

'That paper's a rag,' he said. 'And *Yorkshire*? Seriously?'

'No, it's under new ownership. It's going to be quality again.'

'Who?'

'The Theodore family. Lady Madeline and … ' Emma smiled sheepishly. 'Her son, Henry. My boyfriend. He's going to be the editor.'

'What?' He frowned. 'You're going to be working for your boyfriend?'

'Well – it's a family newspaper. And I suppose I'm almost part of the family.'

He took off his glasses and dropped them on the desk. 'Christ,

Emma. And there was me thinking you were a proper independent London girl. And up North? *Really?*'

This wasn't helping. But she didn't want to mention her brothers; it always made people too sad and uncomfortable.

'Anything I can do to change your mind? Promotion? More money? I'm guessing not.'

'Thanks, Kyle, but no. I've given it a lot of thought and I'm sure it's the right thing to do. I'll get to write features – long ones – and ... Henry and me, we've been doing the long-distance relationship for ages. It's difficult.'

'I see.' He looked her in the eye. 'You and him on the same page editorially?'

'How do you mean?'

'C'mon, Emma. You know how it works. He'll be an influencer. Local bigwigs and politicians will want him on side.'

'Oh, right. I think we agree on most things. Not so sure about his mum, though. And she's the owner.'

She realised she'd given this little thought. Henry was firmly behind the Tories, and had been delighted when David Cameron had become PM after the last general election. And Lady M was apparently active in local politics. Emma, meanwhile, was red with a strong dose of green.

'I'm hoping I can focus on the environment, and maybe women's issues. Henry's going to bring me up to speed on rural life in Yorkshire.'

Kyle smiled. 'By 'eck,' he said. 'Good luck with that. It's another country up there.'

She laughed. 'I'm actually going back to my roots – my parents are both from up that way and my father's parents are still there. It'll be lovely to be near them.'

'Well, Emma,' he said, 'I'll miss your impassioned pleas on behalf of vermin. I'm not sure your Yorkshire farmers will be convinced. But ... ' he sat back with his hands behind his head, 'if you find it an uphill struggle at first, remember what you've achieved here. Readers – even kids – have been emailing the

*Voice* in ever-increasing numbers. They've learned a lot from you about the wildlife of North London. I mean, who even knew that extended beyond pigeons?'

'Pigeons are actually—'

'That Fox Watch thing you did was spectacularly successful. And the bloody bats. Heck, you even got me interested.'

Emma swallowed. 'I'm really going to miss Batman.'

'Not as much as he'll miss you, I'm guessing. As will I, and all of us here. Break it gently to Nick the Sport, he's going to be gutted.'

Tears were threatening, and Kyle noticed.

'You know what your problem is, don't you?'

She shook her head, not daring to open her mouth.

'Too soft. But you've had a hell of a year, and I admire how you've kept going. And I also like how you stick to your guns. When you believe in something, you go for it, like a dog with a slipper. Or a fox with a chicken, maybe. Keep that up, Emma.'

The remaining weeks in London passed in a blur. Prince William married Kate Middleton, and the city broke out in a rash of patriotic red, white and blue. Press coverage of the event seemed strangely focused on the bride's sister Pippa Middleton's bottom.

Emma watched at home with Isabel and Greta, and spotted Lady Madeline and Henry in the congregation.

'That's a bit strange, taking your son as your plus one,' said Isabel. 'She doesn't look much older than him. What the fuck's she wearing?' Lady M's peculiar hat looked rather like one of those medieval hoods.

'But she's working it,' said Greta. 'How many women could pull that look off?'

'She was a teen mum,' said Emma. 'Back when pregnant women had to be made honest through marriage. Knowing Jason, he wouldn't have taken a lot of persuading. One doesn't say no to Lady Mad.'

The three girls left for Morocco the next day, and the holiday brought it home to Emma how much she was going to miss her two friends. Would she make new ones in York? It was never easy for her, being the daughter of celebrity A-listers and now sister of the missing boys.

Crystal's birthday party, a glitzy affair at the Ritz, also turned into a farewell for Emma. Everything was changing. Crystal would soon finish university, and she and Pearl were going travelling. Belle would be by herself in London, and Emma was still worried about that.

A week before she left, she confided in her mother about her plans to look into what the police had been doing – or not – about the investigation.

'Oh, that's wonderful, Emerald,' said Belle. 'Yes, it's been going on for so long. We need to find them. Someone *must* know something.'

'I'll need to find my feet first, but once I've got to know the area and hopefully reconnected with DS Shore ... I'll leave no stone unturned, Mum.'

Belle covered Emma's hand with her own and gave her that look, the one with her head slightly to one side, the one where she fixed Emma with her ice-blue gaze and didn't drop it. Belle was about to ask a big question.

'Can I ask ... you haven't mentioned Rowan in so long. I worry about him, I guess because of Teddy. I'd ask you to go see him when you're back in Yorkshire, but ... did something happen there, sweetheart? You said things were resolved, but were they, really? I saw the dedication, in the book.'

Emma wondered how much to say. She looked down at her hands in her lap. 'Can I talk to you about it?' She'd kept it all bottled up, it had been like a rock in her stomach, all this time.

Belle nodded. 'Of course.'

'Just between us?'

'Absolutely.'

She took a breath. 'He was pretty pissed off about losing his job. But it was like he was resigned to it, felt he deserved it.'

Belle shook her head. 'Poor thing.'

'When I saw him before, at the school, I wanted him to know we didn't hold him responsible in any way. I was kind of desperate for him to know we believed in him. That I wasn't going to give up on him.' Emma paused.

'What happened, Emerald?'

'He ... well, he kissed me.'

Belle shut her eyes for a moment. 'Oh lord, no.'

'Then he said, when the boys were found, I should break up with Henry and we could be together.'

Belle gave a quick shake of her head. 'But you were far too sensible. Once you'd had time to think. Right?'

'No, I wasn't. Yes, I loved Henry, but I thought I loved Rowan more.'

'And then they weren't found. So that's why nothing happened.'

'No, that's not why. He didn't wait for news on the boys – he dumped me almost immediately. He moved to the farm, and sent me a letter. Said he loved me too much to inflict himself and all his baggage on me. I mean ... what a cop out. He'd been having therapy, but I guess that went out the window when he left the school. He gave up, basically. Said to leave him alone, that he could never be what I wanted him to ... ' She shut her eyes as the tears tried to push their way in.

'He did right,' said Belle, firmly. 'The best thing he could do for you *was* to leave you alone. Rowan's a brilliant man, but he's not relationship material, and he knows it. He's very self-aware. You know that in your heart.'

'He said he was dumping me because he loved me, Mum.' She blinked back the tears.

'And he's a wonderful man for doing that. Accept it, Emerald.'

'I have. I've sent him one text in a year, and I've heard nothing from him at all. But I'm worried about him all over again. I found out the locals give him a hard time, because they think he had something to do with the boys' disappearance. We can't let that go on, Mum. We have to put it right.'

'Another reason to get some answers.'

'Yes.'

'And how does Henry feel about you looking into it all?'

'I haven't told him.'

Belle pulled a face. 'Ah.'

'I need to find my feet first. I can't just march in and say I'm going to do this big thing. I'll need to earn my stripes reporting on village fairs and flower shows and all the rest of it. And that'll give me a chance to get to know the area properly, get a feel for the ... I suppose you'd say the nuances of Yorkshire life.'

Belle laughed. 'Nuances? Oh, I can tell you all about those.' She put on a Yorkshire accent. '*You can always tell a Yorkshireman, but you can't tell him much.*'

Emma grimaced. 'Oh god.'

'They're friendly, but stubborn – bloody-minded and bloody argumentative.'

'Well, I guess Dad was one.'

'He liked to brag about his roots, but growing up at Sandal Manor and Middleham – he was hardly your average Yorkshireman. Now Rowan – *there's* your stubborn and your argumentative. And your hatred of anything pretentious. He's straight up, I'll say that for him.'

'And messed up.'

'You said it.' She smiled at Emma. 'Henry's the man for you. He's every girl's dream.'

Emma rolled her eyes.

'But you know,' she continued, 'you're a mature, independent woman now, and very capable. If it doesn't work out, you'll be fine by yourself.'

Emma nodded. 'Yes, I totally would. Thanks for listening, Mum.'

She acknowledged for a moment how Teddy's death and the boys' disappearance had resulted in a wiser, more compassionate Belle. How these events had brought them closer together. She'd miss her mum.

Emma left work a few days before she was due to head north, to give herself time to pack up and spend a last evening with Belle.

She also organised viewings on a few flats in York; she'd be staying with Henry until she found somewhere she liked.

Emma's favourite vegetarian lasagne was in the oven and the mouth-watering aroma filled the kitchen. Jacquetta jumped onto her lap and she stroked her soft coat as the cat began to purr. Out of the French doors, the last of the blossom on the apple tree was ghostly white in the twilight. The old wooden swing still hung from a branch; it was moving gently, caught by a breeze, and in the shadows Emma imagined she saw Riv sitting there for a moment, Freddie behind him, pushing.

'Did you see them?' Belle said softly, following her gaze.

'The swing was moving.'

'It's Jacquetta. I think she's some sort of conduit.'

'For god's sake, Mum.' Emma worried for a moment about her mother being here all alone, her daughters scattered far and wide. Tonight she seemed distracted – and now she was seeing ghosts?

'Mum, you will come up soon?' she said, as Belle poured them each a glass of wine. 'And I'll pop down in a month or so.'

'Stop fretting, Emerald. I'll be fine. You know what?' She smiled mischievously. 'I might even go on a few dates. Just for fun.'

Emma grinned. 'Do it, Mum!'

'With women, too.'

Emma blinked.

'I love how things have changed. I've always wondered . . . '

'Okay, well, I guess this is your time and that's all good. Just . . . be careful. You're probably quite vulnerable.'

'Nonsense. I'm perfectly capable of looking after myself.'

'Are you sure? Really?'

'Yes. But . . .' Belle gave her a long look. 'Are *you*?'

'Of course!'

'Good. Because . . . oh, I don't know. I couldn't decide . . . but you'll find out soon enough.'

'Find out what?'

Belle's demeanour had suddenly changed, and a knot was forming in Emma's stomach. Was this something to do with the boys?

Belle went over to the kitchen worktop, fished under today's newspaper and pulled out a sheet of paper. 'Your grandpa emailed this to me this morning. I don't know whether it'll make a difference to Rowan or not, but I should imagine he was keeping his identity secret for good reason.'

'Rowan?' Emma's heart leapt into her mouth as she spotted a photo of him on the page. She recognised the image – it had been used to promote his play, back in 2006. In it his hair was tousled and his eyes dark and tormented. The family had laughed about it at the time, imagining the photographer saying, 'Look tortured.'

## BEST-SELLING AUTHOR REVEALED AS MISSING BOYS' TEACHER

Emma winced. She looked up at Belle, who nodded at her to read on.

*The* Chronicle *has learned that R. P. King, bestselling author of the psychological thriller* Bent, *and Rowan Bosworth, former English master at exclusive Middleham College, are one and the same.*

*Bosworth, who also wrote the West End hit* Twisted, *was sacked by Middleham following the disappearance of Elfred and River Snow, and in the light of information pertaining to the death of his wife. Since leaving, Bosworth has been living alone in the Wensleydale area. He declined to comment on why he chose to write under a pseudonym.*

*Bent, which delves into the mind of a psychotic killer, has been in the* Sunday Times *bestseller list since its launch last August. The fate of Belle Snow's sons remains a mystery . . .*

Emma didn't recognise the reporter's name – Ed Studley. One of Henry's new team, perhaps. Henry must surely have sanctioned this. But how had the reporter discovered that R. P. King was Rowan?

'This is awful, Mum. It could wreck Rowan's writing career.'

'Yes, it is awful, but maybe he'll be okay. It's not like he does book tours or festivals, and it's only a local story.' She looked away from Emma for a moment. 'Well, for now.'

'But he'd probably *like* to do appearances?' said Emma. 'I mean, god, it sounds like he never goes out. All these insinuations – it's making him a prisoner!' She looked at his photo. That beautiful, haunted face; those slightly narrowed eyes. 'The locals shun him,' she said, more quietly, 'and now people who read his book might think he's ...'

Rowan's words, spoken all those years ago on Glastonbury Tor, came back to her: *God, the stuff I find out about myself when I'm in the zone.*

'Why would someone out him like this?' she said.

'Anyone could have leaked it,' said Belle. 'Someone at his publisher? For money? Or knowing Rowan, perhaps because he upset someone.'

'I thought the *Chronicle* was going to be above chequebook journalism,' snapped Emma. She took a long drink of her wine. Her hand was shaking. 'Henry knew, Mum. He saw the manuscript. And he might have seen the book – your copy. When he came down for Crystal's party.'

Belle's eyes widened. 'Shit. Sorry – language. But yes. I saw him looking at it. I remember wondering if he'd spotted the dedication.' She frowned. '*Henry*, though? He wouldn't do that, surely? Attempt to blacken someone's reputation, because ... well, because he might be jealous? Because Rowan dedicated a book to you?'

Emma sighed. 'I may have told him I had a teenage crush.'

'Oh, Emerald. That probably wasn't wise, given the situation.'

'No, I told him before the boys went missing, ages ago.'

'Is that all you told him?'

'Yes. But I've defended Rowan to Henry, on numerous occasions.'

Belle stared at her wine glass, tapping her long green fingernails on the stem. 'If Henry's responsible for outing Rowan, then that's pretty brutal.'

'It is. I'll get to the bottom of this, Mum.'

'Well,' said Belle, getting up to see to the lasagne. 'Maybe Henry does have a dark side, after all.'

## Chapter Twenty-Four

Emma was furious with Henry, but had decided to ease into it.
She needed to time it right. It wouldn't be a good idea to go
in with all guns blazing on the first day of her new life.

She arrived in York on a sunny Saturday lunchtime, her new
satnav guiding her to Henry's riverside apartment. She pulled over
and texted *Here!* and moments later Henry appeared and waved
her into a parking space in front of the building. He was wearing
shorts, and a snowy white T-shirt that emphasised his broad chest
and muscular arms. A pair of sunglasses was pushed up onto his
red-gold hair. After a long absence, Emma was often taken aback
all over again by just how lush her boyfriend was. She found herself
grinning, in spite of herself.

He swept her up into a hug. 'You're here! You're actually here.
Let's leave your clobber for now,' he said, eyeing the boxes and
bags piled on the back seat of her Mini. 'We'll unload after lunch.'

On the drive up, she'd been wondering what to say about
the Rowan article. She'd already rung her mother and given her
detailed instructions, knowing Belle's famous name would get her
straight through to the reporter Emma had in mind.

'After you,' Henry said, pushing open the front door to the
apartment.

The white walls, cream furniture and pale rugs were dazzling
in the afternoon sunlight flooding through the window. Emma

gasped as she took in the arrangements of red roses that sat on every surface, their heady fragrance filling the air.

'Oh my gosh.'

'Welcome back to Henry Towers,' he said. 'My little Snow queen.'

'How lovely!' she said. 'But I thought white roses were the thing in York?'

He laughed. 'Well, you can take the boy out of Lancaster ... '

That evening, she considered raising the thorny topic of the article, before the Sunday papers arrived on Henry's doorstep tomorrow. He'd assume she hadn't seen it, as it was a local piece. But the dinner and the roses – it was all so perfect, she couldn't bring herself to.

'We won't talk work tonight,' he said. He'd pan-fried the salmon and she'd made the salad, and they sat by the large window looking out over the Ouse. The sun was just starting to go down, burnishing the river with gold – twilight was later up here. 'But tomorrow, there's someone I want you to meet. I thought it would be a good idea, before you start on Monday. We could go to the pub for Sunday lunch.'

'You're being very mysterious. Who is this person?' She picked up the bread knife and cut a few slices of ciabatta.

'Your buddy reporter.'

*Oh, exciting!*

'Name of Ed Studley.'

The author of the exposé.

Henry swept up the crumbs she'd made, tipping them back onto the bread board.

'He's one of the few people I've kept on from the old staff,' he said. 'He's pretty hard-nosed, but I think you'll benefit from that. And the other reason I kept him on is because he's brilliant at finance. He'll be writing the money pages.'

'I didn't know regionals had money pages,' Emma said, attempting to keep her tone neutral. 'We didn't at the *Voice*.'

'People always want to know about money.' He was quiet for a moment, looking away from her, out the window. 'So yes, Ed has quite a nose for a story. He broke one this week I should probably tell you about.' He was looking uncomfortable.

Emma thought quickly. How should she play this? She didn't want to spoil the mood. 'You mean the one about Rowan being R. P. King?'

His eyes flew to hers. 'You've seen it?'

She registered his shock. 'Yes.' She kept her source to herself. 'And I assume as editor, you okayed it?'

Henry sat back in his chair and ran his fingers through his hair. 'I thought you'd be angry.'

'I *am* angry. But now didn't seem the best time to bring it up.' She was quiet, waiting to hear what he had to say.

'As soon as I saw the book in the shops, I realised who R. P. King was. When it became a bestseller I knew his identity would come out, eventually. It was a scoop. We couldn't leave it for someone else – it's important the *Chronicle* gets the stories.'

She looked him in the eye. 'Or did you in fact decide to out Rowan when you picked up Mum's copy and read the dedication?'

He ignored her question, his face giving little away. 'Like I said, I couldn't ignore it. You're a journalist, you understand. I put Ed on it so it was impartial.'

'And he didn't get edited?' Emma didn't drop her gaze.

'I was hands off, because I was personally involved. I left him to it. But I guess it came out sounding like a stitch-up. That wasn't what I intended.'

'I thought the *Chronicle* wasn't going to be sensationalist *crap*.' She spat out the last word.

He kept his cool, but she sensed him squirming. 'The net result will probably be good for Bosworth – watch the copies fly off the shelves this week.'

'Yes,' she said, 'and then watch readers jumping to conclusions, thanks to the *Chronicle* insinuating things about Abigail's death, dropping massive hints about imagined parallels between the author and his protagonist. Do you think he'll ever be able to go back to teaching after this?'

The way Henry raised his eyebrows implied the reason Rowan would never go back to teaching had little to do with writing under a pseudonym. He sat forward and loaded his fork again. 'Emma, *anything* to do with the boys' disappearance is big news. It wasn't personal. I was doing my job. It'll probably be picked up by the nationals and it'll get the *Chronicle* back in the game. We need stories like this.'

She decided to say no more. It was the first night of her new life in York. She'd made her feelings clear. And tomorrow, he'd find out she was perfectly capable of playing him at his own game.

On Sunday morning Emma awoke to the promising aroma of coffee wafting through the bedroom door. She heard Henry clattering around in the kitchen and smiled to herself, stretching luxuriously. They'd made an effort to move the conversation on last night; there had been an uneasy truce. They'd polished off the wine, turned the lights down low and put on soothing music. Then he'd surprised her with a 'welcome to up north' present – an exquisite opal and diamond necklace. It had probably cost as much as she earned in a year, and when she tried it on it made her skin glow.

The romantic evening had dampened Emma's lingering anger, and when she finally fell asleep in Henry's arms, it was with a contented smile on her face, because tomorrow, and the day after, and the day after that, neither of them would be getting on a train or driving up or down a motorway.

She was about to head for the shower when Henry appeared, carrying a tray with a plate of scrambled eggs on toast, a glass of orange juice, a mug of coffee and a red rose.

'Not going to do this every day, but you're new in town so … enjoy,' he said, planting a kiss on her lips. 'Back in a moment.'

She sat up, rearranging the pillows behind her, and pressed a button on the remote that opened the window blinds. The river was revealed; she could see joggers and walkers on the opposite bank.

Henry returned with his own mug of coffee and a pile of Sunday papers.

'You not eating?' said Emma, eyeing the pile.

'I've already had mine,' he said. 'Been up since seven. I wanted to read through some stuff before we see Ed.'

Emma had forgotten about lunch with Ed, he of the hard nose and money talents. The same Ed who'd implied Rowan was hiding behind a pseudonym because he was ashamed of his past. A past that included two missing boys and a dead wife, all of which had led to him being fired from his job at Middleham.

Henry hopped up onto the bed and began reading the *Sunday Times*.

Emma fished out the *Mail on Sunday*, and was pleased to see Belle's photograph on the front. She glanced over at Henry, but he didn't seem to have noticed.

## BOSWORTH – BELLE SETS THE RECORD STRAIGHT

*Rock star Belle Snow, mother of missing boys Elfred and River, spoke to the* Mail on Sunday *this week about the recent revelation in the* Yorkshire Chronicle *that R. P. King, author of the bestselling novel* Bent, *is the pseudonym of playwright Rowan Bosworth. Belle's sons were in Bosworth's care when they disappeared in February last year. Bosworth was a teacher at the boys' school, Middleham College, and subsequently left his post to take up writing full-time.*

*'There has been a lot of misinformed finger-pointing' said Belle. 'It's time to set the record straight. People use pseudonyms for all sorts of reasons, and Rowan Bosworth has always preferred to avoid the limelight. Although my husband Teddy helped him enormously when he was starting out, Rowan wanted to stand on his own two feet, be known for his work, not his associations. I can quite understand his desire to remain anonymous.*

*'I would like to make it clear that my family has nothing but love and respect for Rowan, and we would ask people, particularly the media, to desist from nasty insinuations about our dear friend.'*

*Rowan Bosworth couldn't be contacted for comment.*

Emma let out a breath.

Henry looked up.

She passed the paper over, and he read the piece in silence.

'Why would she do that?' he finally said. 'How can she be so sure?'

'Because she's known Rowan since he was a teenager. Because she and Dad helped him, believed in him, saw what he went through with his wife. And probably mostly because she wants him to know, after your paper tried to hurt him some more, that he still has our full support. Even though he feels he doesn't deserve it.'

'Hmph,' said Henry, going back to his own paper. 'And the *Chronicle* hasn't come out of that well. Ed should've got a quote from Belle; he could've pre-empted that response.'

'And spun it some more?' said Emma. 'Twisted her words?'

He looked her in the eye. 'Rowan Bosworth strikes me as a pretty clever bloke. Yes?'

She nodded.

'Good at reading people, understanding how the mind works, what throws it off – that's what he's known for.'

Emma could tell where this was going. 'Yes, he's interested in the human psyche, what motivates people.'

'And he was known for hanging out with Teddy and his cronies, who were pretty notorious in their day. But you and Belle were one step removed from all that.'

'I suppose so.'

'So maybe you don't actually know him as well as you think. And I'd take a guess he's good at manipulating people. Maybe he knows exactly how to get you and Belle on side. Ever thought of it that way?'

Her mother's words: *He's brilliant, he's charismatic; he draws people in. But he doesn't care too much about them. Rowan's all about himself.*

Emma felt herself growing hot. 'He's a complex man, and yes, he can be mean sometimes. But he's *not* a killer, Henry. Do you honestly think we'd be defending him like this if we had any doubts?'

Henry picked up his mug of coffee. 'Okay, message received. Let's let it lie, Emma. Your eggs will be cold.'

She picked up her fork. The conversation had left a bad taste, but at least she and Belle had set the record straight. She wondered if Rowan, up there on the moors, had been aware of any of it. Did he even see the papers? Read the news online? Maybe he didn't.

Emma didn't warm to Ed Studley. He was a fidget, obsessively checking his phone as his left leg jiggled up and down. He banged on about house prices, and yawned widely when Emma said how great it was that the Green Party finally had their first-ever seat in parliament.

'So, it must be dead weird for you being back up 'ere again, after your brothers going missing,' he said, finally acknowledging Emma after a long discussion with Henry about share prices. He raised his bushy eyebrows at her. His face was pale and freckled, with brown eyes that were forever flicking over her shoulder at the people coming and going from the restaurant.

Henry and Emma exchanged a glance.

'No, it's not weird,' said Emma. 'But what *is* weird is the fact that nothing new has come to light since I was last properly here, which was more than a year ago. It might be good for local media to push on that, to find out why. Instead of focusing on more ... peripheral aspects of the case.'

Henry cleared his throat. 'Ed, you saw Belle Snow's reaction piece in the *Mail on Sunday*?'

'Sounds like she's in denial to me,' said Ed, in his strong Yorkshire accent. 'Doesn't want to believe Teddy Snow's mate could be responsible. I'd say she's feeling guilty, for leaving them with 'im.'

'You should have asked her for a comment,' said Henry, frowning. 'Then the *Chronicle* wouldn't have been left with egg on its face.'

'I tried to get a comment from Bosworth,' said Ed. 'I door-knocked, but 'e slammed it in me face.'

'You saw him?' said Emma, before she could stop herself.

'Rude bastard. Told me to fuck off.'

Emma tried to hide a smile.

'What did you ask him?' said Henry, glancing at her. 'Did you mention the boys?'

'All I said was, could I talk to 'im about his success as a novelist. He wanted to know how I'd found 'im.'

Henry went still beside her. 'What did you tell him?'

'Said my editor had worked it out, cos he were a clever bloke. I might also 'ave mentioned said editor's girlfriend was the missing boys' sister. I wanted to get 'is reaction.' He sat back in his chair, looking smug.

Henry closed his eyes for a moment.

Emma said nothing, but she was screaming inside. All she could think was, would Rowan think she'd told Henry the identity of R. P. King?

'That was when 'e told me to fuck off,' said Ed, when the silence lengthened. 'After he'd asked the name of my editor.'

Henry sighed, not meeting Emma's eye. 'Oh well. At least *I* don't keep my identity a secret.'

''e knew your name,' Ed said. 'What was it 'e said?' Emma saw him thinking back. 'Something about *Bingley*, I think.'

Emma snorted – she couldn't help it. 'Oh my god.'

Henry turned to look at her.

'Sorry, Henry. I may have mentioned the family nickname, when I first told him about you.'

He didn't look amused. 'This goes no further,' he said to Ed.


Neither said much as they walked back to the apartment. It felt to Emma as if a battle line had been drawn. Henry had outed Rowan, but in doing so had played his hand.

'I'm sorry about all that,' Henry finally said. 'Once again my timing has been the worst.'

When she said nothing, he turned to look at her. 'I'm guessing you weren't impressed with Ed.'

'I don't need a buddy,' she replied. 'Give me some time to familiarise myself with the area and your staff; put me on the easy stuff. I'll do the flower shows and the planning applications, all that. When I'm part of the furniture . . . ' there was a pang, as she thought of Kyle and his chaotic desk, 'then I'll nag you about more words and responsibility.'

He put an arm round her shoulder. 'It's a deal.'

It had been a shaky start to this new phase in her life, and she was realising they still had a lot to learn about each other. But she needed to stay positive. And, most importantly, she needed to remember the real reason she'd moved north.

# Chapter Twenty-Five

Emma immediately felt at home in the *Chronicle*'s newly reno-vated offices. The pace was less frenetic than at the *Voice* – it felt more county town, less big city. While Emma had soon real-ised Kyle's Cockney bark was worse than his bite, that bark had been loud, stroppy and sweary, while Henry's clipped tones were considerably gentler – but no less effective.

It was clear he was a popular editor. As he introduced her round the office on her first day, he dropped in some little fact about each member of staff's particular interest, or child, or pet.

'How was *The Wind in the Willows*?' he said to a reporter he introduced as Preshti.

'Great, Henry,' she said, 'until Mr Toad fell off the stage and fractured his arm.'

Henry grimaced. 'Oops.'

'Thanks so much for letting me leave early yesterday.'

'No problem.'

'Did you tell Ed I won't be needing his buddying?' Emma asked under her breath as they moved on, spotting him across the office. His shirt sleeves were rolled up and ... he actually had a pencil behind his ear.

'I never told him I was considering it,' he replied, leading her over to the corner by the window. 'Thought I'd get your reaction to him first.'

'That's a relief.'

'This is you,' he said. 'I saw you scoping this spot when we came in before. It's all yours.'

It was a nice big space, the desk already set up with a new iMac and a stack of stationery and pens. 'Ooooh,' she said, opening a pale blue leather-bound notebook.

'Just feeding your stationery addiction. And this desk here—' he indicated the empty space opposite, 'is Susie Bishop, the features editor. She's on holiday this week.' He frowned at the papers, pens, chewing gum packets, family photos, and hair ties scattered across Susie's desk. 'Obviously she isn't taking my clear-desk policy seriously. I'll have to resend that email.'

'Surely tidiness isn't a thing in newsrooms,' said Emma, peering at a photo of a forty-something woman in ski gear on a snowy mountain. She had a cloud of curly brown hair and a wide smile, and her arms were around two boys who looked about nine and seven.

'But who doesn't clear their desk before they go on holiday? Plus Mother's just spent a fortune renovating these offices. The least we can do is keep them looking respectable.'

Emma peered at the shelves next to her own desk. There were guides to Yorkshire; books on the local wildlife, National Parks and National Trust properties . . . 'You got me books?'

'Homework.'

'I want to hug you,' she said quietly, 'but that wouldn't be appropriate.'

'No. None of that here. But feel free to thank me properly when we get home.'

Emma was surprised at how readily the *Chronicle*'s staff seemed to accept her, given her relationship with Henry. They were friendly and chatty and happy to fill her in on everything local, and by the end of her second day most had managed to broach the subject of her lost brothers, like it needed to be said, to be got out of the way.

'Everyone's been so nice,' she said to Henry as they relaxed on the apartment balcony at the end of her first week, enjoying the river. The brick buildings on the opposite bank glowed red in the evening sun, and a matching red pleasure boat chugged along on its sunset cruise, a splash of colour on the deep blue water. Phonetically speaking, the name Ouse seemed unfair.

'They don't seem ... you know, suspicious of why I got the job, wondering if I can actually do it.'

'What's not to like about you?' he said, sipping a glass of beer.

'Famous parents? Rich? Boss's girlfriend? From down south?'

'You're unpretentious; they like that up here. And that always comes as a surprise, given your family. Plus you're an experienced journalist, you've got the credentials. And of course ...'

'My brothers.'

'Well, yes.'

Emma picked up her wine. 'Susie's back on Monday. I hope she won't think I'm a threat, seeing as I want to do features.'

'I sat you together so you could learn from her,' he said. 'She's old school – tough as old boots, a great journalist.'

They were quiet for a moment, then Emma said, 'Preshti's brother's selling his terraced house, apparently. Quite central. She thinks I might like it. I'm going to take a look.'

'Terraced?' he said. 'Sounds small.'

'It's got three bedrooms, so my sisters and friends could come and stay. I can't believe how much more house you get for your money up here.'

'We'd need to find out if it was a good investment.'

Emma bristled a little. 'I'm more interested in whether it's got character and a nice garden. A private one. And it'll be my money. Well, mine and Mum's.'

'Yes, but it's a big step, buying your first property. And if we buy together, further down the line ... you know. We want to maximise our capital. I'll come take a look with you.'

'I think I'll get a cat,' she said. 'You should get one too! Or a dog. You should get a dog, Henry.'

He wrinkled his nose. 'Messy and smelly.'

'A cat, then. Jacquetta likes you.'

'Jacquetta is not a normal cat. She makes me uncomfortable. She's a demon in cat form.'

Emma laughed. 'Funny you should say that. Mum thinks she's some sort of medium to the spirit world.'

'Yes, well. Belle.' He gave a small shake of his head. Clearly he was still smarting at being outmanoeuvred on the Rowan pseudonym business. 'I sometimes think your mum's away with the fairies, not grounded in reality.'

Emma's smile faded, and there was an awkward silence.

'Let's have some music,' said Henry, obviously feeling the need to fill it.

A short while later the sound of 'Orange' floated out from the living area. The song took Emma straight back to that afternoon in the music room at Glastonbury.

'You can't beat Heat's early albums,' Henry said, sitting down again.

Emma swallowed. 'Good for winding down on a Friday night. Mum's a fan. She loves Marty.'

His eyebrows went up. 'Have you met him?'

'He came for lunch once, when we were staying in Somerset. He taught the boys how to play this, when they were showing off their party pieces to him and Rowan.'

The eyebrows went down again and his blue eyes seemed to darken.

'Actually, would you mind if I changed the CD?' she said. 'It's bringing back too many memories.'

'I'll do it,' he said, getting up.

She sat remembering that afternoon, the boys sitting like twin cherubs on the piano stool, Rowan ruffling Riv's hair: *Very good, maestro.*

Henry reappeared as Franz Ferdinand lifted the mood. 'We're expected at Montfort for Sunday lunch,' he said. 'I thought we could go early, get a ride in.'

Emma's heart sank. Face a horse and Lady M all in one day? She grimaced. 'Must we?'

He didn't smile. 'Afraid so. Also, if I'm going to be mercenary about it, I get a lot of leads from her. She knows everything that's going on in Yorkshire, gives me tip-offs about local stories.'

Emma grinned. 'As in, *A source close to the winner of Yorkshire's best black pudding competition said . . .* '

There was a small smile. 'As in, *A source close to the council committee understands the controversial planning application for a superstore to be built on a Site of Special Scientific Interest is likely to be approved this week.*'

'Ah, I get you,' she said. 'Heck – is she really that much in the know?'

'Formidable spy network. Very little of significance happens that she doesn't know about.'

The ride across the Dales was sublime. The stable-hand saddled up a large docile pony for Emma, and they trekked along pretty bridleways, the warm, plump belly of the delightful Stanley rolling beneath her.

Henry was considerably higher off the ground than Emma, on a bay mare called Tudor, whose glossy red-brown coat co-ordinated nicely with Henry's own well-groomed hair. He was rather breathtaking in his black polo shirt, tight cream jodhpurs and tall black riding boots. It came as no surprise that he looked good on a horse.

When he'd appeared out of the stables changing room, she'd looked down at her own jeans, Greenpeace T-shirt and Chelsea boots, saying, 'Oh dear. City girl fail.'

'We'll get you some kit before next time,' he'd said, handing her a riding hat.

They'd had a quick cup of tea before leaving, but there had been no sign of Lady M. Birch had said she was out and about on the estate, and would join them later.

As they reached the high point on the bridleway, stopping to take in the view, they saw her below, galloping towards them on a magnificent grey horse.

A group of walkers quickly scattered as she flew past. She wasn't slowing down for the plebs, it seemed.

Henry raised a hand as she approached, slowing to a trot.

'Why don't the bloody ramblers stick to the walking tracks?' she snapped as she stopped, facing them, not even acknowledging Emma. 'If I mow one down I suppose it'll be *my* fault. What part of *bridle*way is so hard to understand?'

Emma bit her tongue. She was a strong advocate for public access to areas of outstanding natural beauty, and agreed with Belle that no one really had the right to own huge swathes of land, simply because some ancient ancestor had been handy with a sword and the King had thought fit to reward them with a chunk of England. Also, presumably, the peasants who came with that land.

Henry and Lady M were looking at her, waiting for her to speak.

'Sorry, what was that? I was too busy admiring this breath-taking view!'

Lady M's expression put Emma firmly into that peasant category. 'I asked how you were finding Stanley. He's a frustrating ride. I can't think why Henry put you on him – he's really for children.'

'Oh, he's a delight.' She patted his neck. 'I'm afraid my riding experience hasn't progressed beyond pony trekking with my sisters and . . . and my brothers, on family holidays.'

Lady M's horse was tossing its head and stepping sideways, and she pulled sharply on the reins. Little Stanley seemed spooked by the large beast in front of him. He'd started to snort.

'Jasper's going to go for Stanley if we don't move on, Mother,' said Henry, looking nervous.

'Hold your reins tighter,' she barked at Emma. 'Pull him up.'

Instead, Emma patted his neck again and said, 'It's okay, Stanley.'

But Stanley wasn't okay. He was still snorting, then with a lurch he suddenly took off downhill, skirting Jasper and breaking into a canter.

Emma squealed as the whiplash hit, and grabbed hold of the saddle.

'Pull him up!' she heard Lady M yell.

She was going to fall off. This was terrifying. She leaned back in the saddle a little, trying to keep her balance. Stanley veered off the path, the grass a blur below them. How was he keeping his footing? She managed not to scream – that would surely only spook him further.

Henry and Tudor appeared level with her, on the path. 'Pull the reins,' he called. 'Keep his head up.'

She managed to let go of the saddle long enough to give them a tug. At the same time she talked to the pony, trying to keep her voice calm. 'Stanley, please stop. That horrible big horse has gone now. If you stop I'll give you an extra carrot or something.' She tugged again, and then again, amazed she was still in the saddle, and finally the pony slowed. 'Good boy, that's it, nice and slow, nice and slow.' She risked a pat.

Stanley slowed further, and finally, after one more tug on the reins, stopped.

Emma blew out a long breath. 'Thank you, darling Stanley, thank you.' She patted him again, then rested her hands on the saddle, dropping her head forward. *Oh my god.*

Henry came alongside, grinning. 'Well played, Emma. That was a great piece of riding. You're a natural.'

She smiled weakly. 'That was utterly terrifying. I thought you said Stanley was unflappable.'

He looked back over his shoulder. There was no sign of Lady M. 'She should have picked up that Stanley was getting spooked. He was snorting. I thought she'd back away.'

Emma realised her hands were shaking. 'I think I'd like to get off now.'

'He'll be fine,' said Henry. 'We'll just take it slow, walk on back.'

*Did she do that on purpose? Why?*

They reached the stable block, Stanley following Tudor into the yard.

'Mother's back,' Henry said.

'I hope she's going to apologise,' said Emma.

Henry dismounted, passing his reins to the stable boy, and came over to help Emma off Stanley. 'I think she forgets not everyone grows up knowing how to ride.'

Emma slid to the ground. 'No one in her orbit, anyway. Remind me to apologise for my peasant heritage. I just *won't* do.' She didn't smile. Lady M was really starting to rile her. 'Can we get a carrot for Stanley? I promised.'

Henry fished in his jacket pocket. 'Here, give him this.' He unwrapped a packet of two sugar cubes and passed one over. 'Not good for them, but I think little Stanley deserves it.'

After feeding the pony, Emma wrapped her arms around Henry's waist and leaned her head on his chest. He smelled of horse and leather; quite delicious. 'I did enjoy that, until Lady M and Jasper turned up.' She paused. 'What's with all the Tudor names?'

'Theodore's a derivation of Tudor,' he said, stroking her back. 'That's Dad's name, of course, but there's a Tudor connection in Mother's family tree too. That chap in the portrait – the black-haired John. She has fun with the theme.'

Emma grinned. 'Wait ... you're descended from Henry the Eighth?'

'Impossible. His line died out with Elizabeth the First, remember. The link's further back down the House of Lancaster line.'

'So in fact, Henry, you're part Welsh?'

'I prefer to call it Celtic.'

Emma nodded. 'Yes, that has a nice ring to it. And Mum will like it.'

'Maybe she'll have little part-Celtic grandchildren one day? And about that nice ring ... '

Emma looked up at him as he took off his helmet and ran his fingers through his hair. 'Henry, for goodness' sake don't say anything like that within your mother's hearing, or I'll be dead meat.'

\*

Dead meat featured in Sunday lunch, but most of the chat involved local politics and the goings-on around the Montfort estate. As they sat in the 'small' dining room, Emma made an effort to remember the names of the local bigwigs Henry and Lady M discussed, as she would no doubt need to know these in the coming months.

Henry had had a quiet word with Birch, and Emma was presented with a grilled trout from the river that ran through the estate.

'Wild-caught,' said Lady M. 'Tell me, Emma, how is it acceptable to eat a trout from a managed stream but not a lamb raised on our hillsides?' She smiled slightly in anticipation of Emma's answer.

Emma considered the question, picturing a cold-eyed fish of indeterminate age, and then a cute lamb, gambolling, killed at a few months old. But that argument wouldn't wash.

'It's mostly a gut feeling, Madeline. I just don't feel comfortable eating lamb any more.'

'Not what you'd call a compelling argument, for someone wanting to write opinion pieces?' Lady M's eyes flicked to Henry before returning again to Emma. 'I think you'll find,' she said, delicately cutting a morsel of lamb, 'that hill farming, which has gone on in these parts for centuries, is vital to the preservation of upland ecosystems.' Her tone of voice supplied the conclusion: *and it is not worth debating this further with one so ill-informed.*

Emma opened her mouth to reply, but she was interrupted.

'Do you fish?' Lady M spat out the question, then popped the piece of meat into her mouth. She would no doubt be expecting Emma to say no, unless it was with a net for tadpoles.

'Yes! Dad used to go fly fishing in Scotland and we'd tag along sometimes. I'm quite good at casting; he taught me how. I always dreaded actually catching something, though, because of the whole hook business.' She thought back to those days; it seemed so long ago. 'And because my brothers took far too much pleasure in bopping the trout on the head, little horrors. Really, it was all a bit gruesome.'

Lady Madeline blinked, then turned to Henry.

Emma stared at her fish, which looked mournfully back at her. *That went well.*

She'd have to up her game, if indeed she was going to write opinion pieces that had some grounding in actual knowledge and authority. Come next week, she'd make a list of people she could visit in the area – conservationists, wildlife organisations, the National Trust managers and wardens.

Emma carefully nudged the pink flesh off the bone and took a bite. *At least this fish isn't cold.*

# Chapter Twenty-Six

On Monday, Susie Bishop blew into the office, threw her bag on the floor, and dropped heavily into her chair, letting out a dramatic sigh of relief. 'Thank fuck for that,' she said, picking up a hair tie and scooping her fuzzy brown hair into a ponytail. 'You must be Emma. Nice to meet you.'

There was nothing in Susie's direct gaze to set off warning signals.

'Hi, Susie. Nice to meet you too. Did you have a nice holiday?'

She let out a bark of laughter. 'Camping in France? You call that a holiday? It was like being stuck at home with the kids but without a dishwasher. *This* is a holiday,' she said, beaming at her desk and then at the office in general, waving to Preshti across the other side. 'Cuppa?'

'Shall I make it?'

'Great idea. Tea with milk and two sugars, please.' She rummaged in her bag, producing a packet of Hobnobs. 'These should see us through Monday.'

Emma grinned. 'Dark chocolate ones. Soul sister.'

At lunchtime, at Susie's suggestion, they went for a sandwich together. 'Away from ear-wiggers,' said Susie as they found a bench in Deans Park. 'No doubt the office has been busily sussing you out. Some nice juicy gossip in their sad little lives.'

'Everyone's been so nice. Quite surprising, really. I thought they'd be more suspicious.'

'Probably because everyone loves the boss. Your only problem is likely to be that you're shagging him and they aren't. Even most of the blokes fancy him ... Just joking,' she added, when Emma looked shocked. 'Sorry, tact isn't my strong point.'

'I'm still coming to terms with the whole straight-talking northerner thing.'

Susie ripped open the cardboard sandwich container and took out her ham salad on white. Emma opened her egg mayo on brown.

'So, Henry tells me you want to write features.' She bit into her sandwich and a slice of tomato fell into her lap. She threw it to a pigeon.

Straight to the point. But in a good way, Emma felt.

'Yes, and he tells me you're the perfect person to learn from. But I realise I need to find my feet first, so I'm very happy to be covering the West Yorkshire Cavy Society Annual Show this week.' She paused. 'Actually, that's true. I love guinea pigs.'

Susie laughed. 'I heard you've got a thing for furry creatures and the environment. Suits me fine, I can't be arsed with it all. Global warming, blah blah. Didn't see much evidence of that in France. Pissed down most of the time.'

Emma passed on the opportunity to explain how climate change often meant increased rainfall.

'Tell you what,' said Susie, 'being stuck on a rain-sodden camp-site with two hyperactive boys was hell. What was I thinking? Somewhere tropical with a kids' club next year.'

'Their dad's not on the scene?' Emma had got the impression Susie was a single mum.

'Fucked off years ago. Oh, and by the way, sorry if that sounded insensitive. My mouth often forgets to check in with my brain before opening.' She met Emma's gaze.

Emma smiled. 'It's okay. My brothers were an absolute night-mare too, but I do miss them. Make the most of your boys.'

Susie shook her head, stuffing the rest of her sandwich into her mouth. 'Christ. Can't imagine how that must be for your family,' she said, chewing. 'I bought your mum's album, sobbed my heart out when I first heard it. Haven't been able to listen to it since.'

They were quiet for a moment. It was Emma's first day working with Susie, but she felt . . . 'Susie, the police investigation – it seems to have completely wound down. We've heard nothing in ages. I was thinking . . . maybe I might look into it. I haven't said anything to Henry, but . . . you might understand where I'm coming from with that.'

Susie looked at her. 'Fuck yes. If it were my boys I'd be down that station haranguing them daily. They need a kick up the arse.'

Emma breathed out. 'So you wouldn't be against, say, an investigation by the boys' sister on why the trail's gone cold?'

'You'd have to get Henry's okay, but he's hardly going to say no, right? Would be a hot read. Would probably be picked up by the nationals too. He's not going to pass up on that.'

'Probably not. The only thing is, I'm pretty sure he's already made up his mind what happened, and I don't agree with him on that, so it's a bit thorny.'

'The teacher? Ed Studley doorstepped him. Didn't go down too well, I hear.'

'No.' Emma gave a small laugh. 'Rowan wouldn't have welcomed that particular opportunity to put his point of view. But Susie – Rowan didn't take them. I've known him for years; he's not a child murderer.'

Susie cocked her head to one side. 'You're still on good terms with him?'

'I'm not on *any* terms with him. He feels so bad about what happened that he's cut himself off from us. From just about everyone, probably. If the police could find out what really happened, he'd get his life back too.'

'Or maybe that's because he's guilty as fuck?' said Susie.

'No. He's a very private person, that's why he wrote his book under a pseudonym. But that shouldn't mean people jump to conclusions, right?'

'Okay, love. Look – do the junior reporter stuff for a while, write me a few features on ... I don't know, barn owls in Barnsley or whatever, and in the meantime think about how you'd approach an investigation like that. Who are your contacts?'

'The police family liaison officer was very helpful. She'd be a good starting point.'

'They're not going to give up their information readily, Emma. They won't want you suggesting they're incompetent. And they're busy people. You're the boys' sister, they'll see it as being driven by emotion, a need for closure, rather than having any solid basis for reinvestigation.'

'But if I make it clear I'm not being critical, that I just want to look into how two boys can simply vanish without trace, leaving zero clues behind ... '

Susie nodded. 'There's a good case for the paper investigating. Sit on it for the time being, but start thinking about how to approach it. If you actually know Bosworth, and he's the main suspect, think who you can talk to about him.'

'But he didn't do it!'

'So you'll need to eliminate him. Like I say, think about how you'd do that.'

Preshti's brother's red-brick terraced house was perfect. It was down a tiny side street ten minutes' walk from the office, with a bow window in front and a clay tile roof. The moment Emma stepped over the threshold she knew it was for her. It was old, fashioned but in a good way, and in spite of being Victorian it was full of light. The downstairs rooms had been knocked through into a living area that opened onto a private garden, long, thin and walled.

The original features had been lovingly renovated – a Victorian fireplace with a wood-burning stove, built-in bookshelves either side. A narrow staircase led up to two bedrooms, one at the front and one at the back, with old sash windows that, incredibly, slid smoothly up and down. Another flight of stairs led to an attic room with a dormer window looking across the rooftops to the towers of the Minster. It would make a perfect study.

'It's overpriced,' said Henry, as they walked home after the viewing. 'But the market's soft at the moment, we can probably get them to knock off ten thou at least.'

'Oh, Henry, I should offer the asking price. The poor woman obviously doesn't want to leave.'

The 'poor woman' was Preshti's sister-in-law. She'd shown them round, and she was clearly unhappy about the move. The way she'd lovingly fingered the curtains ('I'll be leaving them all, they belong here'), trailed her hands along the oak kitchen workbench ('I love this old wood, it's recycled') and said, wistfully, as she showed them the garden, 'We've had some great times with the kids out here. It faces south, so it's perfect in summer, and easy to grow things . . . '

'Why are you selling, if you don't mind my asking?' Emma had asked.

'Husband's job. His firm's moving everyone to Manchester. He was lucky to be kept on . . . I suppose.'

'I feel bad for her, and embarrassed enough about Mum paying for it,' she told Henry. 'I'd like to help her out.'

'You're paying cash in a buyers' market, Emma. Offer twenty K below, at least.'

Emma sighed. 'Just leave me to it, will you, Henry?'

At her desk, Emma opened the beautiful blue notebook. She'd been saving it for her investigation. There was something about new notebooks, the promise of them. She wondered if, by the time she'd filled this one, she'd be any closer to knowing the truth.

Nearly two months after starting at the *Chronicle*, this was the first real opportunity she'd had to start her investigation, what with buying the house, learning the ropes of the new job, getting to know York.

Emma had exchanged contracts on the house this week. She'd paid full price, and would be moving in soon. Her time living with

Henry had been lovely, mostly. The only points of tension had flared around the correct organisation of the fridge, dishwasher, food cupboards, cutlery drawers. Yes, she'd miss living with him, but was bursting with excitement about her new place. A house of her very own, to do whatever she wanted with. Choosing flowers for the garden, colours for the bedrooms; filling those bookshelves. A cat. Definitely a cat.

She needed to stop daydreaming and get on with work. She'd met her deadlines for today and the council meeting she'd been due to attend was postponed, so she was cruising for the rest of the afternoon. Susie was working from home today; when she was in there was no chance of slacking. 'You're much better at research than me,' she'd say, piling it on.

Emma smoothed the first page of the notebook with the side of her hand, then wrote: *People to contact?*

Top of the list: *DS Shore.*

*Mr Pickford*

*Anyone else at the school? Other boys? Friends of F&R*

*People who reported sightings – Aysgarth? Find out who.* She underlined that last bit.

She stared out of the window again, at the Minster. Then, taking a breath, she wrote down: *Rowan?*

Could she really do a thorough investigation without speaking with him? But the thought of that. What would it do to her?

If he really was the prime suspect, she should, as Henry kept pointing out, be more objective about that. If she could demonstrate to Henry and others that she *was* objective, then her investigation would have more credibility.

She needed to think outside the box she'd created for herself, to try and open up her mind. Maybe even – she allowed the thought in – explore the possibility that the police were right, that Henry was right.

Means. Motive. Opportunity.

His words, spoken on Glastonbury Tor: *The dark side. We all have thoughts and emotions we're trying to suppress. Sometimes they bubble through ... My own fucked-up-ness is undoubtedly the result of my shit childhood ...*

If she was going to be objective, who could she talk to about Rowan? She remembered their conversation in the Dog and Duck, when he'd told her he was having counselling.

She wrote: *Meena?*

The counsellor probably wouldn't share anything about Rowan. But if Emma was visiting the school anyway?

Who else could she talk to?

*Jane Warwick. Ask her about Abigail.*

*Neville?*

There was that question mark over why Neville had blamed Rowan for Abigail's death. The accusation of emotional abuse. Plus, Neville had been the boys' godfather; he'd known them all their lives. If she was going to be thorough, she should speak to him.

She had her list. Next, she'd do some online research. Over the year and a half since Freddie and Riv had gone missing, she'd kept up to date with the news items, the gaps between them ever lengthening, but she needed to collate all the links, to revisit each and every mention of the boys, in case anything – anything at all – caught her eye, seemed unusual, jogged a memory. She created a folder on her computer: *Monsters*.

By the end of the afternoon, she'd sent off the preliminary emails that would enable her to move forward: to DS Shore, to Mr Pickford at Middleham, to Belle, asking for contact details for Jane and Neville Warwick. Just before she left, a reply popped in from Belle. In it, she suggested Emma should go down to London for a weekend and she'd invite Jane over for Sunday lunch. She also warned Emma off seeing Neville. *Out of respect for your dear father's memory, stay away from that man.*

But what had Neville ever done to Teddy, other than loudly suggest his death had been caused by debauchery? The pair had been thick as thieves. Surely Belle's comment was far more about her resentment of Neville's pernicious influence over her husband.

She took a chance on the email address on nevillewarwick. com, and put in the subject heading: *Contact from Emma Snow*. Her message asked whether she could meet with him in regards to a follow-up piece she was doing for the *Chronicle* on the boys' disappearance, bearing in mind his willingness to speak to the paper before, about his views on Rowan Bosworth. As far as Neville knew, Rowan was no more to Emma than an old friend of the family.

That evening she received a reply:

> Emma, my darling girl. How absolutely marvellous
> to hear from you. Never a day goes by without
> my thinking of your dear father. I would be
> beyond delighted to buy you lunch or dinner — I
> rarely venture to the wilds of the North, but
> do please get in touch next time you're in the
> civilised world.
>
> Your loving godfather,
>
> Neville.

She emailed back, suggesting dinner on the Saturday night. She'd tell Belle she was meeting Greta and Isabel.

Emma moved into 34 Gregory Lane on a warm day in September. She took the day off work, and although Henry offered to come over to help, she told him she'd be fine by herself. Truth be told, Henry was so well ordered, her make-it-up-as-you-go-along approach to unpacking would probably drive him to distraction.

She'd been amassing plates, cutlery and other essentials over the past month, piling it all up in Henry's spare room, along with the boxes of stuff she'd brought up from London. She'd been shuttling back and forth in the Mini to bring it all over.

One of the boxes was labelled 'Emma Starter Pack'. She'd come across it hiding under a box of books. 'Open on arrival at no.34', it said on the lid. When she did, she found teabags, coffee, Hobnobs, chocolates, fruit, wine, crisps and a carton of milk in a cool bag.

'He's such a doll,' she said out loud, taking the goodies over to the kitchen worktop and filling up her new kettle.

The furniture had been delivered, the boxes were all here, and she sat in her new armchair with a mug of tea, gazing around her. *My own space.*

A little while later there was a knock at the front door, and she opened it to see Henry with a bunch of flowers and ...

'Oh my god! You didn't! Oh my *GOD!*' Her tone rose with each little sentence, until it was too high for the human ear.

In his other hand was a cream-coloured kitten with a smudgy brown nose and startlingly blue eyes. It looked at Emma and opened its mouth, and the tiniest squeak came out.

'He's a ragdoll,' said Henry, stepping over the threshold. 'Gentle, affectionate, and intelligent, so they say. And very beautiful. Emma as a cat. He's a pedigree, although,' he frowned a little, 'the breeder seemed a bit dodgy. Anyway, there's cat food in the car and now you two can get to know each other while I go get us a takeaway.'

He passed her the kitten and went over to the worktop to put down the flowers, his eyes taking in the chaos on the floor. 'You don't seem to have got far with your unpacking.'

'No, but I've had my first cup of tea, thanks to the starter pack. Henry ...' With her spare arm she hugged him, the kitten watching her with interest. 'Did I remember to tell you I love you today?'

# *Chapter Twenty-Seven*

E mma and Henry's first serious row blew up in November.
Perhaps unsurprisingly, it was sparked by Lady M. Emma
brooded darkly on the fallout as the London train sped south-
wards. She caught sight of her frown reflected in the train window,
and made an effort to smooth it out, to stop mulling, chewing,
obsessing.

Logic told her no relationship was row free, unless one partner
was completely passive, perhaps. Emma was probably the more
passive of the two. She bit her tongue when Henry tidied up after
her in her own house, rearranged her fridge, shooed Perkin off the
chairs; when he quibbled about prices in the supermarket, always
going for the two-for-ones even when they only needed one.

Little things.

It was bad timing, as Emma had wanted to get Henry's green
light for her investigation. One of her first steps would be to contact DS Shore, which she'd need to okay with him. But before
she'd had chance to broach the subject, the fox-hunting bomb
had gone off.

In spite of the ban, in place since 2005, the issue was still
hotly debated, and people were still hunting illegally. Emma had
canvassed everyone from farmers to conservationists to hunt saboteurs on the issue, and by the time she'd finished working on it,
her feature was well balanced and full of statistics to back up her

anti-hunting stance. Susie had edited it, and after adding a few words to make it clear this was an opinion piece, approved it with her blessing.

And then she'd passed it to Henry. He'd massacred the copy – rewritten the conclusion to make it neither pro nor anti, deleted all the quotes from the saboteurs and their naming of names, taken out all references to suffering, and even removed the part about foxes being Britain's third-most popular wild animal (after otters and hedgehogs).

'Those cute little lambs you refuse to eat? Any idea what foxes do to those?' he'd snapped.

He'd made her feel stupid, ill informed. Then the argument had grown spiteful, descending into *Your horrible mother's far more important to you than I am.*

And when it had reached this heated-up, irrational stage, Henry had let slip that he and the estate manager had been flushing out foxes with pairs of hounds, on one of those weekends when Emma had pleaded decorating as an excuse to avoid Sunday with Lady M. (Every weekend since she'd moved into Gregory Lane, in fact.)

Emma had been speechless. She'd stared at Henry, her mouth open.

'A nice clean shot, Emma. No suffering. I'm pretty handy with a gun.'

Yes, it was a kinder death than being torn apart by the pack, but the thought of Henry taking aim with a shotgun, pulling the trigger. *How could he do that?* The image in her head was too hard to deal with.

And then off they'd gone again, the whole townie sentimentality versus the realities of countryside management.

She took out her phone, opened her messenger thread with Henry and stared at it for a moment. *I'm sorry. I should have told you what I was doing . . .*

Her finger hovered over the send arrow, then she deleted the draft.

He wanted her to be objective. Well, his 'edit' of her piece hadn't been objective. It had been a sop to his mother. She'd probably known Emma was writing it. Yes, she was the owner of the *Chronicle*, so she was entitled to influence editorial opinion. Emma knew how it worked. But . . .

There was no point in brooding like this. She needed to take her mind off it.

She fished in her backpack for *Never Live Long*, Rowan's new book. She'd spotted it in the station bookshop, and so far had only read the back cover blurb – standard psychological thriller stuff – and the dedication: *In loving memory of Abigail.*

She was pleased he was still writing, hadn't lost his mojo after the *Chronicle* had outed his identity.

*Abigail.*

Emma wondered how tomorrow's conversation with Neville would go. Given Belle's and Rowan's dark hints at the impact his behaviour had on Abigail, she was anticipating some difficulty remaining objective.

Her conversation with Jane would probably be more enlightening. If she would talk honestly about what had happened to her daughter, Emma would at least be able to discount those media rumours about the part Rowan may have played in Abigail's death. Or had Ed Studley been instructed – manipulated, even – by Henry? Would Henry really attempt to tarnish an innocent man's reputation simply because she'd once had a crush on that man? Or had he seen in her eyes that it was far more than a crush? Those eyes of his, which sometimes seemed to read her mind.

Enough. She opened the book and began to read.

That evening she and Belle chatted over plates of pasta. Yes, everything with Henry was lovely, Emma said, apart from his ghastly mother, who treated her like a peasant and had just vetoed her exposé of illegal fox hunting, forcing Henry to turn it into a *For and Against* piece, with the bias heavily *For*.

'Ugh,' said Belle. 'That's simply not on, Emerald.'

Emma nodded vigorously, her mouth full of penne.

'I wonder what Jason ever saw in her,' continued Belle. 'And he's so gentle and nice. Hard to believe he's still on good terms with her.'

Emma finished her mouthful of food. 'Perhaps he likes being bossed around,' she said, remembering Aunt Kate shooing him out to mow the lawn. 'Some men do, right?' A picture of Lady M in her riding gear, whip in hand, popped into her mind, and she giggled.

'Kate's pretty bossy too,' said Belle. 'No wonder Jason spends most of his time abroad.'

'But maybe,' Emma said, 'if he'd been around more when Henry was growing up, Henry wouldn't be so bloody ... *attached* to his mother.'

She then described the bolting pony scene, laying the blame firmly on Lady M and her monstrous grey horse. As she relived little Stanley taking off down the hillside, feeling herself growing hot with indignation, Belle burst into laughter.

Picturing the scene through her mother's eyes, Emma smiled. It probably had looked quite funny. She remembered Henry's grin as he said, 'Well played, Emma,' and her smile faded. She was missing him. If only they'd made up before she'd left.

Later, Emma told her mother about her investigation. Belle was happy she was finally making a start. 'Just tread carefully with Jane on Sunday,' she said. 'It was such a terrible thing, losing her only child.'

Before she went to sleep, Emma took her blue notebook and wrote:

*Did Abigail always suffer from mental health issues?*
*How were these affected by Neville's infidelities/marriage problems?*
*Did things change once she started going out with Rowan?*
*How would Jane/Neville describe Rowan and Abigail's relationship?*
*What were the problems between Neville and Abigail and Rowan?*
*Was Rowan in any way responsible for Abigail's death?*

Neville had booked them a table at The Ivy, naturally.

As Emma spotted him – he was calling across the restaurant to an actor she vaguely recognised – she slowed down, wanting to get the measure of him before he noticed her.

It had been six years since they'd last met, at Teddy's funeral. She felt a pang as she watched him. She probably ought to loathe this man, who'd strongly insinuated in the press that Rowan's behaviour had contributed to Abigail's death. And her mother still held him responsible for Teddy's louche behaviour.

But when Emma had been a girl, she'd loved her flamboyant godfather's visits, watching him and Teddy hamming it up together, entertaining the children. It had been Neville who'd launched her father's career, spotting his talent during a university drama production. Neville had made Teddy into Britain's king of stage and screen. He'd showered the children with extravagant gifts, and she fondly remembered him joking about how they should aim for 'a naughty life' rather than a godly one.

But then Teddy's fame and money, and the pair's resulting power in the industry, had led to that slide towards 'debauchery', as Neville himself had described it.

Now, he looked smaller than she remembered. Less colourful, more ordinary. His suit was crumpled and his untidy grey hair was thinning.

He saw her, and half-stood in his seat. 'Emma! What an absolute treat! How the devil are you, my dearest girl?'

It was all said in an actorish voice, as if for the benefit of those around them, but she noticed the emotion in his eyes. He'd genuinely loved Teddy, and maybe Teddy's family too.

'Uncle Neville. Thanks so much for this. It's lovely to see you again.'

She kissed his proffered cheek, and then the other one. His cologne was overpowering.

The first half hour passed in small talk. Emma listened quietly as he entertained her with showbiz gossip. She refused the offer of wine, wanting to keep a clear head.

She let him prattle on until the main course, and then grabbed her moment. They'd already had the brief, customary *so awful that there's no news on your dear brothers* conversation.

'Neville, you know I'm a reporter for the *Yorkshire Chronicle* now?'

He nodded as he chewed on his steak.

'I'm doing a "Where we're at" piece, about my brothers' disappearance, and I'm interviewing everyone who knew them well – anyone who's had anything to do with the case.'

'I see, yes. That must be hard for you.' He sipped his red wine, his rheumy eyes on her.

'Neville ... ' She lowered her knife and fork. 'You made comments to the paper about Rowan Bosworth, implying he was responsible for Abigail's death.'

His eyes narrowed at the mention of Rowan's name, then he looked away from her and took another large drink of wine.

'You also suggested he wasn't suited to teaching, or fit to look after schoolboys. As a direct result of those comments, he lost his job at Middleham. Now he's living as a recluse. So ... I'd like to talk to you about Rowan.'

'What is it you want to know?' he said, still not meeting her eye, his own fixed on the steak he was slowly and deliberately slicing.

'You accused him of emotionally abusing your daughter. What were you basing that on?'

He was quiet for a moment. 'You know Rowan, don't you? I remember, you two got on.'

'Yes – we've kept in touch over the years.'

'He and I fell out after your dear father died. Rowan had the most ghastly childhood, and he'd become overly attached to Teddy. For some reason he seemed to blame me for Teddy's death. He turned against me – I gave him a stellar career, and he threw it all back in my face.'

'After Abigail died?'

'Yes.' Finally, he met her gaze. 'As you'll know, Rowan's fascinated by the human mind. And most of all, by the effects on the mind of others' behaviour. Especially abusive behaviour.'

Emma frowned. 'I see.'

'It all stems from his life experiences,' he went on, warming to his theme. 'His early work was mostly about exploring his own mind. But as part of that, he likes to mess with other people's, and watch how they respond. He controls, he manipulates. His relationship with Abigail was all about that. He finds out what presses people's buttons, and then he presses them. And watches. Then writes.'

Emma looked at him steadily, trying to keep her expression impassive.

'He controlled Abigail,' Neville went on. 'He called it love, but it was more of an obsession. I watched my daughter turn from a quiet, sensitive girl into a depressive who never left the house. She took drugs; she was totally dependent on Rowan. And eventually she died. Because of him.' He dabbed at the inner corner of one eye, and then the other, with his napkin.

Emma said nothing.

'Your poor, darling little brothers,' he finished. 'What in god's name was Belle thinking, putting them into Rowan's care?' He shook his head.

Emma took a breath, wanting to get the next question right.

'Neville, it's been suggested to me that you were in love with Rowan, and perhaps your view on his and Abigail's relationship has been coloured by that?'

His expression changed – from sorrowful to guarded. 'He was my protégé. He was a genius. I found him attractive, yes ...but he wasn't bi.'

'Were you perhaps jealous of your own daughter, though? I heard she found it hard to cope with your behaviour towards Rowan.'

'Perhaps. But it was most certainly Rowan that sent her over the edge.'

*And losing her baby, surely.* Emma wondered why he hadn't mentioned that.

'What would you say to Rowan, if you saw him now?'

'That I will *never* forgive him.' The theatrical tone was back.

'That I wish I'd never set eyes on him. We welcomed him into our fold, and our family. I gave him a stellar career, but his presence in our lives – it tainted everyone he came into contact with. Even your mother, who wasn't my biggest fan – she resented Teddy's attachment to Rowan. I can't imagine why she's defending him now. How can she do that, when the truth must be staring her in the face? I can only put it down to denial. Or guilt.'

'Truth? What truth?'

'Come come, Emma. One doesn't have to be Sherlock Holmes to work it out. It's not too much of a leap to conclude that he was abusing your brothers, and maybe they plucked up the courage to tell someone and ... well, he couldn't have that. So they disappeared.'

Emma's reserves of objectivity were now totally depleted. She needed to leave, to get away from Neville and his warped thinking. She was feeling nauseous; she couldn't face another mouthful of food.

'Thank you, Neville, for sharing those painful memories. It must have been hard.'

'If it helps get that psycho locked up, then it was well worth it, my dear.'

Later, unable to sleep, Emma lay staring into the darkness, mulling over Neville's words. She tried to get into his head. He'd been infatuated with Rowan; he was a man spurned, rejected, in favour of his own daughter.

Who was telling the truth? Who was responsible for Abigail's descent into despair? Neville? Or Rowan?

Perhaps Jane would give her the answers she needed.

# Chapter Twenty-Eight

'Y ou're looking so well, Emma,' said Jane as they drank coffee by the living-room fire after Sunday lunch. 'Yorkshire's obviously agreeing with you.'

Jane was a tall, matronly woman who'd embraced middle age rather than fighting it. She was about the same age as Belle, but looked ten or fifteen years older. An actress known in the nineties for comedy roles, she was now working in theatre management. She'd finally divorced Neville after Abigail's death.

'I do like it up there,' Emma replied, 'and it's so nice being near Henry at last. Also, I don't know if Mum said ... ' Over lunch, they hadn't progressed much beyond the familiar *Any more news on the boys? ... No, nothing at all ... How awful for you ...* 'One reason I took the job on the Yorkshire paper was to be nearer to the boys' school. I mean to find out more about what happened. It's basically a cold case now, left open by the police, but they're doing nothing proactive. They won't, unless anything new turns up.'

Emma picked up her notepad and pencil. Jane eyed them warily. 'I know how it feels to lose a child,' she said. 'Your mother and I have that in common. She told me you want to discuss Rowan, but you can't possibly think he was involved.'

This was a promising start. 'Are you okay with me making notes, Jane?'

'Of course. But I'm going to let you know when something's off the record. Agreed?'

'Absolutely.' She took a breath. 'Rowan spoke to me a little about Abigail, but I'd like to get another perspective on their relationship. Mum said she'd always suffered from anxiety, is that right?'

Jane began to talk about her daughter, staring into the flames. She teared up once or twice, but was frank and open. She described a quiet, shy little girl who'd preferred animals to people, who'd always had difficulty making friends. Abigail had been sensitive, taken everything very much to heart – a dead bird, something awful on the news, a sad book or movie.

Her teenage years had been difficult. She hadn't fitted in at school and yes, had suffered from anxiety, and that was when her fraught relationship with food had begun. And then Neville had come out.

'If you don't mind my asking, how did *you* handle that?' asked Emma.

'Oh, I discovered he was gay just after we married. He especially loved pretty young men. Being gay wasn't as acceptable back then, so he'd kept it hidden. But I found out soon enough. The two of us always rubbed along, so I ... well, I lived with it.' She paused, sipping her coffee. 'I enjoyed the life his career gave us, so I turned a blind eye. Everything was okay. Until Rowan appeared on the scene.' She met Emma's eye. 'This next part is off the record. Understood?'

Emma nodded, her heart in her mouth.

'Your father spotted the boy's talent immediately, and introduced him to Neville. And that's what Rowan was, then. A schoolboy.' She sighed and shook her head. 'A directionless boy loaded with talent he had no idea what to do with. And Neville decided he should be the one to help with that. But his interest in Rowan was way beyond professional.'

'I'd heard that,' said Emma.

'He became obsessed with him. Called him his beautiful genius. Teddy told him to back off, but he wouldn't listen. Rowan could handle him most of the time, when he was at university and only saw him occasionally. But Neville was managing his career, making sure he owned him, basically. And Neville got Rowan noticed by all the right people. Yes ... it was all manageable. But then Rowan met Abigail.'

Emma wrote in her notebook: *Neville 'owned' Rowan.*

Jane then described how Neville had taken Jane and Abigail to Edinburgh for the Fringe Festival, and Abigail had immediately fallen for Rowan. He'd been lovely to her – kind, interested; they'd gone to see some of the Fringe shows together, just the two of them.

Neville had been wildly jealous of his own daughter, and when it became obvious she and Rowan liked each other, he'd banned her from dating him, saying Rowan was unsuitable – far too volatile. 'A complete screw-up, he called him,' said Jane.

'But they carried on seeing each other?' said Emma.

'Yes, and once Rowan graduated and came to London, things got serious. Neville changed, then. His obsession with Rowan only got worse, seeing him all the time. That was when things between him and me took a dive. I have to say, Emma, I wasn't thrilled with Rowan and Abigail getting married. He was nowhere near as unstable as Neville made out, but he was obviously a troubled soul, and he was so intense with her. With Abigail being so sensitive, I worried what would happen if he cooled off. She was head over heels. Rowan – he blew hot and cold, with everyone.'

*Yep.*

'I was afraid he'd give up on Abigail, with all her issues, or find someone else, especially with Neville doing everything he could to split them up. He and Teddy dragged him along to show-business parties, and your father encouraged all sorts of ... well. It was a horrible time, that summer. Abigail was home for the university holidays, and Rowan was staying with us.'

She stopped for a moment. Emma said nothing, not wanting to break her concentration.

Jane sighed. 'Abigail couldn't handle it, Rowan partying when she was too anxious to go out. Part of that was because she was taking drugs. She'd started using while she was at university. Rowan told me. He didn't like it – thought it would mess too much with her mind, and it did.'

Emma wrote: *Abigail took drugs at uni. Rowan disapproved.*

'When things deteriorated between Abigail and her father,' Jane went on, 'she retreated into her shell even further. Stopped eating again. Rowan was busy with his work – *Twisted* was doing really well – and couldn't always be there for her.'

It was around then that Jane knew she couldn't stay with Neville, she said. His on-going infatuation with Rowan was sending Abigail over the edge – and now Abigail was pregnant. 'I hadn't loved him for years, but I started to hate him, for what he was doing to our daughter. In the end I kicked him out.'

'Shall we get another drink?' Emma said, sensing Jane's distress.

'No. I'll be okay.' She took a breath. 'You know what happened – with the baby?'

'Yes, Mum told me. I'm so sorry.'

'It was a terrible time. Rowan and Abigail were completely devastated. I begged them both to get help – therapy – but they just kind of curled in on themselves, the pair of them. And Neville ... Rowan finally sacked him as his manager, now that your father had gone, and Neville was shattered. And furious.

'Once Neville was out of the picture Rowan started doing okay, getting better. But for Abigail ... it was all too much. Losing the baby, the business with Rowan and Neville. She ended up back in hospital ... once, twice, and then the last time she wasn't strong enough—'

Jane burst into tears, dropping her face into her hands.

Emma had tears in her eyes too. Poor Abigail, poor Rowan.

Jane took a tissue from her handbag and sat quietly crying for a moment. 'Sorry—' she started.

'No!' interrupted Emma. '*I'm* sorry, for bringing it all up again. It must be so painful for you.'

'It is. My little girl. She was like a fragile bird.'

'So Neville's accusations – it was revenge?' said Emma.

'More like the bitterness of a scorned man. Professionally and personally.'

'How can Neville live with himself?'

Jane's expression hardened. 'He's a narcissist,' she said, drying her tears. 'And I often think . . . if I'd kicked him out sooner, before everything became so intense . . . Poor Rowan. When Abigail died he was inconsolable. He felt responsible, he kept saying he should have taken her away, got her out of the situation. But he had no money.'

'Surely—'

'No. All that time Neville was Rowan's manager, he controlled him through money. Clever accounting. Rowan was practically broke. And he never had a head for money. He only ever cared about the creative side of his work.'

Emma wrote: *Neville controlled Rowan's money. Kept him broke.* She was trying to keep the emotion at bay, but her hand was shaking.

'This is all so helpful, Jane. You see . . . it's been implied in the press that Rowan may have had something to do with Abigail's death, because of those rumours Neville started about psychological abuse. Now I know for sure the rumours were all to do with the wrong person.'

'Yes,' said Jane. 'Absolutely.'

Emma looked at the questions in her notebook. She had everything she needed.

Later, she lay on her bed, exhausted by the conversation with Jane. She was reading Rowan's book. Again she could hear his voice as she read, and now the experience made her ache all the more. Suddenly she longed to see him, so much that it hurt.

*Everything I love turns to shit.* Watching his wife die, feeling he'd failed her. Losing his baby son, and Teddy, the man they'd named the baby after, who'd been like a father to Rowan. Neville, pointing the finger of blame when Abigail had died; an already fragile girl tipped over the edge by her father's behaviour. No wonder Rowan had trouble trusting people, letting them close.

He made more sense now – that angry young man, the one who'd wanted nothing to do with any of them. She understood why he'd run away, back to Yorkshire. Then he'd been happy, for a while, until Belle had decided to park her sons on his doorstep. And not long after, as if hexed by a Snow curse, things had turned to shit again.

*Oh*. It came to her.

She sat up.

*Neville*.

Her heart began to beat faster.

*Why did I not see this before?*

She slid off the bed and ran downstairs to the living room. Belle muted the TV as she registered Emma's expression.

Emma launched straight in. 'Mum. Jane says Neville's a narcissist. He likes beautiful young men. He pushes boundaries.' She waited for Belle to catch her meaning.

The blood drained from her mother's face. 'What? You mean . . . My god, Emerald. Surely not.' She shook her head. 'No. No way. He loves pretty young men, but boys? Little boys? I don't think Neville would do that. I never saw him looking at Elfred and River in that way. Like he looked at Rowan.'

'But I remember you saying one time, leaving the boys with Neville would be like asking a wolf to look after a couple of lambs.'

'Did I? Well, I wouldn't have meant it like that. More that he'd have fed off them, made money off them, not treated them right.' She stopped. 'But Emerald – you must tell the police so they can check it out.'

'I will. I should be seeing Liz Shore soon.'

Back upstairs, as she packed up her things, her phone rang – Henry. She stared at his name on the screen, wondering whether to answer. She really couldn't face this conversation right now, but she hadn't spoken to him in two days, hadn't even replied to his texts.

She answered. 'Hi, Henry.'

'Oh dear, you sound tired.'

She wasn't going to tell him why; he didn't know she was making a start on her story. 'Oh, you know. Heart-to-heart with Mum, she's not that great. This thing that's happened – it still wallops us when we're together.'

'Ah, right. But she must be happy to have you there again. I see how much you pick her up, you're a great support.'

'Maybe. Can I talk to you about all that tomorrow?'

'All what?'

'The boys. I know we've been avoiding the subject for a while. But there's something I'd like to do.'

'How do you mean?'

'When I get back – can we talk tomorrow? Not now, I'm bushed.'

'Sure, okay. Emma . . . '

She took a breath. 'Henry. Those things I said about your mother – they were uncalled for. You were only doing your job, and I do appreciate she's the *Chronicle*'s owner and she's pro-hunting.'

When Henry didn't respond, she carried on. 'I appreciate I put you in a difficult position. But I stand by what I wrote, and I'm going to see if another paper will run it, because this is important to me.'

'Emma—'

'And I do understand you not wanting to stand up to your mother because she is in fact terrifying.'

She waited for him to laugh, but there was a short silence, then she heard him sigh. 'Emma, you can't use the paper to push your own agenda. I know you feel strongly about these issues, but your reporting needs to be more balanced.'

'It was! I canvassed all the opinions.'

'You quoted extremists.'

They'd already had this conversation. 'Henry . . . I'm too tired. Sorry, but I'm not going to—'

'No, *I'm* sorry.' At last, he sounded it. 'I . . . I've been shite since you left. I hate it when you're not here; I'd forgotten how awful it is. I'm sitting on your sofa with Perkin—'

'What? I thought you'd be at Montfort Grange.'

'Nope. I decided Mother could look after herself. I came over in case Perkin needed feeding, and because I needed a cuddle, and Perkin was the only one who could help. And Mother isn't more important to me than you. No one's more important to me than you. And Perkin's missing you too, though we are about to watch *Top Gear* together, so things are looking up.'

Relief was spreading through her body like a warm balm. They were okay. As long as she had as little to do with Lady M as possible, they'd be just fine.

On the train home, she pondered further on Neville.

Motive, opportunity, means.

*Motive*: she'd rather not think about that.

*Opportunity and means*: how could he have known the boys would be out and about on that Sunday? Unless he'd lured them somewhere. But how would he have done that? They didn't have phones, and if he'd written to them, wouldn't that letter have been found?

But Neville was clever. If he'd been fixated on the boys, stalking them, perhaps, he would have found a way.

And in pointing the police and the press (*and me – nice try, Neville*) towards Rowan, there was the added bonus of revenge. *If it helps get that psycho locked up, then it was worth it.*

It took Emma quite some time to persuade Henry that the investigation was a good idea.

'I can't justify it,' he said. 'You're personally involved. It'd be emotionally driven and there'd be a complete lack of objectivity.'

Her heart sank, but she straightened her shoulders and prepared for battle. 'Can we just find another word? And justify it to whom? Your mother? I thought you believed in editorial independence?'

'To myself, as editor. And I'm not prepared to compromise the paper's relationship with the police. Even approaching them about it would put them on the defensive.'

But over the next couple of weeks, Emma calmly and relentlessly argued her case, knowing there were sound reasons for the *Chronicle* to do the story. She reminded herself of Kyle's parting words: *When you believe in something, you go for it ... keep that up, Emma.*

Susie backed her up, and Susie on side was a wonderful thing. Henry had enormous respect for his features editor, and she promised to monitor progress and make sure Emma's research didn't encroach into her day-to-day reporting.

Between the two of them they'd finally worn him down, convincing him that a piece by the missing boys' sister, bringing that unique insight, would be a compelling read, and would probably be picked up by the nationals, too. He could never resist that.

DI Shore was as warm and sympathetic as ever, greeting Emma with a hug. 'I'm so sorry we're meeting again under such frustrating circumstances,' she said. 'I'll give you whatever help I can, but I have to tell you I'm constrained in what I can share, this being an ongoing investigation.'

*Really? Haven't seen much evidence of that!*

'I understand,' said Emma. 'And I want to reassure you I'm here in a professional capacity, not as a family member.'

Liz didn't look convinced, but she talked Emma through the early leads, showing her on a map where the boys had been sighted. However, she refused to discuss the interviews with Rowan, or the school staff, or to share any of the forensics information. 'I'm afraid that's just not possible. The case is still very much open.'

But she did give Emma details of one couple who'd reported seeing the boys, checking first that they'd be okay with Emma contacting them. It was somewhere to start. Next, Emma would follow up with the school, to arrange to speak with some of Freddie and Riv's friends.

As the detective started to collect up her papers, Emma said, 'Liz, can I ask – back in 2010, did you talk to Neville Warwick? The boys' godfather?'

Liz thought for a moment. 'I'd have to check. May I ask why?'

'I talked to his ex-wife recently. She called him a narcissist, and ... well, Neville's got quite a reputation when it comes to pretty young men. I think it would be well worth checking out where he was on that day.'

Liz made a note.

'Will you let me know? If Neville can account for his movements?'

'It'll take some time,' Liz said, 'and I may not be able to share the outcome while the investigation's ongoing. But thanks for this. And Emma – speaking of alibis, may I quickly fact-check another with you before you go? Purely routine, but I'd appreciate a statement. Sorry – I should have remembered this loose end earlier.'

The detective took out a form, and carefully wrote something on it. Then she looked up. 'During our routine checks into the whereabouts of family members and close associates, Henry Theodore stated he was with you on the Sunday the boys went missing. Can you confirm that?'

*Henry?* Her confusion must have been obvious.

'Like I said, it's purely routine.'

'Valentine's Day weekend,' said Emma, slowly. A wave of sadness hit as she saw herself for a moment – her old self, the one with a lightness of being. 'Yes, he came down to London, to surprise me.'

Liz wrote on the form.

'And what time did he leave?'

She thought back. 'About lunchtime. He had a long drive home. It's four-and-a-half hours from London to Lancaster, I remember him saying.'

Liz looked up. 'That's very precise.'

'Henry's a very precise person.'

Liz resumed scribbling. 'And did you have any further communication that day, after he left?'

'I can check my phone. He usually texted me to say he'd arrived home.'

'Yes, if you could. And how did Henry get on with your brothers?'

This was beginning to feel ridiculous. But Liz was only doing her job.

'He met them just once, when he was down for a weekend.' She thought back. 'I think he was fairly appalled.' She grinned.

'Appalled?' Liz wasn't smiling.

'They put their pet frog in the shower as a surprise, and Riv thought it was funny to knock on the bedroom door when he thought we might be cuddling.'

*I'd officially like to murder your brothers.*

Liz read the statement back to Emma before she signed it. 'Thanks, Emma. If you could just confirm that time for us, I think we're done.'

*Who's doing the interviewing, here?*

Back at the office, she scrolled through her phone. Henry's romantic little text telling her he was home had been sent at 6.05 p.m., from Montfort. She'd forgotten that.

A Valentine's Day visit to his mother? *Bit creepy.*

She left a message for DI Shore with details of the text. It felt disloyal, but detectives needed to do their thing.

As should Emma.

*Henry?*

She tried again to think like a detective.

Means. *I'm pretty handy with a gun.* Firearms weren't thin on the ground at Montfort.

Motive. No. Not unless that dark side extended way beyond a jealous streak.

Opportunity. What were the chances of him driving past them on his way home? Montfort wasn't that far from Aysgarth.

Again, no. The very thought was absurd.

# Chapter Twenty-Nine

Emma wriggled into the month's-salary-but-what-the-heck dress she'd bought for tonight's Best of Yorkshire awards. The *Chronicle* was sponsoring two categories – Sportsperson of the Year, and Performance Artist of the Year – and Henry would be presenting those. It was a big night for him, and she wanted to make him proud.

The figure-hugging dress was dark green velvet and off the shoulder, with a low neckline and a deep V in the back. Perhaps an impractical choice for January, but she had a beautiful pashmina to slip over it.

Her hair, encouraged into long curls with the curling iron, tumbled loose, almost to her waist. She pushed it back and picked up the long emerald-and-gold earrings Belle had given her for Christmas. The Snows had spent the break at Sandal Manor, Emma neatly side-stepping the invitation to join Henry at Montfort Grange. The Boxing Day Meet had happened again, and Emma had a strong suspicion an actual fox was involved. When she'd asked the question, Henry had avoided it, and her eye.

The earrings caught the light as she fastened them in. They were exquisite. The three sisters always received a name-related Christmas gift from Belle. Pearl privately moaned that she wasn't fifty, but this year Belle had sourced something black and Tahitian, and Pearl had been thrilled.

Emma slipped on a few bracelets and rings. Not too many, or people would start telling her how much like her mother she was again. Then on went the high heels that would bring her up to Henry's nose level. A dab of Coco Mademoiselle and a final touch-up of her lips. She was ready.

Looking at her reflection in the full-length mirror, she put her head on one side, then nodded. When she made the effort, she thought she did 'glamorous' rather well. Catching sight of Perkin's blue eyes on her, she said, 'What do you reckon, little boy? All set to slay the men of Yorkshire, or what?'

The little cat meowed silently. She could tell he was impressed.

The ceremony was at a large hotel on the outskirts of the city. Alighting from the taxi, Emma was slapped in the face by the cold. Teetering in her heels and lifting her hem clear, she stepped carefully around a pile of slush banked up against the kerb. Yorkshire was at peak bleak, and again Emma couldn't help picturing Rowan in his windswept, snowed-in, moorland farm. Ever since her discussion with Jane, she'd had trouble keeping him off her mind.

The hotel's automatic doors swooshed shut behind her and she stood for a moment, letting the warmth of the lobby soothe away the chill. She was meeting Henry in the Bronte Bar, and she spotted the name over a door on the far side of the reception.

As she entered the bar, someone touched her arm. 'Hello, Emma Snow.'

Her heart stopped.

*Rowan.*

She turned to see him smiling at her. His eyes widened slightly. 'Well, look at you, Princess Emma.'

She attempted to unravel her tongue. 'Hello, King Rowan. What does the P stand for?'

'What?'

'R. P. King. What does the P stand for?'

He laughed, then said in a low voice, 'That'd be telling.'

They stared at each other, and time stretched out. It was as impossible to look away from those dark eyes as it had ever been.

*The eyes of the man who stole my heart, who told me we'd be together, then dumped me.*

'Why are you here?' she asked. 'I wouldn't have thought this was your cup of tea.'

'My idea of hell. But my publisher wants me to be less reclusive. I'm getting an award, so I thought I'd come out of my cave. My editor's here somewhere.'

There was so much she wanted to say to him. But she couldn't, not here. And as she gazed at him she was clobbered all over again by an emotion so strong it almost took her breath away.

He noticed.

'Fuck the small talk,' he said. 'How are you doing, Ems?' He put a hand on her back, slipping it under her hair, and guided her to the side of the room. His touch on her bare skin was like a lick of fire.

He picked up a glass of champagne from a waiter's tray and handed it to her.

'I'm fine,' she said. 'Most of the time, anyway. If I keep busy, don't think too hard about the boys, about . . .' Her words ran out.

'You're still with Henry,' he said. 'He's your editor these days, I see.'

'Did you know I was up here?'

He gave a small laugh. 'Of course I knew. I may live in the middle of bloody nowhere, but the papers still make it through. Your fox-hunting piece was got at. Was that him?'

*He reads my stuff!*

'Yes. We had a row about it.'

He frowned. 'What the fuck are you doing, Ems, working for your boyfriend, writing about new roads and school fundraisers. In Yorkshire. You should be in London, getting your voice out there. Unedited.'

She answered quietly, 'So should you, maybe.'

He shook his head. 'No.'

'I wanted to be nearer Henry,' she said, 'and when he became editor—'

'Cos his mama bought him the paper.'

'Well, yes.' She sipped her champagne.

'How's that all going?'

'Lady Mad? We don't see eye to eye. She thinks I'm an ignorant peasant.'

Suddenly she was seeing it all through his eyes. She needed him to know ... 'But Rowan, I also came up here because I can't sit back while the police do nothing.'

He didn't reply at first, looking away, scanning the room. Then his eyes met hers again, and they were narrowed. 'What do you want them to do?'

'Anything! It's gone cold. Mum and me, my sisters, we need to know what happened. *Someone* must know something. And ... I'm looking into it all. I met with the police recently. I'm going to get some answers, I'm determined.'

Another pause. 'The police were thorough,' he said. 'They still suspect me. You know that?'

She felt herself grow hot. 'This is also about clearing your name. Mum and I feel awful about all the finger-pointing. I hope you saw Mum's defence of you in the Sunday paper?'

'Yes. My publisher sends me things. I also read the insinuations in your own rag.' His voice was grim.

The way he was looking at her ... he was throwing up walls again. This was all so familiar. And meanwhile her feelings had resurfaced with astonishing speed. She was knocked sideways; she could hardly think straight.

'How are you, Rowan?' she said. 'Really. Are you doing okay? I'm so pleased about your books.'

He ran his fingers through his hair. It was long and shaggy and she wanted to touch it. Badly.

'You can't make a living as a writer. I'm always broke. But my costs aren't huge.'

'Just you and George? I often think of you two, walking across the moors.'

'No. George died.'

Emma gasped, and then she couldn't help it. Her eyes filled with tears.

'Oh no. Rowan. That's ... '

'Old age, Ems,' he said gently. 'He was an ancient dog.'

She shook her head, not trusting herself to speak.

'Yorkshire hasn't toughened you up, I see.' He gave her a long look, which grew softer, then he reached out a hand and took hers.

A fierce jolt ripped through her.

'Hey, don't ... ' His thumb stroked her hand. Then he dropped it. 'I got another one – look.' He took out his phone and showed her a photo of an adorable black Labrador puppy.

'George the Third?' she said, blinking back her tears.

'Teddy.'

She wanted to hug him, wanted to feel his arms around her. She looked at his lips, drowned in his eyes.

'Rowan ... can I come and see you? Talk to you about what happened with the boys? For the piece I'm writing. Off the record, if you want.'

But before he had a chance to respond, Henry appeared by her side. 'Hi, sorry I'm late.' His clipped, self-assured voice jarred after Rowan's soft Yorkshire tones. 'Did you read my text?' He was looking dashing in a white dinner jacket and black bow tie. Rowan's jacket was black. No tie at all.

Henry did a double take, looking at Rowan, whose eyes were still on Emma.

Emma took a breath, attempting to centre herself. She didn't meet Henry's eyes; her own would surely give too much away.

'Henry, this is Rowan Bosworth. He's up for an award tonight. Rowan, meet Henry. My editor and—'

'Henry,' said Rowan, holding out a hand, his expression inscrutable.

Henry was half a head taller than Rowan, and as Emma finally looked at him she saw his eyes sweep over Rowan's open-necked shirt, his long hair, before returning to his face.

'Rowan,' he said, shaking his hand. 'Congratulations. What's the award?'

Rowan looked him squarely in the eye. 'Fucked if I know. Best book by a suspected child murderer?'

Emma's mouth dropped open. She looked sideways at Henry, who clearly had no idea how to respond. It wasn't often he was wrong-footed.

'Mr King,' she said, turning to Rowan. 'That was rather uncalled for.'

He smiled at her. 'Sorry, Princess.'

A pretty brunette in a black dress and pearls appeared at Rowan's side, and hooked her arm through his, smiling up at him. 'Sorry, Rowan, there was a queue.'

'Siobhan, this is the *Chronicle*'s editor, Henry, and this is Emma Snow, the loveliest person in the world. Universe. Siobhan's my editor,' he said, looking at Emma.

*And a bit more than that.* Little needles were stabbing at her heart.

'These are the people that mess with our work, eh, Ems?' His eyes moved to Henry. 'Somehow, I never saw Emma on the fence when it came to fox hunting.'

Henry didn't flinch. He put an arm round her waist. 'Emma's heart's too big. It's a shame the rest of the world – the universe – doesn't care about things as much as she does. It's an editor's job to be that one step removed, right, Siobhan?' He gave her the full blue-eyes.

'Oh, absolutely! Yes.' She smiled back at him. 'Perfectly put.'

'Well, hooray for Henry,' said Rowan.

Emma attempted to swallow her laugh, and choked on her champagne.

'You alright there, girl?' said Rowan, patting her on the back.

Siobhan then moved the small talk forward, asking Henry about the paper. He explained the awards he was presenting tonight.

The conversation was white noise. The only thing Emma was aware of was Rowan's eyes on her, and the look in them. As she met them again, she tried to read them, but she wasn't sure. Desire? Regret? Exasperation?

Possessiveness?

Henry was speaking to her.

'Sorry, what was that?'

He frowned. 'We should go in. It starts in ten.'

'Oh, right. Yes.' She smiled at Siobhan. 'It was nice to meet you.' Then she looked at Rowan. 'Maybe see you in the interval?'

'There isn't one,' said Henry, taking her arm.

'Oh. After?'

'We're going on to the Partingtons, remember?'

She'd forgotten. 'Right.'

Her eyes were still on Rowan.

'Enjoy your evening, Ems,' he said. 'Call me.' He winked.

Had he meant that? Or had it been for Henry's benefit?

# Chapter Thirty

Emma switched to autopilot for the late dinner with the Partingtons – a wealthy York couple who owned a chain of bathroom stores and spent a great deal of advertising money with the *Chronicle*. As Alistair Partington discussed business with Henry, his wife Theresa told Emma how much she loved Woodville's music, and about the time she'd seen them at Wembley. Then she asked Emma about her role at the newspaper – cue funny stories about local personalities and reporting on pet shows. Finally Theresa got round to the difficult question concerning Emma's brothers.

*This is who I am, now.* Emma was becoming maudlin after yet another glass of wine. *I'm the sister of the missing boys, the daughter of the rock star, the girlfriend of the editor.*

She wanted to be more than this. She'd been Emma from the *Voice*, known for her championing of environmental causes. Now she wanted to be Emma Snow, respected journalist, swaying local opinion, pushing for change, making a difference.

Rowan's words about new roads and fundraisers had stung. But she'd needed to serve her time, get to know the people who mattered. *My own people*, she thought darkly, glancing at Alistair. *Not Henry's.*

Finally the dinner was over and a taxi arrived to take them back to Gregory Lane. Emma yawned, then tipped her head back against the headrest and closed her eyes.

'How did I do?' came Henry's voice. They hadn't been alone together since the ceremony.

She opened her eyes and looked at him. 'You were great, of course. Very relaxed. Most excellent words. And you looked hot. Good job, Henry.' She gave him a little punch on the arm, and realised she was quite drunk.

He realised it too. 'You probably shouldn't drink that much when we're with important clients. But you're so beautiful tonight, I'll overlook it this once.'

'Why thank you. So are you.' He was. He was *outrageously* handsome in his dinner jacket, with his tidy golden hair and his snow-white dress shirt and his blue-blue eyes and his *tallness*.

'I didn't know Bosworth was going to be there.' The light-hearted tone had gone. 'Just as well I wasn't giving *him* an award. Christ, what an obnoxious man.'

Emma closed her eyes once more, resting her head back again. 'Straight-talking northerner. At least you know where you are with Rowan. And he's not obnoxious, he was just having a go at you for messing with my foxes. Rowan always had my back.' She remembered him touching it, and a shiver ran through her.

She could practically hear Henry frowning.

'But yes, he can be rude,' she admitted, when he said nothing. 'And *bloody* difficult. All those things. But he didn't take my brothers.'

'Seriously?' said Henry. He drew the word out. 'I've known him for five minutes and I wouldn't leave a child of mine with him.'

'His dog died. It's so sad. He's got no one.' Now she felt teary again. Tired and emotional. 'Well, he's got a new puppy, but George was so adorable.'

'No one?' said Henry. 'I'd say he's in bed with his editor right now.'

Emma breathed in sharply. She'd been so busy remembering his words, his touch, the look in his eyes – trying to interpret it all – that she'd almost forgotten his date for the evening. *Was* he spending the night with her? If she was up from London, she'd no doubt be staying in York. Rowan probably wouldn't want to be driving back to Wensleydale on a freezing January night, so ... A one-night stand? More than that?

The realisation was horrible. She supposed she'd been expecting him to live like a monk, up there on the remote moorlands. It was probably a foolish, unrealistic notion. He'd managed to have two relationships – that she knew of – when he was a teacher at Middleham. Now he had a life as a successful writer.

And he'd ended things with Emma, nearly two years ago. Unequivocally. Why couldn't she let it go?

*Where's your pride?*

By February, Emma was wondering why she'd ever agreed to move to Yorkshire. The northern winter was relentless. Today, she was on a mission to draught-proof her old house. There was central heating, the walls and roof had been insulated, all the windows had double glazing, but somehow it was always a challenge to keep warm. Other than to visit the compost bin, she hadn't been in her garden for weeks. There was no point in hanging out washing – often it just froze on the line.

It was a Saturday morning, and as she knelt on the floor, trying to attach a seal to the kitchen door, Perkin appeared in front of her, flicking his little tail in her face. Then he sat down on the draught excluder and fixed her with his steely gaze. It was as if Henry had installed a substitute all-seeing pair of blue eyes for when he wasn't around.

Henry was at Montfort Grange for the weekend, as his mother was holding a political fundraising banquet tonight. Both Lady M and Emma were happy for her co-host to be Henry. He'd tried to persuade Emma to attend, but she just wanted to cosy up with Perkin by herself. This week marked the two-year anniversary of Freddie and Riv's disappearance, and increasingly she was feeling she'd let them down. She wanted to take some time to think about them, to hold them in her heart. And to think more on her investigation.

It was ramping up. She'd heard back from Mr Pickford, and he'd agreed to let her meet Freddie and Riv's closest friends, as well as him and Meena.

'Shall we forget this?' she said to Perkin. She dropped her DIY stuff back into the pink ladies' tool kit Henry had rather patronisingly bought her – but it *was* useful – and went to put the kettle on.

As it boiled, she checked her phone, and saw that she had a reply email from the woman who'd reported seeing Freddie and Riv near Aysgarth. Jody Platt said she'd be happy to talk to Emma, and included her phone number.

Emma brought up Google maps. It was an hour and a half away, not far from Middleham. The weather forecast was good – no threats of snow or freezing rain or freezing fog or any of those other fun driving challenges Yorkshire enjoyed throwing in the path of the unsuspecting weekend motorist. She quickly made up her mind and dialled Jody Platt's number.

As she drove the familiar road to Middleham, memories came at her thick and fast. She put music on her stereo – upbeat songs to try and lift her mood – but it was hard.

She passed a sign: *Aysgarth 2*.

*Did you cycle down this road? Where were you going?*

She reached the Platts' address, a neat bungalow in the village, and was welcomed in. It took a while for Jody and her husband, Malcolm, to relax, as they fussed about with the best china and a chocolate cake clearly made in readiness for a visit from Belle and Teddy Snow's daughter. She did her best to put them at ease, admiring Jody's collection of Beatrix Potter figurines, and sharing how those characters had helped spark her love of wildlife.

Finally they were comfortable enough for Jody to relate how she'd seen two fair-haired boys on bikes wobbling along the road towards the waterfalls. They'd been wearing backpacks; she remembered because they'd looked top heavy.

'What could they have been carrying?' Emma wondered out loud.

'In February – extra clothes, probably,' said Malcolm.

Emma questioned them further: did they look as if they knew where they were going? Did they look happy? Worried?

'Tired,' Jody said. 'Like they'd had enough of riding along in the cold.'

*So why didn't they turn round? Go home?*

'What time was this?'

'About ten thirty, eleven o'clock.'

*Way before they were meant to meet up with Rowan for their walk.*

Emma learned nothing new, but was glad she'd come. She'd spoken with someone who'd seen her brothers after Rowan had. That made her feel a little happier.

'Is there anywhere else around here that a pair of boys might have wanted to go to on an adventure?' she asked. 'Other than the falls?'

'Not unless they're into cheese,' said Malcolm.

'Cheese?'

'Wensleydale. There's the creamery; it's open to the public.'

Wallace and Gromit came into Emma's mind. Wensleydale was Wallace's favourite cheese in *A Close Shave*, a film the boys had loved. It was a fun thought, but somehow she couldn't see them wanting to cycle all the way to a cheese factory, just because they loved Wallace and Gromit.

But Wensleydale was ringing bells for another reason – Rowan's farm. Her stomach quickly tied itself in knots as she wondered whether to get in touch.

Thanking Jody and Malcolm for their time and their delicious tea and cake, Emma returned to her car and sent a text. If she got a reply within the usual two-year timeframe, it would be a miracle.

I'm in Aysgarth doing an interview. Any chance of meeting Teddy? And you of course.
Ems x

It took only a minute.

Dalehead Farm off A684. Shut the gate x

She grinned to herself, tapped the address into her satnav, and set off.

Even in February, the scenery was breathtaking. Beyond the drystone walls bordering the road, beneath big skies where blue came and went between scudding clouds, was the wide valley of the River Ure, the land rising to flat-topped moorlands iced with snow.

The satnav told her she'd reached her destination. 'Thank you,' she replied. 'I most certainly have.'

An old sign beside an open gate read *Dalehead Farm*. She drove through then hopped out to close the gate. After the heated insides of her little Mini, the cold air was a shock, but it was scented with a mix of frozen earth and something indefinable, something ... country. It was intoxicating. Or maybe it was just the thought of what – who – was waiting for her.

As she pushed the gate shut, she noticed something else on the sign. It was only small, and it had been scrubbed out, but she could still make out the letters: *PAEDO*.

As she stared at it, imagining how it must have made Rowan feel, a border collie came running up, followed by a middle-aged man in a flat cap. 'I'll shut that for you,' he said.

Emma quickly whipped into journalist mode. 'Thank you.' She gave him a wide smile. 'Do you live locally?'

He looked at her with suspicion. 'This is my land.'

'Oh! I thought it belonged to Mr Bosworth. What a lovely dog.' She bent down to pat it.

'Are you from the papers? Cos if you are, you can bugger off.'

'I'm a friend of Rowan's. My name's Emma Snow.' She waited for the penny to drop.

His eyebrows went up. 'By 'eck. Sorry, lass. It's just – I keep an eye out. He gets unwanted visitors from time to time.' His eyes fell briefly on the sign. 'Local morons doing graffiti and whatnot.'

'That's awful. Rowan's a good friend to our family.'

'And to me. Known him since 'e were a lad.' The farmer hooked the gate.

*This man lived next door to Rowan when he was a boy.*

'Did you lease the land after Rowan's parents left?'

'Aye. Good riddance to 'em. Father was a reet piece of work. Dick by name, Dick by nature. And his mother was . . . ' He shook his head. 'Not my place. You'll be getting cold. You'd best get on.'

'Yes, I suppose so. Nice to meet you, Mr . . . '

'Haworth.' He frowned. 'Sorry about your brothers. Terrible business. Rowan's . . . '

'He loved them, I know. Mr Haworth, I work for the *Chronicle*. I want to help clear Rowan's name, but until the boys are found . . . one way or another . . . '

'Aye. Well, I wish you luck. He's a good lad.'

She drove on down the track, and soon a low, rambling farmhouse came into view. It was a less bleak and windswept version of the one she'd imagined – made of stone, with tiny sash windows and a slate roof, a big porch with an ancient wooden door. Smoke was puffing out of a chimney, and off to the side was a large barn falling into disrepair. There was an area of grass bordered by a stone wall, beyond which were winter fields, crusted with frost and ice.

The front door opened as she switched off the engine, and Rowan appeared, dressed in a thick Aran sweater and jeans. He leaned against the door jamb as she approached.

'Hello,' she called. 'I just met your neighbour. He seems like a nice man.'

'Yep. See, I have friends.' He grinned. 'Welcome to my cave.'

He moved aside to let her pass, but she stopped, looking up at him. 'It's so nice to be here,' she said, then she reached up and kissed his cheek. 'I don't care how many times you try to see me off, I'm going to tell you I miss you and *I'll* always be your friend too.'

He gave her a small, lopsided smile. 'You could stop being so nice to me. I treated you like shit. Come and have a cuppa, then we'll test your Yorkshire mettle on a walk round the fields.'

He pushed open a door from the dark hallway and she was hit by the warmth of a log fire crackling in the open fireplace. She looked around her, and let out a sigh of pleasure. 'Ooh, Rowan. This is lovely!'

Those images she'd had, of him huddled in a dark, stone, farm-house kitchen with hideous ancient furniture ... instead here were low oak beams, rich red rugs, a battered but inviting sofa with a woollen throw and cushions, armchairs pulled up to the fireside, and books. So many books. Bookshelves completely covered one wall, and there were more in a bookcase. Over by the window was a writing desk with a computer and an old-fashioned lamp.

The room smelled of wood smoke, and stretched out in front of the fire was a young black Labrador.

'Hello, Teddy.' She crouched down to pat him, then looked around her again. 'I thought it'd be all cold and dark, but ... '

'It was. Some of it still is. But this room – fire, dog, books. All you need in life, right, Teddy?' He patted the dog, then patted Emma's head. 'And the occasional visit from your best friend in life.'

She looked up at him. 'Is that what we are now?'

'Milk? Sugar?' He went to leave the room.

'I'm your best friend and you don't even know how I take my tea.'

'Not too strong. A splash of milk. No sugar because you're already sweet enough and then some.' He disappeared.

She sat down on the edge of an armchair, holding her hands out to the fire, enjoying the warmth.

He returned with two mugs of tea and sat down opposite. The firelight flickered on his face.

'I love this room so much.'

'So you said.' He smiled. 'Knew you would.'

Her heart ... she was trying, and failing, to stop it doing the thing again.

A trophy on the mantelpiece caught her eye – a dog rose, carved out of wood. She got up for a closer look: *Yorkshire Book of the Year*.

'Hey – congrats on this,' she said, over her shoulder.

He came to stand by her side, and her heart began to race. He was so close; he was going to touch her.

But instead, he reached past her and picked up something tucked behind an old clock – a folded sheet of white paper. 'Look,' he said, passing it to her.

HAPPY BIRTHDAY ROWAN

The letters were each in a different-coloured felt-tip pen, the *HAPPY BIRTHDAY* across the top, and the ROWAN down the side of the home-made card, each letter starting a word:

Rambunctious

Orsome

Wonderful

Amazing

Nice

In the space to the right was a sketch of a wild-haired Rowan and a badly drawn black dog.

A lump formed in her throat as she opened it up.

Happy Birthday Rowan

Don't do anything we wouldn't do! That doesn't really leave much, ha ha!

Love from Freddie and Riv (and George) xx

She closed it. 'Rambunctious?' she said, her voice catching.

'It was a word I used to describe them. I was trying to increase their vocabulary.'

She put the card back, then turned to him, tears in her eyes. *Please hold me, Rowan.*

Instinctively he moved towards her, then stopped and awkwardly rubbed her arm. 'Maybe I shouldn't have shown you. Sorry.'

'I'm glad you did.' She sniffed, wiping her tears away.

He bent down to stroke Teddy. 'Why did you want to see me?'

She took some deep breaths. 'Why? You just said I was your best friend.'

'But you said you wanted to see me. About the boys.'

'Right. Yes.' She sat down in the chair and picked up her tea. 'I'm trying to get a picture, of that last day. I visited one of the people who spotted them near Aysgarth. At around mid morning, this woman said. They had backpacks; they looked heavy. What could have been in them?'

Rowan sat down opposite her and leaned forward, his elbows on his knees, his hands wrapped round his mug. 'Lots of food, probably. They were always on the scrounge from the kitchens.'

'Right. And when you saw them, they didn't look ... I don't know. Shifty. Like they were up to something?'

He thought for a moment. 'No, not really. Going to come clean and say I was thinking on my plot, so I was kind of dismissive, told them to come back later and we'd take George out.'

'And around that time – nothing out of the ordinary? Nothing to give you a clue as to what they were planning?'

His face darkened a little. 'You think I haven't thought about this?'

'No, I mean yes, of course you have. It's just ... '

He was growing restless, she could sense him shutting down again.

'Finish your tea,' he said. 'Let's go for a walk.'

Teddy lifted his head at the sound of the magic word.

'C'mon boy.' Rowan stood up and headed out of the room.

Emma shook her head a little. She needed to tread carefully.

They walked across a field, ice crunching underfoot. Their breath formed clouds in front of their faces, and they shoved their hands deep into their jacket pockets. She noticed him keeping his distance.

The path led alongside a small woodland. 'Badger sett,' he said, pointing to an unruly mound of earth. 'Ems, you should come out here one evening when the weather's warmer. There's foxes in there too. And Haworth's involved in this barn owl project. They're usually flying around, at dusk.'

'It sounds magical.'

'The local hunt wants to get at the foxes, but if they try it . . . '

'Kill them.'

'Yes. Bastards.' She loved the way he said it, the short sharp 'a'. She laughed, and playfully put an arm around him. 'Rowan Bosworth, my soul brother.'

He glanced quickly at her, frowning, then increased his stride, breaking free.

Back at the farm, warming up by the fire, he was quiet. She got the distinct impression he wanted her to leave. *Why?*

'I suppose I should be heading off – long drive back.'

'Be careful, the roads will be icing over when it gets dark.' He looked away from her, into the flames.

His whole demeanour had changed. Again.

*Why are you like this?*

She stood up; he stayed where he was, and she stopped by his chair. She couldn't help it – she reached out and put a hand on his shoulder. 'Rowan—'

'Your Henry – seems like a decent enough bloke, though I went to school with a million of him.'

She didn't remove her hand. 'He's nice, yes. But Rowan . . . ' She swallowed. 'He's not you.'

He shook his head. 'Leave it, Ems.'

She didn't understand. She could feel it, the pull between them, stronger than ever. It wasn't one-sided, she knew it wasn't.

'Why, Rowan? Why did you finish it?'

'Fuck's sake, Ems. You need me to spell it out?' He stood up abruptly.

'I know what happened,' she said, her face inches from his.

'What?' His dark eyes flew to hers, and there was fear in them. What had he thought she meant?

'I talked to Jane Warwick. I wanted to be sure Neville's accusations of emotional abuse were unfounded.'

'You saw Jane?'

'She told me what happened, with Neville. How it all affected Abigail. She says Neville's a liar, a narcissist. None of it was your fault.'

He raked a hand through his hair. 'But it was. I should never have left Abigail alone with Teddy. He wasn't thriving, she couldn't feed him properly. She was ... ' His voice caught, and he shook his head. 'And you wonder why I send you back to your charming, unfucked-up Henry?'

She held his gaze, kept her voice level. 'You let me close, just for a while. You asked me to wait for you, and then you finished it. So yes, I *do* ask why you can't be with me.'

He looked away. 'You need to leave me be,' he said after a moment. 'You need to let me go.'

'Are you with Siobhan?'

'What? No, of course not. Siobhan's with Lottie.'

She breathed out. 'Oh, I see.'

He looked at her again. 'Henry'll give you a nice life. That's what I want for you.'

She shook her head. 'That dinner we went to, after the awards. We talked about bathroom fittings. I got drunk. Seeing you again knocked me for six.'

He gave a small laugh. 'You and me both, Ems. Look ... ' He paused. 'I don't want to cut you off. I don't.' He raised a hand, as if to touch her, but dropped it again. 'I'd love us to be friends. Seriously, I meant that. But only friends. Stop asking for more. I can't give it to you.'

They would never just be friends. And in spite of his words, she still didn't understand why. But she couldn't ask again. He'd firmly shut that door.

'Okay, Rowan. Yes, friends. If that's what you want.' Their eyes met, and there was so much left unsaid. Then he nodded.

She went through to the hallway and opened the front door, stepping outside.

'Drive carefully.'

She turned round. 'Bye. There's no point in asking you to call me, because I know you won't.'

# Chapter Thirty-One

Over the following weeks, Emma was too busy reporting on local stories to move her investigation forward. While it was frustrating, she was grateful Henry was now putting her on meatier assignments. A scandal erupted over the finances of a local charity, and he asked her to cover it.

'Ed's pissed off,' he said, as they sat in his office. 'He wanted it, but I think you'll be more clear-thinking on this than him. He knows the players too well; you'll be more—'

'. . . objective,' she finished.

He grinned. 'Yes, that. Go to it, Emma, but tread carefully. The Yorkshire mafia's fingerprints are all over it.'

'What? Seriously?'

'More commonly known as the Rotary Club. Watch out for umbrellas.'

She laughed. 'Funny.'

'I do my best. Off you go then, my little bloodhound.'

Then Susie asked her to take an in-depth look at changing farming practices in the light of recent EU carbon-reduction initiatives, for a special edition on the environment. It was Emma's area of expertise, but she needed to bring herself up to speed on the new laws and regulations, which meant lots of time-consuming research.

So it was late April by the time she made it to Middleham. In the meantime she'd heard nothing from Liz Shore, and nothing from Rowan – of course.

Memories piled in as she pulled into the gravel area in front of the building. She glanced over at Middleham Tor, partially hidden behind a veil of grey mist.

Mr Pickford welcomed her into his study, and she took out her blue notebook. The friendly man who'd fawned over Belle was now awkward and fidgety. He was having trouble meeting her eye. No doubt the publicity surrounding the boys' disappearance had been deeply damaging for the school.

And he had nothing new to say. All she wrote down was the date, and *waste of time* as a little doodle at the side of the page.

'Sorry I can't be of more help,' he said. 'If it's any consolation, the school has considerably tightened its processes, particularly with regards to checking teachers' credentials before employing them.'

Emma looked him in the eye. 'Perhaps it would also be useful to be aware of any children leaving the grounds in the many hours between breakfast and dinner.'

Mr Pickford cleared his throat and went over to the door, opening it and calling, 'Portman, Desai – come.'

The boys were two of Freddie and Riv's closest friends.

'Mr Pickford, I'd like to speak to them alone, if you're happy with that. I want the boys to feel free to discuss anything with me.'

The headmaster nodded. 'Of course.' He went to leave, then stopped. 'Your brothers' schoolwork. I arranged for it to be sent to your mother, but I believe Mr Bosworth kept some of it. You're entitled to ask for that back, if you want it.'

She remembered Belle saying a box had arrived from the school with their belongings. It had been a tough moment for her.

'I see. Thank you.'

He left the room, and two boys came in, one with big brown eyes, the other with floppy fair hair and a cheeky smile.

'Hello there,' she said. 'I'm Emma – Freddie and Riv's sister. Thanks for coming to talk to me. What are your names?'

'Ajay,' said one. 'I'm Freddie's best friend.' She loved his use of the present tense.

'I'm Miles,' said the other. 'I saw you before. Mr Bosworth said you were his girlfriend.'

'Oh yes! I remember. He was joking.'

'Is Mr Bosworth coming back?' asked Miles.

'Maybe one day,' said Emma. 'He misses you guys, I'm sure.'

'We miss him too,' said Ajay. 'He was the coolest teacher.'

Emma smiled. 'Yes. Well, I'm sure you've been asked this question a zillion times before, but I'm trying to find out what on *earth* those two scallywags were up to when they went off on bikes on that Sunday morning.' She paused. Her notebook was in her lap.

The boys looked at each other, then back at her. Ajay shrugged. 'Yeah, the police asked us. So did Mr Pickford. We have no idea. They were always sneaking out; I *told* them they'd get into trouble. Freddie was the worst, Riv just followed him.'

'You say they were always sneaking out,' she said, sitting back in her chair and crossing one leg over the other. 'Where did they go?'

'Up the hill, sometimes,' said Miles, nodding in the direction of the tor. 'Exploring in the woods. To the sweet shop in the village, maybe.'

'And their *project* stuff,' said Ajay. 'It was like their code word for breaking out. We're going to work on our *project*.' Both boys laughed.

Emma's interest was piqued. 'What sort of project would that have been?'

'They were quite into nature stuff,' said Miles. 'Always collecting things. Like acorns and feathers, and Riv found a dead woodpecker one time – he hid it under his bed but it stank.'

'Owl pellets,' said Ajay. 'They look like dried dog poo. They collected them. Weird.'

'They were into owls and other birds and saving animals,' said Miles. 'Especially foxes. Their mum's that singer who does things with Greenpeace. Belle Snow.'

'Yeah, she's my mum too,' said Emma.

'Oh. Course,' said Miles.

Emma wrote down: *nature collection – birds, owl pellets, foxes.*

She talked to them some more, and enjoyed hearing about Freddie and Riv's pranks, the things they'd got up to in the dorms. It tugged at her heart, and yet it made her happy to learn they'd been popular and had enjoyed life here. They hadn't been running away from something horrible, hadn't been bullied.

The last person to come to the headmaster's study was Meena, the school counsellor. She was wearing jeans and a pink sweatshirt with the words *Tea is the Answer to Most Problems* on the front.

'Lovely to meet you, Emma!' she said. 'I hear you met my son.'

'Did I?'

'Ajay.'

'Oh! I didn't realise. What a nice boy.'

'Yes, he is.' She sat down next to Emma, and put a hand over hers. 'When something like this happens, it makes you stop for a minute, appreciate what you have.'

Emma swallowed, and met her kind gaze. 'Meena, I wondered if there was anything you could share with me, from your discussions with Mr Bosworth – Rowan – when you were counselling him. Anything that might help me get a clearer picture of what happened.'

'Absolutely not,' Meena said firmly. 'Sorry.'

Emma tried again. 'I'm looking into everything, as the police aren't actively pursuing the case and it's difficult for my family, not knowing what happened to my brothers. Also you may have noticed some laying of blame in the press, based on allegations by Rowan's former manager, Neville Warwick, who ... ' She paused, wondering how much Meena knew.

Meena looked uncomfortable.

'Neville kept most of Rowan's money,' Emma went on, 'and accused him of mentally abusing his daughter – Rowan's wife. And ... they lost their ... ' She stopped, hoping Meena would pick up where she'd left off.

Meena nodded. 'Their baby. Yes. And then Rowan lost his wife.

He was carrying a huge burden of guilt, we talked it through . . . he was doing so well. But Emma, I don't think any of this is relevant to your brothers' disappearance, no matter what his manager said.'

*Thank you!*

'No. I don't think it's relevant, either.'

'We all miss Rowan,' said Meena, shaking her head. 'He was a great asset to the school. It's a terrible shame. If his name was cleared, maybe he could come back.'

'Maybe,' said Emma. 'That's the other reason I'm looking into everything. For his sake. To clear his name.' She stopped again, letting the silence stretch out, waiting for Meena to fill it.

'Do you know about his parents?' Meena said, finally.

'The Bosworths? Not great, I hear?'

'No, his real ones,' said Meena.

*Oh!*

Emma kept her expression impassive. 'No, he hasn't discussed that with me. I know he was adopted.'

'He was trying to find out about them, as part of his therapy. I thought it might help him deal with this whole rejection complex he has, if he knew why he'd been given up.'

'And did he find out?' Emma asked, her heart in her mouth.

'I don't know. You'd have to ask him yourself.'

'I will.'

She wrote down: *Real parents – did R find out?*

'I saw him a couple of months ago,' said Emma. 'He's doing okay. I think he misses teaching, but his writing's going great.'

'Oh, he's *so* talented,' said Meena, her face lighting up. 'We all love his books!' Her smile faded. 'He's very much missed. When you see him, tell him to come back for a visit.'

Somehow, Emma doubted Mr Pickford would be on board with that.

*Well*, she thought as she drove home later, *I haven't found out much, but what I do know is that the people who get to know Rowan properly – Meena, Freddie and Riv, me, Dad, Mum, Jane, Abigail . . . love him to bits.*

And the rest could go take a running jump.

Back home that evening, she opened the blue notebook again and wrote: *Project??*

May in Yorkshire was glorious. Finally, the hedgerows burst out their blossoms, bluebells carpeted the woodlands and colourful hanging baskets brightened the streets of York.

Much as Emma dreaded going there, Montfort Grange was achingly beautiful, nestled in its green valley, sheep grazing the hills, the fields criss-crossed by drystone walls.

Unlike the surrounding countryside, Lady M hadn't managed to shake off winter, and was frosty as ever. Henry kept the conversation going, and it helped that there were, as usual, extra guests for Sunday lunch. There was much talk of the Olympics, due to take place in London later in the year. The Olympic torch had arrived in Cornwall and would be passing through York next month.

The vicar and his wife were here again, and Caroline asked if there had been any further news on Emma's brothers.

'Nothing much,' said Emma. 'Though I'm really hoping something will turn up. The police have put me in touch with people I can speak to. I'm writing a . . . I guess you'd call it a "*Where we're at*" piece for the *Chronicle*.'

She sensed Lady M's laser glare.

'You didn't tell me about this, Henry,' she said, turning to her son. 'Is that a sensible use of company time? Emma's unlikely to be . . . clear-sighted on the subject, and the paper's relationship with the police is of utmost importance. Implying they're not doing their job properly will set that back.' She drew her eyebrows together. 'Really, Henry, I can't believe—'

'Emma feels it's something she needs to do,' he interrupted. 'She's doing it more or less in her spare time.' He smiled, attempting to diffuse the situation. 'Not that I let her have much of that.'

*He doesn't need to explain it to you!*

'Well clearly it must have been the master.' Lady M's gaze swept across everyone at the table. Her voice brooked no argument. 'He's the obvious suspect. The whole business of motive, opportunity and means. And I hear he's quite an obnoxious man.'

*Obnoxious man.* The words were familiar. Emma glanced at Henry as she felt the heat rising up her neck.

'*Motive?*' Emma said, trying to keep her voice steady. 'Why would—'

'He was part of that fast crowd of your father's, Emma.' Lady M deigned to look at her. 'And that dreadful libertine Neville Warwick. Drugs, homosexuality ... God knows what other perverted sexual practices. I saw Bosworth's play, too. The devil was most certainly in them all.' She stabbed at a lump of red meat on her plate. 'There's no doubt in my mind that Bosworth abused your brothers. Perhaps they finally plucked up the courage to seek help, and Bosworth had no option other than to silence them.'

'Mother, please ... ' murmured Henry.

Emma, felt sick. *Enough!* She put down her knife and fork with a loud clatter, making Caroline jump. She opened her mouth to respond, but Lady Madeline wasn't finished yet.

'He'd be behind bars if they could only discover what he's done with their bodies.' She shook her head a little. 'And to think, I considered sending Henry to that school.' Lady M's eyes fell on the vicar. 'There are dark forces at work.'

The vicar nodded slowly.

Emma's hands were now in her lap, and she was digging her nails into her palms. The silence around the table was deafening, and she had a sudden impulse to scream, to break it. The worst part about this was, she sensed Lady M's argument had made sense to them all. They'd probably read those things about Rowan's past in the *Chronicle*, too.

She took some deep breaths and looked at Henry. His expression was difficult to read. For his sake she'd try to remain calm. *Objective.*

She fixed her gaze on Lady M. 'Rowan was only seventeen

when my father discovered him,' she began. 'Just a schoolboy. When Neville became Rowan's manager he completely controlled him financially, so he couldn't leave, and yes, Neville was a terrible influence. And my father could have done more to stop that.'

There was just the sound of cutlery chinking on plates. Emma continued to stare Lady M down. 'But Rowan wasn't ... like them. He was in love with Neville's daughter, Abigail, and he married her, against Neville's wishes. Rowan's been maligned in the press, unfairly so.'

She glanced at Henry.

'Rowan loved my brothers dearly – he'd known them most of their lives. He'd never have ... touched them. He's devastated by all this. I need to find out what really happened. I intend to.'

Lady M's eyes were like flints. 'Birch?' she said eventually.

'Yes, Lady Madeline.'

'Could you bring more gravy?'

She turned her gaze back to Emma. 'I'll discuss this further with Henry later.'


'Mother wants me to kill your investigation,' said Henry, as they drove back to York.

Emma bristled. 'Why? Does she think you're indulging me? Does she not realise this is going to be an important piece for the *Chronicle*?'

'She thinks you're wasting company money. She called you "deluded". And you know what, Emma?' He glanced over at her. 'She knows everyone, so she's probably basing that on something solid, as well as on her own instincts. There are still no other potential suspects, right?'

Emma sighed. 'No. None. But it wasn't Rowan.'

'And how do you know that, for sure?'

'I just do.'

'Well – that's likely to stand up in court.'

'It won't go to court. Not unless ... '

'Someone finds them.'

All at once, Emma was overwhelmed with it all.

*Freddie, Riv. Where are you?*

She was carrying on, no matter what Lady M thought. She'd do it in her own time if she had to.

But the next day, Henry quietly told her to continue, and apologised for his mother's Sunday lunchtime tirade.

She made notes; brainstormed. She pored over the map, going over every word of the conversations she'd had.

There were question marks against the 'school project' the boys had made up to explain their escapes, and . . . Rowan's parentage. But what could that have to do with anything?

It was a warm June evening, and Emma was walking from the office to Henry's apartment. He'd been out all day at meetings and was cooking for them tonight.

He was already home, and had left the front door open.

'Shoes!' he called, as she walked across the carpet.

'Sorry!' Every time.

Henry was at the kitchen worktop, on which sat a silver bucket holding a bottle of expensive champagne. The kitchen was immaculate – but then Henry believed in clearing up as you go. Emma had never understood how that was possible. She sniffed the air, but there was no hint of what was for dinner.

'This all looks a bit fancy,' she said, eyeing the champagne.

'You don't know what today is?' he said, expertly popping the cork. He poured two glasses and held one out.

She thought hard. Should she know? 'Can't say that I do. Is that bad of me?'

'It's a year to the day since you made the move north. Happy one year as a northerner, love of my life.'

'Is it?' She clinked her glass against Henry's.

A whole year. She wasn't sure how she felt about that. What had she achieved since she got here?

She'd bought a house. Well, Belle had bought her a house. It was now fully painted and decorated and she loved it. She had an adorable cat, though Perkin was getting very up himself. He insisted on lying between her and Henry in bed. Henry had taken to calling him The Usurper.

She was writing longer pieces, including more on the environment. Two had been followed up by nationals.

But she'd achieved next to nothing as far as her missing brothers were concerned. She was unsure what to do next. Liz hadn't come back to her about Neville, and the only other loose ends were those dangling over Rowan.

*Rowan.* Of course, he hadn't been in touch. So much for the 'best friends' nonsense. As always, she missed him. And she wondered, had he found out about his background? And did that have any bearing on his state of mind?

The 'project'. She could ask him about that. She could ring, or text, but he wouldn't answer.

She could just turn up.

But would she be using the investigation as an excuse to keep in touch? Was she just being the stupid moth again? Unable to resist that flame, up there on the moors? Or did he really hold some key to a lock she hadn't yet identified?

Emma chided herself – she was focusing on the wrong man. She wound her free arm round Henry's neck, standing on tiptoes to kiss him, and as she did, she properly registered the smart trousers and crisp white shirt.

'Should I have gone home and put a frock on?'

'Yes,' said Henry. 'Look at the state of you, Snow.' She was wearing her work jeans and a stripy blouse. 'Just as well I assigned Susie to the case.'

'Susie?'

'Go take a look in the bedroom. Hope you like.' He looked at his watch. 'You've got half an hour, Cinderella. Get to it.'

On the bed lay a beautiful sequinned dress. It was flesh-toned with shoestring straps that crossed over on the cutaway back. Alongside was a pair of glittery high heels with a note tucked in – Susie's writing: *Go girl!* In a little bag was some lacy underwear, cosmetics, and hair tools.

Well, this was all rather thrilling and mysterious, but . . . *All this, because I've been here a year?* A suspicion sidled in.

Henry's reaction when she emerged confirmed Susie had got everything spot on. 'Oof,' he said, opening his eyes wide. 'Just in case I was forgetting I'm dating the most beautiful woman in Yorkshire.'

'Why thank you. Where are we going?'

'The only place worthy of such a princess.'

The satnav gave the game away. They took the scenic route to Castle Howard, along winding lanes beneath the wide summer sky. At the touch of a button, the Maserati's roof quietly flipped back so they could fully enjoy the soft greens and golds of the countryside.

'Sheriff Hutton,' said Emma, as they passed through a pretty village. 'Why does that ring a bell?'

'The castle, probably,' said Henry. 'Not much left of it now.' They glimpsed a ruin, beyond the church. 'It was one of Richard's.'

'Which Richard?'

'Crookback. He parked his nieces here when Henry Tudor's invasion was imminent. Some of the wilder rumours even say the two princes were here too.'

Arriving at Castle Howard, they swept up a wide avenue and stopped in front of the magnificent building – even more spectacular than Montfort Grange (just). A man in uniform greeted them and took them inside, carrying the overnight holdall Henry had packed.

Dinner was in a private dining room dripping with crystal, exuberant floral arrangements and gilt. The room could comfortably have accommodated a royal banquet.

'How on earth did you swing this?' asked Emma, as they started on their entrées. Classical music from hidden speakers softened the cavernous echo of her voice.

'I know the owner,' Henry said. 'We were at Eton together.'

'Of course you were.' Emma thought for a moment, about Henry's 'normal'. He was a fully signed-up member of the rich and powerful. This evening was spectacularly romantic, and yet ... she was reminded of her childhood, when she'd lived a slightly lesser version of this life – country houses, staff, spreads in *Hooray!* magazine, picturing Belle, Teddy, and their Snow-clone children in whatever 'gracious home' they happened to be in when a new Woodville album or Teddy film needed publicising. When all Emma had wanted was a normal life.

'What is it?' he said, catching her look.

She picked up her smile. 'This is amazing. And Henry – thanks for letting me carry on with my investigation, in spite of your mother.' She put a hand over his. 'I do love you.'

*I do, I do.*

He smiled back. 'I love you too. And I say it more. You should say it more.'

'I will.'

Later, after they'd polished off the champagne, Henry asked, 'Ready for dessert?'

'I might bust out of this dress. But if you insist.'

Henry nodded to the waiter, and soon a spectacular cake with white and dark chocolate decorations was set down in front of them. In the middle were piped the words: *Marry Me.*

Emma's hand flew to her mouth. 'Oh my gosh!'

But she'd been anticipating this. Had she not, she wouldn't have dared call herself an investigative journalist.

She looked from the cake to Henry's face, then back to the cake, as she tried to untangle her feelings.

'There's a ring to go with the cake,' he said. 'And it's not an emerald one. But if you don't like it we can get you something else. Do you want to see?'

'Yes.' It felt like a practice answer.

He produced a box from his jacket pocket and opened it up. An enormous rock set in an ancient gold band flashed and twinkled in the candlelight.

'Jesus!' she exclaimed. 'That's ... '

'Quite old,' he finished. 'Family heirloom. Worth a fortune. I'll have to get it properly insured if you actually decide to wear it.'

'What else would I do with it?'

'A bank vault would be sensible. We can get you an everyday ring,' he said. There was a pause. 'So?'

And then she saw the uncertainty in his eyes. Her heart went out to him. He *was* lovely.

*But he's not Rowan.*

She dismissed that thought. Rowan was a no, a not ever. He wasn't even a friend, never mind a best one.

'Yes, Henry. Thank you so much for asking me. I'd love to marry you.'

'Oh my god, your mother,' she said later, as they lay in each other's arms in a sumptuous castle bedroom.

She felt the sigh resonate through his chest beneath her head.

'Honestly, Emma? I don't get it. Everyone loves you. *Everyone.* You're bright, you're kind, you're—'

'Keep going,' she said.

He laughed, then sighed again. 'I think it would be the same whoever you were. Though ... she does keep going on about Arabella Rees-Pocock. I don't know why she liked her so much.'

Arabella had been two before Emma.

'Probably because she had the correct number of surnames.'

'And she's an Olympic show jumper. And rides to hounds. Really, Emma, you could try harder.'

She chortled. 'Maybe it's time I got reacquainted with Stanley?'

'I'll buy you something bigger but just as winsome. Let's wait until Mother gets back before we announce our engagement.' Lady M was spending the summer in the South of France again. 'There'll be hell to pay if she's not the first to know.'

'Not even Belle?'

'Would you mind? Mother's back end of August.'

'So many weeks without seeing your mother. How will I cope?'

'Emma, you've met her four times. In how many years?'

'Fair point. Where will we live, Henry?' Emma hated the thought of giving up Gregory Lane. 'Can we live at mine?'

'We can talk about that. It's very small – might be better to rent it out, it'd bring in a decent sum. You can choose us somewhere bigger.'

Emma was quiet. How much of herself would she need to give up to become Henry's wife? She'd need to think this through, make sure that 'yes' was a one-hundred-per-cent yes. And she knew, in her heart, she needed to see Rowan again, before she locked herself into an 'I do'.

# Chapter Thirty-Two

Emma was taken by surprise when Rowan answered his phone. 'Ems. How's things?'

'Hi, Rowan! Well, this is a first. You actually picked up.'

'I'm bored as fuck. Just finished my latest book and I don't know what to do with myself. I might even take a holiday. How do you fancy a week in . . . Romania? Transylvania has a certain appeal.'

Emma snorted. 'Oh yes, you'd make a lovely vampire. Count me in.'

'What can I do for you?'

She drew a breath. 'Rowan, you said before, about seeing your place at dusk. If I promise to be totally one hundred per cent best friend and no awkward stuff, can I come? There are a couple of things I want to talk to you about but I promise not to . . . touch you, or anything.'

That hadn't come out quite as she'd intended.

He chuckled. 'A hands-off badger watch. Sure. This week works for me, if the bloody rain stops. So would next week, and the one after. Fuck me, I really need to get a life.'

Emma was aware that the happiness bubbling inside her was way out of proportion to the unusually positive vibes she was getting from Rowan.

'Friday? After work? I could be there by six if the traffic's not too bad.'

'That's way before dusk. I'll have to cook you something.'

'Works for me! I'll bring wine.'

'Okay, girl. Don't forget your wellies. And a camera. There's been a lot of action recently, especially owl action. Haworth's barn owls are breeding well.'

'Right! Super! See you Friday, then.'

She'd chosen Friday because Henry had a conference in Newcastle, and wouldn't be back until Saturday morning. It would be simpler that way.

The rain that had fallen steadily for the past weeks had finally stopped for breath, and it was a beautiful late-August evening as she drove through the Dales, the hills casting long shadows across the river valley. It probably wouldn't be dark until gone nine. That would give her three whole hours with Rowan. Dinner and wildlife watching. The prospect was delicious, and she couldn't keep the smile off her face as she sang along to Adele's 'Rolling in the Deep'. She wondered if Belle had met Adele yet. Emma would love to interview her.

As she shut the farm gate behind her, she saw Mr Haworth again, watching her from the far side of the field. He raised a hand and waved.

The front door was open, and she called out Rowan's name. Teddy appeared, wagging his tail, and she crouched down to greet him. 'Hello, sweetheart.' She put her arms round his neck. 'Look at you. I could gobble you up.'

'Thought you'd be veggie.' She looked up to see Rowan in shorts and T-shirt, a bottle of beer in his hand, leaning on the hall wall.

'Sort of,' she said, noticing his ponytail. *Ponytail?* 'I climb down off the fence occasionally, if it's ethical.'

'Ethical,' he said. 'Maybe I'll get you to read my manuscript again. I've been exploring a few boundaries. One person's ethics is another's unwarranted constraints.'

*Heh?*

'A bit heavy for a Friday night,' she said, passing him the bottle of wine she'd brought. 'But you know what? I love a bit of philosophical debate. Makes a change from *Did you remember to buy loo cleaner?*'

'Are you living with him now?' asked Rowan, sipping his beer.

'No, I've got my own place.' She realised how little he knew of her life. 'I wish you'd come and see it. It's in an old terrace – I think you'd like it. Henry's got a swanky riverside apartment. Fantastic views but ... so much white. So *very* neat and tidy. Not many books.' She paused, frowning. 'That was disloyal of me. It's beautiful.'

'But not really you?'

'I'm saying no more. I should be more loyal.'

'Loyalty is a great virtue. And I appreciate yours to me. Let's get you a wine.'

*He's in a weird mood tonight.*

He led her through to the kitchen, and once again she sighed with pleasure as she looked around. An ancient wooden table had been roughly painted pale blue; there was clutter everywhere, but it was homely, not disorganised. A large copper saucepan bubbled on an old range, and more pans hung from a rack on the ceiling. In the centre of the table, an unruly bunch of wild flowers was crammed into a Mason jar.

The only nod to modernity was a gleaming coffee machine. The sublime aroma of baking bread filled the air.

'What are we having?'

'Soup.' He picked up an opened bottle of red wine. 'Want to open yours, or will this do you?'

'The red would be lovely.' She grinned. 'Soup, Rowan?'

'I'm shit at cooking,' he said. 'But I know how to make bread. Don't judge me till you've tasted my bread. Also we have Wensleydale to go with it.'

'Of course.' She put on a Wallace voice. '*It's like no cheese I've ever tasted.*'

Rowan answered: '*Gromit, that's it! Cheese!*'

She laughed in delight. 'You can quote Wallace and Gromit?'

'Your brothers were fans.'

They went quiet. 'Here you go, Ems,' he said, handing her the wine.

'I'd love to read your new book,' she said, to fill the silence.

'It's a bit heavier than the other two.'

'More black?' she said, eyeing his black T-shirt.

'A bit of that. Shall we eat outside? You might get to see the barn owls hunting.'

'Oh, that would be lovely. Have we got time for a tour of your house first? I'd love to see the rest of it.'

'If you want.'

He led her up the stairs, and pushed open the door of a light, sunny bedroom. It was simply furnished; whitewashed, with a few animal prints randomly hung up on the walls. In the centre was a double bed, and she couldn't help picturing him in it, his dark curls on the pillow, his beautiful long eyelashes resting on his cheeks as he slept. She quietly blew out a breath.

'That's me now,' he said, then immediately moved on down the landing. 'This was me before.' He pushed open another door. The tiny, dark bedroom had been left as it was, with a single mattress, a worn rug, a battered chest of drawers and nothing much else. There was a shoebox on the drawers with *ROCKS* written on the top in black felt tip, and a pile of old books. A small, cracked window looked out over the barn.

Emma grabbed her moment. 'It must be strange, being here again, when you didn't have the happiest childhood. What was your mum like?'

'Useless.' He shut the door firmly. 'Let's go eat soup.' He ushered her ahead of him, back to the stairs.

'But she wasn't your real mum, so I guess—'

'She was.'

*What?*

They reached the bottom of the stairs, and she turned to face him. 'But I thought . . . '

'So did I. I looked into it. Meena thought it might help to

find my real mum. Turned out she *was* my real mum.' He ran a hand over his head. 'Jesus, Ems. What sort of a woman pretends she isn't your real mum? What sort of fucked-up society was it back then?'

'But your dad . . .'

'Not my real one. As he loved to remind me. Kind of explains why Mum put up with so much crap from him. He called her a slag a lot, too. But I think she probably was. Emma – move. The soup will be boiling away.'

She stood aside and he went into the kitchen, shooing Teddy out.

'Did you find out about your real dad?' she asked.

'No. She didn't name him on the birth certificate. Do us a favour, take the bread out. Oven mitt's around somewhere. And butter – in the fridge.'

Emma spotted the glove and opened the range, sliding out the loaf. It was golden and perfectly risen. She bent to sniff it. 'I can't believe you bake bread. Can I marry you?'

He was ladling soup into bowls. 'You promised not to ask me today.'

'Oh well, never mind. I'd never marry a man with a pony-tail, anyway.'

'You going to just stand there sniffing that bread? Butter, Ems. Bread knife in that drawer there. Breadboard over here. Follow me.'

She collected everything up and soon they were sitting at a wooden picnic table in a small garden at the back of the farmhouse, sipping soup which was every bit as delicious as the warm bread. Teddy lay at Rowan's feet.

'What is it?' she asked. 'Carrot?'

'And some other stuff. Thai things. Hey, go easy on the bread, save some for the cheese.'

She let out another sigh of pleasure – a long, dramatic one. The little garden was sheltered and warm, and looked out across the picturesque valley. Bird feeders hung from an old apple tree. It was quiet – just the gentle calling of the sheep on the hillsides.

'It's so lovely here,' she said.

'You're a proper northern lass now.' His smile was full of affection.

What that did to her. She knew . . . it was time to be honest. She had to be clear in her mind. Had to know for sure.

Now he was watching a pair of crows across the wall, fighting. 'God, those two buggers are always at it. The battle of Bosworth's field.'

She laughed. He was so . . .

'Rowan?'

He turned to look at her, and read her expression. His smile faded. 'Don't. You promised.'

'Henry's asked me to marry him.'

He looked away, back at the crows. After a while he said, 'So marry him. You're happy enough, right?'

'Happy enough,' she repeated. 'Is it wrong to want more than just enough?'

When he didn't reply, she decided to leave it be. Tonight was so perfect, she didn't want him doing that thing again. From warm to cold. Friendly and fun to brooding and prickly.

'Sorry,' she said, in a lighter tone. 'Blame it on the bread. In the face of such perfection, I needed to be sure I was making the right decision.'

He smiled. 'You'll be happy. You're a happy person. Ready for cheese?'

They finished their meal and set off across the fields. In spite of her resolution, she felt the tension mounting.

'I went to the school,' she said. 'I met a couple of the boys' friends. Ajay and Miles. They said you were the coolest teacher – Freddie and Riv used to say that too. And I saw Meena. Everyone misses you, apparently. She says to go visit.'

He stared ahead, scanning the fields, saying nothing.

'Do you think you'd go back? If ever this mystery is solved?'

'Don't know. Maybe.'

They'd reached the woodland. He was carrying a small

backpack, and took out a folded rug, spreading it on the ground, then produced the rest of the cheese and two bottles of beer.

She sat down, wrapping her arms around her knees, resting her chin on them.

'You only had one wine,' he said, 'you can probably have this too.' He flicked the tops off the beers. 'Now if you'd stop yacking we might see a badger.'

They sat in silence for a while. Dusk was thickening the air, and a stillness crept over the hills. A barn owl swooped low over the field in front of them, scouting the hedgerow. 'Oh!' Emma said quietly. Then as it disappeared, 'Dammit, you told me to bring a camera. I forgot.'

'You'll just have to come again.'

She turned to look at him. 'Can I?'

They were sitting close. Putting down his beer, Rowan leaned back on his elbows.

She sipped her drink, watching him. 'It was strange, being back in the headmaster's study. I sat right there on that same sofa. The one where you sat next to me and told me to keep writing. I was eleven.' She smiled fondly at him.

'You're a good writer now. A lot more confident.'

'You still read my stuff?'

'I've always read your stuff.'

She was aware of watching herself watching him. Like she was outside of her body. This pull between them. She was hyperaware of it, stronger than ever. Was it because she couldn't have him? Had never been able to have him? For whatever reason – because he had someone else; because he lived at the other end of the country. Because he felt responsible for her brothers' disappearance.

Why wouldn't he talk to her about it? She'd just told him Henry had asked her to marry him, and he'd cheered her on. And yet, she knew. He wanted her. She could see it in his eyes. He was denying himself, out of some misplaced loyalty to her family, to her. Because he thought he wasn't good enough, because he was too messed up.

She remembered Meena's words: *This whole rejection complex he has.*

Maybe he was too afraid of being hurt – the result of a loveless childhood, what he went through with Abigail and the baby. Neville. Damaged; unable to trust.

She'd broken through all this before. Could she do it again, so she could once and for all move on with her life?

'Stop staring at me.'

She smiled. 'You're too cute.' She was careful to keep it light. 'You're wasted, living up here like a monk.'

He looked up at her. 'Now you're flirting with me. Stop it.'

Before she could think too hard about it, she reached across and pulled out the elastic band that had slid down his ponytail, dropping it on the rug. Unable to resist, she gently combed her fingers through his hair, spreading it out across his uneven shoulders.

He froze, not moving, not saying a word.

She lay down on her side, propped up on one elbow, her face inches from his, and looked into his eyes. Lifting her hand, she stroked a finger down his cheek. 'Rowan,' she said softly, 'I can't marry Henry until we've had this conversation.'

Still he said nothing, didn't move. She leaned forward and kissed him, gently. He resisted, staying still, his eyes fixed on hers, his lips tight shut. But he didn't move away. She closed her eyes and kissed him again, and this time she didn't stop. She was aware of the cooling air, an owl hooting from across the field, the woolly rug beneath her on the stony ground. The remembered scent of Rowan, the taste of him. All her senses were heightened, a fire was moving through her.

At last his lips parted beneath hers, and she felt his hand on her head, holding her close as the kiss deepened, and the world faded away and there was only him.

Then all at once he pushed her back and rolled on top of her, pressing himself into her, kissing her hard; on the lips, then moving down to her neck, burying his face in her, and it felt as if her whole life had been leading here, to this moment of truth.

She gasped as a trail of heat followed his lips down her body. His knee nudged hers, and she opened her legs with a moan. 'Oh my god,' she breathed, as he slipped between them. 'At last ... '

But her words triggered something, and he sat up abruptly, dropping his head into his hands. 'You said you wouldn't,' he said into them. He sounded like a small boy. 'I can't. Please, for chrissakes, Ems, leave me alone.'

She felt like she might explode. With longing, with love; with frustration.

She lay on her back, her chest heaving. 'Why, Rowan?' She pushed herself up to sitting and grabbed his hand, pulling it away from his face. 'Look at me.'

She waited until he did.

'I love you,' she said. 'I've always loved you. I want to be with you.' Her voice was shaking with emotion. 'I don't know why you won't let me love you. I think you might love me too.'

There were tears in his eyes. 'Of course I love you. I've told you before that I love you. But so does your Henry, and you must love him, because you've been together all this time. You tell me he's nice ... ' He broke off and squeezed his eyes shut. 'Emma. I'm not nice. I'm not remotely nice.' Opening them again, he looked her in the eye. 'Everyone I love dies. You need to leave me alone.'

Then he stood up and pulled the rug, yanking at it. She moved off it, and he stuffed it in the backpack, then emptied their beers onto the earth and shoved the bottles in the backpack. Soon he was stomping back across the field.

She followed, and tried to mine her anger, to chase away the hurt – hurt at not being allowed to help him. At being shut out. At not being worth the effort of trying all over again to come to terms with his past.

'Fine,' she muttered. She headed straight for her Mini. 'I won't come again,' she said grimly, as he stood watching. Her pride was in shreds. 'You're a complete fuck-up, Rowan. I should have listened to you. To everyone, actually.'

She saw him flinch. He took a few steps towards her.

'I'm sorry,' he said, quietly. 'Speak to Belle.'

'What?'

'You need to speak to Belle. Tell her I know. Tell her ... I'm sorry.' He looked at her for a long moment, and she couldn't fathom his expression. It was as if something had been tortured out of him.

He turned on his heel and went into the house.

Emma couldn't sleep. She tossed and turned, reliving the evening. The kiss. The way it had felt. The *rightness* of it. The anger had gone, and now there was only deep hurt.

*Speak to Belle ... tell her I'm sorry.*

He was apologising for the boys again.

'Tell her I know.'

*What* did he know?

# Chapter Thirty-Three

Emma phoned Belle first thing, but it went to voicemail. She kept the tone of her message casual, not wanting her mother to think there was news on the boys.

As she made coffee in the kitchen, Henry's name flashed up on her phone.

'Hi! How was Newcastle?'

'Can I come over?'

'Oh! Sure, yes. Why don't you bring croissants or something. I haven't had chance to go shopping yet.'

There was a short pause. 'Right. See you in a bit.'

He'd sounded cool. It was as if he could read her mind. She felt the guilt weighing down on her. Was she a terrible person? She'd kissed Rowan – was she no better than that 'slag' of a mother of his?

The memory refused to give her a moment's peace. Along with the memories of those other kisses. Each had been a profound moment of beauty, as well as ... She took a breath. She'd never known desire like that. The want, the way her body seemed to dissolve with longing, every rational thought evaporating, demolished by this need; demolished by him. As if the two of them was the only thing that mattered in her life. Had ever mattered.

How could something so strong, so beautiful, be 'wrong'?

But it was. And he didn't want it.

As she sank into a chair, Perkin jumped onto her lap and she lifted him to her face, burying her nose in his fur. 'What can I do, little boy?' she asked. 'I don't know what to do.'

Henry arrived with a bag of pastries, and busied himself putting them on plates and brewing more coffee. He also washed up her plates and cups from Thursday and Friday. She watched him with a combination of exasperation, fondness and guilt.

He didn't speak as he moved about the kitchen, finally putting the coffee and food on the table.

'Yum,' said Emma, biting into a pain au chocolat.

'Why didn't you do a shop?' he said, looking her in the eye.

'Oh, I went out.' She thought quickly. She couldn't claim drinks after work, obviously. 'It was such a lovely evening, I went for a walk and then a swim.'

'Until past ten thirty?'

Her heart missed a beat. 'Huh?'

Those eyes.

'I came back from Newcastle early. Couldn't be bothered with the final dinner. You weren't here.'

'Oh. You should have waited.'

'Where were you?'

Emma was a terrible liar. Always had been.

She sighed. 'Oh god. I'm sorry. I wasn't being underhand and sneaky, I just knew you wouldn't like it.'

He raised his eyebrows, taking a bite of his croissant. He was playing it cool, she'd give him that. There was no huffing or Rowan-style anger.

'I went to Wensleydale. To see Rowan . . . ' It came to her. 'He's still got some of the boys' schoolwork – Mr Pickford told me we were entitled to get it back. I knew he'd never bother to send it, and I thought . . . well, I thought it was time I saw him, anyway. To be honest, how can I do a proper investigation without talking to the last person to speak to the boys?'

He didn't reply for a moment. He hadn't taken his eyes from hers; they were narrowed. 'And?'

'He made soup. And then we went looking for badgers, but we didn't see any. His farm's really nice. I thought it would be bleak and remote but it's in the dale; it's lovely.'

She was gabbling.

'I didn't find out anything useful, but it was good to talk. He still feels responsible for what happened.'

He gave her a look.

Had her eyes given anything away? She didn't know. Every time she said his name, pictured him, things happened to her heart.

Henry sipped his coffee, watching her. 'Mother's back from France. I thought we might go over to Montfort, share the news of our engagement. Are you ready for that?'

'Oh my god. I don't think so, Henry. I'll need a little time to work up to that one.'

He sighed. 'Okay. I'll go by myself.'

She was surprised he'd so readily agreed. 'Maybe next weekend? We could stay overnight. I could rekindle my relationship with Stanley?'

He didn't smile. 'Maybe. I'll see what she's up to.'

'Right, well. Thanks for bringing breakfast. I guess I should go do a shop.'

He took their plates and cups to the sink, rinsing them and putting them neatly in the dishwasher.

She put her arms round him from behind. 'I'm sorry, about not telling you where I was going. I knew you wouldn't like it.'

He turned, and his expression was dark. 'I want you to stay away from that man. For god's sake, Emma, he's probably a killer.'

For a moment she was speechless. 'Of *course* he's not!'

'You're deceiving yourself. Get real. The world's full of violence, and people doing terrible things. You should know – you work for a bloody newspaper. Not everyone is good. Not everyone cares about cute animals and saving the planet. Not everyone looks for reasons to excuse bad behaviour. He's rotten to the core. Has to be. You've read his books, you've seen the play. He's obviously crossed the line from imagining to doing. I don't want you seeing him again.'

Then, before she could respond, he kissed her, pulling her hard against him. There was no tenderness in it.

She pushed him away. 'You see? Why I didn't tell you? It's like we just go in circles, the same stupid conversation, over and over. Rowan did *not* take my brothers.'

'I'll call you tonight,' he said, and left.


Henry didn't call her that day, or the next. He appeared on her doorstep on Sunday evening, bearing a huge bunch of flowers.

His face was hidden as he stepped over the threshold. 'Sorry,' he said, from behind a sunflower. 'I've been spending cooling-down time.'

She opened her mouth to speak, but he carried on. 'Of course you had to see Bosworth. You're investigating. I was just horrified at the thought of you being up there alone with him.'

'They're beautiful, thank you.'

She'd had time to think things over – Henry had been horrible, but she'd also done wrong.

She went to take the flowers from him, but he pulled them back towards his face. 'Brace yourself.'

'What? Why?'

He lowered the flowers, revealing a livid bruise around his left eye, extending halfway down his cheek.

'Jesus, Henry! What happened?'

'Tudor chucked me off. A rock broke my fall.'

'Oh my god, are you okay?' It didn't look okay.

'Fine. Perhaps I should've taken Stanley. I wasn't on form. Too busy brooding instead of concentrating. I hate it when we row.'

'Oh, Henry, me too.'

He put down the flowers and took her in his arms, and they held each other tight. Again she felt the warm balm of relief trickling through her limbs.

\*

Belle rang back that evening, but Henry was in the room so Emma didn't mention Rowan.

The next morning, as they left for work together, Emma felt herself returning to an even keel, like a sailing boat that had been dangerously close to capsizing finally righting itself. At the office she texted Rowan: *Thank you for Friday. Sorry, I won't come again. Can you send F&R's stuff please? Mr Pickford says you still have some of their schoolwork.* She typed in the address.

As expected, there was no response.

It – if ever there had been an 'it' – was well and truly over. She resolved to do as he'd asked, time and time again: *Leave me alone.*

She was hurting, but she knew it would pass, like it had passed before.

The melancholy scent of autumn was in the air. The leaves were turning, already giving up on 2012 – *that's it, we're done!* – after the wettest summer in a hundred years. There was a sense of winding down. The Queen's Diamond Jubilee, with all the street parties and the rainy summer fêtes, seemed a long time ago. The Olympics were already a memory.

On Friday evening, Emma took out her blue notebook. She tried to free her mind as she looked at the words she'd jotted down.

*Project???*

*Nature collection. Birds. Owl pellets. Foxes.*

How to move forward? What would a detective do? They would draw up a list of everyone who'd been around the boys, and eliminate them one by one. They'd look at the logistics . . .

She brought up Google maps, took a screenshot of the area around Middleham, and printed it off. Putting it down on the table, she circled Middleham and Aysgarth with a red pen, then annotated the map with distances, times – *last seen at school, spotted by Jodie Platt . . .*

Her eyes scanned west . . . Wensleydale.

*Wensleydale.*

Rowan's farm was just up the road from where the boys had last been seen. *Holy shit*. Had this been staring her in the face all along?

But Rowan had been at school.

*Was he? He said he had no alibi.*

She forced her mind to go where she hadn't allowed it before. Maybe Rowan was prime suspect for good reason.

*Everyone I love dies.*

A shiver ran down her spine. She pictured it. The boys heading off on bikes. Rowan realising they were gone. Getting in his car, going to find them. Spotting them somewhere around Aysgarth. Putting their bikes in the back, then taking the boys to the farm. Maybe promising they could meet a fox, a badger.

And then . . .

She shook her head. No . . . *No*. Surely, no matter what darkness he had inside him, it wasn't that sort of darkness.

But as her mother had told her more than once, she needed to listen to her head, not her heart.

Neville. Rowan. One an egregious narcissist, the other damaged, and dark.

*You need to speak to Belle. Tell her I know. Tell her . . . I'm sorry.*

What did her mother know, about Rowan? She hadn't followed up on the phone call, because she'd been putting off thinking about him.

But it was harder to block those thoughts in the early hours. She tossed and turned, as images pushed their way into that half-sleep, where the line between reality and nightmare blurs. Where truths, unfettered, make themselves known.

Her father, making love to other women, snorting cocaine; part of that 'circle', as Grandpa Snow had called it. That notorious circle. What depravities had they explored? *The devil was most certainly in them all.*

And Rowan had been part of that.

But Teddy had always looked after Rowan. Protected him.

*Thank god for Teddy – he's a buffer between me and Neville.*
*He was the dad I never had.*

Emma's eyes flew open in the dark.

Jane saying: *Teddy was like a father to that boy.*

*Like a father . . .*

She sat up and flicked on the bedside light, gasping for breath.

*Rowan Bosworth, my soul brother.*

The look he'd given her.

*You need to speak to Belle. Tell her I know.*

Emma pressed a hand to her mouth.

*No. Oh my god. No!*

*She didn't name him on the birth certificate.*

Emma slid out of bed, not knowing what to do with herself. She felt sick. Picking up the empty glass from her bedside table, she went into the bathroom and refilled it, drinking deeply, then sat down on the toilet, taking deep breaths.

She went back to her bedroom. Sitting on the edge of the bed, her head in her hands, she began to think properly again.

Teddy's patronage of Rowan. The way he'd always looked out for him. Inviting him to their country houses in summer. She remembered, as clearly as if it were yesterday, his pride when he'd introduced the genius he'd discovered to Neville, after the school play. His big arm round Rowan's shoulders as they'd stood together on the stage.

Emma looked up at her ashen-faced image in the mirror. As much as she hated the conclusion – surely the truth – everything made sense now. Rowan's sudden about-face, from when he'd said they could be together, to his rejection of her, in that letter. It had been when Meena was counselling him, when she'd suggested he find out about his background.

Trying hard to be just friends – *the occasional visit from your best friend in life.* But still having those feelings. Those utterly impossible feelings.

Incestuous feelings.

Because he was her half-brother.

Emma let out a groan and dropped her face back into her hands. The tears came. *Rowan*. How could fate be so cruel?

She curled up under her duvet, sobbing, finally falling into another disturbed sleep, later waking with a jolt. Her bedroom was muted grey; the sun was rising. Her nighttime discovery rushed in, hitting her all over again and the tears returned. What could she do? *You need to speak to Belle.*

She thought back to her mother's attempts to keep her away from Rowan, always pushing her towards Henry. *No wonder.*

*How could she not tell me? How could she let me carry on like that?*

She pulled up the train timetable on her phone. She could be in London by mid morning. She dialled Belle's number.

More lies, but this had been a white one. Emma rang Henry, saying she was 'popping' down to London as Belle was having a lonely moment, and hadn't seen any of her daughters in far too long.

'She must be quite bad,' Emma said. 'You know Mum's not a drama queen. I'll be back tomorrow night.'

She wasn't sure how she'd managed to sound so cool, so normal. Her world had just come crashing down around her. She was in love with her own brother. Each time she thought that thought, she felt nauseous again.

By noon, she was in Hampstead.

'What's this about then, Emerald?' said Belle with a knowing smile, as they sat at the kitchen table. Emma looked out of the window, wondering how to start. The grass around the old tree was scattered with rotting apples, wasps buzzing around them. It seemed a lifetime ago when the children had picked them, the boys going for the high ones, lobbing them into the baskets the girls held below.

That noisy chaotic home, never a moment's peace, never a quiet space. And now here was Belle, all alone.

She looked at her mother again, and from that little smile, guessed she thought Emma was about to tell her she was pregnant, or engaged.

'It's not to do with me and Henry, or my job. It's about Rowan ...'

Belle frowned. 'I thought that was all in the past. Please don't tell me—'

'I can't *believe* you haven't been honest with me! What I've been through. What Rowan's been through.' Her voice rose as the emotion hit. 'Last time I saw Rowan, quite recently, I kissed him. *Properly* kissed him. Again. And he kissed me back, and then he stopped and ... Mum, he *cried*. Because he can't be with me, and you didn't tell me the real reason why. That it was nothing to do with him being messed up. Nothing to do with his loveless child-hood. How could you not tell me? *How?*' She began to cry. 'I love him, Mum. I love him so much. He told me to tell you that he knows. And that he's sorry. But *he* doesn't need to be sorry, does he? It's *you* who needs to be sorry.'

'For god's sake, Emerald. Calm down.'

But she saw in her mother's eyes that she knew.

Emma drew in a deep breath and shakily blew it out. 'Tell me, truthfully. I'm in love with my own brother, aren't I? And *you* let that happen.'

Belle's mouth dropped open. 'No, Emerald. No!' Her hand flew to her mouth.

'Yes! How many times did I need to hear people say it – *Teddy's like a father to that boy* – before the penny dropped? And yet it didn't. I had to wait for poor, poor Rowan to tell me where to find out the truth. From *you*.'

'No, Emerald. Please – you've got it all wrong.' Belle grabbed Emma's hand, but she snatched it away.

'Don't, Mum. Just don't.'

'Emerald ... Rowan's not your brother. He's your uncle. Grandpa Snow is his father.'

## Chapter Thirty-Four

B ut it was still incest, thought Emma, as the train took her
back to York.

Did Sir Richard even know he was Rowan's father? Those awful
things he'd said: *What's a man like that doing teaching young boys?*

She pictured Grandpa Snow, searching for any resemblance to
Rowan. He'd been dark and slim too, when he was younger, though
their faces weren't alike. But then, Teddy had looked nothing like
his father, either. Teddy had been tall, broad-shouldered, fair-haired.

She'd go and see Rowan, tell him she knew the truth. And most
importantly – she pictured him flinching as she'd called him 'a
complete fuck-up' – she needed to apologise, and to let him know
she was here for him. His best friend.

His niece.

She blinked as she stared out of the train window. *Uncle Rowan.*
If it wasn't so bizarre, if her feelings for him hadn't been so strong,
it would almost be funny.

The next morning, Emma quickly wrote the conclusion to an
article she'd been working on, entitled *2012 – THE YEAR OUR
WEATHER TURNED DANGEROUS.* She read it through, then
sent it to Susie.

'It's good,' said the features editor. 'Henry could feed this one
through to the *Telegraph.* Reckon they'd follow it up.'

'Great,' said Emma.

Susie pushed her reading glasses up onto her head. 'Emma, love. Are you alright? You've been on Planet . . . somewhere very distant, this morning.'

'I'm okay, yes. But I need to go see someone – it's to do with the investigation. Will you cover for me? If anyone asks, I'm . . . um—'

'I've sent you out to interview that bloke who won the Olympic medal in the rowing.'

'That'll do.'

'Mum's the word.'

Emma was on the road north by midday. How would this go?

*I'm going to see Rowan, to tell him I know he's my uncle. How weird is life? I won't want to kiss him this time, will I?*

She opened the farm gate, drove in, shut it again. There were no signs of life.

Getting out of her Mini, she sensed an emptiness to the house. The front door was shut; there was no barking dog, no smoke puffing from the chimney.

She knocked, and the sound echoed inside. She peered through the kitchen window. It looked reasonably tidy in there; all the washing-up was done. Like no one was home.

*Dammit!* She took out her phone and rang him. It went to voicemail. She didn't leave a message.

Rowan wasn't home. Where was he? She couldn't believe it – she'd come all this way and he wasn't home. On impulse, she started looking underneath the paraphernalia in the porch. Bingo! A key, under a watering can. Presumably burglars weren't a threat up here. Or were a bit dim.

She let herself in and called out. *Funny how you can tell when there's no one home, like the house lets you know.* Going into the living room, she bent down and held a hand over the ashes in the fireplace. They were cold.

*Think like a detective.*

She went through to the kitchen and touched the range.

Cold. She opened the rubbish bin and gingerly poked around. A squashed milk carton, dead teabags ... scrunched up kitchen roll, and the broken pieces of a plate.

She shut the bin and looked around the kitchen.

Then opened the bin again, and fished out one of those pieces of kitchen roll. The one that had blood on it. Also the others, beneath it, that had blood on them. And then the bits of plate.

*What happened here?*

Had he broken a plate and cut himself on it? She stared at the bloodied shreds of paper, as if asking them to explain themselves.

Taking out her phone, she photographed them, and the plate, then put everything back in the bin.

She returned to the living room – she'd take a last look around downstairs before leaving. It felt awful to be snooping on Rowan, but she was thinking like a detective.

There was a pile of exercise books on his desk, and her heart skipped a beat as she recognised her brother's handwriting on a stapled-together sheaf of lined paper: *Foxes, by Freddie Snow.*

The books were all named. Rowan must have been getting the boys' schoolwork ready to post to her. She sat in his desk chair and began to read Freddie's project. Tears pricked the backs of her eyes as she took in childish drawings of foxes, trees, rabbits.

*Habitat: woodlands, fields, urban environments*

*Diet: small mammals like mice, birds especially chickens, worms ...*

Rowan's red pen on the last page: *A-*

His comment: *Excellent work, Freddie. Watch out, Mr Attenborough!*

She smiled sadly, running her fingers across the page before going through more exercise books. The marks were good. Her brothers had been bright.

There was another stapled-together project: *Owls, by River Snow.* Something that looked like dried mud was sellotaped to a page, with a blue arrow pointing to it. *This is an owl pellet. Owls cough them up. Sometimes you can see bits of dead voles in them but not in this one unnfortunitely.*

Rowan's red pen, correcting the spelling.

*Owls.*

The memory of the barn owl swooping like a ghost in the dusk.

*Owls.*

Mr Haworth was involved in a barn owl breeding project.

She sucked in a breath. *Oh my god.*

Supposing Rowan had brought the boys to see Mr Haworth's owls. She knew he took them out of school without asking, like he'd taken them fossil hunting at the coast. Perhaps Mr Haworth had invited the boys back, any time they liked.

*PAEDO.* The word had been graffitied on the farm sign. Perhaps it hadn't been aimed at Rowan. Perhaps Mr Haworth was . . .

*Holy f–.*

Supposing they'd cycled to the farm that Sunday. Mr Haworth had shown them his owls again, and then . . .

She looked out of the window and her eyes fell on the barn, which was over the wall, on the land Mr Haworth leased from Rowan, presumably. Was this where the barn owls lived?

*If I went in there, would I find two bikes?*

She tidied up the books, then found a pen and paper.

Rowan – I came to see you today. I've talked to Mum, I know about your real father. I'm so sorry for the things I said to you, I was angry and hurt. Now I understand. I hope you're okay, I'd love to see you to talk it all through.

Please please call me.

Emma xx (your niece – WTF?)

PS You should find a better hiding place for your key

She let herself out and put the key back under the watering can.

The old barn was padlocked. *Damn!* She walked around it, in case there was a way to see in.

'Hello there.'

Emma jumped at the gruff voice behind her.

'Rowan's not here,' said Mr Haworth, as her heart thumped.

She looked at his face. What did a child murderer, a paedophile, look like? This wasn't the Middle Ages, or a Disney movie. People who were evil were no longer expected to look evil. He looked like a Yorkshire farmer.

The border collie was by his side, and she bent to pat it, to hide her panic.

'I don't know why I thought I might find him in here!' she said, her voice a little higher than she'd have liked. 'Is this where you breed your barn owls, Mr Haworth?'

'No, lass. I don't breed them, I just encourage them. Planting corridors and the like. Reducing pesticides. They're making a comeback; it's great to see.'

'Oh, that's wonderful. Perhaps I could talk to you about that sometime, for the *Chronicle*?'

'Any time you like, love.'

'Can I take your contact details?' Her phone in her hand was reassuring. It would take no time to hit the emergency dial.

He gave her his number.

'Do you know where Rowan might be?' she said, after inputting it.

'Done a runner, sorry to say.'

'A runner?'

*I'm alone here, in the middle of nowhere, with the man who may have killed my brothers.*

Mr Haworth looked beyond her to the farmhouse. 'Rowan does this from time to time. When things get tough, 'e takes 'iself off. Goes walking or something. Silly bugger should've told me where 'e was headed, he's a law unto 'iself.'

Was this because of their row?

Haworth must have seen something in her expression.

'Don't be blaming yourself; 'e's a tricky lad. He had a visitor – flash bloke. He disappeared after that.'

*Flash bloke?*

'When was this?'

'Week or so ago. Expensive car. Aston Martin, I think.' He took a step towards her. 'Why don't you come in for a bit? I can make us a brew.'

'Thank you, but sadly I have to get back to York.' Emma took a breath and looked him in the eye. 'Mr Haworth – did you ever meet my brothers? Freddie and Riv?'

He frowned.

'They were very interested in wildlife,' she continued, 'especially owls. They were doing a project. I thought perhaps Rowan might have brought them to talk to you about the barn owls?'

'Nay, though he asked if 'e could.' He stroked his bristly chin. 'I guess he never got round to it, before they disappeared.'

'So you never met my brothers?'

'Like I said, no.'

'Right, well ... I've left a note for Rowan. Will you tell him I was here, when you see him?'

'I will.'

'It was good to see you again, and can I ring you about an owl piece?'

'Any time you like.' He smiled. 'I think ... Rowan has a soft spot for you. Am I right?'

'We've been friends for many years.'

'I'd say it's a bit more than that, eh?' His expression was kind. 'He's a tough nut to crack, that lad, but I reckon you could do the job.' He bent down to pat his dog. 'He needs someone in his life,' he said, looking up at her. 'That awful business with his wife, I think 'e's over it now. He should move on. To you, I think.'

She felt herself blushing. A Yorkshireman will always give it to you straight. 'I'd like to see more of him, yes. He's very dear to me.'

'Get to it, lass.'

She laughed.

'I'll open the gate for you.' He set off down the field, his dog running ahead.

'I'll expect to see thee soon!' he called, as she drove through.

As Emma headed back, the pieces of the jigsaw clicked into place. The broken plate and the bloodied kitchen roll. The 'flash bloke' in the Aston Martin, which was probably a Maserati.

Henry's black eye.

Rowan's disappearance.

Henry hadn't been to see his mother that Sunday – he'd been to see Rowan. They'd had a fight. And now, Rowan was missing.

And she was back to square one with her brothers.

Who was in the picture, now?

Neville: possible.

Mr Haworth: instinct told her that was a no. But instinct wouldn't cut it. She'd need to mention the farmer to Liz, so he could be eliminated.

Rowan: from a completely objective point of view, he was still the most obvious suspect.

*I'm not nice. I'm not remotely nice.*

His writing, delving deep into the dark side of the human psyche.

*I've been exploring a few boundaries. One person's ethics is another's unwarranted constraints.*

Henry, with his incisive, journalistic mind – detached, objective, able to spot truths where she couldn't – had pegged Rowan as the culprit right from the start. Certainly there had been jealousy in there, and she'd put all the newspaper spin down to that. But he genuinely believed. He'd been horrified, thinking of her alone at the farmhouse with him. And when he'd found out she'd been to see him, it had pushed him to act.

Like a knight bearing her favour, he'd charged up to Wensleydale in his Maserati and laid into Rowan, warning him off once and for all. If it wasn't so awful, it would be quite sexy.

She shook her head. No, it wasn't sexy. She pictured Henry in Rowan's kitchen, telling him to stay away. Rowan giving him some sardonic answer, probably winding him up. Perhaps he'd told Henry they'd kissed, that he could have had her if he'd wanted her. Provoking him, until he'd lashed out, punching Rowan, knocking him against the table, a plate falling off and smashing. Then Rowan lunging for Henry, socking him in the eye.

She squeezed her eyes shut for a moment. The image was horrible.

Then Henry leaving, putting his foot down hard in the Maserati, spraying earth as he sped away from the farmhouse. Rowan, clearing up the kitchen, brooding. Then going off with Teddy, needing to walk in the hills.

Or had Rowan run away because he knew the game was up, and Henry had let him know it?

*For my lovely Ems, who believed.*

Did she still believe in Rowan? Or was it time to get real?

NOW

# Chapter Thirty-Five

## York, September 2012

Emma's desk phone rang. She was *never* going to meet today's deadline.

It was Henry. 'Emma, can you come through?' There was something in his voice.

'What is it?'

'Just come through – and close the door behind you.'

She looked across the office, and saw him perched on the edge of his desk, waiting for her. He wasn't looking her way.

*Oh god, he's going to kill the investigation. He's actually going to kill it.*

And for all the wrong reasons.

As she made her way over to his office, Emma was aware of a chill creeping along her veins. *No way am I giving up. Not now.*

'Emma,' he said, as she shut the door. 'Sit down.' Frowning, he raked his fingers through his hair.

'What's going on?' she said, not sitting down. If she was going to fight her corner, she'd rather be standing.

'You saw the papers this morning?'

*Oh.* She let out a breath. He was going to congratulate her on being picked up by the *Telegraph*.

'You mean the *Telegraph*?'

'The body found in Leicester. Under a car park.'

'Body?' she said, stupidly. What did this have to do with anything? *Unless* . . .

'Emma . . . '

She sucked in a breath, suddenly petrified by the look on his face.

'Please, Henry, not Rowan.' It was barely more than a whisper. Time seemed to stand still as she waited for him to answer. And in that infinity she glimpsed a future without him.

From the way Henry looked at her, she knew she'd given herself away. But she didn't care, *couldn't* care, about anything, except his next words.

He shook his head. 'Why on earth would you think that?' Then that look, that brief narrowing of his eyes, passed, and he came over and took her hand.

*Not Rowan.*

'It was the body of a child,' he said. 'Aged about ten.'

The silence between them.

*One child. Just one.*

'But I had a call from a contact down at the *Leicester Mercury*. Half an hour ago, they . . . Emma, there are two. Two bodies. The second child looks to be a bit older, maybe twelve. Word is, off the record – the police think they're boys, from their hair and clothes.'

*Two boys.*

'Oh god, Henry.' She edged backwards until she felt the desk behind her, and sat down heavily.

'Preliminary guess – like I said, off the record – is that they've been dead for two or three years. Not sure what state . . . I mean, it'll probably need DNA testing. Teeth, whatever. But Emma, they both have fair hair. And obviously there's speculation . . . '

Emma couldn't think straight. 'Leicester, though?' she said, finally, staring at him. 'How could they have been there? Maybe it's not them?'

Did she want it to be? Would it be better than the not knowing?

His gaze was full of sympathy. 'If they were abducted . . . Look, let's wait for news. My contact's on the case, he's feeding through everything he can. All we can do is wait.' He put his arms round her, rubbing her back. 'I expect you'll want to contact Belle, if the police haven't done so already. They'll probably have to, even before anything's confirmed or otherwise. Press speculation will be rife – two fair-haired boys of the right age, missing for a similar number of years.'

She pulled away. 'Yes, I ... I should ring Mum.' She turned to leave.

'Emma ... '

She stopped and met his eye again, saw him searching for words. 'It's okay, Henry. I'll be alright.'

All she felt was a numbness. A strange dissociation from reality. Perhaps she was in shock.

'Do you want me to come—'

'No,' she said. 'I'd like to be alone. I need some air. I'll call Mum while I'm out.'

Emma returned to her desk to collect her phone, ignoring the curious stares of her colleagues, then headed for the lift.

She walked slowly past the ancient walls of York Minster, weaving between the tourists and gaggles of schoolchildren, and found an empty bench in a quiet corner of Deans Park. She sat staring at her phone, then put it down in her lap and closed her eyes, revisiting those moments in Henry's office, allowing the feelings to resurface. Those terrifying seconds when she'd thought, for an infinite moment, that Rowan had been found dead. When she'd glimpsed a future without him.

And then, Henry's words: *Emma, there are two. Two bodies.*

Not 'bodies'. Her brothers. Unconfirmed, but somehow she knew it was them.

She deflected the image Henry's words had conjured, instead picturing Freddie and Riv full of life, full of mischief.

The tsunami of pain hit, and she dropped her face into her hands, racked by sobs, tears leaking through her fingers.

*I'll never see them again.*

When she was all cried out, she took some deep breaths – *be strong* – and called Belle.

That afternoon, Emma and Belle went to Leicester, and were shown the ragged remnants of the clothes the boys had been wearing. The two women held each other tight as they broke down in tears, recognising Riv's *Fantastic Mr Fox* T-shirt.

DNA tests confirmed their identities.

## BELLE'S LOST BOYS DISCOVERED BURIED IN LEICESTER CAR PARK

It was the biggest news story of the year – bigger than *Curiosity* landing on Mars, bigger than the Queen's Diamond Jubilee, maybe even bigger than the Olympics.

Belle and Emma stayed in Leicester to assist the police, and they in turn protected the two women from the media glare. Everyone was very kind. Emma even received a bouquet of flowers from Lady M, with a note: *I'm so sorry, Emma. Please pass on my condolences to your mother. Warmest regards, Lady Madeline Beauregard.*

The bodies were being forensically examined. Thus far, Belle and Emma had been informed there was no obvious injury to either. No broken bones or skull fractures.

It was too late for CCTV footage, but the police had determined the bodies must have been buried in 2010, before the car park was concreted over. This tallied with the date of the boys' disappearance.

The police informed them the bodies would be released as soon as Forensics were done. Belle wanted them to be buried at Sandal Manor's chapel. It was where she and Teddy had married, and the boys had always loved spending time with their grandparents.

Emma returned to York at the weekend, Belle carrying on to Sandal to be with Grandma and Grandpa Snow, who would help with the funeral arrangements.

Henry came round to cook dinner. Emma was exhausted after the drive, wrung out after the events of the week.

'Maybe after the funeral, we should have that week in Santorini,' said Henry.

'What?' Emma was only half-listening as she sat on the sofa reading the latest *Chronicle*. Then, as she registered his words, she added, 'I couldn't possibly.'

'C'mon, Emma,' said Henry, slicing an onion. 'You need a break. Belle will be fine, staying with your grandparents. And obviously your feature – that's not happening now.'

'Not happening?' Emma swung round to look at him. 'What do you mean? The police still have no idea who did this – or even how the boys died, yet.'

'We have to leave it to the police, now. We'll have to share anything you've found out with them, in fact. Your notebooks and ... everything. Pass it all on.'

Henry was probably right. And because of that, she made a mental note to lock away some of her paperwork, password protect the hell out of everything on her computer. Her notes! God. Everything she'd written down about Rowan; those question marks. The notes from her conversations with Jane and Neville. She'd go to the office early tomorrow, put things in order.

Rowan. Had he seen the papers? He must have done – the boys' photos were everywhere again.

Later, Henry finished loading the dishwasher and brought Emma a mug of tea. 'Feeling less wiped out now?'

'A bit. That was a delicious meal, thanks so much. I don't think I could even have summoned the strength to *pierce lid with fork*.'

'Must have been exhausting,' he said. 'Are you up to telling me more of what the police have found out?'

'Only what I already told you. Still waiting on more forensics.'

'Right.' He skewered her with that gaze. 'Look, Emma ... ' He ran his fingers through his hair. 'I know you've been putting off your conclusions, but you have to face up to things. Where it's all pointing.'

'Henry, I'm absolutely shattered—'

'You can't keep putting it off. You're in denial.'

She wondered for a moment, whether to raise the topic of his visit to Rowan's farm, but she couldn't summon the energy. That conversation would have to wait.

When she didn't answer, he said, 'Well, I guess we can leave it to the police, now.' He glanced at his watch. 'Look, you're shattered. Why don't you have an early night? I'll go back to mine and we'll make up for lost time tomorrow.'

'Oh.' There was a moment of surprise – she'd assumed he'd be staying over. 'Okay, I guess I could use some extra sleep.'

He kissed her goodbye, and she shuffled off to her room, using her last remaining energy to change into her PJs, brush her teeth for almost no seconds, and set her alarm for 6.30 a.m. The clothes could stay on the floor.

She slept deeply. It was mercifully dreamless and uninterrupted, unlike those nights in Leicester.

As she lay in the grey light of dawn, trying to rouse herself sufficiently to switch off her alarm, she remembered Belle's muffled sobs on their first night there.

How long would it be before they heard again from the police? They needed to bury their boys, to say their goodbyes.

*No evidence of broken bones or head injuries.* What had happened to Freddie and Riv?

Turning off the alarm, she remembered why she'd set it so early. She had to protect her notes. Swinging her legs out of bed, she headed to the shower.

An hour later she was at the office. As she approached her desk, she saw herself sitting there, such a short time ago. The old Emma, the one who, subconsciously, had held on to that tiny glimmer of hope that her brothers might still be alive.

The tears that had been threatening nearly made it through as she registered that some kind person – Susie? – had tidied her desk for her, after she'd left in a panic for Leicester. Her notebooks and papers were stacked neatly, her pens back in their pot.

She started with the paperwork. There wasn't a great deal: newspaper reports, and the small amount of police material Liz had given her access to.

She flicked through her notebooks. Her scribbled handwriting, the date at the top of each page.

Her lists of names; her notes from her various meetings:

*Project ???*

*Nature collection. Birds. Owl pellets. Foxes.*

*Was Rowan in any way responsible for Abigail's death?*

*Neville controlled Rowan's money. Kept him broke*

She switched on her computer. As she waited for it to wake up, she carried on looking through the notebooks. Some of the notes in the one with the blue leather cover – she'd rather they were kept private. She put it in her handbag.

A notification appeared on her computer screen: *Disk Not Ejected Properly.*

She stared at the words, then remembered she'd copied some files onto a memory stick for her laptop, which she'd taken to Leicester.

Opening the file *Monsters*, she selected *Privacy*, and the option to reset the password. From *FreddieRiv* to . . . what? She'd need to remember it without writing it down.

*RowanIsInnocent2012*

Did she still really believe that?

# Chapter Thirty-Six

The forensics team were done, and the bodies were released. But there had been no breakthrough. It was all so familiar – the feeling of being in limbo, of not being able to move on.

Rowan hadn't replied to any of her texts, and wasn't answering his phone. She'd called Mr Haworth, wondering if the police had been in touch with him – if they had, he didn't mention it – but Rowan was apparently still away.

Emma had let the fact that Rowan had 'done a runner' slip to Henry, and he didn't hesitate to give his opinion as to why: now that the boys had been found, it would only be a matter of time before the police issued a warrant for his arrest.

The boys had been moved to a funeral home. Emma couldn't bear to think of those two small coffins, the sight of which she'd soon have to confront. She ordered two floral arrangements – a white owl, and a fox's head.

DS Shore had asked to see Emma again, and was coming to the office. Emma had a feeling Rowan was going to be the main topic of the interview, and was dreading it. Should she tell Liz about the family connection? What about Grandpa and Grandma Snow? Did Lily know Sir Richard was Rowan's father? If Emma told DS Shore, would Lily find out? Probably not, unless …

Unless Rowan was arrested. And then surely it would all come out.

Emma massaged her temples. This was too hard.

'Alright, love?' called Susie.

'Rarely been worse.'

Henry had offered his office for the meeting with Liz, as he was out lunching with a local politician. Emma showed her in, and braced herself.

'Thank you for the information about Rowan Bosworth's neighbour,' Liz began. 'He's given us an alibi, and we're checking that out.'

'Good. What about Neville Warwick?'

'Sorry,' said Liz. 'I'm still unable to share that. However, what I *can* tell you is that to get more of a picture, we checked out those claims Warwick made about Rowan Bosworth's abuse of Abigail. The police at the time dismissed them after looking at the psychiatric reports. There was no reason to think he abused her.'

Emma sighed. 'No, of course he didn't.'

'We also followed up on the financial situation between him and Rowan. Warwick's records bear out your suspicions that he defrauded Rowan of substantial amounts of money.'

Emma frowned. My *suspicions*. How did Liz know about those? She went cold.

*My notes . . . Henry.* Had he shown Liz her notebooks, while she'd been away in Leicester?

Emma thought quickly – what had she written about Rowan? She took a breath. 'Do you still suspect Rowan Bosworth?'

'I'm not in a position to share that information, Emma. I'm sorry.'

'He's . . . he wasn't just their teacher.'

Liz smiled her warm smile and said, 'No, I appreciate he was a friend of the family.'

Emma made the decision. 'A bit more than that, actually. I recently found out he is in fact a relative. It's why he was close to my father – it wasn't only because Dad mentored him. Dad – Teddy Snow – was actually Rowan's brother. They had the same father.'

Liz's eyes widened in surprise, then she frowned. 'Why were we not made aware of this before?'

'I didn't know. Only my mother knew, and . . . well. Dirty laundry and all that. Everything about our family tends to end up in the press, so we're a little overcautious.'

'I see,' said Liz. She wrote something down in her notebook. 'Would you excuse me for a moment? I need to make a quick call about that.'

*Why?*

A short while later she returned. 'There's an anomaly here,' she said, sitting down again. 'I'd like to clear it up.'

'Anomaly?'

'The DNA. We matched DNA from the boys' remains – sorry, I know that sounds horrible – to the DNA collected at the school. Their combs, toothbrushes, and so on. And to the DNA we found in Rowan's car, which proved they'd been in it. At the time, Rowan's DNA was found in the car too, of course.'

'Right.' Emma wasn't following.

'Our team would have picked up if the boys' DNA and Rowan's DNA had shown a familial relationship. I've asked them to run what we call an avuncular test, to be sure, but Forensics are saying they're not related.'

Emma stared at Liz. 'Not . . . How certain can you be?'

'Pretty certain, but I'll let you know.'

If Freddie and Riv weren't Rowan's nephews, then Emma wasn't his niece.

Her head was spinning, she couldn't think straight.

If she and Rowan weren't related . . .

'Rowan's gone off somewhere, I don't know where he is,' she said in her confusion.

'That's not something you need to be concerned about,' Liz replied. 'I came here mostly to update you on Neville Warwick, and to reassure you that we're working with the Leicestershire Police to bring this to a conclusion.' She stood up. 'This is a difficult time for you and your family, and I appreciate everything you've done to assist us. We'd like to come to the funeral.'

'Yes, of course. That would be kind of you.'

Unexpectedly, she took Emma's hand. 'This is absolutely the worst thing to happen to a family, losing not one but two children … I want you to know, Emma, we're doing everything. I don't think you'll be waiting much longer for closure.'

Back at her desk, Emma gave up trying to concentrate on the piece she was writing. Her mind was churning like a washing machine revving up to maximum spin. She told Susie she'd work from home, and left.

Perkin kneaded her lap as she sat on her sofa, mulling things over. She didn't trust the science. It must be wrong. Grandpa Snow was Rowan's father, that made sense. And presumably, his name had been on the birth certificate Rowan had sighted. Rowan must have lied about his mother not naming the father.

Did Grandma know Rowan was Grandpa's son?

Emma made up her mind. She'd go to Sandal and talk to Belle and her grandparents. She called to let them know she was coming, and arrived later that afternoon. Immediately, she asked her mother for a quiet word.

There were purple shadows beneath Belle's beautiful eyes. Poor thing, what she'd been through. But it would be good to bury the boys, say their farewells. Things would surely be easier afterwards.

'Mum – there's a question mark over the relationship between Rowan and Grandpa Snow,' she said, as they sat in the window seat looking out over the gardens – the spot they always gravitated to for these heart-to-hearts. Autumn leaves were being raked up by the gardener. 'According to Liz Shore, although she needs to get it double-checked, the DNA doesn't indicate a family relationship between Rowan and the boys.'

'What?' said Belle, looking confused.

'Who told you,' said Emma, 'about Rowan being Grandpa's son?'

'Teddy. And he heard it from *both* his parents. Richard came clean when Teddy told him about this genius who'd written the school play. Teddy was up here those two weeks before we saw the show, if you remember.'

Emma thought back. 'But why would Grandpa Snow have admitted he was Rowan's father? Why didn't he just keep schtum?'

'Lily wanted him to tell Teddy, because she knew Teddy would look after Rowan. He was something of a lost soul, always a loner.'

'Grandma's so kind.'

'She is. Richard had been paying Rowan's mother – Celia, her name was – an allowance. Hush money too, I guess you'd call it. Celia went away while she was pregnant, then left the baby with a family member, I think. Later she married Dick Bosworth, and they pretended they'd adopted Rowan to save Richard's and her own reputation. Her husband's too, I suppose. It was a comfortable arrangement, things were often done like that, back then.'

'But it wasn't *that* long ago.'

'You don't realise how much things have changed. Anyway, Lily thought it was only right and proper that Teddy should know he had a brother, especially when Teddy thought Rowan was so brilliant, plus he had no other siblings. But she asked Teddy not to tell Rowan the truth about their relationship, to protect their father. The press would have had a field day.'

Emma's head was still spinning. Could the DNA thing be wrong?

'Rowan called his mum a . . . quite a rude name,' said Emma. 'He implied she slept around. Could Grandpa not have been the father?'

Belle gave a small laugh. 'Oh my gosh. Imagine that – if after everything, he wasn't.'

'Can we just ask them? Grandma and Grandpa.'

Belle looked nervous. 'I don't know; you know what Richard's like. I think he'd rather die than admit—'

'Bloody hypocrite!' interrupted Emma. 'He said awful things about Rowan – his own son – and about what people in Dad's *circle* got up to. And there he was . . .'

'Yes, indeed,' said Belle.

Emma huffed. 'Let's speak to Grandma, then.'

'She's in the conservatory. Why don't you go find her. It might be easier for her if it's just you.'

Emma found Lily planting out seedlings into pots.

'Hello, darling,' said her grandmother. 'I find there's nothing like working in here to soothe the mind. This is a difficult time for us all.'

Emma gave her a hug. 'It is, Grandma. And ... I don't want to make it harder – for any of us – but I found out something recently, about Rowan Bosworth. It's why I've come here this afternoon.'

'Rowan?' Lily frowned as she pressed earth round a seedling.

'Yes, but it's all become quite confusing. I need to be clear in my head, as it has some bearing on the police investigation.'

Lily wiped her hands on her gardening apron and looked Emma in the eye. 'I'm guessing ... you found out who Rowan's father is?'

'I think I did.'

'There's no need to beat about the bush, Emma. I'm far too old to care what people think. Your grandfather does, but I don't. What do you need to know?'

Emma was taken aback by her grandmother's forthright response. 'Oh, right. Well – apparently, Rowan believes Grandpa is his father.'

Lily sighed. 'So he found out. I thought he would, eventually.'

'Yes, he saw the birth certificate.' Emma pressed on. 'And so, obviously, Freddie and Riv were Rowan's nephews. But the police are saying Rowan's DNA, and Freddie and Riv's DNA, don't indicate that relationship. I don't know the details – percentage probabilities or whatever. The police are doing another check to be sure.'

'Oh my lord,' said Lily. She started fiddling with her seedlings again, avoiding Emma's eye. 'Richard and Rowan ... yes. Rowan is almost certainly Richard's son.' She looked up. 'His mother had quite a reputation, but honestly, I knew her and she wasn't that bad. Richard certainly believed her when she said the child was his.'

Emma's shoulders slumped.

'Is that bad news?' said Lily. She put a finger under Emma's lowered chin and tilted her face up. 'Is it such a terrible thing? I thought you liked Rowan.'

Emma said nothing, but her eyes must have given her away.

'Oh. How are things with you and Henry, dear? He's such a nice man.'

Emma didn't know what to say. She looked into her grandmother's kind eyes. 'Honestly, Grandma, all these secrets and lies. I can't stand it! My head's all over the place. First Rowan's a friend, then he's an uncle, then no – he can't be an uncle, and now you're saying yes, he is my uncle.'

'Why is it so important to you, darling?' her grandmother pressed.

'It doesn't matter.'

'But I can see it does, Emma. And if you tell me why, I can help you with that.'

'With a comforting hot chocolate and marshmallows?' Emma was on the verge of tears again. *God, what a week.*

'No, with the truth. Why does it matter, about Rowan? Is it because you're in love with him?'

How had she guessed? How had she known?

Emma nodded slowly. 'All these years, Grandma. All these years I've been in love with my own uncle.'

Lily smiled. 'No, Emma. You haven't. The DNA is correct. Rowan's not your uncle. Rowan *is* Richard's son, yes ... ' She paused. 'But *Teddy* wasn't Richard's son. Teddy's father was a man I had an affair with, a lovely man by the name of Tom Archer. Your real grandfather. I met him in France, when I was over there for a summer cooking school. I'm afraid I let Richard think Teddy was his; I thought it would be for the best.'

Emma was frantically trying to reorganise all the thoughts in her head – again. *Grandpa Snow isn't my real grandpa.*

'I actually thought Richard might not be able to have children,' Lily continued, 'when I never conceived again. Perhaps he isn't in fact Rowan's father. But maybe that's not important. What *is* important is that you and Rowan aren't blood relatives. I guess if Richard *is* his father, you'd be ... step ... what would you be?'

Emma couldn't work it out. She didn't really care. All she cared about was those words: *you and Rowan aren't blood relatives.*

'So Teddy and Rowan weren't brothers,' Lily said, picking up her trowel. 'But I never told Teddy, as he had no other siblings, and he was so delighted to find out about Rowan. He did love him like a younger brother.'

'But ... does Grandpa know now? That Teddy wasn't his son?' Poor Grandpa.

'I told him after Teddy died. It sounds harsh, but I had my reasons. We never told Belle, though. Richard didn't want anyone else knowing, so I kept it secret. I'll tell her, when the time is right. Not now, I think.'

Emma puffed out a long breath. 'God. Do you think every family's like this? Secrets, lies, affairs ... sorry, I'm not judging. I can hardly talk. And look at Dad!'

Lily chuckled. 'Oh yes. I think every family has a skeleton or two. Your generation's luckier than mine. Better, I think. Yours doesn't judge, the way mine did.' She sighed. 'Society would say I was a bad person for having a holiday romance and coming home pregnant. The reason I took the trip alone was because I'd found out about Richard having an affair. He may not have been Teddy's real father, but he was like him in many ways. I want you to know, Emma – Tom and me, it was a beautiful thing; a brief moment in time. I'll never regret it.'

Emma smiled. 'No, you shouldn't. I'd like to know more about my real grandpa, sometime.'

'I did love him,' said Lily, 'but I was married, obviously, and Richard and I rubbed along well enough. I missed Tom – and if I hadn't met him, I wouldn't have had your father. Or you and your brothers and sisters. I don't think love is ever "wrong", Emma. You love Henry, I can tell. But you love Rowan too. You'll have to make a choice, but don't ever regret having loved them both.'

Emma smiled as she pictured a young Lily in France. 'You know what? After learning how Dad carried on, and now I know Grandpa cheated on you, it makes me kind of happy that you had a hot fling. Perhaps I'd better brace myself for what Mum gets up to on tour, do you think?'

'Well,' said Lily, with a wink. 'Wouldn't *you*, Emma?'

'How did things go with the police?' Henry asked on the phone that evening. Emma was lying on the bed in the pink bedroom.

'Liz had some interesting stuff to share. I'll let you know when I see you.'

*And I'll be asking you how Liz knew about Neville keeping Rowan broke.*

'Stuff about Rowan?' said Henry. 'No arrest yet?'

She wasn't going to be drawn. And anyway, he'd know if there had been. He always knew. 'No, they still seem pretty much in the dark.'

'I've done the maths,' said Henry. 'Leicester and back, four hours. He could have driven down there, dumped the bodies, and been back in time for a few hours' kip before breakfast.'

'Really, Henry?' she said. 'And why would he have done that? The middle of Leicester. A car park. When he had vast areas of wilderness on his doorstep?'

There was a short silence.

'Okay,' he said. 'I get that you'd rather not discuss it. Are you alright? This is so tough on you – going to Leicester, and now with the funeral to face.'

'I'm getting through. Being with my family helps. Is it okay if I stay here until after the funeral? I've got my laptop – Susie can tell me what needs doing, workwise.'

'Of course, you didn't need to ask. And I'll tell Susie to handle everything; you're on compassionate leave.'

'Thanks, Henry. I appreciate that.'

They said their goodbyes, and it was all too polite. The distance between them was widening. Emma lay staring at the ceiling, overwhelmed by sadness.

Coming out of her trance, she texted her neighbour to ask her to feed Perkin. Then, as she reflected on the events of the day, turning her mind to her grandmother's revelation, a smile crept over her face.

*Rowan isn't my uncle! I love Rowan, and there's no good reason now why he can't love me too.*

# Chapter Thirty-Seven

The next day, the *Chronicle* published an 'update' on the case of 'Belle's Boys'. Henry's fingerprints were all over it.

'Have you seen this?' Lily asked at breakfast, nodding at the paper as she poured cups of tea from a bone china teapot. As always, the tea was brewed from loose leaves, the milk was in a jug, and the matching cups and saucers were laid out on a snowy tablecloth. Emma skimmed the article quickly. A familiar photo of the boys, and a report that the 'private family funeral' would take place this week, now that the bodies had been released. Thankfully, the location wasn't named.

That was followed by a paragraph on how the boys' school-teacher, who'd left Middleham 'under a cloud of suspicion', had disappeared since the discovery of the bodies. And a reminder that Rowan Bosworth was a writer of dark, often violent novels, written under a pen name to conceal his true identity.

The byline was Ed Studley.

'Fuck's sake,' muttered Emma. Grandpa Snow gave her a look, and she apologised for swearing.

'Is that true, that Rowan's disappeared?' asked Lily.

'He sometimes goes off when he needs to think,' said Emma.

How did Henry think his smear campaign was going to endear himself to her? Beating Rowan up and then trashing his reputation? What was he actually thinking? Was this ramping-up of his anti-Rowan propaganda a response to a sense that he was losing her?

Emma's mood didn't improve when Henry rang later, informing her that his mother would be accompanying him to the funeral.

'What? Why!' Emma squeaked.

'I'm sorry, I really am. But she's going to be your mother-in-law, so it's the right thing to do. And she wants to come. She's not as uncaring as you think, Emma. She's trying to be supportive.'

Emma said nothing, squeezing her eyes shut for a moment. She didn't have the emotional energy to argue.

'Fine. Just . . .'

'Yes, I'll try to keep her out of your way,' said Henry, 'if that's what you want. Perhaps, afterwards,' he continued, his voice suddenly chirpier, 'you and I can share news of our engagement? Not an official announcement, as such, but as your family will all be there it would be nice to tell them, don't you think? Might cheer everyone up.'

Emma felt hounded, like a fox on the Montfort Grange estate. How could she stop this? She'd given up trying to think ahead when it came to her personal life. The best, admittedly vague, plan she'd come up with was to wait until after the funeral, go find Rowan and tell him they weren't related, then end things with Henry. It would no doubt mean an end to her role at the *Chronicle*, but some things in life were more important. There were other newspapers.

'Henry, I don't think that would be at all appropriate,' she said, attempting to sound firm. 'The funeral will be incredibly hard for all of us. It's about remembering Freddie and Riv. Announcing our engagement wouldn't feel right.'

There was a brief silence. 'Okay, I understand.'

They said their goodbyes, and Emma blinked away the tears that were threatening. To take her mind off the Henry-shaped hole in her future, she thought about Rowan, picturing herself saying the words: *You're not my uncle. We're not related.*

*Where is he?*

Were the police looking for him?

*We're working with the Leicestershire Police . . . I don't think you'll be waiting much longer for closure.*

Outside the window of the ancient manor, where so many had lived and died, the sun was coming up. Day after day it rose, and the world carried on turning, and all over that world people were hurting, grieving, trying to carry on. Because – what else could they do?

*Today, we bury my brothers.*

Emma lay in bed, staring at the ceiling. A spider was crawling slowly across it. What was it like, to be a spider? Build a web, wait. Catch a fly, wait for fly to die. Eat fly. Repeat. Die.

What was the point? Of the spider. Of the fly.

She remembered Rowan's 'tangled metaphor' as they climbed Middleham Tor. *There you go, idiot dog. Something for you to point-lessly chase after and pointlessly bring back.*

Freddie and Riv, their barely-begun lives brutally cut short, probably through some cruel stroke of fate that had an opportunist paedophile spotting them in the middle of nowhere; Belle, her beloved husband and sons lost to her, travelling the world singing her sad songs; Rowan, that unloved little boy, bullied by his father, bullied at school, losing his baby son, watching his wife die.

Emma, writing from the heart, trying to touch other people's, to make them stop . . . just stop for a moment, and appreciate this world, to make them want to protect it, like she wanted to. Failing, mostly, it would seem. Today's newspaper, tomorrow's fish and chip wrapper.

What was the point of any of it? What if she just didn't get up today? The thought of what lay in wait was too hard.

But . . . Belle, Crystal and Pearl. Grandma and Grandpa Snow, and her other grandparents, who would be arriving this morning. All would be feeling like this right now. Together, they would get through it.

Love – *that* was the point. It was the only part of life that made sense.

She swung her feet out of bed, went over to the window and pulled back the curtains. The sun was rising, pale and golden, over the low hills on the horizon. The sky was clear – it was going to be one of those lovely Indian summer days.

In spite of it all, the world *was* a beautiful place, worth carrying on for, worth fighting for. She breathed deeply. *I can do this.*

Mrs Berry fussed around the family at breakfast, insisting on doing everything, banishing silence with kitchen sounds – kettle boiling, toaster popping, fridge opening and shutting … more tea, more coffee, more toast. But no one had much of an appetite. They focused on details: Lily making sure the catering was sorted for later, Grandpa Snow vigorously polishing his shoes, Belle canvassing opinion – hair up or down? Everyone keeping busy.

And then the hearses arrived. Emma held Belle's hand tightly and Crystal held Belle's other hand, and the family went outside, down the steps.

The small, white coffins lay in the hearses, the funeral directors standing respectfully to one side. A beautiful floral owl with fern leaves for its feet was propped up on one of the coffins, which had *RIV* stencilled in blue on the side. On the coffin stencilled with *FREDDIE* was a fox's head made of orange gerberas. More flowers, from Belle, and the boys' grandparents, were arranged around the coffins.

Belle was gripping Emma's hand like a vice. Nobody spoke. Then Belle asked for the back of Freddie's hearse to be opened. She laid her hand on the little coffin, whispered Freddie's name, and closed her eyes.

Emma lay her hand beside her mother's, picturing her brother's sweet face, hearing his voice, his giggle, and her sisters followed. They moved to Riv, and Emma ran her fingers gently along the white wood.

*What happened to you, my darling brothers?*

'They're home now,' said Belle softly.

Grandpa Snow, awkward in the presence of so much female emotion, cleared his throat and suggested they get in the limousines.

The procession made its way over the short distance to the family chapel, and they exited the cars in front of the guests gathered outside. Emma saw Henry and Lady Madeline, DS Shore with a small group of police officers, Grandma and Grandpa Rivers, Mr Pickford and his wife ... Jane Warwick was here, and Aunt Kate and Uncle Jason. And just off to one side, by himself, stood Neville.

'What's *he* doing here?' said Belle sharply.

Crystal put a hand on her mother's arm. 'Don't get upset, Mum. He was practically part of our family, once. Let it go.'

Emma realised she'd been looking for Rowan, but of course, he couldn't come. Not when half the people here probably thought he'd murdered her brothers.

Henry came over and wrapped her in a hug, and she closed her eyes briefly, comforted by his familiar warmth.

'Emma,' said Lady Madeline, nodding at her as she pulled away. In head-to-toe black, she looked like a crow. She wore large sunglasses. Not appropriate.

Emma turned away; the pall bearers were hoisting the coffins onto their shoulders.

They made their way to the graveside, and the coffins were carefully laid on planks above the hole in the ground. The celebrant gave a reading, and a prayer, and then Belle read A.A. Milne's 'The End':

> '...*so I think I'll be six now*
> *Forever and ever.*'

Her voice was gentle, clear, full of love, and Emma didn't know how Belle got through it without breaking down.

The sisters held tight to each other's hands. Emma looked away from the gaping hole, from the coffins, staring hard at the grass beyond – anywhere else. But as Belle read the touching little poem, she thought, *Why am I trying to hold this in? Why should I care if people see how sad I am?*

She looked at the coffins, and an image of the boys playing in the old apple tree swam into her mind's eye. Leaning her head on Crystal's shoulder, she cried.

And then the pallbearers were lowering the boys, placing them side by side in the hole, and there was only the sound of muffled sobbing. Belle stepped forward and threw in a handful of earth, which clattered onto the coffins. Then two stem roses, white on white.

*'Ashes to ashes . . .'*

The funeral was over. People began walking away, blowing their noses, leaving Belle and her daughters alone beside the grave.

'That was beautiful,' Emma said, hugging her mother.

Over Belle's shoulder she saw Henry and Lady M, waiting for her.

'I can't face Henry's mother,' she said in Belle's ear. 'Could you—'

'Stay here,' said Belle. 'I'll tell them you want some time alone.'

'Thanks, Mum.' She gave her a final squeeze, then Belle went over to Henry.

He looked at Emma, and she smiled then turned away, her eyes moving down to the grave.

'Are you coming?' asked Pearl.

'I'll see you at the house. I'll walk back.'

As the guests returned to their cars, a quiet stole over the grave-yard, bringing with it a deep connection . . . nature, softly humming its song. Emma's senses tuned in, and she was aware of a gentle breeze passing through; the autumn sun warming the chapel's ancient walls; a skylark singing; patches of pale lichen spreading across centuries-old gravestones. Moss, its vibrant green softening the grey lines of the tombs. Life, pushing back against death.

A movement on the far side of the graveyard caught her eye. A fox. It trotted the length of the stone wall, its coat vivid against the green and grey, then stopped, looking at her for a moment, its ears pricked, amber eyes in amber fur, a splash of white around its black nose.

Then it was gone.

She sensed Rowan's presence before she saw him, half-hidden behind a tree by the wall.

Checking behind her – everyone had gone – she made her way over.

'Ems. You okay?' he said as he came to meet her. He was wearing his dark wool coat, and he'd had a haircut.

'Not really. That was hard. Lovely, but hard.' She looked into those eyes, wanting to drown. 'I really need a hug.' She started unbuttoning his coat.

'What are you doing?' he said, looking down at her.

She slipped her arms inside, around his waist, and rested her head on his chest, and a deep peace washed over her. After a moment's hesitation, his arms came round her, holding her tight.

'Rowan—'

'Thought I'd better stay out of sight.'

She looked up at him and smiled. 'Or Henry might beat you up again?'

'Did he tell you?'

'I worked it out. I'm quite the detective these days.' She took a breath. 'I have also been acquainting myself with the finer points of genetic profiling.'

'Ems,' he said, shaking his head a little, stroking her hair. 'Maybe save all this for later? You'll be wanting to get back to the house. Look . . . I should tell you, the police—'

'Rowan – you're not my uncle.'

His hand stilled; he said nothing.

'Richard's your father, yes. I found that out, like you did. But he's not my grandfather. Grandma had an affair, and Teddy was the result. Teddy wasn't your brother. We're not blood relatives.'

He searched her eyes, frowning, trying to make sense of what she was telling him. 'Are you shitting me, Ems?'

She smiled and shook her head, slowly. 'Oh dear, Rowan. I was hoping for better words. I just gave you the reason to stop sending me away. The reason why you can now kiss me and not be committing creepy incest. In fact – now would be good.'

'And how do you know this?' he said. She saw the suspicion in his eyes; he wasn't letting himself trust, not yet.

'From the police. The boys' DNA and yours – it shows no genetic relationship. And in the light of that, Grandma came clean to me, about Teddy's real dad. Teddy and you have different fathers, different mothers. So you're not related to Teddy. Ergo, you are most certainly *not* my uncle. Like I said, you can kiss me now.'

A bewildered smile – a look of wonderment – was spreading across his face.

'Emma Snow,' he said, incredulously. 'You absolute beauty.'

He bent his head to kiss her. It was tentative, as if he still couldn't quite believe it ... and she was suddenly overwhelmed. She started to cry again.

He took her face in his hands, wiping her cheeks with his thumbs. 'All too much?'

'Yes,' she sobbed. 'It's the saddest day of my life, and the happiest, all at once.'

He kissed her again, gently, sweetly, and she never wanted it to stop.

'More of those happy days to come, I think,' he said. 'Once you've properly told Henry to fuck off. Today?'

She nodded. Yes, it was time.

'You'd better go. They'll all be thinking another Snow child's been abducted. Sorry, crass remark. Look, Ems. Next time I see you, things will have changed. I'll call you—'

'Will you?' She'd gained some composure now. 'That'd be a first, Rowan.'

'I will do better, I promise. Go, now. No – wait. Kiss me again, and then go.'

She did, and he pulled her close, then closer still, and now the fire took hold. All the intensity of emotion – the pain of seeing those coffins lowered into the ground; the love for her family, for Rowan – it all coalesced into a longing that swamped her. The touch of him, the taste of him, his hands moving down her back, stopping, pressing her into him. Her insides were liquefying; she ached for him, she wanted him to consume her.

He stopped. 'Ems . . . I want to take you to bed and never get up again. But right now, you need to go.'

'Yes, I should.' She caught her breath, reeling. 'Any more of that and I won't actually be able to walk.'

He laughed softly, then his gaze moved over her shoulder as something caught his eye. 'Look.'

A barn owl, pale and silent as falling snow; ghostly, flying towards them across the graveyard, briefly illuminated as it caught the sun. Its eyes – coal-black circles in a round disk, almost like a human face. Swooping low over the stone wall then away across the stubby cornfield. And then . . . another, right behind it.

Long, slow wing beats; gliding, and then the pair reached the end of the field where it dropped away downhill.

They were gone.

'Do you believe in ghosts?' she said.

# Chapter Thirty-Eight

Sandal Manor's main hall echoed with the low buzz of conversation as Emma arrived back. Mrs Berry's teenage son and two of his friends were moving among the guests with refreshments. There was tea and coffee, but most people were having a restorative wine, and the mood was already brighter than it had been at the chapel.

She joined Belle, who was talking to Mr Pickford and his wife. '. . . it was lucky the science lab was well insured,' he was saying.

'I remember that phase,' said Belle. 'The explosions one. They'd moved on from matches by then.'

Mrs Pickford grimaced.

'Remember when they discovered what you could do with a magnifying glass on a sunny day?' said Emma with a grin.

'You threatened to call the RSPCA,' said Belle.

'The Royal Society for the Prevention of Cruelty to Ants,' they said together.

'And they burned *Leeds FC* on the lawn, for Teddy,' said Belle.

Emma smiled sadly. 'Little monsters.' When all this was over, she'd tell her mother about the owls.

DS Shore appeared next to them, waiting to speak.

'Thank you for coming, Liz,' said Emma. 'And your colleagues. We really appreciate it.'

'May I have a quick word with you both?' she asked.

They moved to the side of the room. 'I wanted to apologise—' Liz began.

'No no,' interrupted Belle. 'We know how hard the police have worked on the case.'

'Mrs Snow – I'm apologising because I just took a call, which confirmed something I'd been waiting on. It's not the best timing, but . . . we need to do this now, before people start to leave.'

'Do what?' said Emma.

Liz looked at Emma. 'You saw Rowan?'

Emma's heart stopped for a moment. *Surely* . . .

'*Rowan?*' said Belle. 'He wasn't at the funeral.'

'Yes, he was,' said Emma. 'I saw him.'

*Next time I see you, things will have changed.*

Emma felt the blood drain from her face. *No . . . oh my god.*

Liz looked across the hall at her two colleagues, who were watching her, and nodded. 'Like I said, I'm sorry for having to do this now. Please, excuse me.'

Belle and Emma looked at each other, Belle in confusion, Emma in horror, as DS Shore went over to the other police officers. Then the three of them moved across the room, past Crystal and Pearl, who were talking to Jane Warwick; past Grandma and Grandpa Rivers, who were with Grandma and Grandpa Snow . . .

The hall fell silent as the guests noticed the officers crossing the room with intent.

They were approaching Henry, where he stood with his mother. He turned, frowning.

The police carried on to where Neville was standing with Aunt Kate and Uncle Jason, and stopped in front of the group of three.

'Oh my god,' whispered Belle, her hand going to her throat. '*Neville.*'

Emma was hit by a wave of nausea.

'Jason Theodore,' said DS Shore. 'You are under arrest on suspicion of the murders of Elfred and River Snow. You do not have to say anything, but it may harm your defence . . . '

The rest of her words were a buzz in Emma's ears. Belle's

eyes were wide as she paled. Emma put an arm round her mother's waist.

'What?' gasped Belle. '*Jason?* No. It couldn't possibly be ...'

Jason was staring at DS Shore, shaking his head. His eyes went over Liz's shoulder, to Lady Madeline and Henry, who had frozen.

Liz nodded to one of the officers to stay with Jason, then she and the other policeman moved back towards Henry and Lady M.

'Lady Madeline Beauregard, you are under arrest on suspicion of aiding and abetting Jason Theodore in the murders of Elfred and River Snow. You do not have to say anything ...'

'Oh my god,' whispered Emma. 'Oh my god ...'

Henry was staring in shock at his mother, then he turned to the police officers. 'This is ridiculous.' His voice was quiet and low, but carried in the silence of the hall. 'On what evidence are you basing these allegations?'

'Utter incompetence,' snapped Lady M. 'I expect better from the Yorkshire Police.'

'It's the Leicestershire Police we have to thank for their efforts,' said DS Shore. 'And Rowan Bosworth.'

'*What?*' blurted Henry.

Emma saw Rowan appear in the doorway, taking in the scene in front of him.

Jason was brought by the arm over to DS Shore. Aunt Kate, a hand over her mouth, was ashen.

Jason looked over at Belle, his face stricken. Emma could feel her mother trembling. 'I'm so sorry, Belle,' Jason said. 'It was an accident – a terrible accident. The boys didn't suffer, I promise you.' He swallowed. 'I wanted to call an ambulance – the police – but Madeline wouldn't ... they were already dead. There was nothing we could do.'

'For god's sake, Jason – shut up!' barked Lady Madeline.

'No, I won't shut up,' said Jason, sounding stronger. 'You're a terrible, terrible person. You care more about your reputation than the lives of those two young boys. And their poor family – imagine not knowing, all this time.'

'Dad . . . ' Henry's face was twisted with confusion. 'For chris-sakes, explain yourself.'

Jason looked at DS Shore, who came over to Belle and said, 'Mrs Snow. You'll have many questions. We may not be able to answer them fully until we've interviewed Mr Theodore and Lady Madeline.' She turned to her officers. 'Take them to the station. I'll stay here and talk to the family.'

Lily stepped forward. 'Perhaps the rest of us should go to the conservatory, give you some privacy.' She nodded at Belle. 'Come find me, darling, afterwards.'

The guests started to leave the room, and the pause gave Emma the chance to take a breath, to try to understand what was happening. She noticed Neville's eyes on Rowan where he stood in the doorway, but Rowan was watching Sir Richard, and Emma saw her grandfather's gaze meet his son's before he followed Lily out of the room.

Jane took Neville by the arm and led him away.

Emma's eyes moved across those who were left.

Henry seemed unable to look away from his mother – as though, if he stared hard enough, this might make some sense.

Lady Madeline's face was blank.

Jason was hanging his head; he kept shaking it.

Rowan came over, his eyes on Emma. She slipped her hand in his, and he squeezed it.

'Rowan gave us the breakthrough we needed,' began DS Shore, as Lady Madeline and Jason were taken away.

Emma looked at Rowan in surprise, and he half-smiled.

'Your sons, Mrs Snow,' continued DS Shore, 'were intending to sabotage a fox hunt on the day they disappeared.'

'Oh, my darlings . . . ' breathed Belle.

'Rowan found information about the saboteur group in with their school project on foxes. He investigated the hunts the group had been targeting, and on the day in question, there was an illegal hunt in the Wensleydale area. Lady Madeline was in attendance, as was Jason Theodore.'

Emma frowned in confusion. *Even Lady Mad wouldn't kill two boys for interfering with a fox hunt.*

'We have yet to establish what happened – it looks as if Mr Theodore will be willing to tell us – but somehow, the boys died that day.'

'But how did they end up in Leicester? Buried in a car park?' said Emma.

'Rowan, do you want to explain?' said Liz.

Rowan slipped an arm round Emma's waist.

Henry breathed in sharply and took a step forward.

'Back off, Henry,' warned Rowan.

'Perhaps you should leave, Mr Theodore?' suggested DS Shore.

'I'll stay,' he said grimly.

'It was a lucky break,' said Rowan. He looked at Belle. 'I made the connection between the fox hunt and the boys. I got in touch with the saboteurs, but they didn't see Freddie and Riv that day. That left the hunters – Lady Mad and her pals, including her ex-husband. The internet told me he was in the country at the time.'

His gaze move to Henry. 'I googled Jason Theodore, and the month – February 2010 – and up popped a photo of your father at the opening of his latest property development, the new Leicester City Council offices.'

He paused as Henry returned his stare. Neither dropped their eyes.

'Rowan went to Leicester,' continued DS Shore, 'and persuaded the police there to excavate under the car park, as the photo showed this hadn't yet been laid when the opening ceremony took place. Rowan was, as we know, correct in his suspicions.'

'But ... Jason,' said Belle, shaking her head. 'I still can't believe it.'

'*Lady Madeline*,' said Emma. She looked at Henry. 'Didn't you say she's always bailing out Jason's failed property developments?'

Henry dropped his eyes, saying nothing.

'She probably threatened him with bankruptcy, or bribed him, or something,' pressed Emma. 'He most often did as he was told, right, Henry?'

Henry nodded.

'She'll have ordered him to dispose of the bodies, even if they died by accident, so her *reputation* wouldn't be damaged.'

'We should know soon,' said DS Shore. 'And of course, the priority now is to find out exactly what happened to the boys. I should get back to the station. I'll be in touch very soon, Mrs Snow.'

'Come with me,' said Rowan, as Liz left. He led Emma into the deserted entrance hall. 'I'm going back to Wensleydale. When you're ready, come see me.'

'Yes. I will.' She put a hand on his arm, looking up at him. 'Rowan – you solved it. I can hardly take it all in but . . . you did it.'

'Yup. I had to,' he said, putting his hands on her waist. 'I needed my life back.' There was a mischievous smile. 'You might say . . . I had a hunch.'

Emma snorted. 'Stop it.'

'And meanwhile,' he continued, 'my beautiful girl was busy discovering she wasn't my niece.' He bent to kiss her, but stopped as Belle burst through the doors behind them, her eyes wide. 'Emerald – no! You know you can't—'

*We never told Belle, though . . .*

Emma grinned. 'I can, Mum. He's not my uncle. You need to talk to Grandma. Trust me on this.'

'What?' Belle turned to Rowan. 'Richard's not your father?'

'No,' said Emma, 'Richard *is* his—'

Rowan put a finger on her lips. 'Save it for later.' Then he winked at Belle as he tightened his arms round Emma's waist, and kissed her.

'I love you so much,' she whispered, when he finally let her go. 'Thank you.'

He chuckled. 'Emma Snow, you're so polite. I'll be off. You know where to find me. Make it soon.'

Emma returned to the great hall. Henry was standing by

the window, looking shellshocked, and Emma's heart went out to him.

She joined him. 'I'm so sorry, Henry. I can hardly believe it . . . your mother.'

He shook his head. 'I can't think straight. And Dad . . . '

She touched his arm. 'And I'm sorry this has all come out at the same time as . . . as me and Rowan. I'd like to explain, when this is all over, why we didn't—'

'I don't want to hear it.' His tone was bleak. 'Why would I want to? I appear to have lost everything today. My mother, my father, and you.'

Emma swallowed.

'Thing is, Emma . . . ' He turned to face her properly. 'I've always known you loved him. You're terrible at lying. And yes, I tried to pin the blame for the boys onto him—'

'Those pieces in the paper,' she said. 'Starting with that first one, with the quotes from Neville, even before you were at the *Chronicle*. They were all down to you.' She hadn't meant to kick him when he was down, but it all came spilling out. 'You listened in on a private conversation with my family, then you went off and phoned Neville.'

'Neville Warwick was more than happy to shit on Bosworth, and he had every reason to.' His eyes were as icy-blue as Perkin's. 'That girl, Abigail – your precious Bosworth more or less kept her prisoner once they were married. She never went out. He made her emotionally dependent on him. She had eating disorders, she took drugs . . . then she died. So yes, I may have been wrong about the boys, but not the rest of it.'

Emma shook her head in disbelief. 'So much for being objective. You heard what you wanted to hear. You didn't think to question Neville's side of the story? Why didn't you speak to Abigail's mother? That was shoddy journalism, Henry, right there.'

'There was no need to speak to the mother, I had what I needed.'

'Oh yes, you most certainly did.' Emma narrowed her eyes. 'Including carefully selected excerpts from my notes – the parts that might have incriminated Rowan – and files downloaded from my computer, which you fed to the police.'

He shrugged. 'You were my employee; you were away in Leicester. It was in the interests of the police investigation that I forwarded your research.'

'Your *employee*? Well, that journalist nose of yours was way off the mark. And your hatchet job on Rowan was verging on the criminal. He's had to live as a recluse because of you. You trashed another man's reputation, mostly because you were jealous.'

'No,' he said. 'You're wrong. I did it because I genuinely believed he took the boys. I thought once your eyes were opened, then you'd stop … ' He paused, and his expression changed. 'You'd stop loving him.'

The fight left him, replaced by defeat.

'I was trying to save you from him, as well as keep you for myself.'

He was telling the truth as he saw it.

'Henry … ' Emma couldn't help it. In spite of what he'd done to Rowan, she still had feelings for this man. She touched his arm again, and he flinched.

'I know it's probably too soon,' she said, 'but … can we stay friends? We were happy, weren't we? We shouldn't let go of that.'

# Chapter Thirty-Nine

D S Shore returned the following morning, and Belle, Emma, her sisters and their grandparents sat around the kitchen table while she explained what had happened.

Jason had been relieved to tell the truth, it seemed. Contrite, willing to do anything to help, as far as he was able.

Lady Madeline – not so much.

On the day of the boys' deaths, she'd arrived an hour or so before the hunt was due to meet, and had been checking out the covert where the fox was thought to be hiding. But the boys had got there first, armed with a banner saying *FOX HUNTING IS MURDER* and a pair of cymbals to frighten the horses.

She'd shooed them out, told them to be on their way, back to school, but they'd refused to leave, lecturing her on the suffering endured by the fox at the kill.

Emma met Belle's eye and smiled a little as she pictured it.

Lady M had changed tack, inviting them into her horsebox to discuss the matter further, saying she'd drive them home after the hunt.

Then she'd locked them in, and their bikes.

Lady M's horsebox was, apparently, the Montfort Grange of horseboxes, with a lounge, bathroom and kitchen. She'd moved it away from where the other horseboxes would be parking, in case the boys shouted for help.

On her return that afternoon, she'd discovered the boys dead. It had been a bitterly cold February day and, unable to switch on the heaters because Lady M had turned off the electricity, the boys had looked for a way to warm up. They'd had a box of matches with them (*of course – when didn't they?*) so they lit all the gas hobs, and later passed out due to carbon monoxide poisoning. There was no flue, or fan, and they hadn't thought to open a window.

Belle started to cry, and Emma put an arm round her.

'They fell asleep and didn't wake up, Mum. They didn't suffer, like Jason said.'

'Fuckin' cow,' muttered Pearl, swiping at her cheeks.

In a panic, Lady M had summoned Jason and, as Emma had suspected, threatened to ruin him if he didn't help her cover it up. Otherwise, Lady M would have been held responsible for their deaths – accidental or not, she'd locked up two young boys and left them without supervision.

Although she hadn't at first realised who they were, Jason had immediately recognised them as his wife's nephews. He'd been distraught, but in the end, as ever, he'd done as he was told. Driven the boys to Leicester in the early hours of the morning, and buried them in the car park that was due to be concreted that week.

It was over. Or at least it would be, when Lady M was in prison. And Jason too, though as Emma drove home from Sandal Manor early on Saturday morning, she found herself hoping his sentence wouldn't be too harsh.

She stopped at Gregory Lane just long enough to pack a small bag and pop round to ask her neighbour to feed Perkin over the weekend. Emma was assuming that this time, Rowan wouldn't send her home.

'This is just a flying visit, little boy,' she said, removing Perkin from the holdall she'd put on the bed. 'But I'll be back soon. Ish.'

And then she was on the road north again, Ed Sheeran loud on the car stereo (Belle had alerted her to this new talent – another of her 'ones to watch'), turning off the A1, the signs flashing by: *Middleham ... Aysgarth ...*

She glanced over the drystone walls. Somewhere along here, Freddie and Riv had parked their bikes and hidden in a covert, ready to defend the fox. She smiled sadly. 'I love you, brave boys,' she said out loud.

She reached the farm, opened the gate, closed it ... there was no sign of Mr Haworth.

Pulling up outside the farmhouse, she turned off the engine and the music stopped, and as she exited her Mini, the silence of the Yorkshire Dales settled over her. Just the bleating of the sheep, the cawing of crows, and the trill of a yellowhammer ... *little bit of bread and no cheeeese.*

She took a deep breath and smiled – Rowan's bread! And his Wensleydale cheese. Would he bake bread this weekend? Maybe she had a lifetime of his bread to look forward to. Her heart was bursting with anticipation at the thought of seeing him, at the thought of everything to come.

Mr Haworth appeared round the side of the house. He really was the very definition of ubiquitous.

'Hello, lass! I saw you come through the gate. He's up near the wood, mending the wall. I'm getting a bit old meself, for lifting stones.'

'Hello! Good to see you, Mr Haworth. Thanks – I'll find him.'

He came closer and met her eye. 'I read about your brothers, love. I'm that sorry.'

Emma had avoided the papers. She didn't need to read their take on it all.

'That Lady Madeline asked to hunt across our land a few times,' he said. 'Rowan told her to eff off. She's a piece o' work. I hope they lock her up and throw away the key.'

'Me too. Well ... '

His face broke into a smile. 'I can see you're in a hurry. Go get 'im, lass.'

Halfway across the field Teddy appeared, racing towards her.

She bent down to pat him. 'Where is he, boy? Where's your gorgeous master?'

Teddy took off back the way he'd come, and she spotted Rowan hoisting a large stone onto a broken-down part of the wall between the field and the woodland.

He saw her and stopped, pushing back his hair, smiling, resting his hands on his hips. His shirt was open, revealing a muscular, tanned torso that belied the writer-hermit-in-a-cave she'd imagined.

She waved and speeded up, finally breaking into a run. And then he was lifting her up and her legs were round him, and she buried her face in his thick black hair which smelled of woodsmoke and fresh moorland air and ... Rowan. She squeezed him between her legs and his arms tightened around her waist, then he was kissing her, and this time there was no reason to stop.

'Hello, lovely non-relation,' he said, carrying her over to the wall, sitting her down on the part he'd been rebuilding. 'Emma-not-in-fact-a-Snow.' He kissed her again, and as it grew intense, pushed her legs apart, pulling her towards him and pressing himself against her.

'Rowan,' she gasped, as his mouth travelled down her neck, 'should we go back to the house?'

'Why?' he said into her skin. He undid the top buttons of her shirt, his fingers brushing her chest, then pushed it open, kissing the hollow above her collarbone. 'I thought you were a lover of the outdoors.'

'But someone might—'

'No, they won't.' He undid more buttons, and slipped a hand inside her shirt, gently stroking her breast, his lips moving down. She gripped his hair. 'Private property,' he said. 'No one comes into my wood.' Then he paused, looking up. Teddy was watching them with interest. 'Avert your eyes, dog,' he said. 'Shoo!'

Teddy looked at them for a moment longer, then took off.

He let her go and took a step back, and she wobbled on the wall, dizzy with desire. 'Tell me,' he said, 'about the boys. What happened?'

'Now?' She admonished herself. 'Sorry, yes, of course now.'

Her heart was racing; she couldn't think straight. All she wanted was for him to finally deal with this longing. She shuffled a little, to regain her balance, and a flat stone skittered to the ground.

He tutted. 'Mind my wall, girl,' he said, picking it up and laying it back in place.

She laughed. 'Mum always told me not to break down your walls.'

'She said what?'

'Never mind.'

He took her hand and kissed it. 'Tell me,' he said, gently, not letting it go, 'about Freddie and Riv. I've avoided the news.'

So she explained how her brothers had suffocated from carbon monoxide poisoning in Lady Mad's horsebox, while trying to keep themselves warm.

He kissed away her tears, then they were quiet for a moment.

'It's kind of a relief, Ems. The nightmares I've had, about them being abused and murdered.'

'I know. Me too.' She leaned her forehead on his.

'But Jason Theodore,' he said. 'Why didn't he tell the police? Why would he bury them for her? How could he live with himself?'

'He was totally blackmailed by Lady Mad. She deserves to rot in hell. Jason, though—' Emma sighed. 'I don't know. I hope they're not too hard on him. I'm sure he's suffered horribly already.'

Rowan raised his eyebrows, shook his head a little. 'Jesus, Ems, we still need to toughen you up. He was a stupid twat; he deserves to have the book thrown at him. You're way too soft. Next you'll be telling me you want to stay best friends with Henry.'

'Who?' she said.

He grinned. 'Turn round.' He picked up the same small back-pack he'd had with him on the failed badger watch and dropped it on the other side of the wall, then nimbly climbed over. Emma swivelled, and he lifted her down.

She kept her arms around his neck and he kissed her again, and finished unbuttoning her shirt, slipping his hands inside, round to her back, tracing her spine with his fingers, stroking the curve of her waist. He pulled her closer and her skin was pressed against his warm chest, and the longing returned in a rush. Then he grabbed her hand and led her a short way into the woods, stopping by an old tree with a smooth, silvery trunk.

At last he let rip, pushing her up against the tree, kissing her lips, her neck, letting loose her hair, tangling his fingers in it; pulling off her shirt, running his hands over her skin ... There was no holding him back. It was like being in the path of a wildfire and her body ignited as he explored it, tugging off her jeans and underwear, his hand between her legs, touching her, stroking her, his fingers slipping inside her, sending her quickly to the edge. Then he lifted her up as if she weighed nothing, hoisting her legs round his hips and finally ...

She let out a moan, her head falling back, gripping his shoulder with one hand, reaching the other up and back, her back arched, her fingers splayed against the smooth bark of the tree. She looked up as sunlight flashed and twinkled through the leaves overhead, lighting up bunches of red berries, dappling her body, and the cool autumn air caressed her heated skin as Rowan thrust harder, deeper, pushing her towards heaven.

'Slow down,' she gasped. 'Stop.'

'Stop?'

But he did, and she looked into his eyes.

'I need you to know,' she said, trying to catch her breath, 'how much I love you. What you mean to me. How much I want you ...'

He smiled, his hands supporting her, and then he moved, just a little, holding her gaze. His pupils were dilated; there was a hint of wickedness and she gasped again as, with aching slowness, he pushed back into her. 'Love you too, Ems.'

Slowly, sensuously, he carried on, not taking his dark eyes from hers. She spiralled into their depths, whispering 'oh god' as he moved faster. And then she gave herself up to the waves of pleasure that gripped her, each more intense than the last, until there was an exquisite burst, like an explosion of white light, and she finally closed her eyes, breathing his name as she flopped forward, spent, her arms around his neck, resting her head against his.

'Christ, Ems,' he said into her hair. 'What you do to me.'

She moved her hands to his hair, stroking it, keeping her legs around him, squeezing him tight. 'I won't ever, ever, let you get away from me again.'

She lay on his woolly blanket, her head in his lap, and he fed her freshly baked bread and cheese.

The sun shone through the branches of this beautiful tree with its bunches of scarlet berries and its smooth (*just as well*) silvery bark, creating a halo of light around his mane of dark hair as she looked up at him.

'What type of tree is this?' she asked.

He bit into a piece of cheese. 'Thought you were the expert.'

'Is it ... ah, wait. A mountain ash?'

'Fuck's sake girl, give it its proper name.'

She grinned. 'A rowan.'

'That there was an Emma sandwich,' he said. 'Squished between two Rowans.'

She chuckled. 'Don't rowans have, like, magical properties, or something?'

'They're known for their power to ward off witches. Probably not a good choice for your mum's garden.'

Emma almost choked on her bread.

'But more importantly,' he said, 'the Druids consider them portals between worlds.'

'Figures,' she said, reaching up, stroking a finger down his face. 'You just took me to heaven.'

Later, in the farmhouse, she sat beside him on the sheepskin rug by the fire. He was lying on his stomach, his head turned towards the flames, and she watched the firelight flickering across his face.

She trailed a finger down his naked spine.

'Maybe don't,' he said, shifting a little as she traced the curve. 'It's part of you, it's beautiful.'

She leaned over and kissed the nape of his neck, then moved her lips down his spine, dropping kisses all along its length.

He flipped over and pulled her on top of him, and she wondered, would this ache ever lessen? Would she ever get enough of this man?


'Will you go back to writing under your real name?' Emma asked later. The room had grown dark; there was only the glow from the fire, reflected on their skin. 'And – what *does* the P stand for?'

'Work it out,' he said lazily.

'R is for Rowan.'

'Also Richard,' he said. 'My father's name.'

Emma made a mental note – Sir Richard would need to make an effort to get to know his son.

'Richard, right. P . . . I don't know.'

'Think about the surname – the real one. Bear in mind the Tudors were Welsh nobodies, with a very dodgy claim to the throne. Not very kingly.'

'Bosworth. I see. That's quite a coincidence, that Henry and Richard battled it out at Bosworth Field.'

'Never rely on coincidence in your writing, Ems. Different outcome, anyway. This time, Richard got to keep the beautiful princess. Emma of York.'

She turned her head slightly, kissed his chest. 'So what's the answer? Will you go back to being Rowan Bosworth?'

'Maybe not.' He stretched luxuriously, then looked at her through those ridiculously long eyelashes. 'I rather like being King.'

# *Historical note*

## The real story, people and places

Elizabeth of York (Emma Snow) grew up at the magnificent fifteenth-century court of **Edward IV** (Teddy Snow) and his queen, **Elizabeth Woodville** (Belle Snow). The eldest of ten children, she was the archetypal medieval princess – beautiful, with long fair hair; accomplished, modest and kind. Elizabeth of York's main claim to fame is probably that she was Henry VIII's mother.

England was finally at peace (mostly) after the Wars of the Roses, during which the House of Lancaster (red rose) and the House of York (white rose) – two branches of the Plantagenet family, who had ruled England for 300 years – had fought for the throne. The Yorks were finally victorious, at the Battle of Towton (1461), reputed to be the bloodiest battle ever fought on British soil.

Edward IV, the victor, was quite a guy. He was England's tallest-ever king, taller even than his lofty grandson King Henry VIII. Although perhaps eclipsed as kingliest king by Henry, he was magnificent – handsome, affable, much-loved by his people; a brilliant warrior who brought peace after years of war.

Edward IV was the first English king since the Conquest to marry for love. Although that sounds deliciously romantic, it all started to slide as he grew older. He was a terrible womaniser and enjoyed a spot of whoring on the streets of London. His ways, which leaned towards debauchery, may well have contributed to his early death at the age of forty.

Edward's queen, Elizabeth Woodville, is famous for her beauty, which captivated the king to the extent that he married her in secret, when the powerful **Earl of Warwick** (Neville Warwick), known as The Kingmaker, was busily organising a political alliance in which Edward would marry a French princess. Unsurprisingly, Warwick was unhappy about Edward's marriage, and it was the beginning of the end of his relationship with Edward.

Elizabeth Woodville and her mother, **Jacquetta of Luxembourg** (Jacquetta the cat), had a river goddess in their family tree (really!), and rumours of witchcraft swirled around the pair. How else would a common(ish) girl bag a king?

During Edward's reign, the last hope of the House of Lancaster, **Henry Tudor** (Henry Theodore), was in exile in France with his uncle, **Jasper Tudor** (Jason Theodore). Henry's mother, **Lady Margaret Beaufort** (Lady Madeline Beauregard), was busy attempting to get Henry back to England, and, later, for him to take the throne.

Lady Margaret was a formidable woman. A noble and wealthy heiress in her own right, her her ambitions for her son are legendary. Married to Edmund Tudor at the age of twelve, she gave birth to Henry when only thirteen, and it was traumatic. She never had any more children.

When Edward IV was dying, he named his brother, **Richard Plantagenet, Duke of Gloucester** (Rowan Bosworth) as Protector, until Edward's twelve-year-old heir **Edward V** (Freddie Snow) was old enough to rule. Richard put Edward V in the Tower of London while preparations were underway for the boy's coronation. It's important to note that it was tradition for monarchs to reside in the Tower before their coronation – there was nothing particularly sinister about this, as it was a royal residence as well as a prison at the time.

However, a respected bishop came forward to say Edward IV's

children were illegitimate, and that the true heir to the throne was therefore Richard. (Edward IV may indeed have been a bigamist, but it has never been proved that he was already contracted when he married Elizabeth Woodville.) A group of officials described as 'the three estates of this realm of England' petitioned Richard to take the throne, and his ascension was subsequently ratified by Parliament in a document called Titulus Regius (Royal Title). Henry VII later had all copies of this document destroyed.

Incidentally, the middle of the three York princes, (the 'Three Sons of York'), **George, Duke of Clarence** (Rowan's first black Labrador), had made a bid for the throne during Edward's reign, claiming that *Edward* was illegitimate. Some historians believe this could be true, as their mother, **Cecily Neville** (Lady Lily Snow) may have had a fling with an archer (Tom Archer) in France while her husband **Richard, Duke of York** (Sir Richard Snow) was away fighting. George's bid failed and Edward IV executed him for treason. The story goes that he was allowed to choose his own method of execution, and was drowned in a butt of malmsey (wine).

Back to Elizabeth of York's story ... Fearing for her family's safety, Elizabeth Woodville took sanctuary with her children in Westminster Abbey. Richard persuaded Elizabeth to let her younger son, **Richard** (River Snow), join his brother in the Tower.

By the time Elizabeth and her daughters emerged, the girls joining Richard's court, sightings of the two boys in the Tower had stopped.

Richard III ruled England for two years. He was loved and respected in the north, which he'd ruled during Edward IV's reign. Richard put great value on knightly virtues, and is known for his loyalty, to his brother Edward in particular.

Richard had scoliosis – sideways curvature of the spine. (He didn't have kyphosis, an outward curve which results in a 'hunch'.) This was confirmed when his skeleton was unearthed in a Leicester car park in 2012. The most obvious effect would have been that one shoulder was higher than the other.

He was a strong, capable leader, and he attempted to bring in laws that would benefit the common man, but such ideas weren't appreciated by the southern nobles he had to deal with.

Before he became king, Richard married **Anne Neville** (Abigail Warwick), daughter of the Earl of Warwick. They had one child, a son, who died young, and after this Anne's health began to fail.

Meanwhile at court, something was going on between King Richard and Elizabeth of York.

After some clever forward planning by her mother and Lady Margaret Beaufort, Elizabeth had been promised in marriage to Henry Tudor, still biding his time in France. This York–Lancaster alliance would consolidate the peace, and would strengthen the Tudor position (Henry's claim was shaky).

But rumours swirled that King Richard was planning to marry Elizabeth if his ailing wife died. The rumours were so strong that Richard publicly denied them. Elizabeth may well have wanted to marry Richard, in spite of their close blood relationship (he was her uncle). There's a fragment of a letter (most of it was burned) in which she seems to be asking for the matter of her marriage to Richard to be hurried up, because there's nothing she wants more.

Did Elizabeth and Richard have feelings for each other? Richard certainly paid her much attention, dancing with her, organising for her to have clothes as lovely as the Queen's (more significant than it might sound). But we don't know. Even in the days when marrying your noble cousin was considered normal, an uncle having a relationship with his niece was decidedly unsavoury. The populace were shocked at the rumours.

One theory is that Richard encouraged the gossip so that Henry Tudor would hear Elizabeth was spoiled goods, and would decline to marry her, scuppering the alliance that would have made Henry an attractive proposition to the people of England.

At the time, Richard was negotiating to marry a Portuguese princess, and for Elizabeth to marry the future king of Portugal. The rumours about Richard and Elizabeth could have been stoked by supporters of the Tudor cause in an effort to derail these negotiations.

But then Henry invaded, and Richard was killed at the Battle of

Bosworth Field. He died a noble death, fighting bravely to the end. He was the last English king to die in battle.

Jasper Tudor joined Henry at court when he became king. Lady Margaret Beaufort held a great deal of influence; she insisted on being addressed as My Lady the King's Mother (and she had better rooms than the Queen). But in spite of often being portrayed as the mother-in-law from hell, Lady Margaret seems to have had a reasonable relationship with her daughter-in-law.

Henry and Elizabeth's marriage is believed to have been a happy one, and unlike Elizabeth's father, Edward IV, and her son, Henry VIII, Henry VII was apparently a faithful husband. He reigned for twenty-four years. He wasn't a popular monarch, lacking the charisma and common touch of his son, Henry VIII. He was suspicious and paranoid, always worrying about rebellions, and he imposed unpopular taxes. He had a reputation for stinginess, but he didn't hold back when it came to spending on manifestations of his Tudor importance. The Tudor rose, incorporating the Lancastrian red rose and the York white rose, was everywhere, and is still highly recognisable today.

Henry and Elizabeth had four children. The eldest, Arthur, died young, and as a consequence Elizabeth was perhaps overprotective of the remaining male heir, Henry, and he in turn was devoted to his mother. And so a spoiled brat was created! And from Henry VIII's point of view, perhaps no wife could ever compare to his mother ...

Elizabeth died in her thirties, and her husband (and son) were said to be heartbroken.

## Who killed the Princes in the Tower – if anyone?

The mystery of the Princes in the Tower remains unsolved, and this whodunnit is still hotly debated. If they were killed, suspects include Richard III, Lady Margaret Beaufort, Henry VII, and the Duke of Buckingham. Sir James Tyrrell, a knight loyal to Richard, allegedly confessed to the boys' murders many years later when on trial for treason, claiming they were smothered in their beds. But he was unable to say where they were buried, and the original document of this 'confession', reported in Sir Thomas More's *History of King Richard III*, was never produced. There is no other contemporary record of Tyrrell's words, and many historians dismiss the confession as fiction – part of the 'Tudor propaganda' campaign.

Perhaps the Princes weren't murdered at all. Perhaps Richard had them removed from the Tower, most likely overseas, for their own safety.

Henry VII put down two rebellions led by pretenders claiming to be the brothers returned from abroad. One of those, **Perkin Warbeck** (Perkin the cat), who claimed to be the younger brother, was acknowledged by a number of European monarchs, including the King of Scotland, and the Holy Roman Emperor. The princes' aunt (Edward IV's sister), Margaret of Burgundy, apparently believed he was her nephew. Warbeck claimed his elder brother had been murdered, but that he had been spared due to his young age and 'innocence'. His rebellion failed and he confessed to having made up his identity – however, the confession was likely given under 'duress'.

A pair of skeletons was discovered beneath a stairway in the Tower of London in 1674, but it has never been proved these were the boys. Old bones weren't a rarity in the Tower. The skeletons were interred in Westminster Abbey.

The Tudors promoted the belief that Richard III had the princes murdered, as the remaining Plantagenets were a threat to the throne. It was in their interest to blacken the Plantagenet name, as the Tudors' hold on power was shaky, and there were still Plantagenets waiting in the wings. Many thought their claim was stronger. Over the courses of their reigns, the two Henrys gradually mopped them up.

The historical heavyweights responsible for the enduring

anti-Richard 'propaganda' were Sir Thomas More in his *History of King Richard III*, and William Shakespeare in *Richard III*.

Thomas More was part of Henry VIII's team, and Shakespeare was writing in the time of Elizabeth I, the last Tudor monarch. Shakespeare's portrayal of an evil hunchback child murderer would become the accepted image of Richard for centuries to come.

More recently, people have questioned this image. It has been proved that portraits of Richard were tampered with, to exaggerate his 'hump', and frown lines were added. (In centuries past, a disablement or disfigurement was taken as a sign that you were a bad person.)

In the 1950s, Josephine Tey's book *The Daughter of Time* approached the mystery of the Princes in the Tower as a modern whodunnit, with a detective concluding Richard was innocent, and the rehabilitation of this king's image properly began.

More recently (2012), the the Looking for Richard project, supported by the Richard III Society, which aims to exonerate this much-maligned monarch, organised the search for and eventual excavation of Richard's remains from a Leicester car park, and interest in Richard III surged again. There is now a strong body of opinion that states he was a capable ruler whose bad reputation was the result of Tudor propaganda. (However, the majority of historians probably still believe Richard III was responsible for the princes' murders. They were brutal times, and the Plantagenets were super-efficient at dealing with rivals to the throne.)

## Footnotes

Richard III knew **Anne Neville** most of his life, as they spent time together at Middleham Castle during their childhoods. They were married for thirteen years. Anne's death is mysterious – she seems to have faded away after the death of their only child. It was likely a terminal illness, maybe tuberculosis, but there was also talk of poisoning, and this was around the same time as rumours surfaced about Richard's possible affair with Elizabeth of York.

**Elizabeth ('Jane') Shore** (DS Shore) was Edward IV's favourite mistress. They had a long-term relationship that lasted until his death, after which she ran messages between Edward's ally, William Hastings, and Elizabeth Woodville, incurring the wrath of Richard III, who charged her with conspiracy.

## Places

Sandal Manor is based on **Sandal Castle**, now in ruins, which is near Wakefield. This was the castle of two Dukes of York, and Richard III chose it as his northern base just before he died at Bosworth.

Middleham College is based on **Middleham Castle**, in the Yorkshire Dales, where Richard III spent several years of his childhood, under the tutelage of the Earl of Warwick, the castle's owner.

# Acknowledgements

Firstly I'd like to thank my friend Alison Reynolds. When were discussing who I might focus on for my third book, she suggested I read Josephine Tey's *The Daughter of Time*. I'd been pondering on Richard III for a while, and this was the push I needed to give him my full attention, which quickly developed into an obsession. I'd highly recommend Tey's novel to anyone interested in Richard and the mystery surrounding the Princes' disappearance. (And hunt down a copy of Sharon Penman's *The Sunne in Splendour* too – you won't regret it!)

Enormous thanks to Ali's sister, Dame Fiona Reynolds, who checked the environmental and countryside content that is a key part of this story. Fiona and Ali gave me invaluable feedback on the plot and characters too. Thank you both so much for your thoughtful insight and enthusiasm, and for your championing of British history and wild places.

My grateful thanks to Matthew Lewis, chairman of the Richard III Society, who was kind enough to give my historical note the once over. Matt's excellent books on this fascinating period of English history, particularly *The Survival of the Princes in the Tower* and *Richard III, Fact and Fictions*, informed much of my story.

Thanks also to my lovely journalist friend Sue Bishop, who allowed me to borrow her name and checked through the newspaper office parts for me.

My old friend (and brilliant artist) Dominic Zwemmer contributed his partisan (ha) thoughts on the Houses of York and Lancaster, and in so doing demonstrated how the Wars of the Roses are by no means over. Thanks, Dominic, and I look forward to yarning further on Richard, hopefully in the pub, when I can finally travel again.

The editing on this book took place during the various stages of UK lockdown, and I'd like to thank my three wonderful editors at Little Brown UK – Emma Beswetherick, Eleanor Russell and Sarah Murphy – for your enthusiasm under what I'm sure were trying circumstances. Thanks also to copy editor Tom Feltham for that final buff. It's been such a pleasure to work with you all.

Heartfelt thanks, as ever, to my wonderful agents Vicki Marsdon and Nadine Rubin Nathan at Highspot Literary for your ongoing support and belief in me. You made me justify Richard's appeal as a protagonist, and in so doing helped me get to grips with this enigmatic man. He was a hard sell, but boy, was he worth it!

Thanks also to my trusty NZ team of first readers – Jane Bloomfield, Suzanne Main and Julie Scott – for your feedback, and for sharing the ups and downs of author life.

Finally, thanks as always to my family – my husband Michael, son James and daughter Helena – for cheering me on with my writing and trying hard to look interested when I give them history lessons at the dinner table.